TREASURE

BOOK TWELVE

THE CIRCLE OF CERIDWEN SAGA

TREASURE

OCTAVIA RANDOLPH

PYEWACKET PRESS

Treasure is the twelfth book in
The Circle of Ceridwen Saga by Octavia Randolph

ISBN Softcover: 978-1-942044-46-8
ISBN Hardcover: 978-1-942044-47-5

Book cover design by DesignforBooks.com. Maps by Michael Rohani. Cover
art photo credits: Hagia Sophia by Arild Vågen; Walls of Constantinople,
Apaleutos25; Theodosian walls at the Selymbria Gate, Bigdaddy1204; The
Xylokerkos Gate or Gate of Belgrade, CrniBombarder!!!; Trajanus saluhallar,
Jebulon – Eget arbete; clouds, landscape, and water, RD Studio stock.

Pyewacket Press

The Circle of Ceridwen Saga employs British spellings, alternate spellings,
archaic words, and oftentimes unusual verb to subject placement. This is
intentional. A Glossary of Terms will be found at the end of the novel.

CONTENTS

LIST OF CHARACTERS

Hrald, son of Ælfwyn and Sidroc, Jarl of the
Danish keep of Four Stones in South Lindisse

Jari, a warrior of Four Stones, chief body-guard to Hrald

Æthelflaed, Lady of Mercia, daughter
of King Ælfred of Wessex

Pega of Mercia, formerly wife to Hrald

Mealla, companion to Pega, a maid of Éireann

Dagmar, daughter of the late Guthrum,
King of the Danes in Angle-land

Yrling, half-brother to Hrald, currently living at Four Stones

Ælfgiva, daughter of Hrald and Pega

Bork, an orphan and young warrior under Hrald's care

Kjeld, second in command at Four Stones

Ealhswith, sister to Hrald, daughter of Ælfwyn and Sidroc

Ashild, late sister to Hrald, daughter of
Ælfwyn and the late Jarl, Yrling

Ælfred, King of Wessex

Guthrum, late King of the Danes in Angle-land

Ælfwyn, formerly Lady of Four Stones,
now wife to Raedwulf of Defenas

Raedwulf, Bailiff of Defenas in Wessex

Sigewif, Abbess of Oundle

Congar, a thegn's son of Cantwaraburh

Wilgot, priest of Four Stones

Edwin, Lord of Kilton in Wessex

Ceric, son of Ceridwen and the late Gyric,
grand-son of the late Lord Godwulf, God-son of
King Ælfred, and older brother to Edwin

Worr, the horse-thegn of Kilton, pledged man of Ceric

Alwin and **Wystan**, captains of Edwin's body-guard

Eadward, Prince of Wessex

Plegmund, Archbishop of Cantwaraburh

Hroft, infant son of Dagmar and Hrald

Eanflad, sister to Ælfwyn, resident at Four Stones

Nelda, a village spinner at Four Stones

Ultan, stable boy in the King's stable at Witanceaster

Sister Bova, brewster at Oundle, formerly
known at Tyrsborg as Sparrow

Vigmund, late body-guard of the King of Dane-mark

Edgyth, Lady of Kilton, mother by adoption to Edwin

Modwynn, late Lady of Kilton,
grandmother to Ceric and Edwin

Dwynwen, Princess of Ceredigion in Wales, wed to Ceric

Cerd, grandson to Ælfwyn and Ceridwen,
son of Ceric and the late Ashild

Burginde, companion and nurse to Ælfwyn

Wulfsige, son of Ælfwyn and Raedwulf

Blida and **Bettelin**, orphaned siblings of
Defenas, in service to Ælfwyn and Raedwulf

Lioba, wife to the steward of Raedwulf's hall

Gunnulf, late brother to Jari, and friend to Hrald

Godwin, late Lord of Kilton, killed by Sidroc

Onund, late warrior of Four Stones, killed by Hrald

Asberg, uncle to Hrald, in command
at the fortress of Turcesig

Edfrid, a priest at the cathedral of
Cantwaraburh, uncle to Congar

Dunnere, priest of Kilton

Garrulf, scop of Kilton

Willehad, a priest in the train of Æthelflaed

Luned, a woman of Wales, step-mother to
Dwynwen, grandmother to Ceric and Edwin

Mul, the stableman at Four Stones

Aszur, a ship-master and trader of Jorvik,
dubbed Gold Tooth by Hrald

Wite, a girl of the village of Four Stones, nursemaid to Hroft

Haesten, late war-chief of the Danes, killed by Hrald

Tegwedd, a Welsh serving girl to Dwynwen

Mindred, a serving woman at Kilton

Deorwine, a Reeve of King Ælfred

Inga, wife to Jari

Haward, a young war-chief of a small holding adjacent to Four Stones

Werburgh, wife to Haward

Siggerith, daughter of the late Thorfast, a war-chief killed by Hrald

Inkera, daughter of the late Guthrum, and half-sister to Dagmar

Bodil, mother to Dagmar

Orri, a warrior of Four Stones

Steinn, half-brother to Inkera

Agmund, son of the late Guthrum

Inger, mother to Inkera

Njall, late father of Kjeld

Sidroc the Dane, formerly Jarl of Four Stones in South Lindisse, a wealthy trader on Gotland

Ceridwen, Mistress of the hall Tyrsborg on the island of Gotland, wife to Sidroc

Lifrid, a fisherman of Gotland

Hrald the Elder, father to Sidroc

Stenhild, wife to Hrald the Elder

Rannveig, a brewster on Gotland, mother of Tindr

Gunnvor and **Helga**, cook and serving-woman respectively at Tyrsborg

Ottar and **Runa**, a couple living with Hrald and Stenhild

Eirian and **Rodiaud**, daughters of Ceridwen and Sidroc

Tindr, a bow hunter

Berse, a weapon-smith of Gotland, formerly a warrior

Juoksa, a boy of Gotland, son of Tindr

Ingirith, once wife to Hrald the Elder

Toki, late nephew of Hrald the Elder, and cousin to Sidroc, killed by the same

Runulv, a Gotlandic ship-master and trader

Eskil, a Svear warrior and ship-master

Brani, a seaman guide of Eskil

The Eparch, Prefect of Miklagårdr

Arni and **Farulf**, two Gotlandic adventurers, perished en route to Miklagårdr

Sigtrygg, a Svear adventurer, perished en route to Miklagårdr

Uffa, a Gotlander resident in Miklagårdr

Belos, an agent of the Eparch

Oleg, King of Kyiv

Sava, a farmer along the River Dnieper

Karlen and **Demyan**, Princes of a river trading post, and nephews to Oleg

Efim, Prince of Gnezdovo

Vermund, King of Novgorod

Ladja, Mistress of Staraya Ladoga

Truvor, the half-Svear son of Lady Ladja

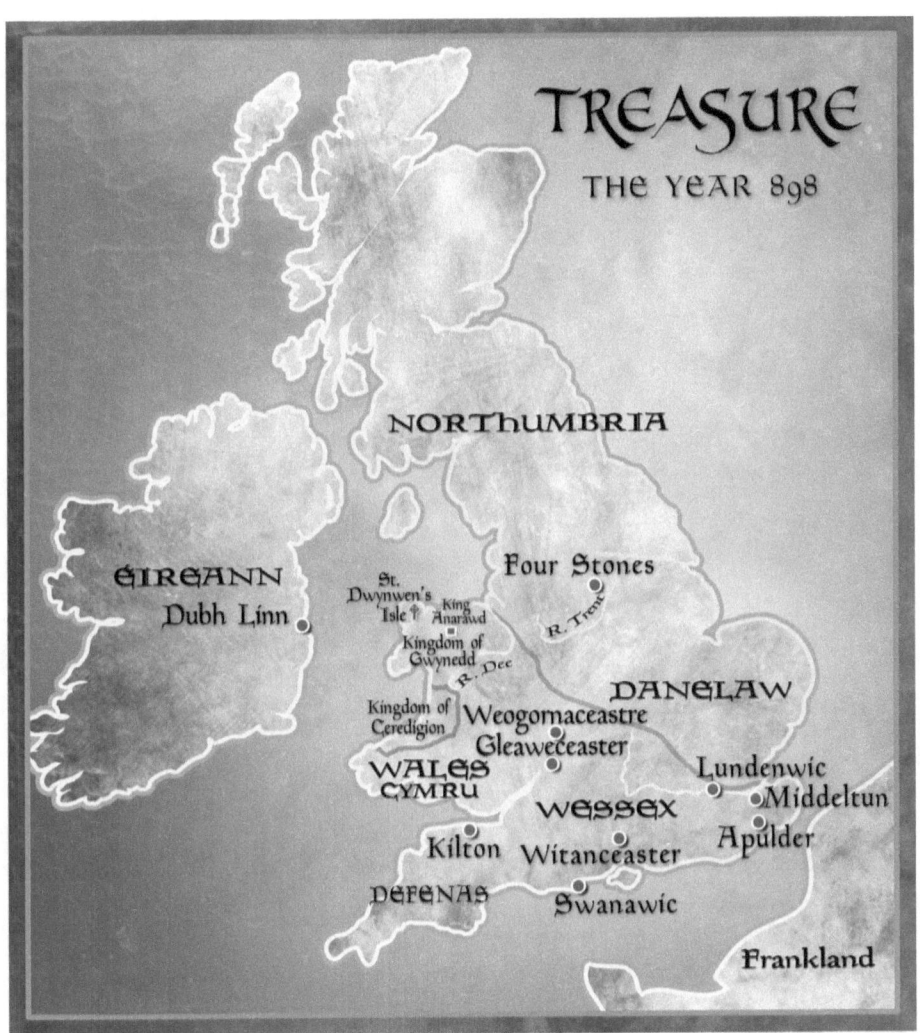

TREASURE

THE YEAR 898

Land of
the Sámi

Land
of the
Sámi

Norse

Uppsala

Svear

Gotland

Land
of
the
Rus

Tyrsborg

Viborg   Danes
Aros   Skanía   Öland

Ribe

Prus

Four
Stones

Pomeraní

Frisia
Dorestad

Polanie

Wessex

Kilton

hunefleth

Frankland

Paris

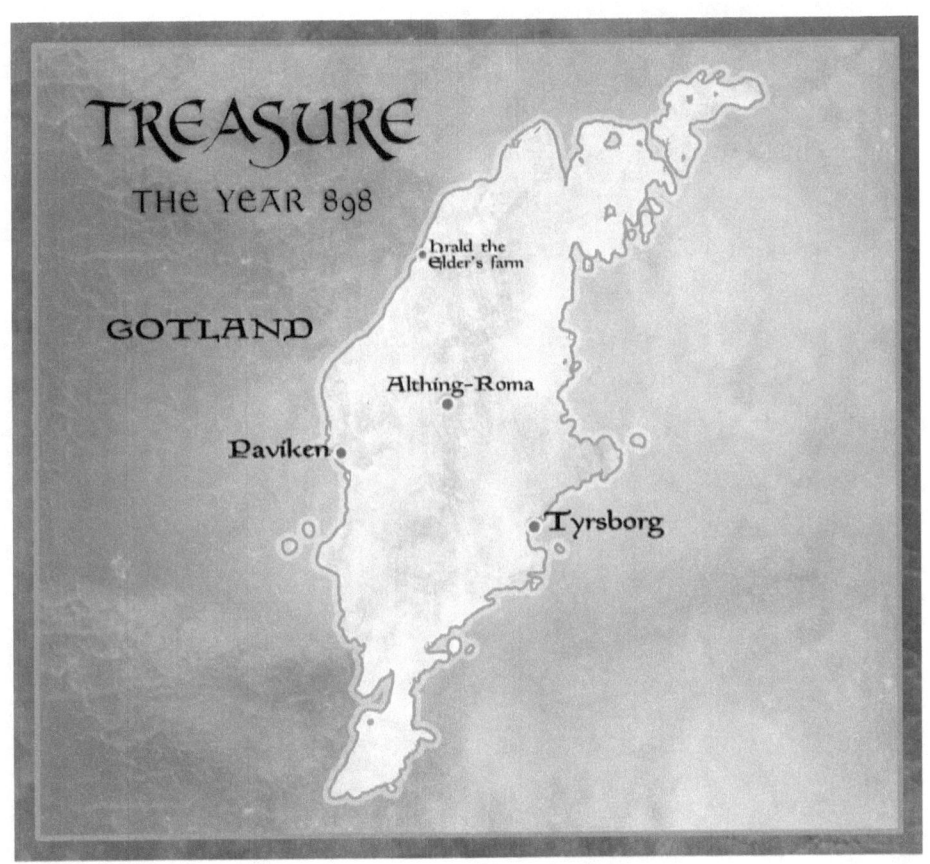

Lake Ladoga

Staraya Ladoga

Gulf of the Finns

Novgorod

GOTLAND

Baltic Sea

Gnezdovo

The Princes' Fortress

Return Route

Kyiv

Dneiper

TREASURE

THE YEAR 899

Black Sea

Miklagárdr/ Constantinople

TREASURE

THE ROAD HOME

Four Stones in Lindisse
The Year 898, Summer

I T was a long six days back to Four Stones, and with so large a party, nearly impossible to shorten. Hrald and Jari rode out through the gates of Witanceaster fronting the same thirty men, two waggons, and five extra horses they had left Lindisse with. Absent only was Pega, former Lady of Four Stones, and Ælfgiva, the small daughter she shared with Hrald. There in Ælfred's royal burh Pega had sundered her union with the young Jarl of Four Stones. She was once again under the protection of the King's daughter, Æthelflaed of Mercia. It was Hrald's task to return to Four Stones so that Pega's treasure and goods might be packed up, and delivered to her back at Witanceaster, before she and Æthelflaed journeyed to Mercia.

Though Pega remained behind, that Lady's longtime companion Mealla was amongst Hrald's party, as she was entrusted with packing Pega's goods. This black-haired maid

of Éireann, ever loyal to her mistress, spoke scarcely a word
all the tiresome journey back. She was so cold to Hrald that
she would not permit him to help her descend from the
waggon board; it would be a breach of the angry privacy she
was keeping. The man acting as driver did so, jumping down,
and helping Mealla to the ground each time they halted, just
as he aided her ascent. It was not stable-yard workers who
drove the waggons. For such forays Hrald always used skilled
drivers from amongst his own warriors, well-versed in the
handling of a frightened team, and not afraid to whip the
horses to speed to elude capture during attack.

The mood was uniformly glum. His men who had
ridden so far with Hrald, with the expectation of a long rest
and feasting, had been denied both, as they had taken their
leave the morning of the Feast of Saints Peter and Paul. Hrald
had been denied much more. He had sent message to Lady
Æthelflaed, informing her of his departure, and asking that he
might come to see Ælfgiva before he left. The answer – "Lady
Pega must act in the interests of her daughter, and refuses"
– cut him as sharply as a honed blade. Was it Pega who
heard his request, he wondered, or had Æthelflaed shielded
her from it? Then he recalled Pega telling him that he was
dead to her. And perhaps dead to their child. Hrald turned
his face, lowering his chin, and remembered her words, the
most stinging blow she could have delivered.

Then there was what he had denied himself. Dagmar was
his true wife in heart, but he would not possess her body. The
one kiss he had given her, holding their son Hroft in his right
arm, and Dagmar, pressed close to his heart, in the other, was
all he could allow himself. That one kiss sealed his return to
her, and homecoming to her son. When he had seen her later

that Fate-ful day to tell her soon they would again wed, Hrald would allow himself nothing more. He had suffered the sharp pangs of conscience nearly the moment he had awakened after their coupling in Witanceaster almost two years ago. Many were the sleepless nights, and questioning days, that followed. The teachings of the Church and his own driven needs had collided. Because she had once been his wife, he could feel no other way. No sin, he thought, lay in loving Dagmar; the fault was in acting upon that love while still bound to another. If he again held her, kissed her, he would not be able to control his impulse to be man and wife. And they were not; not in law nor in the eyes of the Church. There must be no taint upon his actions now. He had broken faith with his God once; he would not sully his reclaimed happiness in doing so again. Yet, he must press her close to his body, for a fleeting embrace. "Soon we will be wed," he breathed into her ear. "And I will bring you back to the treasure room . . . "

As promise it was thrilling for him to utter, and she had trembled in his arms as he whispered it. Those words must be enough, for both of them. With the scent of her hair still about him, he broke from her. He had but a day to marshal his men, have Jari see to the provisioning, make sure the horses were sound enough to again take to the long road ahead. He had silver aplenty with him, and left Dagmar with a fat bag of it, for any wants which might arise. His final words to her were, "Until I come for you." He kissed their son and tore himself away, shoring himself with the knowledge that the sooner he left, the sooner he could claim Dagmar as his rightful wife.

The ride was thankfully uneventful, sober as it was. Hrald often rode back to check on the rear guard. Even its youngest members, Yrling and Bork, were subdued. Yrling knew nothing more than his brother's marriage to Lady Pega was at an end; Hrald had told him himself the morning before the planned feast. "Dagmar was my wife before Pega. My first wife. She made a mistake. Then I made a greater one, and sent her away." That was all Hrald would tell him. Even Jari refused Yrling any details. Yrling figured all would need to wait until their arrival at Four Stones for Hrald to say more.

They neared Four Stones on the afternoon of the sixth day out. The outer watch stationed along the road had greeted them, and Hrald rode on with little more than a nod. As they approached the outermost fields of the village, Hrald turned to the Tyr-hand at his side.

"Jari. Will you ride ahead," Hrald asked.

His next words were long in coming, but the Tyr-hand could guess what they might be, and supplied them.

"I will make sure you enter as quietly as can be," Jari answered.

Hrald gave a grateful nod of his head. "Ask Kjeld and Ealhswith to meet me in the treasure room."

As Jari had promised, the party's arrival was subdued. No ward-man whistled out their approach from the ramparts, and though the folk of the village stopped in their work and looked up at them, their greeting was restrained, sign that they had been told to go about their business. If any, looking closely at the waggon board on which Mealla sat, lips tightly compressed, noticed the Lady of the place not at her side, waving at them, they bethought themselves the Lady tired after so long a journey, and resting under the tarpaulins with her little daughter.

They passed within the open palisade gates, a troop of tired, dusty, and thirsty men, on horses equally fatigued. Ashild's white stallion, looming before them in the paddock, marked them. He tossed his great head and whinnied, a shrill challenge to Hrald's bay. Hrald's own animal stretched out his arched neck and answered with challenge of his own. The white horse lifted both front feet and leapt in the air with a snort. The pale hooves struck the ground with force. Even Ashild's horse knew, thought Hrald. But Bork had come up from behind, was off his own horse, and ready to take Hrald's into the stable for a rubdown.

Mealla, having suffered the long journey comfortless and alone, was eager to escape the eyes of the yard folk now looking at her and the other arrivals. The driver helped her down, and called to a couple of the serving men to take her packs and follow. She went straight for the bower house, clutching her hand basket as she did so.

Jari awaited the arrivals. He dismissed the men; they must care for their mounts, then their kin would welcome them. Bork was already at work in the stable, removing the saddle packs from Hrald's horse, and would have his own to see to as well, once the bay was rubbed down and watered. Yrling lingered, his horse's reins in his hand, looking at Jari. Would he be invited in to hear what Hrald would say, he wondered. Jari gave a shake of his head, dismissing him. But Yrling did not move. Hrald turned, and saw his younger brother there. He must hear, he thought, and nodded at both Jari and Yrling that his brother should follow. Yrling was young, but he was as well a son of Sidroc, just as he was. Yrling must hear from Hrald's own lips the change that had been wrought.

Kjeld and Ealhswith stood just within the hall, their uncertainty on their faces. Neither could assent to awaiting Hrald in the treasure room, and so they stood here, at the bottom of the short flight of steps, the patterned floor of red and black stone flowing behind them. Four serving women were already approaching, with basins for hand-washing, and trays bearing ale. Hrald saw the drink for what it was by the crockery holding it. This was no ordinary welcome; ale was not adequate. And the stronger mead was for celebrations.

"Is there wine," Hrald asked, as his first utterance. He was looking at the two serving women, but it was Ealhswith who answered.

She knew the stores, enough to know that there was in fact wine. She turned to the two women, and in soft tones asked that wine be carried in.

Kjeld unlocked the treasure room, surrendering his key to Hrald. The Jarl walked in, to be confronted with the many chests and boxes belonging to Pega. But also meeting his eye was the solid old table, its chairs, the shelves hammered up upon the wall, and the many wooden pegs driven into those walls. There stood the chests and casks holding the armaments of Four Stones, and the great body of its treasure in bronze, silver, and even gold, treasure amassed by his own efforts, those of his father Sidroc, his great uncle Yrling, and of the Lord before him Yrling had fought, Merewala. On the wall, and hung in honour was the shield his father had made for him on Gotland, the same Ashild had once carried.

Hrald's bed was there as well, one covered with a spread laced together of wolf-pelts, the fur of grey and white still thick. It had always been there. That fur throw was inextricably linked in Hrald's mind with Dagmar, and making love to her upon it, so linked that he had never been able to order its removal. It had adorned the bed every day of his life that he had slept in this room. He saw the wolf-pelt spread anew, mute but meaningful symbol of his own past, present, and future.

The wine was brought. Hrald gestured that all sit. There were but four chairs, and Jari remained standing, as did Hrald, while Kjeld, Ealhswith, and Yrling took their seats. With a glance Hrald asked Jari to sit as well, and the Tyr-hand lowered himself into the final chair.

"Pega is not with me," Hrald began. His eyes moved from Kjeld to his siblings, fixing them in turn with his gaze as he went on.

"She has sundered our union. She did it with good cause. Two years ago I went to Witanceaster to see King Ælfred" – and here he looked to his sister – "about you, Ealhswith. I found Dagmar there. She lives as guest of the King. The Dane I had cast out with her was killed, along with his King, in Dane-mark, and she returned to Wessex in the company of some nuns and priests. She led a quiet life until I saw her. I spent a night with her. A babe was born of that night, one I knew nothing of until last week, when I came upon her with our son in Witanceaster.

"Pega saw her as well; saw Dagmar and the boy, and me standing with them. It ended our union; she went to Lady Æthelflaed, whose anger at me is great. Pega's goods and treasure will be packed by Mealla, and I will carry it back to Witanceaster where she awaits. I have forfeited the bride-price; this is my choice. When I return from Witanceaster I will bring Dagmar with me. Soon after we will wed, at Oundle, and she will again be Lady of Four Stones."

This news so stunned Kjeld and Ealhswith as to leave them speechless. It was a re-ordering of the life of the hall, sudden, and complete. The young mind of Yrling was filled with stark yet vivid impressions, those of passion, discovery, and impact. His brother Hrald had moved for what he wanted, this woman Dagmar, and now she would be his. This was what it was to be a man.

It was Kjeld who first found voice. He had clear memory of Dagmar, of her attraction, and the grief she had caused Hrald. But his first utterance was that of a friend. He stood and spoke, taking up the bronze cup before him.

"You have a son. I raise a cup to you, and to his mother."

Jari looked at Kjeld, a meaningful glance, in which his surprise and also gratitude was clear. The Tyr-hand rose to his feet, and raised his cup in salute as well, forcing Hrald, standing there looking at all, to take another sip. Yrling also stood, mute but aware of the magnitude of the moment. Kjeld asked no question; he drove to the main point: Hrald had a male heir.

Hrald's sister sat there, her slender hands around the base of her silver cup, eyes wide, and lips parted. Her brother had more to tell, and must continue on. But she spoke first, in attempt to find some happiness in this unexpected twist.

"Dagmar," she offered, eager to relieve herself of her secret. "I too saw her at Witanceaster. She comforted me about Edwin. She is coming back," she ended, and looked about her with widening eyes as if she might appear at any moment.

Hrald had no idea Ealhswith had met with Dagmar over those fraught days; the girl had hid it well. He realised his own surprise at her, keeping such news.

"Yes," he answered. There was no gladness in his voice, for what he must say. "Dagmar, and our boy. But much is forfeit; the bride-price. Ælfgiva, who I may never see again. And you, Ealhswith."

"Me? I am forfeit?" The puzzlement in her voice was mixed with girlish wonder.

"Lady Æthelflaed has asked for you. She – she can make a great match for you. I am to bring you back with me; you, and Pega's treasure."

"I – I am to leave . . . ?"

Ealhswith had felt honest pride in how she had administered the hall and stores in her brother and Pega's absence. But there would be no reciting of what she did, to merit Pega's praise; Pega was not here, and would not be here. And soon, she would not be, either. But a great Lady had requested her, and as her brother told it, she was being paired with Pega's immense treasure, almost as if she were part of it. Which, she realised, she was; Lady Æthelflaed would not have otherwise claimed her if this breach had not occurred. Pega had been kind to her; Pega was kind to all. Yet Dagmar was returning, a woman she admired so much. She knew not what to ask, not in front of Jari and Kjeld and Yrling, and kept her silence.

For his own part Kjeld now became aware that with the end of Hrald's union with Lady Pega, Mealla was likely lost to him. He could not give rein to this thought; he had not been there to greet her, as Jari had told him to await Hrald in the hall. A single glance from her would tell him the truth of their future, he was sure.

A sudden shaft of light pierced the gable window: the time-marking Sun, dropping down the sky to cross the horizon. It struck the table, and most of all Ealhswith, sitting there with lowered head.

Hrald spoke again, and to all. "I will tell the hall tonight."

Kjeld paused outside the door of the treasure room. Jari and Yrling had left with him; Hrald's sister remained within. But Kjeld did not go far. He had no tired horse to tend to, no kit to unpack. Despite the many thoughts tumbling in his brain, Mealla was foremost. It could not wait; he must see her at once. He had no idea where the black-haired maid might be; he had but once mounted the steps to the partial upper floor of the hall leading to the weaving room – the day of her arrival with Lady Pega. Then he was laden with a wooden chest, too heavy for a single man to wield, but he had in his pride made it up with it, and laid it on the floor where she had instructed, with, he had hoped, scant sign of effort. He stopped a woman in the hall to ask if she had seen Mealla ascend; the answer was a shake of the head; she had watched her march off, head held high, clutching her hand-basket to her bosom, in the direction of the Lady's bower house. This too was forbidden Kjeld; no man entered there. But off he went; he must. As he neared the path leading to the garden gate he saw Pega's great grey coursing hound Frost within the garden, standing near the wooden table. The dog cocked his head at Kjeld, then knew him for who he was. The plumed tail thumped against the table leg in greeting. Kjeld had cared for the animal while Pega and Yrling had been away. The hound offered no challenge to him now. Still, Kjeld would not breach this sanctuary.

The maid of Éireann had wasted no time. Kjeld saw the bower house door to be open, and at least two other women at work within. The greater quantity of Pega's possessions, and all her silver and gold, were housed in the treasure room, but she would have goods here in the bower house, as well as up in the weaving room. Mealla was already at work, packing. Kjeld could hear the lilt of her voice as she directed the actions of the serving women with her. He could not enter the garden; no man but Hrald and such a guest as had been the Bailiff of Defenas were invited in. But he stood there, and Mealla, crossing the floor within, saw him. She stopped in her action, laid down what was in her hands, vanished for a moment, and then with a squaring of her thin shoulders came out to meet him.

As she approached, Kjeld could think of nothing so much as a black-bird, that creature whose song gave such pleasure, whose glossy wing so matched Mealla's black hair. Now she would fly; he could see it. It was not only the anger written on her face, but the directness of her approach. She stopped before him, the closed gate far from the only barrier.

"Hrald has told us," he began. "Me, and Yrling, and Ealhswith."

Mealla took a breath. "Then there is nothing more to say," she snapped.

"There is," Kjeld countered. "Are you then bound to leave, as well?"

"Ha! That I am. I am bound only to Lady Pega. None but she."

This last was not required, but he saw Mealla's ire was such that she could not temper her tartness now.

The maid of Éireann had been simmering with it, ever since turning that corner with her Lady in Witanceaster and seeing the Jarl standing next a strange woman. She had need to stifle her outrage for Pega's sake, but rolling into the forecourt of Four Stones and walking to the bower house had brought all to a near-boil. There was Lady Pega's timber church, which she had lavished much attention and silver on. Seeing it now was to Mealla nothing short of an affront. Mealla had not, and would not enter that sanctuary a final time. She wished to take the church apart, piece by piece, and cart it back to Mercia, and to her mistress. Pega had woven and sewn the snowy linen altar cloth, as well as the smaller linen corporal upon which the Sacrament was placed. Pega had further embellished both with delicate cut-work at their borders. Mealla regretted every hour her Lady had spent bent over this work. Mealla could not take those back with her, they belonged to God now, but she could not help fear what heathenry might befall church and hall in Pega's absence. Now this Dane Kjeld stood before her, and she must attend to him as well.

Kjeld had no answer for Mealla's response, so near to a rebuke it was. He could not ask for her hand; it was out of the question. His feeling for her ran deep enough that a direct rejection, one to his face that she seemed readily able to supply, would cut them both. He stood wordless, looking at her. Two crimson dots had risen in her cheeks; her anger had forced them there, upon her milk-white skin.

Mealla looked down at her palm. Something was clasped there, and she took a step nearer Kjeld and offered it him.

It was the silver pin he had given her, formed in the shape of a long-winged bird, a tiny, milky Moonstone for its eye. A sharp-beaked bird, gracefully rendered in that cool metal. With her long and narrow nose, there was a likeness there, Kjeld had thought. And Mealla certainly had the ability to puncture his spirits when she felt the call to do so. Still, she had worn it often, and with seeming pleasure. Now she wanted no part of it, nor him.

"Nej," he told her, refusing to accept it. "I bought it from a woman of Éireann, and with another it must remain."

She shook her head, making her dusky curls spring gently by her face.

"Keep it," he pressed, "as memory of me."

Another shake of her head made him speak. "There is no harm in it. And if you wed, and no longer wish to see it, you can give it to the Church."

This drew her stinging response. "Ha! Not likely I will do that! Seeing what I have seen."

Seeing how Hrald and Pega had ended, Kjeld knew. All was lost with Mealla, but he might salvage a hope for their vanished future, that both could hold in private recollection. He offered it now. "If things had been different . . . "

"And they are not."

"They might have been," he answered. "Keep the pin. It is all I ask of you."

Mealla lowered her chin. She had been holding the silver ornament out to him all this time. Now she withdrew her hand, and allowed her fingers to close upon the keepsake. Indeed, she thought, looking upon his earnest face. What might have been.

When Jari and Yrling left the treasure room they walked to the door leading to the stable yard. They had not yet reached the threshold when Yrling turned to the Tyr-hand. He was so taken by the change in his brother's life that he had thought of nothing beyond the action Hrald had taken to cause it, but now something struck him, and he must speak of it.

"Could there be a fight?" he wanted to know.

Jari pressed his lips together, then gave a grunt. "Not likely. Hrald has done too much to aid Wessex. And though Lady Pega is of Mercia, that benefit extends to her home as well."

Jari thought back. The troop from Four Stones had sat in the King's hall two nights before they must leave, sat and supped, without either their Jarl nor Pega. Neither made an appearance. But Yrling had been there, taking in all.

The Tyr-hand spoke of this. "Ælfred's daughter Æthelflaed – you might have marked her at the high table, sitting by her father and mother – she controls Mercia; she and her husband, Æthelred. It was she who made the match between Hrald and Pega, and it was she who Hrald spoke to. And, he did what few men would have – forfeited the bride-price in a union sundered by his wife."

"What was it?" Yrling asked.

"A waggon full of weaponry, casks and chests of it, including pieces worthy of any King."

Yrling nodded, but his face showed his uncertainty. It prompted Jari to lay a hand on the boy's shoulder.

"It will come right," he promised.

They parted. Jari's wife Inga awaited him, and had as yet but scant greeting from her returned man. Yrling found himself entering the stable, looking for Bork. He had no one else to speak to; Kjeld had vanished.

Bork was finished with Hrald's bay. The stallion had been washed, rubbed down with a clean handful of straw, then burnished to a shine with linen towelling. The long black mane and tail were combed smooth by Bork's skilled fingers, and the animal now stood in fresh straw up to his hocks in his box stall, his downy muzzle in a manger of oat-mixed hay. Bork was now working on his own horse, and to his credit, gave the animal as much care as he had to Hrald's. He stood, soothing the gelding with the linen held in his right hand, while his left smoothed over the gelding's dark coat after every stroke. Yrling came to stand on the horse's off side, and looked at Bork over the animal's withers.

"Lady Pega had ended the marriage," Yrling said. "She will return to Mercia. A woman named Dagmar is coming here. And with Hrald's son."

Bork's hands stopped in their action.

"Lady Dagmar," he said. "She is Guthrum's daughter, the great King who united all for the Danes here." Bork paused before going on. "She came here not long after I did. They were wed at Oundle. In the rain," he remembered.

"Then a few months later the Jarl found her . . . " Bork's voice trailed off. "I heard only a messenger came, a Dane, with a gift for her. Then the Jarl found her in the treasure room, with him. He threw them both out."

"Threw them out."

"Já. That hour. He would not kill the Dane, nor his wife. He only threw them out.

"He was sad after this, more troubled than I have ever seen a man."

Both paused, taking this in.

"And now this woman Dagmar will come back," Yrling said. None of it boded well, despite what Jari had said.

Bork had spent another long and thoughtful moment. "I am sorry for Lady Pega. She was kind to me. But it was Lady Ælfwyn who took me in; she and the Jarl."

Yrling was forced to nod. "Jari said there will not be war. So that is good."

Bork bobbed his head. "And the Jarl has a son," he ended. And no woman could have caused him such grief, save one who had given him much joy, Bork said to himself.

⚇⚇⚇⚇⚇⚇⚇⚇⚇

It was Ealhswith who stayed behind with Hrald; she must. As stunned as she was at the collapse of her brother's marriage, she could not quell her excitement at the return of Dagmar. She did not delay in telling Hrald. "Dagmar is coming, I want to stay. To live with you, and her."

Hrald gave a slow shake of his head.

"Ealhswith, Pega cares for you. You will be with her, and Mealla and little Ælfgiva. You will live in a royal hall."

She did not respond to this, and instead wished to know more. "This happened with Dagmar when you met mother and me at Witanceaster."

"Yes."

"It was a long time ago," she reflected.

"Almost two years. My boy is just over a year."

Hrald gave thought to this. It was then Ealhswith had been refused by Edwin, and she had wept in Hrald's arms at his rejection. Since then no other match had been put forth for her. For his own part, Hrald could admit he had not been looking on her behalf. His contacts with Wessex and Mercia were too slight, and though Ealhswith could readily wed one of the Danes who held large holdings in Anglia or further north by Jorvik, such a pairing would not prove the strategic match that all seemed to think her capable of. It led him to speak of this, but as gently as he could.

"In all this time, you have met no one."

She cast her eyes down, as if in admission of this.

"How could you," he asked, "living as you had at Defenas with mother, and Raedwulf. He keeps a quiet hall, as much as he can, to counter his life on the road with Ælfred, and at Witanceaster."

Ealhswith could not mention a young man she had met. Abbess Sigewif of Oundle had dismissed Congar of Cantwaraburh out of hand, given the circumstances of their discovery. But the Abbess had been kind enough to shield her brother from the truth of her adventure, and potential disgrace. How could Ealhswith mention him now, fearful that the whole truth would come out, when Sigewif had protected her from just that. Congar was likely back in Cantwaraburh, as a novitiate, or perhaps had fled to Rome to seek his fortune. Ealhswith had no choice but to say nothing.

Hrald returned to the life awaiting her. "You will live with Pega," he repeated. "And the King's daughter, Lady Æthelflaed. She promised a match for you to benefit all."

These would be the benefits. He must warn her of the danger.

"But do not allow the Lady to push you, to rush you into a union without your full consent. If she tells you she has a suit for you, listen with respect, but declare you must have time to think."

She looked her question to him, but could not form it into words. It seemed he was fearful of Lady Æthelflaed, and how she might pair her. Yet Æthelflaed was the King's daughter. For years Ealhswith had wished to be of service to her brother, to win his approval and regard, to do some great act for Four Stones. Now she seemed to be called to do so, but his caution filled her with sudden wariness.

"Do you . . . do you think we could stop at The Fold in Defenas, on the way to Mercia?"

There was true plaintiveness in her question. Hrald could only answer with the truth.

"It is hardly on the way, Ealhswith." Yet despite the detour he thought Lady Æthelflaed would oblige his sister's desire. Outraged as the Lady was, she might relish telling their mother and the Bailiff of Hrald's actions. They had led to the failure of the union with her former ward, fracturing not only a young family but the bond between Mercia and Four Stones. Still, he must encourage Ealhswith in her desire; she would wish to see their mother. "But you should ask this of Lady Æthelflaed; she will want mother's approval of your going to Mercia with her."

Even as he said this, Hrald could imagine the result: their mother's shocked reaction at Pega telling her what she had discovered at Witanceaster. And he would not be there. Not to counter the baldness of the truth; there was no denying his act. But his absence meant his mother could not hear from him directly as he asked pardon for the harm he had caused them all.

Hrald allowed the silence to speak for both of them. Ealhswith must be content with this, at least, her next words were those of quiet obedience.

"When – when will we leave?" she wished to know.

"It will take a day or two. You will have time to pack."

"Aunt Eanflad," she said of a sudden. "She will be left alone."

Eanflad was in many ways always alone, and as long as she was left so, seemed content. But Hrald must answer.

"Soon Dagmar will return. She was always kind to her, was she not?"

Ealhswith must nod her head at this. At last she had an order from Hrald she could follow. There was a path ahead to make him proud of her. She found herself dropping in a small curtsey to him, to mark the event.

Hrald was left alone in the treasure room. He looked about the space, unchanged from when he and Pega had left it, so unlike their lives, and the lives of many others dependent on them. He should go to the bathing shed and scrub the grime of the road off him. But he knew it would be crowded with the men who had made the journey with him, and he did not want to see any, until he spoke to them all. One of the yard men tapped on his door, and carried in the packs from his saddle. Within the treasure room Hrald had a basin large enough for face and chest, and asked for water. When the man returned, the hall was already busy with serving folk, moving the trestles around the fire pit, carrying the table tops to rest upon them, setting the benches in position. Hrald washed himself, and put on fresh clothes. He chose nothing that marked an occasion of note, but did place his father's heavy cuff of red gold upon his wrist.

The young Jarl of Four Stones waited until the hall was filled. When men returned from any venture, the hall was always noisier than usual, for the tales being told. Not much could be shared about this one; his men knew little, and the din was muted. Hrald came out to see the high table much as it always was – Jari seated to the right of Hrald's own chair, and his wife Inga next him, and Wilgot the priest next her; Kjeld to the left of his chair, the rest of the table filled with his best men and, if they were wed, their wives. Ealhswith was standing to one side, a pitcher of ale meant for the high table in her hands. It was full, and heavy, he saw; she had one hand on the slender handle, the second supporting the bottom of the vessel. Ealhswith would serve out the first cup as she had done in Pega's absence, but then retreat to the women's table, where she usually sat. At the table set aside for young warriors Yrling and Bork sat, side by side, not at either ends as they once had.

As soon as Hrald approached, the hall quieted even further. The chair on which he sat was large, carved of oak, and high-backed. He saw Pega's chair had been removed; likely Jari had thought to do so. Its absence gave him easy access to his own. He put one booted foot upon the seat of his chair, and then, in an act never seen from Hrald, stood upon the table top itself. Those before him responded in a stifled gasp, an intake of breath which seemed shared by all.

He lifted his arms for quiet, a gesture which silenced all but the scraping of benches as his folk angled to get better view of him. They saw the thick band of gold encircling his wrist; the older men there had clear memory of Sidroc bearing it, gift of Guthrum, when Hrald was yet a child. The son wore it well, reminder as it was of his lineage.

All eyes were upon Hrald as he addressed the men and women of his hall.

"Lady Pega has sundered her union with me," was his first, and stunning declaration.

"I will leave soon to carry her goods to her, at Witanceaster. From there she will travel to Mercia, where our union will be dissolved.

"When I return I will do so with one you know, Dagmar, daughter of Guthrum. She will again be my wife and Lady of the hall. And she will bring with her our son."

It was the least Hrald could say, but contained in it all vital to know. A son had been born to him with his first wife, and therefore Pega had ended the marriage by her own volition. Dagmar would be returning, as Lady, and with their child.

His words did not break the spell which hung about him. When Hrald climbed upon the table, it was no mere sign of dominance, though the raw power of the gesture said much. He was able in a stroke to command the attention of all in the crowded hall, and to signal the importance of what he was about to say. He still held that attention, his listeners sitting mute and nearly motionless in the wake of what they had been told.

Jari and a few of the older men were carried back long years by his act, to the one time they watched Yrling leap up upon that same board. It was a few days after the taking of Four Stones, and outside the door of the remaining hall lay the still-smoldering ruins of what had been burnt in the taking. Yrling had raised his arms to silence his men, made riotous with drink. He told them that order would now be imposed. Hrald was now signalling a new order for himself, in the return of Dagmar as his wife.

Hrald lowered his arms, but remained upon the broad board of the high table. Kjeld at his left rose from his bench, as did Jari on Hrald's right, the latter in a movement so forceful he would have overturned the bench if Inga and the men sitting there had not been weighing it down.

"A son," Kjeld called out. "The blood of Sidroc and of Guthrum flows in your boy, my Jarl!"

Few words spoken were better timed than these uttered by Kjeld. Lady Pega and her riches and her link to the royal halls of Mercia and Wessex might be lost, but here was the gain, a return to an earlier day, the first generation of bold conquerors and their winnings.

The hall erupted, in bellows and gladsome cries, and shrill whistles of approval. Men pounded on the trestle tops, calling out "Hrald!" and "Guthrum!"

Hrald looked about him. His news was as unexpected as could be; and it had taken long moments for the folk before him to absorb it. Speculation had run wild amongst his men on the ride home, but one look at the missing Lady's companion, or at stone-faced Jari, quelled any notion of questioning them. Now here was the truth, a revelation of vast impact.

Hrald's eye fell on his sister Ealhswith. She still stood there, ale jug in hand, beads of moisture running down the side of the pottery walls. The two women who would follow her to replenish her vessel stood in her wake. The girl looked lost amongst this clamour, her eyes locked on the spout of her pitcher. Jari saw her too, and spoke in a voice of command, one of happy celebration.

"Mead," he called, his voice ringing through the hall. "We will have mead and drink to Jarl Hrald and Lady Dagmar!"

Ealhswith turned with the women who trailed her, and with several serving folk vanished up the passageway leading to the kitchen.

Hrald's men were laughing now, their wives looking wonderingly about, some questioning others, but many smiling as well. Hrald turned to step down and take his seat. His eyes met those of Wilgot the priest, staring up at him. The man was open-mouthed at this report, his state of disbelief written upon his lined face. Hrald could do no more than nod at the cleric.

Hours later the Jarl of Four Stones stumbled into the treasure room. His bed was empty. He was drunk, as were many of his men. It was all he could do to pull off his clothes and drop into his bed. Once there, his hand ran over the fur of the wolfskin spread. He had broken Pega's heart. He had lost his little daughter. And he had incurred the wrath of Æthelflaed. But Dagmar! Dagmar was coming; he would bring Dagmar back here, and with her the son they had made together. The hall had no Lady, but she was coming. He would bring Dagmar back, and soon. On the morrow, early, he must go to Wilgot, make full confession, be shriven. That must be first.

He slept, at last, the fitful sleep of one stunned by drink. It was late, far past dawn, when he awoke; the growing light in the treasure room told him that. He pushed off the covers and stood. His head was sore, but his mind swirled with thoughts of his next, and needed steps.

He must see Wilgot, and be shriven. Then he would go about selecting new men to return with him, fresh horses too. Jari would insist on making the trek; this he knew. The kitchen yard would need two days for provisioning them, the baking of extra loaves, time to dry meat by the fire, and to package up barley and other grains in sizes easy for the men to carry. Ealhswith – and Hrald thought of her with a pang – she would need time to pack herself up. She must choose a serving maid to accompany her, that was certain. Ealhswith might also ask one of her friends to go with her, as companion; if so Hrald would be certain to make a generous settlement to her parents. Any maid leaving with her might go on to a rich life with Ealhswith, but would likely never see her folk here again. Oundle – they must stop at Oundle, so Ealhswith might say Fare-well to their grandmother Sister Ælfleda, and say a prayer at the tomb of Ashild. And Hrald must speak to Abbess Sigewif, tell her himself what had transpired.

He shook his aching head at these needful tasks, and stood there by his rumpled bed. The noise from the hall was muffled and indistinct. Many would be getting a late start after such a night as they had spent. He pulled on his leggings and found a fresh tunic. There came a rap at his door, a strong double rap, followed by the voice of Kjeld, calling Hrald's name.

Hrald slid back the bar and opened the door to his second in command. Behind Kjeld were two serving men bearing trays of steaming food and drink. The men placed the trays upon the table, and with a nod to their Jarl, left. Kjeld and Hrald stood facing each other across the small table. Hrald's dark hair was wild from sleep, and he kept blinking his eyes as if to help focus them. He was not alone in greeting the day thus, Kjeld knew. When the hall was finally settling last night, with the younger men taking themselves off to the second hall, Kjeld had been there at the high table, still. Some who slept in the main hall were already in their alcoves, though not all the trestle tables had been knocked down. Kjeld watched Jari approach the table where the youngest warriors supped. Bork was on his feet, but Yrling was sprawled over the table top, his arms flat out before him, his cheek resting against the wooden board. He still held a cup in his hand, as a small child might. Jari tried to rouse him with a hand on his back, to no avail. The big man stooped down and lifted the inert Yrling up and over his shoulder. With Bork weaving unsteadily at his side, Jari led the way out the door and to his house, where Inga had been long abed.

Kjeld was not drunk. He had wished to become so, to dull the pain of losing Mealla. But Kjeld could not. He was second in command, and must be ready to defend Four Stones if his Jarl was not. Hrald had needed that mead, Kjeld knew it. He and the men on active watch last night, and a handful of others were the only ones who had kept to ale.

Now Kjeld spoke.

"You need food. And broth. Sit, and we will eat together."

They did so. The first sip of the hot meat broth almost rebelled in Hrald's mouth, but a spoonful of the oat porridge gave a lining to his belly to drink more. Kjeld ate, and Hrald followed suit, as much as he could. When they both put down their spoons, Hrald spoke.

"What you said last night, about Dagmar, and my boy. I thank you for that."

Kjeld paused under this thanks. "It is only the truth," he answered. "The daughter of Guthrum, greatest of our war-chiefs, will again be your wife. And she has given you a son."

Hrald's dark lashes dropped over his eyes, thinking of the babe.

"His name is Hroft," he offered. "He was my great-grand sire, on Jutland. A farmer."

"And a fine name," Kjeld returned. "She did well in choosing that."

Hrald felt close to tears.

"I cast her out, Kjeld. I cast her out."

"Other men would have killed them both," Kjeld reminded. "You did no wrong."

Hrald gave a violent shake of his head. "I wronged us both!

"She dropped to her knees before my mother, begging for her help. But our shock was such that . . . " Hrald could not voice it, but went on nonetheless. "It was as if I cut off my own limb, in sending her away."

Kjeld could only say the next. "She is back now, and with your boy."

Hrald gave a nod, his eyes fastened on Kjeld's own.

"Já, and we will wed at Oundle, as soon as I bring her from Witanceaster."

Kjeld's question shown on his face, and Hrald addressed it. "Lady Æthelflaed made clear the union would be annulled upon their return to Mercia."

"All will be well," Kjeld answered. The same was not true for Kjeld, and Hrald gave thought to this.

"Mealla," he asked. "Have you spoken to her? Pega told her to remain here, and wed you."

Kjeld looked to one side. "Mealla has a mind of her own."

"I am sorry, Kjeld . . . " It was all that Hrald could tell him.

Kjeld gave a shake of his head. "She never said she would wed me."

Hrald could only nod at this truth.

They sat in silence. Hrald drank more broth, and a spoonful or two more of the oats.

"I must visit Wilgot," he said. "Will you help Jari choose the men to ride with me," he ended.

Hrald splashed his face with water and combed his hair. He felt he could see no one, not even Jari, before he had spoken to the priest, and received absolution for his sin. Few were in the hall as he moved through it, and when he headed through the stable yard his face was so resolute that none tried to hail him. He passed the church – Pega's church – a church she would never again see – and strode on to the priest's house. If he were not there he would wait for him; it was as simple as that.

Wilgot was there, his door ajar to allow the morning rays entry into his small house. As Hrald placed his foot upon the wooden step that fronted the door, he heard the scraping of a stool or chair as it was slid back. Hrald called out.

"Father Wilgot."

"Come in."

The priest was standing as Hrald entered.

"You may close the door," Wilgot told him. He looked well aware of the need for privacy. The room darkened to deep dusk at Hrald's action, an atmosphere conducive to the telling of secrets.

Hrald bowed his head and addressed the priest. "I would make confession, Wilgot."

He was more than ready to do so. The fact that when he had visited Ceric Hrald had made a false act of contrition to Dunnere, the priest of Kilton, disturbed him greatly, as did his lapse in never mentioning his infraction to Wilgot, his own priest. He would carry this burden no further; it was one he would free himself from as speedily as he might.

"You have heard my sin," Hrald began.

"As all did. That of adultery. And the begetting of a child outside the bonds of Holy Matrimony."

Wilgot let this hang in the air between them a moment, a weighty and true charge, a mortal sin which did damage to the wronged party, and greatly harmed the soul of the transgressor. Then he went on.

"You have proven faithless to your Faith, and lived outside the Church. Both its teachings and its precepts, in thought, and in practice."

The litany of sin rolled on in Wilgot's head. Faithless to your good wife as well, she who built a church here at last, he thought. You have endangered your daughter, now deprived of her parents' stable union, and brought forth another child, one conceived in lust. And this past year you have stood before me many times, unshriven, and received the Holy Sacrament, falsely.

Wilgot was not a man of passion, nor even strong feeling, but his enumerating these gross failings in Hrald now made it difficult for him to moderate his tone. He sat upon the bench and turned his head away, signal to all penitents to kneel.

Hrald did so, crossing himself and reciting the opening petition. Yet Hrald hardly knew how to frame it. "I have sinned, Father," he began. It took a moment for him to name that sin. "I have lain with a woman not my lawful wife," was what he said.

"And what more," prompted Wilgot.

Hrald was silent, considering. The priest answered for him.

"Your sin was compounded by neglect. From fear or shame or pride you did not seek absolution. You hid your sin from all. All save God. And now the evidence of that sin is known, and your sin is fully known, by all.

"Are you fully contrite, both for the sin of adultery, and the act of omission, in admitting your guilt?"

"I am, Father."

Hrald could say this now, for it was his own fault he had cast his true wife, Dagmar, from him, only to wed another, the innocent Pega, whom he had gone on to harm.

Wilgot paused.

The Jarl of Four Stones was expecting a penance imposed on him of many cycles of prayer, as well as the suggestion that a certain large sum of silver be given over to the poorer folk of the village. He dropped his head the further, and lowered his eyes to receive it.

"Your penance is the following. You will make pilgrimage to Cantwaraburh. You must be simply dressed, with no weapon other than your knife.

"You must go on foot. And you must go alone.

"At Cantwaraburh you will again make confession, of what you have learnt through reflection upon your journey there. Plegmund is the Archbishop; apply to him, and tell him all so you may be fully shriven."

Wilgot had turned his head so he might glimpse how the Jarl received this. There was a flutter of Hrald's lowered eyelids, nothing more.

Behind those lowered lids Hrald's mind tried to compass this mandate. It was a humbling penance, and one which, despite its solitary nature, felt public, an act of exposure. He must make the journey alone. Hrald had never ventured to Cantwaraburh, that great Benedictine shrine built by St Augustine, but both Abbess Sigewif and her priests had done so, in a convoy of guarded waggons. On foot, Hrald thought it a walk of six or seven days, perhaps more. Once there he must present himself to the most revered Churchman in the land, and there again confess his sin. Somehow telling this to Wilgot was not enough; his sin was so great another must absolve him of it.

Wilgot went on. "Once you are shriven you need not walk back, or alone. You may join others travelling, or buy an animal to return on."

Hrald remained silent, head still bowed. Wilgot ended on a note meant to convey encouragement. Yet from the priest's lips it sounded more warning than reassurance.

"If God grants you protection on your journey, that will be a sign of grace. And of hope."

Wilgot's next words seemed uttered with near reluctance. He made the sign of the cross in the air over the penitent. "Thereupon, I absolve thee from thy sins, as far as it is my power to do so, in the name of the Father, and of the Son, and of the Holy Ghost. Amen."

The priest rose. Hrald crossed himself and rose as well. There was something more he must free himself from. He took a small ring of twisted gold from his belt and handed it to the priest, with a murmured request. "For the poor."

Wilgot looked down at the ring, that once worn by Hrald's wife. The priest gave a nod and set it upon the table. He had a final word to impart.

"I understand the requirement that you leave at once to carry Lady Pega's gold to her. You may defer this penance until your return from Witanceaster," he ended.

Father Wilgot bowed his head in dismissal.

The Jarl stepped over the threshold, leaving the door behind him open, as the priest had indicated. He squinted against the harshness of the Sun. Hrald had found only partial absolution here; he would not be fully absolved until he had completed his penance. He must go to the Cathedral of Cantwaraburh, on foot, unarmed. And alone.

TWO LADIES OF MERCIA

Witanceaster in Wessex
The Year 898, Late June

"KILTON."

Lady Æthelflaed uttered that single directive to Pega in her royal hall at Witanceaster. Pega's eyes, red-rimmed and tired, widened. Æthelflaed came toward her with extended hands, and took both of Pega's in her own. The Lady's voice was low, yet with that ripple of firmness that she often employed in dealings of State. She gave Pega's small hands a slight squeeze.

"I look upon the future Lady of Kilton," she told her.

Pega could not answer.

"Edwin, the young Lord of that place, still seeks an appropriate wife to be his Lady," Æthelflaed explained. "And he already wants you, Pega. Three years ago, before your marriage, he came to Gleaweceaster to buy cattle from Lord Æthelred. It was there, at that visit, Edwin spied you, walking at my side as we entered the cathedral. You left great impress upon the young Lord. Once his business was concluded with my Lord-husband, he asked of you. Æthelred knew I had already set you aside for Four Stones, but the young Lord's interest was such that he allowed Edwin to speak to me. His attraction was, shall I say, immediate, and predicated on nothing more than seeing you at my side at Divine service.

"He has not wed; he has found no woman to meet his standards. Now I can present to him she whom he sought – you."

Pega's chin dropped. In her grief and weariness she felt no prize, but rather a proud discard who had sundered her own marriage upon learning an ugly truth. Her murmured answer gave proof of this.

"I have been wed, or at least been a man's woman."

Here Æthelflaed gave Pega's hands so firm a squeeze she almost winced. "None of that, my dear girl. We all thought you to be rightfully and lawfully wed. Do not cast yourself in that light, you who are innocent of wrong-doing."

Pega gave a shallow nod and went on. "And I have a child." As if this were a dark mark against her.

Lady Æthelflaed freed her hands, the better to pounce upon this seeming deficiency and turn it to the advantage it was.

"Yes, my Pega. You have brought forth a beautiful and healthy daughter, and with no harm to yourself. What better assurance could Kilton ask than to enter into this union knowing you were capable of bearing more? There is no risk of a faulty womb, or weakness in your person. You shall bear him sons."

Æthelflaed took a turn about the room. "I have not seen Kilton, though it has ever been a favoured hall to my father. A royal granting in fact, from his own father to Edwin's grand-sire, Godwulf. Godwulf and his wife, Lady Modwynn, greatly increased its wealth. Now it is under the direction of Lady Edgyth, widow of the late Godwin, who herself brought a fortune to Kilton.

"It is a curious line; Edwin is the second son, and hers by adoption. Ceric, first born, is a thegn who serves with my brother."

"I know of Ceric," Pega murmured. How could she not; Hrald had spoken of him countless times.

"That elder brother, Ceric, is a God-son of the King. He has made my father glad in his marriage to a Princess of Ceredigion."

Pega knew of this union, if not of King Ælfred's high approval of it. When Hrald left Witanceaster two years ago, he had travelled with Edwin to Kilton, so Hrald might visit Ceric. When he returned to Four Stones he had mentioned the pretty child his friend had wed. Pega found herself biting her lip at this remembrance. Hrald had been fresh from the bed of that woman Dagmar when he went to Ceric.

She gave a small shake of her head to banish this spectre. Æthelflaed was asking her to give thought to the importance of the family of Kilton, a rich and honoured hall. The older brother was wed to a Princess of a Welsh Kingdom. And now the young Lord himself, Edwin, might still want her.

The Lady of Mercia was looking carefully at Pega. Her ward had not recoiled; no abhorrence shown on her face. But then, Pega was exhausted from the revelations of the day. Still, Æthelflaed must press her advantage in this; there was no time to waste. She would write to Edwin at once, and propose a visit in the near future, so that he would not enter into any other contract.

In return, Pega posed a plaintive question to her guardian.

"To wed again," she posed. "In such unseemly haste?"

"Unseemly – no action of yours has been unseemly," Æthelflaed returned. "Yours was a putative marriage; and thus invalid. You soon shall be free as an uncaged bird. Nothing will smooth this upset the quicker than movement to a new place, and new, and important, standing. Standing as the Lady of Kilton."

Smooth this upset, Pega repeated to herself. The rent in her heart felt far greater than that. Yet she knew the Lady's swiftness of action to be needful to the occasion; such things were decided in a stroke. A path lay open; it must be trod; a chance offered; it must be seized. She hung her head, too weary to protest more.

"I ask for nothing now," the Lady went on. "You need make no decision. Dismiss this from your mind. You need rest above all. But know that your welfare is foremost. There will be no union with Kilton, until you have met Edwin and fully approve of him and his hall."

From the open window came the dull clang of a brass gong being struck; the signal for all to gather in the great hall. Æthelflaed was needed there.

"I must leave now, Pega. Try to sleep. We will speak more of this on the morrow."

The new day found Æthelflaed leaving her hall at first daylight. Her guests were still abed, or at least the Lady of Mercia could hear no sound issuing from their chamber. She would greet them later; now she must catch her father early, before the cares of the day descended. Æthelflaed knew to go straight to the small timber building which served as the King's study and writing room. Ælfred always arose before dawn, knelt at his bedside to say morning prayers, then retired to this sanctuary of quiet so he might reflect upon the duties before him.

The presence of not one but two guards outside the closed door told the daughter of the King she was correct in thinking him within. But her father was not alone. In answer to her knock and her naming herself, the door was opened, and by her brother Eadward. He had only arrived late yesterday, and the family had but a hasty reunion at the high table. Æthelflaed was not sorry to see Eadward there; she might deliver her news to both male kin at once. The King was seated at one end of his writing table, its surface covered with inked parchments, but neatly ordered all the same. Eadward was standing before it, mayhap having entered only a short while before.

After kissing father and brother, Æthelflaed began.

"I bear tidings of some import," she began. She looked to her father. "You asked me of Pega last night. She was not indisposed. She was grieving."

The faces of both men sharpened at this news, and Æthelflaed went on.

"She was not ill, but forsaken. Jarl Hrald has fathered a child on the woman Dagmar. Pega, to her great sorrow, discovered this shortly after her arrival here yesternoon. She came across Hrald holding a boy-child, and standing with Guthrum's daughter, his arm about her."

Æthelflaed paused here. She had expected surprise, indignation, even shock on the face of her father. Instead, he gave a solemn nod of acceptance.

She would restate it, and in words forceful enough to convey the seriousness of the offence. "Hrald has fathered a bastard with that woman. He had in fact never ceased loving her. Pega has begged for my protection, which I have granted. I have assured her the union with the Jarl will be speedily dissolved."

It was Eadward made answer. "Just so," he uttered, as if to himself. Yet he wore his surprise upon his face, unlike their father.

"I know of this child," the King began. "He is my God-son."

Æthelflaed found herself sinking into a chair. Eadward too showed his surprise.

"Your God-son," Æthelflaed repeated.

"And my Lady-wife stood as God-mother," Ælfred went on.

Æthelflaed took this in, silently. She was not certain she could control her voice, even if it could be found. Her own mother had held the babe, and offered him to the priest for immersion at the font.

Her father had stood as God-father for several children of importance. The expediency of statesmanship had sometimes demanded it, as had been in the case of Haesten's two sons at the encampment at Middeltun; her own husband Æthelred standing by proxy for the younger boy. In the case of Ceric of Kilton, Ælfred's serving as God-father was far more, proof of true affection and loyalty. A similar bond seemed to be extended to this grand-son of Guthrum, as well. It was much to take in, but accept it she must. This man before her was not only father, but King to Æthelflaed. She could not challenge him, nor his judgement.

The King went on in his telling.

"The boy's mother is the daughter of the greatest opponent I ever faced. Guthrum pushed me – all Wessex – to the brink, after taking every other Kingdom. Yet he knew when to stop, and when to forge with me the Peace of Wedmor. And he held that Peace for long years. As did Sidroc of Four Stones, who signed that Peace before us both.

"Lady Dagmar came to me from Hunefleth in the train of my own priests returning from Paris. She humbly asked my protection. I granted it. She lived here the quietest of lives. I knew of her coming child; she told me, but did not confide to me the father. It was to me a mark of high integrity that she protect his name. When she returned to Witanceaster with her new-born babe I must honour the memory of her father Guthrum, who accepted Christ at my request, taking the baptismal name of Æthelstan. He was himself my God-son.

"I did not know until you told me the boy's sire is Hrald." Ælfred took a long moment in recollection. "Sidroc's own son. And no other Dane has upheld the Peace as has Hrald.

"That is the long and the short of it, my daughter. The Lady Dagmar asked for my protection. I granted it. Just as you have done for Lady Pega."

Æthelflaed found her feet. She drew herself up, a woman not tall, but of befitting regal bearing. There could be no re-drawing of the circle, with Hrald outside the paling. If anything, he had been drawn to the bosom of the royal family through the birth of his son with Guthrum's daughter. Æthelflaed could openly revile neither, not when her own King and her mother had stood as God-parents to the babe.

The King looked down at the table top, considering next steps. "The union of Lady Pega and the Jarl will be annulled," he reflected.

"I have promised her so, and speedily, father. It was entered into under a false pretense. He is to return at once to his hall to retrieve Pega's treasure and goods. As soon as she and I are back in Weogornaceastre, where she wed, the Bishop will annul the union, freeing her."

Ælfred nodded.

"The Jarl, to his credit, forfeits the bride-price," she went on.

Both father and son lifted their heads at this.

"A hefty sum in recompense," Eadward assessed. His father had told of the waggon- load of weaponry Hrald had rolled in with, in offer for Pega's hand.

Æthelflaed's retort could not fully conceal her indignation. "Only his due, for the pain inflicted on my ward."

"And the disruption to your plans, my dear," the King answered. "I know considerable effort went into this match, one brilliantly achieved by you."

The Lady was in no mood to suffer praise for this now-failed union. She gave her head a shake of dismissal. Her news had not elicited the surprise she had expected, yet there was more to tell.

"I have another pairing in mind. Pega as the Lady of Kilton."

"Kilton." King and Prince voiced it almost at one and the same time.

"An inspired pairing, Æthelflaed," her father praised. "Young Edwin has had rare ill fortune in finding his match. I had perhaps looked too far afield for him, first to Four Stones itself, then to Frisia.

"Kilton . . . " he mused.

"Pega will complete the hall," his daughter told him. "Her treasure is beyond peer. And she has proven she can bear a healthy child. Something the house of Kilton has had sorry lack of."

"Lady Edgyth is the best of women," the King was now recounting. "Pega will be, I think, very much to her taste."

Eadward must speak of one of Kilton's men, and did so of he who had long served at his side in treacherous circumstances.

"Ceric. His bond with Four Stones is life-long. His mother, the Lady Ceridwen, who lived there, and carried Gyric of Kilton from certain death from its cellars. His friendship with Hrald. And his union, and child, with Ashild." Eadward was forced to give a shake of his head, thinking of Pega's arriving there.

"Warrior that he is, he will accept this, as he has all else." He looked to his father.

"Your continuing friendship to both the Jarl and Lady Dagmar will mean much to him."

The King nodded. "I have ever held regard for Hrald's mother, Lady Ælfwyn. I met her at her hall in Cirencester, when she was but a maid of seven and ten Summers." Ælfred took a slow breath. "Gyric of Kilton was with me . . . "

Each side of the reunited couple had its own long history intertwined with her father's. Æthelflaed could not escape this.

She had one more morsel to impart.

"I have asked for the Jarl's sister, the maid Ealhswith."

This was as unexpected as was the sudden turn to Kilton.

Eadward lowered his eyes a moment to take this in.

"I know the young woman," the Prince offered. "The Bailiff of Defenas asked me to escort her to Lundenwic."

His sister's sudden attention to this fact prompted him to go on; her eagerness to hear more was barely concealed.

"In face and form she is as lovely as they come."

Eadward had indeed found her person to be attractive. Now he paused, and found himself adding more to this assessment. "But – demure," he added, as if this trait had given reservation to his judgement. "Docile, even. She lacks spark."

The Lady of Mercia gave an impatient toss of her fine head. "In short – she is not her sister."

Æthelflaed had thrown this out as a challenge. All had heard tell of the fire-brand Ashild, whose rebellious ways had led her to disaster. Her next words to Eadward were also a challenge.

"Had you known Ashild?"

"Only by repute," Eadward must admit. "Sadly." Ashild had been no beauty, he had heard, but her attraction must have been great for a man like Ceric of Kilton to have loved, and wed her.

Eadward again gave thought to Ealhswith. A hostage of real value for Æthelflaed, he considered. What he asked was, "The Jarl's sister, Ealhswith. Your plans for her?"

"To wed her to advantage."

This was crisply stated, and left to stand. The Lady of Mercia could not now crow in triumph that her demand for the girl was additional recompense for the way Hrald had harmed Pega.

Ælfred gave his head a solemn nod. "I am sure the maid will be in the best of hands, my daughter. May you achieve with her an honourable pairing, and one of long duration."

Pega remained in seclusion for the two days leading to the Feast of Saints Peter and Paul, that occasion which had called her to Witanceaster, and to the undoing of her marriage. She refused to leave Æthelflaed's hall until she could be certain Hrald had quit the burh. Mealla went out, taking Ælfgiva so the child might run about in the small but green precincts of the cathedral, but these ventures were of short duration. The maid of Éireann kept her eyes so steadfastly upon the romping toddler that even if a whole troop of Hrald's men had appeared before her she would have seen nought but their booted feet.

Mealla was out with the child on such an airing when Hrald sent message to Pega, asking leave to see their daughter. It inspired a sudden panic in Pega's breast, that Hrald might come across Ælfgiva and pluck her from Mealla's arms and ride off with her. No action would be more unlike Hrald than this, but then, Pega did not truly know him; she did not think him capable of the action he had taken to end their union. She delayed responding until Æthelflaed returned, and by then was in such a state of distress that the Lady took the scrap of parchment out of her hand and made answer herself.

Her companion was much on Pega's mind. She must steel herself against the loss of Mealla as well. Pega had lost her marriage, and did not wish Mealla to lose the chance to wed a man she knew loved the raven-haired woman. Yet when she brought up the subject of her companion remaining at Four Stones to wed Kjeld, Mealla objected with such obdurate passion that Pega must relent. Pega held a small purse which she had tried to press on Mealla, one meant as a wedding gift. Mealla went so far as to raise her own hand to stay Pega's, as if it held a thing odious.

"'Tis my choice and none other's whom I wed, you have said so yourself," the maid of Éiriann contended. "Never will I remain under such a roof!"

Pega felt sure her meaning was a pointed rejection of the man who held the hall. And how in good conscience could she bid her friend to remain under the protection of one who had treated Pega so badly? They ended in tears in each other's arms, each consoling each.

When they had dried their faces Mealla glanced sideways at the pouch still in Pega's hand.

"But," she teased, "you might tell me what it holds . . . "

A smile forced its way to Pega's lips, if only for a moment, at this stratagem to make her laugh.

"Three pieces of gold."

"Gold! Three pieces worth? 'Tis enough to build a ship and circle the fine island of Éiriann, leaving a trail of riches at every shrine our Blessed Saints had founded."

Her mistress had ready answer for this. "Needless to say, when you do wed, it shall be yours."

Mealla only shook her head. Three pieces of gold. So much would be a mighty burden. She could not help but think of Kjeld, who had worked so hard to accrue what silver and weapons he had. He was proud of what he had won, and prouder still of those items he had been awarded. Three pieces of gold might cast all that into deep shade. Mealla had an abundance of pride, too much for her own good she had been told, but the second in command at Four Stones also had his.

That night Pega must array herself for the feast. She took the new rose-pink gown Mealla had sewn for her from her clothes chest, just as she slipped the minikin version she had stitched up for Ælfgiva over the girl's yellow curls. Pega could delay her entry in the royal hall no longer, and now that Hrald had left there was no fear of meeting him within. Still, she fought tears at every moment, recalling the high expectation of this feast, and how proud she imagined feeling appearing before the King at the side of her well-regarded husband, the Jarl of Four Stones. Now she felt akin to a widow, or a worse blow to her pride, a woman discarded.

Æthelflaed entered her chamber as Pega completed her dressing. It took but a single look to read the sorrow stamped on the young woman's brow.

"The King has great sympathy for your plight, my Pega, and wished me to convey this," she began.

In truth, Ælfred had said nothing at all about the wreck of Pega's marriage; all the talk had been of Dagmar and her son, her father Guthrum, and of Hrald, and his sisters, living and dead. Recalling this gave rise to fresh umbrage in Æthelflaed's own breast, an anger she must, like so many, stifle in service to her greater ends. To tell the girl that the King had stood as God-father for Hrald's son was out of the question; it would serve no purpose save to wound Pega the deeper.

Pega, looking down, picked up a fine veil of linen, one tinted with the merest blush of pink. To her surprise, Æthelflaed took it from her hands, and herself laid it over Pega's fair hair. She pulled the golden pins fastening her own veil from her head, and slid them with care, one each near Pega's ears, securing the fabric in her hair.

"Golden hounds, with garnet eyes," she murmured. "They are yours now. They will recall you to your dog Frost, who you will soon have."

"You are so kind, my Lady," Pega answered, her voice catching in her tightened throat.

"We shall enter the hall together, and you will sit at my side," Æthelflaed went on.

Pega knew that if Hrald were here, if her marriage were still intact, she would sit by him a few places down, off the Lady's left side. Now she would be at her very hand, as if taken again into the innermost circle of the royal family. As signal to those watching it would be telling. But it could not be helped. Sooner or later all would know of the end of her union.

That night Pega felt her body to be in attendance at the feasting-board, but that her heart and mind dwelt in some shadow-land far beyond the timber walls. Yet she was aware that as the three of them walked in, Pega in her rose-pink gown at Lady Æthelflaed's side, holding the rose-gowned Ælfgiva in her arms, heads turned to look with admiration.

The hall was mercifully full, the noise quieting only when a door behind the high table opened, and King Ælfred appeared, with his personal priest, the Welshman Asser. The King's eyes swept across the hall. It was a look which Pega knew was practised over decades. He appeared to take in the faces of all the subjects before him, and in an instant acknowledge them in a way which held true meaning to those who met his eyes. The King then looked to those honoured guests seated at his own table. As his gaze fell on Pega he smiled upon her, a smile of indulgence, kindly offered, and gratefully received. Though she sat without her husband, there was no question in his eyes. He knew; it was clear to Pega that Æthelflaed had told him. Æthelflaed had taken care of all.

The next day Pega ventured forth with Ælfgiva. They went first to the narrow greensward of grass by the cathedral, with an eager Ælfgiva pulling her mother by the hand to reach its verdant confines. Encumbered by her daughter, hearing but not listening to Ælfgiva's voice as she responded to her prattling child, Pega's heart seemed to give voice within her breast. Hrald was out there, on the dusty road, heading north to Four Stones. Come back, come back, Hrald. Come back to me, her heart spoke, before she could quell its longings.

She stopped herself. Hrald would not come back. She had ended their marriage with such decision, he had not been able to speak a word. But then, it had not been her after all, she told herself. The image arose of Hrald standing side by side with Dagmar, his left arm still about her waist, their son upheld in his right. It was he who had ended her marriage. That one pose, that encounter with the other family to which he had deeper alliance had shattered her union. Pega squeezed her eyes so tightly closed that she must stop in her progress. When she opened them a hot tear was rolling from each eye, and she lifted her hand to brush them away.

⁂

When Hrald had been gone a week, Æthelflaed invited Pega into her chamber. Generally the Lady came to that which Pega was sharing with Ælfgiva, and this summons signified a discussion of some note to Pega.

Æthelflaed was sitting in a chair by the open west window, a basket of spools of coloured thread on a low table next her, and in her hand, a length of linen long enough to serve as altar cloth. Once her serving woman had left, she gestured to Pega that she sit opposite her. The Lady glanced up from her thread-work.

"You are fond of Ealhswith, are you not, Pega?"

"Ealhswith?" Pega had been trying to think of no one and nothing at Four Stones, but she must answer. "Of course I am fond of her, Lady. Ealhswith is an admirable girl."

"Would you deem her kind and obedient?" came the next, and surprising question.

Pega nodded. "Most kind. And most obedient. Indeed," she went on, thinking more on the girl, "she has perhaps been overlooked for these very qualities."

"You are astute, Pega, and I thank you for your candid view." Æthelflaed released the linen from her grasp, and smoothed it in her lap with her hand.

"It is my intention that Ealhswith be overlooked no more. In fact, she is returning with Hrald, and will come with us to Mercia. I have asked for her."

"Asked for her?" Pega's lips parted the slightest amount. This meant only one thing, that Hrald's young sister was forfeit to Æthelflaed; the Lady had demanded it be so. There was no other way Pega could think to frame this, but she managed a smile with her response.

"We were always good friends, Ealhswith and I. I will welcome her company."

"I know you will. I mean to wed her to some advantage. I believe from what I have heard that the girl may have been cosseted, as well as ignored. Such has kept her from developing her character. I am sure your presence did her good at Four Stones, and will do even more good in future. She can learn much from you."

Pega dropped her gaze at this. One thing Ealhswith could glean was how to be a forsaken wife, a lesson Pega hoped would never be forced upon her. But if Ealhswith was to be re-formed in another mold of the Lady's fashioning, how much more so would Pega be? She was already as good as wed to the young Lord of Kilton.

"Must I see Hrald, when he arrives?"

"Indeed not. It will be your choice to do so."

"But I find it likely he will again request that he see Ælfgiva. I would perhaps grant him that."

Mothers of minor children were always granted custody, except in the rarest of cases, but to forbid a father to see his own offspring without due cause was to court an appeal to the hallmoot. In this case, knowing how favourably the King looked upon that father in question, Hrald could apply to Ælfred himself. Æthelflaed could not indulge her anger at the Jarl of Four Stones, that was clear.

"You could be present," the Lady went on. "Or I could be there, with Mealla, so that the child feels perfectly safe."

Tears formed in Pega's eyes; Ælfgiva loved her father and of course had always felt safe with him. After this one meeting he would become as a stranger to the child. A surge of anger rose within her, followed by pity for her daughter. She could feel none for Hrald, who had flung all away.

CHAPTER THE THIRD

STRONG ATTACHMENT

Four Stones

HRALD emerged dazed from his conversation with the priest Wilgot. As he walked back to the hall a growing sense of clarity overtook him, one born of urgency.

He could not bring Dagmar directly back to Four Stones. As soon as he returned he must embark on his penitential trip to Cantwaraburh. He must complete that journey; be shriven by Archbishop Plegmund himself. Only then could he return here and take up the new life he would build with his wife and son.

His men were behind him, at least last night with their bellies full of mead they were. Jari and Kjeld he could trust to the last degree. But there was another, and age-old ally, and he must see her. She dwelt at Oundle, that place of refuge in time of need. He must tell Abbess Sigewif what had transpired in his life, in hope she would aid him.

On the ride home from Witanceaster his mind had touched upon the fact that Sigewif must know sooner rather than later of his past acts. Now in the light of a new day,

facing the long journey back to Ælfred's royal hall, only to
return with one more difficult ahead, he knew he must see
the Abbess now. Today, in fact. He would not tax his bay; in
the paddocks were several of that stallion's sons as strong as
he to carry Hrald there. He would leave within the hour.

Entering the hall he was not sorry to see Jari and Kjeld
sitting together at the high table, thoughtful looks upon their
faces.

"I ride now to Oundle, but will be back before night," he
announced.

Jari began to at once rise, but Hrald lifted his hand to
stay him. "I want you here, my friend. I must ride at some
speed, and your back has had no time to rest. I will take two
men with me, in place of you."

The scowl on the Tyr-hand's face spoke more than his
coming words. "No one rides in my place. Not two men, not
twenty." The resoluteness of this statement forced Hrald to
relent.

"We will take fresh horses then. Ask Bork to look over
my animals and saddle up whichever is fittest for us both."

Hrald looked to Kjeld, as his hand went to his belt.
"Again, we will return at dusk," he told him, handing him the
key to the treasure room.

Hrald spoke little on the ride, one not conducive to conversation, as they took their mounts through cycles of walking, trotting and cantering to reach Oundle in haste. Luckily
the two streams which met their path still flowed with water,
though high Summer was upon them, and their beasts could
lower their necks and drink their fill as they needed.

Luck was again upon them as they reached the palisades
of the foundation, and were welcomed in; the service of Sext

had just concluded. The Abbess, with the Prioress Mildryth at her side, was in fact walking from the stone church as Hrald and Jari appeared. The two surrendered their horses to the waiting stablemen. With a bob of his great head towards the women of the cloth Jari excused himself to the monks' kitchen yard, knowing a deep cup of Sister Bova's ale would welcome him.

Hrald was offered the same as the Abbess led the way to her writing chamber. Once inside she was able to regard her visitor more carefully. Hrald looked the worse for wear, there was no denying it.

"I rescind my offer of ale," she told him, with a slight smile. "I will have mint-water brought. It refreshes, quenches thirst, and leaves the mind unmuddled."

"I thank you, Abbess Sigewif," Hrald answered. With his dark hair tousled from the ride, and uncharacteristic shadows about his eyes, he looked in need of deeper replenishment than any herbal concoction could offer. There was in fact an almost haggard quality about him, which placed Sigewif, in possession of an acute ability to read others, in a heightened state of awareness.

After summoning drink for them both, Sigewif sat down at her writing table, and gestured that Hrald sit opposite.

Hrald was silent a long moment as the Abbess considered him. He had told Jari, then at Four Stones Kjeld and his brother and sister, and last night the entire hall. At each telling he had used much the same words, yet they grew no easier to utter. It all seemed scant preparation to tell so august a personage as she who sat before him.

Sigewif, by her quiet attendance, was like oil upon a roiled sea. There was nothing expectant about her manner, nothing pressing in her bearing. She sat before him with an air of interest removed from any personal gain, regarding him with the same benevolent expression she had used with Lady Ælfwyn, and that Lady's offspring, all their lives. Her single sternness with Ealhswith, and occasional exasperations with Ashild, had been warranted exceptions.

A novice returned with the expected refreshment, a pitcher carrying the herbal brew in her hands. Instead of the silver cup the Jarl was always offered, the Abbess brought forth two slender but tall beakers of pale green glass. She poured out the drink for them both, a mix of mints, costmary, and dried rose hips from the abbey's gardens, steeped in hot water, stirred with honey, strained, and then set to cool in the spring house.

Hrald took a draught before he spoke; his throat was indeed dry.

"Reverend Mother," he began, for given the nature of what he was about to tell, he must use this more personal form of address with her.

"I have returned from Witanceaster without Pega. She has sundered our union, for she learnt that I, two years past at that royal burh, had seen Dagmar again, and lain with her. We now have a son from that night, whom I learnt about, and saw for the first time while there.

"Pega and Ælfgiva have remained with Lady Æthelflaed. All of her goods are being packed now, and I will return with her treasure to Witanceaster before they proceed to Mercia.

"I arrived back at Four Stones yesterday. Just this morning I confessed all to Father Wilgot, for my transgression I had withheld from him in the past." Hrald lowered his head. "As I have withheld it from you."

He raised his eyes for his next words, those of a request he hoped the Abbess would grant.

"When I return from Witanceaster, I will do so with Dagmar. She will again be my wife. I ask that she and our boy might lodge at the convent for safekeeping, until I have completed my penance."

"Safekeeping," the Abbess echoed. Hrald's news was wholly unexpected, and this was the first time she had allowed herself speech. It was clear she must respond to this unusual choice of words.

"Yes, that is so, Reverend Mother. After I bring them to you, I must myself leave. Father Wilgot has assigned my penance. It is that I go to Cantwaraburh, and there confess to the Archbishop."

The Abbess took a breath, but nodded. "With your fast horses, you and Jari and those who escort you should be gone no more than a week," she suggested.

Hrald was forced to again lower his eyes. "That is not the requirement, Abbess. It is that I walk to Cantwaraburh, alone. And unarmed."

The Abbess made no attempt to contain her surprise. "Walk to Cantwaraburh?"

She lowered her chin, her eyes gazing at the table. Next she murmured, as if to herself, "These are news, indeed."

Though this fact lodged only in her own bosom, the Abbess had no high regard for the priest Wilgot. He was, she well understood, the best cleric that could be found to come to Four Stones years ago when Lady Ælfwyn requested one. Sigewif found the priest lacking, not only in matters of theology, though she had rarely entered into discussion with him on such matters, but lacking as a man. The conditions of the penance he had imposed, the exposure to danger Hrald would endure, struck her as highly disproportionate to his offence. The ways to the cathedral town were at times plagued with brigands and hungry vagabonds. Cantwaraburh held not only the cathedral, and thus attracted the devout carrying alms, but also housed a royal mint. It was to her mind outrageous to subject Hrald, a young man of such responsibility, and heretofore spotless character, to such hazards.

Yet it had been done; the penance, harsh as it was, meted out. Her task now was to aid Hrald in those ways open to her. She began with a question.

"The hall knows?" Hrald had only lately arrived; he might not yet have shared this news with his folk.

He gave a nod in answer. "Kjeld eased the way for me, after I told them. He called out acclaim for Guthrum, and his daughter. And our son."

Sigewif inclined her head, as if hearing this herself. She had not often seen the young man who had become Hrald's second in command, but he had left impress on the Abbess when she had. It had been Kjeld who Ælfwyn had sent to carry her to Four Stones at Ashild's death. She had seen Kjeld at sundry other occasions, including his escorting Ealhswith here. Sigewif had always found him well-spoken, as well as forthright. He had used the same powers in Hrald's behalf at a critical moment, and the Abbess was grateful for it.

Her next words were uttered in quiet firmness.

"I will welcome Dagmar, and your son," she said, the one promise that Hrald had hoped to hear.

Hrald would build on his request. "The union with Pega will be speedily annulled, Lady Æthelflaed assured me."

Sigewif gave a nod. She could only imagine the distress with which that noble Lady had met these tidings.

But Hrald was going on. "I would like to wed Dagmar at once after my return, and wed her here."

Yet he was guilty of adultery, and felt compelled to add the next. "I have not known her embrace since the night which resulted in our son, nearly two years past. We have refrained until we are again wed."

As tempting as it must have been for the lovers, Sigewif was not surprised at this sign of continence and restraint, not in Hrald. Restraint at any point in such matters was worthy of approbation, and the Abbess said as much.

Her thoughts now circled to that young Lady who had served as Hrald's second wife, and presented him with a daughter. "I will write to Pega," she told him. "She was held in great regard by the community here, a worthy successor to your own mother."

Hrald almost winced. The praise was true for Pega, but set so high a standard for Dagmar.

Sigewif saw this and addressed it.

"Lady Dagmar will grow into her role, Hrald. I do not overlook the fact that as a child she had none of the advantages of your mother, nor Pega. Yet Dagmar is a young woman of high intelligence. I am sure her devotion to you and your son will guide her. As I will."

Hrald's grateful words were from his heart. "I thank you, Abbess. If you will shelter her, advise her, it will mean much to us all."

Indeed, as Lady of Four Stones many would rely on Dagmar's skill and judgment. And she had not Ælfwyn to advise her; she would be quite alone.

"You have not told me your son's name," the Abbess said next.

Hrald released a breath.

"It is Hroft," he told her, and for the first time in their interview a smile shown, however briefly, on his face.

"I look forward to holding him in my arms, Hrald," she answered, and then reached out to place her hand over his.

Hrald had known little sleep, scant food, and long hours in the saddle. This kindness was almost more than he could justly acknowledge. "I thank you, Abbess," he murmured.

He wished he need not tell the rest, but he must.

"There is more," he went on. "Lady Æthelflaed made demand for Ealhswith. I am to take her to Witanceaster with me, to then lodge with the Lady and Pega in Mercia."

Sigewif lowered her own eyes at this. Hrald was to be deprived of all his close female kin. His mother Ælfwyn resided now in Defenas; he had lost his little daughter Ælfgiva to her mother Pega; and now Ælfred's daughter called for Ealhswith. And Hrald's older sister Ashild rested here in the stone church of Oundle.

The Abbess released a soft breath. "Doubtless Æthelflaed has a worthy match in mind for the girl."

All Hrald could do was give a single nod of his head.

The Abbess went on. "It is, I think, what her mother would want for Ealhswith; a marriage to a man of Wessex, or Mercia. And Ealhswith as well is perhaps best suited for this, and will be closer to her mother."

Hrald must agree. He had always assumed it himself for his little sister, that instead of wedding a Dane she would be called to the Kingdom of Wessex and wed some well-born man there. Æthelflaed's new involvement brought the old families of Mercia into play for the girl's hand, as well.

Hrald would offer an observation about his sister. "It is strange," he reflected. "After Ealhswith stayed with you at the Feast of the Visitation, Pega felt certain she had found some vocation here. At least she asked speedily to return, which Pega took as an impending decision to ask if she might remain with you. I thought Ealhswith might think of going as a nun.

"I was surprised, but then I realised how scant were her prospects otherwise. She had met no one who wanted her, no one with whom she could form a true attachment."

The pause before Sigewif spoke was telling. Yet she must counter this last, as only she could.

"Ealhswith is capable of strong attachment," she answered.

It was stated as fact, one beyond questioning. But then, the Abbess had rare insight into the hearts and minds of the young; Hrald knew this. He went on.

"I must leave now, to be back before dark. Tomorrow or the next day I will return to you, with Ealhswith, that she may bid you and our grandmother Fare-well."

The Abbess nodded. It might be the last time the girl could do so, or visit the resting place of Ashild. Fate could take her to a marriage far from here, and the dangers of child-bed were constant.

Hrald stood, that he might find Jari and make sure their horses were ready. The Tyr-hand was lying, knees bent, on his back upon an old work table in the kitchen yard, a pose Hrald and others had caught him in before.

"Your back is aching," Hrald said. He had not wanted Jari to ride with him, yet nothing would stay him.

Jari gave a grunt and swung his feet down to the ground as he straightened up. "No more so than that horse which carried me," he tried to jest.

The Abbess came to see them off. After she had waved them through her gates, she returned to her study chamber. She would write at once to Pega; the letter might be carried away by Hrald as soon as on the morrow. Sigewif considered her writing table, its stack of neatly trimmed parchment squares, tin pan of new and used goose quills, scrapers, and tiny pottery pots awaiting freshly made ink. She then considered all that Hrald had told her, and the unspoken longing, pain, and grief behind his actions. Sigewif would write what comfort she could to Pega. Her hand rose to her brow, as if to assuage a pain which had arisen there.

"Poor child," she murmured. And she added, "All of them."

The ride back with Jari was again undertaken largely in silent companionship. The one meaningful note Hrald offered was that he would be bringing Dagmar to Oundle on their return. This made sense to Jari; Hrald had already said they would wed there, so having her lodge at the Abbey a day to two would allow him to approach the place as a true bridegroom would, to his bride's home. Hrald said nothing about the penance he must undertake. There was no reason to rile Jari over it now. The task ahead of them was to safely transport Pega's treasure and goods to Witanceaster. They must put all their thought and energy to that end.

In their absence Ealhswith had been diligent in her packing. With the help of the serving women it was accomplished in but a few hours. There was a deep chest already laid by in the weaving room with the linens and woollens Ealhswith had woven, intended for her bridal day. This would be hauled down, as well as her clothes chest, along with a covered basket holding her favourite spindle, weaving tools, needle case, and coloured threads she favoured. She had no need to ask that a loom be broken down for transport; she knew from her mother that wherever she would lodge there would be looms enough. But as she worked at gathering her things, with her Aunt Eanflad steadily moving the shuttle through her own loom and beating up the weft, she felt a pang of remorse to be leaving her alone. Eanflad was solitary in all her ways, and not seemingly unhappy at it, but this was greater, it felt the woman would be left friendless.

Ealhswith could counter this. She walked out the hall yard and went to the croft of a woman in the village, one of the many skilled spinners who provided thread and yarn for the wants of the hall. Nelda had been to the weaving room many times to deliver her yarn for the waiting looms. Would she consent to come every day to the weaving room, and do her spinning there, and so keep Eanflad company?

"You need not speak to her," Ealhswith assured the woman. "You know she is shy. But if you should sing as you stand and spin, it will give her pleasure. You may even hear her hum along. You need come only until Hrald returns, with Lady Dagmar as his wife."

Nelda looked surprised, but hid this as well she might. "I welcome Lady Dagmar," she answered, and gave a curtsey as if that former Lady of the hall were now before her.

"I am glad to hear you say that," Ealhswith could return. "I welcome her as well, but must go to Mercia and stay with Lady Pega."

That night in the hall Ealhswith again went round the high table, pitcher of ale in hand. Again two serving women followed her, with jugs from which Ealhswith could refill her own. She had sat at the high table with Kjeld in her brother's absence; now she, as she had last night, would retreat to the woman's table where she generally sat. But when she had filled all the cups, Hrald gestured her near. His folk must know of another change within his hall.

The Jarl had no need to step upon the scarred boards of the table and raise his arms. The mere summoning of his sister to his side quieted those before him. As faces turned to them, he called out his news so it could be heard by all.

"My sister Ealhswith has been invited by Ælfred's daughter, Lady Æthelflaed, to be her guest at her hall in Mercia. She will be leaving with me."

It was the best face Hrald could put on it. His sister was forfeit, little better than a hostage, but at least this declaration was what he hoped his sister would remember of the way he allowed her to leave; that it was no less than a royal summoning, and Ealhswith would be guest of a woman who was nearly a Queen.

Last night it had been Kjeld who had led the way with his response. Tonight it was Ealhswith's own friends, those maids and widows she sat with at the women's table, who took the lead. They answered these words with smiling gasps, and stifled squeals of delight.

Hrald looked to Ealhswith. A flush of colour had arisen on her face, and she too was smiling.

In the morning the stable-yard was busy with the lading of waggons and saddling of horses. Hrald hoped to get a start before noon, and their final provisions needed time to be prepared and packed. Before this was well underway Hrald again asked Jari, Kjeld, and Yrling to meet him in the treasure room. Another was invited, Bork. When all assembled Hrald gave his orders.

"Yrling, you will remain behind with Kjeld," he began.

Yrling began almost to rise in his place in protest; he had already packed his kit and saddled his horse, though Hrald had said nothing about his coming. Yet Yrling could hear a command when it was meant as one, and he lowered himself to his chair, though his mouth was still opened in objection.

"Kjeld is second here," Hrald told his brother, "holding that title not only because he is a good warrior, but a good leader. You will be as his shadow, and see how he keeps the men in order. You will learn much."

This must content Yrling; at least it seemed a kind of confidence in his own promise. All was undone with Hrald's next words.

"Bork. I want you with me. You will ride as part of our rear guard, and oversee our horses for the short time we are at Witanceaster."

"But I serve as rear guard along with Bork!" Yrling could not keep from claiming this, as though it was rare honour and not the least desirable of all road details.

Hrald had no time nor appetite to debate his little brother. "It is a long journey, there and back; you know this.

We could be set upon. I could die. My son as well. If that happens, Kjeld and Jari will help you hold Four Stones."

The bald starkness of this telling was enough to silence Yrling, and to remind all of the expectations of the Jarl.

"What you can do now, Yrling, is help Mealla with the hounds." Hrald had already decided that of the four young Pega's hound Frost had fathered, he would send Frost with that male who most resembled her beloved dog. It was lighter in hue, but otherwise nearly the twin of its sire, and young enough to live long years when Frost had died of old age.

"They are both well trained," Hrald went on, "but make sure we have good leads for them when needed. Mealla will be in charge of them, and the drover and Bork will help her."

At the end of the table lay Hrald's saddle bags, full and ready to be tied to his saddle rings. The Jarl's next words were in dismissal to three before him.

"Stay Kjeld, and I will give you the key."

When they were alone Hrald took the key, ready on a shelf by his bed, and handed it to his second in command.

"Will you serve as escort, to the end of our pasture lands?"

It would give Kjeld more time in Mealla's company, a chance for her to speak to him, even change her mind. Hrald was not sure if Kjeld would agree, but must offer it just the same.

Kjeld's face, firm of jaw and open of expression, softened at this. He gave a quick nod at this request. "I will serve as escort."

They rolled out through the palisade gates just past noon. Hrald, having confessed twice, felt the lighter in spirit, despite his tiredness. His first, and formal admission had been to Wilgot, the second, and heartfelt, in simple converse with Sigewif. He had not time to absorb the sensation, but an inkling of freedom of conscience was there, one which after he had completed his penitential journey could blossom into fullness. For now he concerned himself with one task only. He fronted a troop guarding a massive amount of golden treasure, and his pressing need was to deliver it safely. As he took his position fronting the ranks he allowed himself a single errant thought, that every step of his horse's hooves brought him closer to Dagmar.

Mealla sat on the waggon board of the first conveyance, straight as an arrow. This was a small waggon, rarely used since Pega had arrived in it. It had been gift of Lady Æthelflaed at her marriage, and the same two sturdy horses that Lady had bestowed on Pega as dray animals were again hitched before it. The tarpaulins thrown over the hooping were as gay as any travelling tinker's cart would sport, painted in pointed lozenges of red, blue and yellow. As a waggon for a bride it had brought a smile to the faces of all who saw it. Given the sober nature of this journey the brightly painted covering seemed a mockery of that earlier happiness, when both Pega and Mealla sat expectantly upon the waggon board. Unchanged and within was all the gold of Pega's forebears, heading first to Witanceaster, and then back to Æthelflaed's hall in Weogornaceastre, where her ward would likely live. Untouched by this family history, Pega's hound Frost and his son were frisking in eagerness by the side of the waggon.

The driver was as stolid as any; his eyes fixed upon the road beyond his horses' manes. Kjeld rode at the side of the raven-haired maid, saying nothing, for there was nothing more he could say. Hrald was ahead, riding in tandem with

Jari, so this time granted Kjeld was theirs alone, but Mealla would not share it.

They reached the outermost limit of the grazing land; before them the clay road wound through forest. Mealla had remained silent. Kjeld reined his horse close to the wheel by which she sat.

"Knowing you has been worth it," he told her.

Mealla pressed her lips together, but was finally forced to look at him. She gave but a quick nod, and turned her face away. Nothing more. But the speed with which she turned her face from his told him of the cost of her silence.

THE WALKING STICK

Lindisse

HRALD returned to Four Stones with twenty of the two score men who had served as escort, carrying Pega's treasure to Witanceaster. The other half he had left at Oundle. Dagmar was now there with their infant son, Hroft. They were treasure enough to demand this protection while under the hallowed roofs of the abbey.

Now all Hrald's attention turned to Cantwaraburh, and his penitential pilgrimage to that shrine. He could not pick up the thread of his life until it was fulfilled. He and his remaining men had arrived back at Four Stones quietly, and on the morrow he would leave it, with even less notice.

Before all gathered for the evening meal he called Jari and Kjeld into the treasure room. Both expected Hrald would discuss the need to ready the hall for his impending nuptials, which Jari and Kjeld supposed would take place in as short a span as it took the kitchen yard to prepare a suitable feast. They were wrong.

"At dawn I leave for Cantwaraburh. It is the penance assigned to me by Wilgot, and one I am eager to undertake. When I arrive there I will confess to the Archbishop. After my return I will wed Dagmar at Oundle, and bring her and Hroft to Four Stones."

Neither listener knew anything of this requirement, so well had Hrald guarded the spiritual redress demanded by the priest.

Jari's mouth had opened, in disbelief. "What, you have not chanted so many Paternosters, or other incantations Wilgot threw at you?"

The prayers, nearly all in the tongue of Rome, were not much more than a mournful drone in the ears of the Tyr-hand.

Hrald's sober reply, unadorned and low, deepened his listeners' concern, as Jari and Kjeld heard the conditions of the journey.

"I will go alone, unarmed, and on foot."

"Unarmed, and on foot?" Jari's umbrage was real, and growing. "He is raving, as mad as a dog to ask you this."

Hrald could only lift his hand in dismissal of Jari's anger. "I will not argue with you, Jari. You do not understand the importance of this. I cannot expect you to," Hrald admitted.

Jari was baptised at a late age, and by persuasion if not outright order, whereas Hrald had been born into and raised in the Church. He believed whole-heartedly in its precepts, even though he had failed to adhere to one of them.

"I must do this thing, and you serve me best by aiding me in this task. You and Kjeld will be in charge of all here, and Asberg is but a gallop away."

He looked to his second in command. Kjeld was as startled as Jari by the penance imposed on Hrald, yet would not risk a comment on it. All Kjeld could do was await the orders Hrald was about to give.

"Let Yrling continue to shadow your movements, so that he can see all that goes into keeping the hall and lands secure." Hrald was more than aware of his brother's innocence. "They are far greater than he can imagine now."

Hrald's next words were meant for both men facing him. "If anything should befall me, Yrling, with your help, will serve as heir, until Hroft is of age."

Such talk was so grave as to make Jari shake his head. It only stirred his ire at the priest, who in the Tyr-hand's eyes had far outstepped the bounds of what should be demanded from the Jarl. He could not suppress the low growl issuing from his throat, a rumble only heard when roused to violence.

Jari raised his maimed hand in objection, then swallowed his anger. He was sagacious enough to ask of Hrald a question.

"You saw the Abbess – what did she say of this punishment?"

"The thoughts of others, even Abbess Sigewif, cannot be brought to bear on my actions. The penance has been laid upon me by a priest; I must fulfill it.

It was clear enough to Jari and Kjeld that the Abbess had grave misgivings about the undertaking, and clear as well that Hrald had not sought her aid in avoiding it.

"I will tell the hall tonight," Hrald ended. He lowered his head a moment, then met the eyes of the two who stood staring at him. Their Jarl named both promise and goal. "When I return and fetch Dagmar, there will be a wedding feast."

Alone in the treasure room, Hrald bethought him
what he must pack for his pilgrimage. There was no supply
waggon to haul food and means to cook it, plentiful bedding,
or waxed tarpaulins to be pulled into tents. Even the same kit
he took in his saddle bags when he had ridden without such
a waggon would be too much, for he must himself carry all
he needed. He had as pack an ash-slat woven basket, with
stout straps of leather; such would hold enough on his back.
A tanned calfskin of no great size, rolled and tied atop his
basket, would add little bulk. It could serve as both ground
cloth, and if needed, a slight shelter when tied between tree
boughs. When it rained he would get wet, as all did who
camped with little gear, but it was Summer and he should
suffer no undue cold.

He laid his leathern kit bag on the table and pulled out
anything he thought he could do without, leaving himself
with a wooden bowl and spoon, a turned cup of the same
material, and two toasting forks of iron which would also
serve as pokers. A single small pot from the kitchen yard
would suffice; he could prop it on rocks and forgo the need
for a tripod to suspend it over the fires he must kindle. He
would take grain, barley and wheat both, and a few vegetables, for it would be a day or two before he might come to
a farm to buy more. At his waist he kept always steel striker
and flint; and he added amply to the store of flaxen tow
fibres from the wooden tinder box kept within the room. He
rolled a single woollen blanket and towel of linen together.
For pillow he would use the pack itself with a sole change of

clothes within. He readied a generous amount of silver, filling two small purses for his belt, the rest tied in a linen pouch to lay in the bottom of his pack-basket.

His clothes – Wilgot had told him he must be plainly dressed. Those which he wore when riding the boundaries of his lands with his men would suffice, and he lifted the lid of a clothes chest he thought might hold them. Hrald was mistaken. It held nothing but a small pouch of red silk, laying abandoned on the dark bottom of the chest. He knew at once what it held, the silver body jewellery he had given Pega as part of her morgen-gyfu. She would have instructed Mealla to leave behind all he had given her. Hrald too never wished to see it again; Pega had donned it on her bare skin the night he returned from his Fate-ful visit to Witanceaster, and Dagmar. He closed his eyes to rid the memory of that night, and entering into the act of love with Pega when he yearned for another. Hrald would discard the jewellery somehow, to Wilgot perhaps, as an Offering for the poor. His hand went to the pouch, and he felt the contents shift in his hand, more fluid than they should have been. He pulled at the drawstring closing the silk. The linked chains had been broken, snapped into many small pieces. Mealla's anger had done it.

Hrald thought of the final time he had seen the maid of Éiriann. He had delivered Pega's treasure to Lady Æthelflaed at Witanceaster; Pega herself did not appear. After the formality of this, he again asked that he might see his daughter. This time the request was granted.

Hrald was allowed a short visit with Ælfgiva, held on the narrow greensward of the cathedral. The girl was flanked by both Mealla and Lady Æthelflaed, and the three stood awaiting him. Ælfgiva had laughed as he neared, and run to him, eager to be held. He had not wanted to relinquish her, but the tenseness in the air between the disapproving Mealla and the watchful Æthelflaed strained the atmosphere about them. He would have been content to merely hold her in his arms, talking with the child, and kissing her brow, but due to the unease she grew restless, and he set her down. She ran back to Mealla, holding onto her skirts and rocking back and forth with an open-mouthed smile on her face. He wished to call to her to return to him, yet hesitated lest she not do so. After a long moment Mealla said simply, "Well," to bring the visit to a close.

Hrald had forfeited Ælfgiva; she would, he knew, grow up far from her father, perhaps to call another man by that name. With a firm shake of his head he stopped himself in his rumination and returned to his packing.

⁂

That night Hrald spoke to the hall. He stood by his chair and addressed those gathered, saying he must leave in the morning to journey to Cantwaraburh, and would return as quickly as he might. As ever, Kjeld would hold Four Stones, and Hrald nodded at him as he said this. Hrald did not say why he was going, but then his men were not always privy to the reasons for his movements. The priest Wilgot was there, sitting as he ever did at the high table. Hrald did not look at him; his eyes were focused down the length of the hall. He saw the surprise on the young faces of Yrling and Bork; lately they had been included in the Jarl's travels, or at least heard of them when Kjeld did. Then Hrald sat, lifting his cup to the serving woman holding the ale.

Hrald was awake well before dawn. He belted on his knife, shouldered his woven back-pack, and stepped out to begin his day. His men were still in their alcoves, but Kjeld was up, awaiting him by the light of a cresset. Hrald locked the treasure room door and wordlessly passed the key into his keeping. Kjeld began to speak, but Hrald motioned him to silence. Still, he could not keep the man from walking with him, out the side door, and thence into the dark morning. The setting Moon hung low in the sky, an orange and waxing half, casting light enough to walk. Both paused to look up at it. By its light they spied a large figure approach from the shadows. Jari. Kjeld placed a hand on Hrald's arm in Farewell, and turned back to the silent hall.

Jari stood alone, awaiting Hrald. He was holding something that looked a spear of throwing length, but then Hrald saw it was a simple pole, into which a hole had been drilled and a leathern thong threaded for the hand.

"A walking stick," Jari offered.

Indeed in its length and stoutness, it was more a staff than stick. Jari named it only this, though used as a fighting staff, any such shaft was an estimable weapon. But Jari would not name it a weapon. It was, after all, far from a spear.

Hrald had to close his eyes in gratitude for a moment at this gesture. He then nodded his thanks.

The men stationed at the gate pulled it open. Those on such duty had witnessed both Sidroc and his son leave well before sunrise, but rarely alone, and never without a fine horse. They wondered, yet like Kjeld, questioned not. Something about seeing their Jarl on foot, with a simple pack on his back, silenced them. Hrald for his own part was grateful. He was submitting, willingly, to fulfill a penance decreed by a priest of the Christian God; he could not care what those who witnessed it thought of his leaving in seeming stealth, and alone. He turned to the men at the gates and said, "I will see you soon. Hold all, as you always have."

Jari took another step or two with him, then with a heaving sigh, turned to the hall yard. He did not see a tall but slight figure, waiting near the gate, watching Hrald.

Jari had left his house in the early dark, treading as softly as he might to keep from awakening Inga. Another was quietly astir in his alcove: Bork. The youth had been listening just for this. The day before he had watched Jari smooth a length of coppiced ash into a walking staff, and Bork had drilled the hole with a hand drill for him, as it was fine work and hard to accomplish with a maimed hand. And Bork with his nimble fingers had threaded the plaited thong of leather through the hole, and knotted it firmly, so it could be slipped over the wrist while walking to secure it.

Bork did not ask the Tyr-hand about the staff, but watching Jari leave his house with it made much clear. He could guess it was for Hrald's coming journey. Bork was not far behind. He thought Hrald would use the main gate to leave, as he was heading to Cantwaraburh, and then take the village road. Bork had a leathern pack ready, with a towel, a blanket, a second pair of shoes, and as much food as he could in good faith ask the kitchen yard for. There was no way he could ask the men at the palisade gate to open for him, but he thought that once they had let Hrald out, they would allow him to follow. He counted on this. In the dark of early morning, the sky showing the slightest sign of lightening, he did not expect to see Jari walking at the side of Hrald, stepping through the gate with him.

The gate was swung wide enough to allow them out; Bork could hear a few words between Hrald and the two men who opened it. Hrald and Jari passed through, and Jari reappeared a moment later and walked toward the hall. As the guards moved to close the gate, Bork stepped forward. They saw his pack, his knife, the shield on his back, and spear held fast in his fist. All knew of his devotion to Hrald. The two guards looked at each other. They did not speak, but gave a nod, and let him pass.

Dagmar walked the nuns' garden at Oundle. It was dusk, and most of the foundation was within the church at vespers. Hroft was asleep in the private cell Dagmar had been given by Abbess Sigewif, tended by a serving woman assigned the task; every courtesy had been extended to them since Hrald had ridden off at noon, back to Four Stones. The deepening gloom drained the colour from the blossoms about her, though the fragrance of maiden pinks was heady as she moved amongst the gravelled paths. The outlines of the brewing shed at the far end of the garden sunk into the timber wall behind it. The retreating light leached the features of the low-slung building of all distinction, and at this hour the shed was empty, the work of brewing laid aside for the night. The path Dagmar trod was still bright enough, as were the fruit trees, standing against the common wall dividing the nuns' and the brothers' gardens. She paused to gaze upon those trees, her mind skipping over the past fortnight, to linger on a few telling moments.

When Hrald returned for her in Witanceaster, he had again taken both Dagmar and their son into his arms. She saw the light in his eyes as he looked upon them, an almost inexpressible joy to her. That single look was something Dagmar had placed in store. She had need of it now, until they could truly be together. Before he rode he told why he had left her here, that he must seek absolution at the distant Abbey of Cantwaraburh. He could not hazard telling her before; he had not wanted her to dwell upon it. Now Dagmar was alone with her thoughts, and her hope.

She let her eyes linger on the darkening fruit trees here at Oundle, and thought of the apple she had left behind. At Witanceaster she had been ready for days for Hrald's arrival. She took only her clothing and personal goods with her, a stool she had grown fond of, and Hroft's cradle. The rest – bed, small table and two chairs, a few other items of utility – she left. House and contents she made gift to Ultan, the stable boy, and his parents, serving folk both, allowing the elders to leave the kitchen-yard common hall and the alcove where they slept. Ultan had ever been of service to her, and though he would continue to make his bed in the King's stable, she could reward him and his folk now. The youth had been there to carry out her goods to the waiting waggon upon her departure.

"Take care of the apple," she told him.

Ultan nodded. "I will, Lady, as will my mother. When it does fruit we will remember you the more, in thanks."

She took a moment when all was loaded, the cradle secured in the waggon bed, Hroft napping within, to lay her hand on the slender tree trunk in Fare-well. Hrald, having overseen the packing of her goods, had been waiting with Jari. Now he drew near to her as she stood by the tree.

"You planted this," Hrald offered.

Dagmar lifted her face to him, a smile briefly crossing her lips. "I did. An attempt to foster good in my life."

In answer Hrald had laid his hand over hers. "Together we will plant an orchard," he promised.

It was little Hroft who awakened Dagmar her first morning at Oundle. His cradle was just off the side of her narrow bed, close enough for her extended hand to reach out and rock the babe back to sleep. Hroft was not fitful but laughing, chortling as his tiny hands gripped the sides of the cradle in attempt to pull himself up and out. Dagmar rose; she could see first light from the single window, and the day looked fair. Hroft was eager to be up, to see, to move. The gravelled paths were awkward walking for him, even if his mother held his hands. A bell would ring, Dagmar had been told, summoning her to break her fast, and until she heard it chime she might take Hroft outside. She dressed them both, and did so. The doors of the nun's cells faced away from the gardens, but rounding the building brought her to them, still mist-enshrouded at this early hour. The church was always open; its stone floors smooth walking. Dagmar carried her restless boy there, pulling the heavy door with one hand as she held Hroft in her other arm.

Someone was already within. A slight figure in a nun's habit knelt on the floor in the corner, fanning an armful of flowers out over the white stone there. The nun looked up. Dagmar thought she knew her, and voiced her greeting.

"Sister Bova?"

The nun stood, and for greeting, bowed her head. Dagmar recalled that the sisters observed silence much of the day; the brewster might be forbidden speech just now. Yet she did not withhold her welcome, for Bova's hands made a generous and loving gesture at the boy Dagmar was about to set down. Her surprise was great at finding Dagmar here, yet the openness of the nun's face, and the warmth of her smile said much. Dagmar feared the return to Four Stones, as she had feared returning here; feared she would be shunned, if not before Hrald, then privately, when alone. Instead this young nun gestured the boy to her, and Hroft stood and made his way to her, first on two unsteady legs, then dropping to his hands and knees into a rapid crawl. The nun beamed, and when Hroft reached for the array of blossoms granted him a blue corn-flower. The little fist went straight to his mouth, bloom first. His mother was there to stop him.

Both women smiled, and Bova, back on her knees, went about her work. It was then Dagmar could see what this was; she stood on Ashild's ledger stone. Dagmar knew her body was here, and now she saw herself the reverence with which it was treated. Bolted to the wall was an upright spear. Hrald had told her of this, and also that preserved in one of the small silver caskets in this sanctuary was the raven pennon Ashild had made for him, soaked with her lifeblood.

Dagmar took in the gravity of all this, and then Bova, having completed her task, rose. Hroft was now crawling to the wall and to the butt of the spear. Dagmar moved to him, plucking the boy into her arms. Bova must leave now, and did so with another smile, and a gesture of gathering both to her heart.

The Abbess sent a young and blushing postulant to bring the new guest to her writing chamber. It was Dagmar's second day of residence at Oundle. She had been within Sigewif's writing room only twice before; the first was on her initial visit to Oundle, with her sister Inkera. Dagmar had ridden with Ashild and Hrald, accompanied by their mother Lady Ælfwyn, and though she had boldly claimed eagerness to meet the esteemed Abbess had rarely felt so out of place as she had in that setting of Christian devotion and learning. The second time Dagmar had been invited within Sigewif's chamber was the day of her wedding Hrald. She and Hrald were damp from rain, smiling and breathless as they signed the abbey register. Despite her best efforts with the quill she dropped ink on her signature, blotting her name. She felt abashed. In light of the dissolution of that union but six months later it seemed a telling act, one which she had never forgotten.

This time she was alone; the postulant, after tapping on the door and opening it for Dagmar to enter, withdrew. Sigewif rose from her writing table, and Dagmar came forward. To her surprise the Abbess gestured Dagmar into her arms, and held her in a firm, if momentary embrace. A fragrance rose from Sigewif as they parted, one subtle but which carried Dagmar back to her prior meetings; the scent of some rare resin, mayhap frankincense or sandalwood.

"You slept, I trust?" Sigewif asked her, after they both were seated. The Abbess answered herself a moment later, and with a knowing smile. "As well as a young mother can, with a teething child."

"Indeed Abbess Sigewif, we both slept. It is as quiet a place as I might ever wish."

"I am glad to hear it. After the long journey rest and peace are generally welcome."

"And I am grateful for your welcoming us. Hrald said it was a safe harbourage, and so it is proving." The shadow that passed over the speaker's face was rooted in her concern for he who was even now heading out on his penitential trip to Cantwaraburh.

The Abbess nodded, but said nothing. The silence prompted Dagmar to speech.

"Hrald's penance – he is undertaking it so readily, despite the hardship, and perhaps danger." Here her voice dropped, and almost faltered, as she found words. "Should I not be forced to do some penance, as atonement for my part in Hrald's adultery?"

Sigewif paused but a moment. "No one is ever forced to penance. It must be an act of true contrition, undertaken willingly, perhaps even joyfully, by those yearning to return to God's grace."

Dagmar's lowered head, and the slight colour rising in her cheek told of her discomfiture. She understood so little of the true nature of the precepts of the Church, and again had revealed her ignorance.

The Abbess could do nought but take pity on her. Dagmar was the daughter of a King, the possessor of striking looks, and had been given a healthy babe. The Jarl of Four Stones loved her enough to have forgiven her gross trespass, losing his innocent wife Pega, her vast treasure, and his daughter in the aftermath. Sigewif could not condone their acts, but could never condemn them; condemnation was God's alone, just as salvation was. Hrald had entrusted this woman and their child to her care. Besides a refuge, the Abbess could offer the comfort of a hearing ear. With Hrald gone, Dagmar was quite alone, and Sigewif knew many might revile her.

"Would you give your own account of your actions, Dagmar? I have heard but fragments of the tale. I welcome the rest, and from your lips."

Dagmar took a breath. The muffled stillness of the writing chamber, the sunlight pouring in from the open casement, even that odour of sandalwood about the Abbess – all enveloped her in a sense of shelter. She would entrust the tale to Sigewif; even that which she had banished from her mind, and told no one.

The telling was unsparing, of her expulsion from Four Stones and its aftermath. It began with the shock she felt at Vigmund's appearance, her critical and foolish error in bringing him to the treasure room and allowing him to hold her, her immediate and profound regret at the pain she had caused Hrald, the disappointment in her actions so clear on the face of Lady Ælfwyn. Dagmar had lost all, cast out to face the harshness and humiliations meted out by Vigmund's cruel use of her body on their cold flight. Then followed the hardships of the journey to Viborg, her attempts to create a life there, which closed with her fleeing with so many others. She detailed all else, from her joining in the train of nuns and priests returning to Witanceaster, to the shock of meeting Hrald there.

To finally speak of it served as a kind of confession, which true Christians enjoyed, an unburdening of the past, and a freeing from that dark well within her into which she had been forced to prison all the bad which had flowed from the mistakes in her life.

The Abbess listened as she always did to such confidences, without interruption or questioning the teller. Her attentive silence allowed, and even encouraged, the deepest level of disclosure from her supplicant.

Her guest ended with her deep worry about Hrald and his safety.

Sigewif's observation on this was delivered in a tone that suggested her own considered opinion of the penalty exacted by Wilgot.

"A severe penance has been imposed on the Jarl. One rather stricter than I had expected."

Dagmar thought that here the Abbess suggested Hrald bore the brunt of punishment, and that she had escaped unscathed from censure, or from needing to make amends. Dagmar's next words were no more than a murmur.

"Perhaps . . . perhaps I need atone for my own sin."

The Abbess uttered a sound akin to a dismissive tut. "A priest would no doubt impose some severe penance. Speaking as Abbess, I would agree. Speaking as a woman, I should argue that you have suffered enough."

She stopped here, but Dagmar's face revealed her uncertainty about the Abbess' expectations.

"I think there has been contrition in your heart for the harm you did to Hrald."

Dagmar closed her eyes at this. How she had suffered for her thoughtless and confused actions.

The Abbess, watching her face, went on. "It is not ours on Earth to judge the workings of the human heart. Christ reminds us that none but he who is without sin can cast the first stone."

Sigewif turned to consider the result of the illicit coupling. "The child has been baptised?"

Dagmar gave a nod. "Yes, Abbess." She paused before going on. "At the cathedral at Witanceaster."

"Cathedral-christened," Sigewif repeated, and not without a trace of satisfaction. "He shall be raised in righteousness," she added.

Dagmar could scarce promise to do so on her own account, but she could on that of the boy's father. "I shall do my best, Abbess. I know Jarl Hrald will."

THE HALL OF KILTON

Wessex

LADY Æthelflaed's rider arrived at Kilton late in the morning. He was astride his third animal of the trip, having been instructed to keep himself on a fresh horse so that he might proceed in due haste. He had also been told to place the letter he bore directly into the hands of Edwin, Lord of Kilton, and to remain at that burh until he had answer.

Thus it was that Edwin was met by the courier. He was returning, helmet in hand from the sparring yard with his brother Ceric, Kilton's horse-thegn Worr, and the two captains of Edwin's body-guard, Alwin and Wystan. The rider was already off his horse; a stable-boy had the reins in hand. The boy turned and gestured to the approaching men. The courier, a wiry and dust-stained youth, approached them, bobbing his head in respect. He was as yet empty-handed.

Edwin nodded back, granting permission to approach.

"Lady Æthelflaed sends the Lord of Kilton God's greeting, and her own," the youth began. It was clear he was not certain which of the men before him was he who he sought, dressed for sparring as they were, and all with good weapons.

"I am Edwin of Kilton," came the answer.

The courier's hand went to his breast. He unbuckled one of the three fasteners clasping his leathern tunic, and withdrew a thin wallet, also of leather.

"A letter for you, my Lord. I am to await your answer."

"I thank you," Edwin returned. "Your horse will be well cared for."

Indeed, the heated animal had already been relieved of its packs and saddle, and was being walked to coolness. Edwin's next words were for the comfort of the rider himself.

"Wystan. Take him to the kitchen-yard for food and drink. The bathing-shed as well if he wishes it," he added, not failing to note the grime on the young man's face.

The two left, and the Lord of Kilton stood there, Ceric and Worr on one side, Alwin on the other, the slight wallet in Edwin's hand. A letter from Æthelflaed of Mercia. He had no idea what tidings the missive held, for good or ill. Those who might best advise him stood about him, yet Edwin's next words could stay their help. He was in fact not sure how to take such a message, with his advisors, or alone.

The eyes of Edwin and Worr met, and Edwin thought how much he needed the guidance and counsel of an older man. Worr felt it too. But Edwin was still ashamed of having struck his brother in the horse-thegn's presence. He could not ask for Worr's help; the best he could do was have Ceric with him.

Edwin looked to his brother. "Ceric. Will you come with me, to the treasure room," he invited.

Once inside the brothers set down their helmets, pulled off their leathern tunics, and then the thickly padded linen tunics beneath them. A serving man brought ale, and with their cups before them the brothers took seats at the table.

The leathern wallet was stitched shut, laced and knotted so closely as to try the patience of any who tried to unpick the thongs which sealed it. Edwin gave up almost at once and sliced it open with the tip of his seax. He pulled out a single sheet of parchment, and held it before him.

Edwin did not get far in his reading; he scanned the first few lines, and then passed the letter to his brother. The import was such that alone he could read no further.

"It is indeed from Æthelflaed of Mercia. She is offering me a wife."

The surprise Ceric felt was unconcealed; the jerk of his head betrayed it. He cast his eyes upon the letter. Ceric saw, and at his initial glance, perhaps more than Edwin had.

The first thing that struck him, other than Edwin's opening pronouncement, was the lettering, in a wholly distinctive hand.

"The Lady penned this, herself," he said aloud.

It was of import to Ceric. Lady Æthelflaed had at her disposal numerous priests and monks, not to mention learned nuns, to write her letters. But such was the gravity of the matter she had taken it upon herself to serve as her own scribe. The hand was not as tightly controlled as that of a scriptorium monk, or professed scribe. It was, though, quite firm, more open – expansive even – like the Lady's ambitions themselves, Ceric thought.

He began to read. He did so aloud, without attempting to colour the contents with his own interpretation.

"MY LORD EDWIN OF KILTON

You stood before me once at Gleaweceaster, inquiring after the exemplary young woman who was my ward. I assured you then that should there be a change in her status, you would be the first to know. Lady Pega, lately of Four Stones, has sundered her marriage with the Jarl thereof. The termination of the union is uncontested. Her dower is that which a King might envy. And in her deportment, grace, dedication, and skill, Kilton will find a perfect Lady.

I need not remind you of Lady Pega's attractions; you noticed and remarked on them yourself. She has borne a healthy daughter, now over two years of age, and thus can be fully expected to bear Kilton the rightful heirs such a burh demands.

Lady Pega and I are currently at Witanceaster. Her former union will be annulled as soon as we arrive my hall at Weogornaceastre. Your response will be carried thence, that I might have it upon my return to my hall. Should you respond favourably, I myself will travel to Kilton with Lady Pega. We will thus be able to reach Kilton by the feast day of St Lewina, Blessed Virgin and Martyr."

It was here Ceric must pause. The Ladies Æthelflaed and Pega were at Witanceaster. There had been some sudden occurrence, and there, to change the status of Pega's marriage with Hrald. Ceric could not help but form the name, though silently: Dagmar.

Dagmar, Hrald's first wife, must be at the heart of this; Hrald had seen her two years past at Witanceaster, and there she must have remained.

Ceric read on; he must.

"I need not tell you that such a union with Pega will create yet a further bond between the hall of Kilton and the royal house of Wessex. Raedwulf of Defenas, a man beloved by my Kingly father, is now wed to Ælfwyn of Cirenceaster, lately of Four Stones. And that Lady is grand-mother to Ælfgiva, Pega's child. I scarcely need mention that through me, Pega has a long and close connection to the royal family of Wessex.

I look forward not only to making your direct acquaintance, my Lord, but in meeting with Lady Edgyth, your mother, a woman greatly esteemed by my own father.

I await your answer.

ÆTHELFLAED OF MERCIA"

Ceric lowered the parchment.

His eyes did not go at once to his brother, but rested upon the wall to one side of Edwin's bed. A large loom, now un-warped for many years, stood against that wall; one that Ceric as a child had been hidden behind with his grand-mother Lady Modwynn during the Twelfth Night attack at Kilton. After the death of Godwin, Lady Edgyth had vacated this room, retiring to a bower house so that Edwin might rightly live here in the treasure room. Edwin had no Lady to use that loom; now one might be coming, to stand before it as

Modwynn and Edgyth had stood. This possibility presented by the empty loom returned Ceric to Lady Æthelflaed and her letter. Here is a peace-weaver for you, Edwin, it seemed to say; though the severed warp threads were no doing of his. Ceric could not help but be struck by the assumption by Ælfred's daughter that Edwin would at once acquiesce to her wishes and wed the woman she was offering Kilton. It felt to Ceric near a threat, this reminder of how close the halls had been, her suggestion that it would be a protection to Kilton that Pega be installed there. Yet some truth lodged there. For after all, Kilton had been a royal granting.

Ceric turned his eyes to his brother and spoke.

"So you have seen Lady Pega," he began.

"I have. When I went to Gleaweceaster to replenish our cattle. I saw her when Pega entered the cathedral there at Lady Æthelflaed's side. I inquired after her to Lord Æthelred, who seemed to think her a target far beyond the strength of my arm pulling the bow-string. At any rate, Lady Æthelflaed deigned to see me, to tell me the girl had been set in reserve. For Hrald of Four Stones, I was to learn later."

Ceric must look down a moment, hearing this. All he could do was go on.

"There is, I am sure, no defect in Lady Pega. When Hrald was here he told me she was a wholly admirable young woman." He must say the next, and did. "But . . . Hrald had been wed before."

Edwin supplied the answer. "Yes. To Guthrum's daughter. A woman named Dagmar."

"You know of her?"

Edwin could not conceal the note of bitterness in his response. "I spied her, again at church, at Witanceaster." He gave a soft laugh at his own expense at this, one painful to hear. But Edwin would say no more of the dark-haired beauty. He could not bear to admit to his brother that he had been attracted to a second young woman either designated for, or discarded by the Jarl of Four Stones.

"Yes, Dagmar. The daughter of Guthrum," Ceric answered. "I think she was the cause of this breach. Perhaps Hrald and Lady Pega were called to Witanceaster. There he saw Dagmar again. And that occasioned the breach."

"You mean Pega had been betrayed by Hrald."

Ceric must answer, though he risked damning Hrald with that brand. "Perhaps so," he finally murmured, with a nod of acknowledgment.

"So Lady Æthelflaed presents me with a slighted woman."

Ceric answered with some little fervour. "It is no fault of hers. Pega sounds innocent of any wrong-doing. Again, Hrald only spoke highly of her."

Edwin shook his head. "It is a mares-nest," he muttered. "What manner of man is Hrald, to conduct himself thus?"

"We know little now," was the answer Ceric offered, one unsatisfying to both brothers.

Edwin sat staring at his older brother, his impatience rising. To Edwin's ears Ceric seemed to be championing both parties. The Lord of Kilton's irritation got the better of him.

"You cannot defend them both!"

Here Ceric's indistinct thoughts on the matter became a firm border. "I can, and I will, as I can condemn neither."

He drew breath and returned to the offer at hand.

"And – do not forget her riches.

"Pega may bring as much to Kilton as our grandmother Modwynn did."

Edwin's answer bordered on the petulant. "She has been wed and had a child. Hrald's child."

Ceric was quick to counter this. "A daughter you will raise as yours, should you wed her mother. Hrald has little claim on the girl, after this.

"And Pega can bear more. Your daughters, your sons." Ceric said this last with decided emphasis, one unmistakable.

Having spoken this, Ceric was forced to think of his child-wife. I have wed a Faery, and she can bear me no daughter, or son. Only the happiness she brings me.

This realisation, once wraith-like, arose unbidden in his mind, growing more distinct in form and substance. Ceric fought against it. His task here was to help Edwin, and he must allow nothing to intrude.

Edwin's own thoughts had travelled on. "Her union will be annulled . . . what does that truly mean?"

Ceric took a breath and considered how best to put it. "That the given marriage was entered into falsely, by one or both parties. Through ignorance, or concealment, one or both could not truly commit to the union, though they said their vows."

"And the children resulting?"

"They are considered legitimate, and legal heirs, just the same. But if Hrald allows, there would be nothing to keep you from naming Pega's daughter your own, should you wish it."

The young Lord looked lost in thought at this. Ceric at last relinquished the letter, laying it down upon the table. Edwin looked down at it, but did not take it up.

"St Lewina's Day – when is that?" he asked.

Ceric could only shrug. "Dunnere will tell us." He gave thought. "Likely in a fortnight, or perhaps more – it is a good distance to travel." The Lady must be pious as well, Ceric considered, to pin the day near to her arrival to a lesser-known saint like Lewina.

Edwin gave no answer other than a nod.

Ceric went on. "Pega. If you saw her once, and liked her, perhaps you should see her again. Then you may judge."

Edwin found himself turning his face away. Everything I look at is in the shadow of Hrald, he thought. Even you, Ceric. You are his best friend.

"Lady Pega," Ceric repeated. He recalled what Hrald had told him. "She is of an honoured family of Mercia, one of the oldest. In her family is gold, gathered by the Caesars. Pega is dear to Lady Æthelflaed, as a younger sister would be. She would not entrust her to you unless she felt you more than worthy, and Pega more than willing."

Ceric paused. "And as alliance, Edwin – think of it. It is direct and powerful alliance with Mercia. It is thus direct and powerful alliance with Ælfred's own daughter, Æthelflaed, and Ælfred's son, Eadward, who will become King of Wessex. And the wealth Pega will bring you – you could expand the hall, build a fleet of war-ships. Anything you needed. Think on what she is bringing you. You have seen her, and she pleased you. Think on that, as well."

A long and reflective moment passed for Edwin. He finally spoke. "You sound like Raedwulf."

"I will take that as praise."

Edwin again turned his head aside.

Ceric must go on. "Edwin. Our role is to protect Kilton. At all cost. At any cost.

"Here is a Lady, kind, fair in bearing, and of coveted wealth, willing to be your wife. Think on this."

Edwin must think on it, yet he was sorely tempted to take up Lady Æthelflaed's letter and write along the bottom, "I must respectfully decline." That would give him some satisfaction.

The Lord of Kilton let this sense of aggrieved relief wash over him, knowing it for the childishness it was.

For after all, how could he refuse? He thought through all he had heard, all Ceric had added. He must accept that Lady Pega left Hrald – she had not been set aside – she had walked away from an unjust and deceitful union. She had pride, just as Edwin did. And she was immensely rich; Lord Æthelred had conveyed as much to him, and both this letter and Ceric confirmed it.

And Edwin could not refuse two choices from the royal house of Wessex. His objection to Hrald's sister was rooted in the girl's father, and was understood and accepted by the King. This rejection would not be. He must accept Pega. But for a long and telling moment he wrestled with himself. Pride was urging him to two conflicting ends; reject Pega out of pride, as a sting to Æthelflaed who had once passed him over; and accept her out of pride: she was no less than he deserved, and she was apparently choosing him over Hrald or any other man in agreeing to this match.

Edwin's hand reached for the letter lying there before his brother. As he did so, the sleeve of his tunic pulled back enough to reveal the tip of a red scar on his wrist, the terminal of the blow Sidroc, Hrald's father, had dealt him on Gotland. As Edwin took up the parchment, he thought of the Dane. Sidroc told him he must pray to God to win a wife, and also to be prepared to sacrifice much for her – to "abandon all you know."

He had not understood it then, nor could he now. Edwin was not formed for the kind of deep passion his brother knew. He saw, each and every day the kind of love Ceric had for that Welsh sprite he had wed, but could scarce imagine it for himself; it seemed a kind of obsession to him. Edwin had no name for that degree of absorption and attention. He is under a spell of some kind, he had told himself. Yet part of Edwin desired this, yearned for this. And he had, alone and in a kind of despair, gone to the church here one night when his brother was away in Wales, and prayed for a wife. He had vowed silver for the poor women of Kilton, which next morning he had delivered to the priest Dunnere.

Yet, abandoning all he knew? What did he know? He could never abandon Kilton. But something had been weighing on him. Right now the prod of besting Hrald was like a cruel and unrelenting spur in his side.

Was that the abandonment he must make, his hope of one day being seen as better than Hrald? And what about Ceric, but an arm's length away? Edwin was forever in his shadow. Ceric excelled him in all things, and Edwin felt all knew it. Edwin too had stood before Lady Luned in Ceredigion, but it was to Ceric that Lady revealed their kinship. She had not told Edwin; he must learn it from his brother's lips upon his return from Wales.

Edwin allowed his eyes to travel over the letter. Here was a veritable Queen, asking for his help. Æthelflaed had suddenly a valuable asset returned to her, one which she must dispose of in the most profitable way possible. Edwin could step into that breach and accept Pega, and her gold, and the gratitude of the houses of both Wessex and Mercia. He must accept what was being granted to him – Pega and all her prestige, even though she was first the wife of he who was his rival. He clenched his jaw at this. The honey did not fully conceal the bitterness of the potion he was being asked to drink.

But he had before been wrong about what he thought he wanted – he had once sought to kill Hrald's father, then realised he desired something quite different, to face his own mother and challenge her with his words. And she had won that challenge, won it with her love.

Edwin dropped the parchment upon the table. Ceric was moved to take it up again. He had a final word to share with his younger brother.

"Edwin. Look at the hand. Compare the letter with the signature. As I said, Lady Æthelflaed penned this herself. That is a mark of high respect."

Edwin gave a reluctant nod.

There was no more Ceric could think to add. He waited for Edwin to say more, then spoke himself, with a question that might, in its answer, disclose Edwin's turn of mind.

"What will you tell Lady Edgyth?"

Edwin released a long and slow breath. "I will give her this letter." Such concern was on his brother's face that Edwin could not help the slight smile cracking his lips. "And tell her I welcome the arrival of the Ladies Æthelflaed and Pega."

Ceric returned to the bower house, to leave his sparring kit. He thought he might find Dwynwen in the pleasure garden, and was right. But he was first greeted by one of her black and white speckled hens, which lifted her feathered head from the leaf litter she poked in and welcomed him with a tut-tut as he entered the pavilion. The fowl from Ceredigion had been granted the run of the garden, and a small wooden house built there for their protection. They were no ordinary hens but Dwynwen's special pets, meant not for the pot or roasting spit but for the pleasure they gave to the niece of King Elidon, who had granted them to her. One of the hens was especially partial to the Princess, and often hopped up into her lap when she sat at the table in the pavilion. Today the hen stood upon the table top, looking down with glinting eyes at the work Dwynwen was bent over.

Ceric paused a moment to study his wife. The breeze was blowing her veil, lifting it away from her face and shoulders, and lifting also the tips of her brown hair. He was not surprised the speckled hen was motionless in her presence. Dwynwen might have been a small bird, or butterfly, and like those creatures was intent on what held her attention. Before her on the table top lay a generous array of seashells she had gathered from the shore below. She was at work, spreading them out, arranging them into a dense and out-curving spiral.

Despite her absorption she looked up as Ceric neared, and greeted him with a smile.

He pulled the second chair and sat across from her. The hen fluttered off to join her sister in the herb bed.

"You told me one day when you were drawing your designs that Edwin's wife would come to him. You were right."

Dwynwen's smile did not fade, but her face took on a new alertness as Ceric went on.

"A letter has just arrived from Lady Æthelflaed, Ælfred's daughter. She wishes to come here, to Kilton. And she will bring with her a young woman to wed Edwin."

Dwynwen's answer was as warm as her shining eyes were bright.

"I am so glad for him."

Ceric slowed his words. "There is one impediment for Edwin. Not in fact, but in feeling. The woman was Hrald's wife."

He went on to share what he had intuited from Lady Æthelflaed's letter, adding what he could about Hrald's attachment to his spurned, but first wife.

Dwynwen listened so thoughtfully that it took her long moments to make answer.

"Such love as Hrald's is Fated," she murmured.

Or fatal, thought Ceric. Nothing would have driven Hrald to such ends save dire need. He must be in great distress, and Ceric could do nothing.

The Princess of Ceredigion studied her husband's troubled face. She placed her hand over his, a hand so small upon his own. Ceric watched her do so, the same giving gesture she had made the first time she had touched him, here, at this very table.

"Hrald will know what to do," she told him. "All else will fall in around his love."

Ceric could only nod. Certainly Dwynwen felt their own love to be Fated, and it had come right, in the end. And what greater stroke of Fate was the uncanny fact that Dwynwen's step-mother, Lady Luned, was his own grandmother? The path his child-bride trod had taken her inexorably to him, in echo of the spiraling circles she so often created.

He let his eyes drop to the shells she had placed in her sinuous design. Shells, seeds, pebbles – Dwynwen often took such things and played with them, laying them out in artful arrangements, only to return them to nature when done. He sometimes wondered if it was a form of divination, or if she received some secret and inexpressible satisfaction from such play; even a message of some kind.

The shell in the centre of this spiral was nearly round, pink-tinged, and pearlescent at its heart, a shell of true beauty. It moved Ceric to speak.

"Will you not save that middle shell, the pink one?"

Dwynwen smiled, but shook her head. "I will free them all, letting the waves wash them," she answered, tilting her head to the sea beyond the cliff.

"The next time I gather shells I will make a new design, one different. Just as every day is different. But just as beautiful.

"So will Hrald," she went on, "build a new design.

"And Edwin will have a Lady soon," she ended with another smile.

<hr />

Even as Ceric and Dwynwen spoke, Lady Æthelflaed's party approached. They must first stop in Defenas, at the hall of Raedwulf, the Bailiff of that shire, and his wife, Ælfwyn.

Æthelflaed sent a rider ahead to The Fold, to warn the Bailiff and his Lady of her unexpected arrival. The Lady's note was brief, assuring them of but an overnight stay, and mentioned none but herself. Hearing Pega and Ealhswith were with her would occasion nothing but alarm in her hosts. The full truth could wait until their appearance.

The courier arrived a full day ahead of her party. The couple opened the letter in the hall, with only Burginde in attendance. She was the first to react to the message within, straightening up on the bench holding her, and rolling up the stocking in her hand she had been darning, to tuck back into her workbasket.

Raedwulf was surprised at the announcement; a visit to the southern parts of Defenas was a clear detour for Æthelflaed, should she be heading from or to Mercia and Witanceaster. He answered Ælfwyn's puzzlement as best he could.

"Some special request she must make of you?" she asked. Ælfwyn held little Wulfsige on her lap; the babe was playing with a strand of his mother's long hair.

Raedwulf gave thought. Or of my Lady, he considered, to himself. His wife was mother of a powerful Jarl of Lindisse, and mother-in-law to Pega, who all near to the Mercian royal house knew was as close as kin to Æthelflaed. Raedwulf watched his little son try to stuff the strand of flaxen hair he held into his tiny mouth, and must smile as Ælfwyn gently relieved him of it.

"We will not speculate," Raedwulf decided, and leant forward to kiss his wife on her brow.

Ælfwyn arose, and with a nod at Burginde, answered with her own smile. "Not when there is much to prepare," she agreed.

The following day a second rider approached, giving The Fold fair warning that Lady Æthelflaed's appearance was nigh. Both the Lord and Lady of the hall were dressed to greet her, Ælfwyn in a linen gown of silvery blue, and Raedwulf in a tunic of charcoal grey. The brilliant sapphire he had given his wife upon the birth of their son rested on Ælfwyn's breast, and Raedwulf wore a chain of linked gold spanning from shoulder to shoulder, gift of King Ælfred. Burginde stood next her mistress, holding Wulfsige, and young Blida had charge of Cerd, who stood next her, his feet stamping with excitement at the sight of the scores of horses approaching.

The train of their visitor was even more impressive than the watchers expected. It was a small army, with no fewer, Raedwulf quickly summed, than two score and ten mounted men, and six waggons.

Eight horsemen in doubled ranks led it, and from the saddle cantles of the first pair were fixed two small flags each, the golden dragon banner of Wessex, and the coiled green serpent banner of Mercia. Behind this rolled a waggon hooped with a snowy tarpaulin, pulled by four fine horses. Æthelflaed sat there upon the waggon board, a range of her serving women and companions behind her.

Ælfwyn's eyes were drawn to a smaller waggon behind this, one gaily caparisoned, its overarching tarpaulins painted in bright lozenges of red, blue, and yellow. This was a conveyance she knew; it was that in which Pega had arrived Four Stones when Hrald brought her home. Ælfwyn could not see who sat within; her view was blocked by the first waggon now slowing as it rolled to a halt, but the sight of the painted waggon made her heart skip in wonderment.

The ensuing arrival was far from what the Lady of The Fold had anticipated. Æthelflaed, daughter of Ælfred, was imparting a great honour on their hall in stopping here, and Ælfwyn had imagined a warm, if formal, reception of so significant a guest. Raedwulf's wife took his arm, and together they moved forward to greet the Lady, until Raedwulf himself reached to aid Æthelflaed's descent from the waggon board.

It was then Ælfwyn turned her head to the second waggon. There sat Pega, marked distress on her young face.

Ealhswith, wide-eyed, was at her side. A white-faced Mealla was just behind them, with little Ælfgiva. Only Ælfgiva looked happy.

Ælfwyn must turn back to welcome Lady Æthelflaed, now standing upon the packed soil of the forecourt. Raedwulf had time to murmur an introduction between the two, for he had also seen the young women in the second waggon, and seen too their faces.

Ælfwyn's bowed head and deep curtsey to Ælfred's daughter was sincere, as was that of Burginde behind her. But the distraction was such that Æthelflaed turned almost at once, gesturing her charges to come forward. The driver had jumped down to assist them, and Raedwulf joined in handing the young women down.

Pega had steeled herself for this meeting, yet upon seeing Ælfwyn her face crumpled under the force of coming tears. She bit her lip in futile attempt to stay her sobs. Tears flowed from the eyes of Ealhswith as well, out of sheer sympathy; yet the emotions churning in her breast were confused.

For a moment of horror Ælfwyn feared the worst for her son; here, unaccountably were his wife, daughter, and sister. Ealhswith, after her first embrace, was quick to reassure her mother. "Hrald is alive; Hrald is well," she offered. Ealhswith could scarce utter the words, so swept up was she in a turmoil of sorrow and concern, one laced with a thrill of excitement at what her own future might hold. Her life was going to change; it had already changed. She squeezed her mother's hand again and repeated, "Hrald is well." But over her daughter's shoulder Ælfwyn saw Pega turn her face away.

Meanwhile Cerd had broken from Blida to run toward
Ealhswith with a happy cry, eager to tell of his pony. Lady
Æthelflaed took command of the confusion.

"I think Ealhswith would like to reacquaint herself with
her nephew." Her voice was low and measured, but pointed
enough.

"Yes," agreed Ælfwyn. The welcome ale in the hall
proper would no longer serve, not under these circumstances. Nor had she a moment to embrace Ælfgiva, who
for her restlessness Mealla had been obliged to set on her
own legs. The child neared Cerd, pointing at him as she did
so. Ælfwyn addressed her daughter. "Ealhswith, please to go
with Burginde and Cerd and Blida. Ale and cakes await in
the hall. Then Cerd may show you and Ælfgiva his pony,"
she promised, looking to her little grandson. Pega nodded at
Mealla, bidding that she stay with Ælfgiva and enter the hall.

Ælfwyn turned now to Æthelflaed. "Will you come,
Lady, and Pega, to my garden bower. We will take refreshment there." A glance at Burginde assured Ælfwyn that food
and drink would soon follow.

So it was that Ælfwyn and Raedwulf escorted the two
through the hall yards and to the bower garden and its
small timber house. Ælfwyn had meant Lady Æthelflaed
to sleep there, and all was laid in readiness to receive her.
Ælfwyn was proud of the little house, as Raedwulf had used
his considerable skill in directing the joiners to create a
snug but almost fanciful structure of upright timbers. The
two window openings and single door sported decorative
carvings of intertwined animals, their long legs and tails
wrapping about each other's bodies, and the steeply
pitched gable roof was laid with the thickest thatch to be

seen in Defenas. All must go unremarked on, as Ælfwyn shepherded her guests in.

There was a pot of purple betony stems on the table when they entered, left to greet the Lady of Mercia. Flowers seemed unaccountably out of place now, and Ælfwyn's first move was to lift them from the table top and place them on the broad sill of the near window.

They had just settled when Lioba, the wife of the steward of the hall, herself appeared, trailed by Blida's elder brother Bettelin. They carried both ale and wine, a jug of water to amend the latter, and the aforementioned small cakes, dotted with nutmeats and dried cherries.

When they were again alone Ælfwyn poured out wine for her husband, and at her own urging, for Pega as well, for the girl was pale as a sheet. She then filled two more glass beakers with ale, for herself and Æthelflaed. The first sip was taken in ceremony, and no celebration.

The Lady of the Mercians did not hesitate to speak. "I will begin with the kernel of the tale, and Pega will augment the story as she sees fit."

Ælfwyn must brace herself, and Raedwulf's presence at her side lent comfort she feared she would fully need. He had in fact moved his chair the nearer to her own, so that paired they might meet whatever tidings were to come.

"The King assembled a handsome gift of treasure to be carried to Rome as St Peter's Pence," Æthelflaed began. "This occasion was to be marked with a feast at Witanceaster, and as I was attending, asked that Pega and the Jarl be invited. They had no sooner arrived and the Jarl gone off to stable his horse when Pega suffered the shock of her young life. She, Mealla, and Ælfgiva made a random turn in the northern precincts of the town, and came upon the Jarl, standing with another family. Or I should say, his other family. The woman at his side was Dagmar, and the child in his arm their son."

There she stopped, the searing truth left hanging in the air before them. Ælfwyn, who knew her son had not resisted the temptation presented by Dagmar's nearness, was none the less stunned by the outcome. Hrald's other family. It was as bald as it was true. His mother resisted the temptation to close her eyes against this news; there was no shielding herself from it, not when the innocent suffered. She looked to Pega, who sat pale and almost motionless next Æthelflaed. Hers were eyes which had shed many tears over this betrayal, though they were dry now. Ælfwyn found her hand lifting to brush away a tear forming in her own right eye. Raedwulf had made but a single exhalation of astonished breath, his sole audible reaction, for he was caught completely off guard.

Ælfwyn asked her first, and hushed, question. "What did he say?"

"His actions spoke for him," came Pega's retort. Though terse, her voice remained low. She thought, and then went on. "He did tell me he was aggrieved at the harm he had caused me.

"I went to Lady Æthelflaed at once, to tell her my marriage was over. I begged for her protection, which she granted. I saw Hrald only to return his ring, and tell him of my decision."

Æthelflaed added to this. "He was however permitted to see Ælfgiva, when he returned to Witanceaster with Pega's dowry. The child was in the care of Mealla during the visit – and mine own care."

Ælfwyn could scarce draw breath. Hrald had perhaps seen his daughter for the final time. Her hand went to her brow. It was not hers to make apology for her son's conduct, but she must say the next.

"Pega, your pain has been immense. I grieve for your loss, and the loss to Ælfgiva of her father."

"Yet I celebrate Pega," Æthelflaed answered, as if to deflect Ælfwyn's compassionate response as an impediment to Pega's disentanglement. "She had the strength of character to remove herself at once from a situation which would have only led to greater harm."

Here Hrald's mother answered, in tone so low Æthelflaed must incline her head to hear better. "I give thanks he could see his child a final time."

Pega's eyes dropped to the table. "It is Christian to answer cruelty with kindness."

The inference that Hrald was less than a Christian was an added thorn pressed into the flesh of his mother. She could give but a slight nod, and lowered her own eyes.

Æthelflaed spoke again. "The Jarl forfeited the bride-price; his own offer," she admitted. "And all of Pega's treasure has been returned to her. We travel with it now. It explains the size of my troop; the King gave me a score of his own men as additional escort."

A few words passed between the Bailiff and Lady Æthelflaed concerning the feeding and lodging of her warriors, the latter insisting that her men would camp as normal, and their supply waggons held provisions enough so that no demand would be made upon the larders of The Fold. "And we shall be off in the morning," she reminded.

"We have ale in abundance to offer them; Lioba has just jugged it," was how Ælfwyn answered this, attempting to hold at bay the thought that she would have but scant time with her daughter, Pega, and Ælfgiva.

Æthelflaed thanked her hostess with her accustomed courtesy. She then turned to Pega. "I have some matters of State to discuss with the Bailiff, dear Pega," she told her. "Perhaps you will join the others. We shall not be long."

Ælfwyn arose as well, to accompany Pega outside. A serving woman waited at the line of young beeches, who could escort Pega to the hall. The two stood together, Ælfwyn's garden around them, one awash in ox-eye daisies, cornflowers, and clinging to wooden frames near the outdoor table, twining yellow honeysuckle scenting the air. Almost at their feet, growing about the roses of pink and white, was the pale blue of forget-me-not, with its tiny golden hearts. This innocent beauty made sharp contrast to the sorrowful nature of this visit, and Ælfwyn found it hard to control her voice.

"May I embrace you, my dear?" she asked of Pega, uncertain if her touch would be welcome. Pega hesitated for but a moment, and with tears welling in her own eyes, pressed herself in her mother-in-law's arms. Ælfwyn spoke by her ear. "My love for you, and your daughter, remain unchanged. And it goes with you," she whispered. "I hope to see you both, and soon."

Upon Ælfwyn's return she once again offered ale and wine to those awaiting. She had poured out more drink during their talk, but the small cakes remained, their sweetness untouched. Ælfwyn's own mouth was dry, and even the action of pouring out ale helped to calm her.

The three remaining sat in silence for a tellingly long moment. The Bailiff of Defenas well knew that Æthelflaed's next news had nothing to do with matters of State, and that Ælfred's daughter must set both tone and pace of what was to come. Raedwulf had been in the company of the noble Lady many times, in fact, since Æthelflaed's girlhood. He had been as well a frequent visitor to her halls in Mercia during the conflicts of war. The Bailiff shared her father's admiration of Æthelflaed's intellect and capabilities, more so, it might be added, than was accorded by the Bailiff to her husband, Æthelred. She would have formulated a plan worthy of her ward, and Raedwulf inquired of it now.

"My Lady," he began, "may I ask if you return to Weogornaceastre?"

"We do," confirmed Æthelflaed. "Pega's former union will be annulled there; I have sent letters ahead to the Bishop. When we arrive my hall there, a letter should await me, one from Lord Edwin of Kilton. I have offered Pega to be his wife."

The silence with which these words were met spoke of the listeners' surprise.

Æthelflaed sketched in the background of the scene she had so suddenly presented. "The Lord of Kilton had seen her, during the cattle murrain. Our beasts were not afflicted, and he had come to procure breeding stock. It was at Gleaweceaster. Edwin inquired of Pega then, and I agreed to speak to him, though I must tell him she had already been placed aside. For Four Stones.

"And now the Lord of Kilton, remaining unwed, might have a second chance to win her. That is my object. It does not restore what was lost in the dissolution of the union between

Mercia and Lindisse, yet it does unite two great families, one of Mercia and one of Wessex.

"And," she added, after a pause, "strengthening my father and brother's Kingdom will ever be my first goal."

"I am sure the answer you seek will await you," Raedwulf murmured.

"I imagine it so," she returned. "In which case we will set off for Kilton almost at once, ready for the union to take place."

"And what of Ealhswith?" asked the girl's mother.

The calm confidence of Lady Æthelflaed's answer suggested she had given it some thought. She had been forced to; she had extracted, under duress, the sister of the Jarl of Four Stones, a maid also daughter of Ælfwyn of Cirenceaster, of undoubted bloodline. That Lady was now coupled with no less than the Bailiff of Defenas, a man beloved of her own father the King, and a counsellor known to be shrewd and insightful. Æthelflaed must strike the right note.

"My interest in her is two-fold. Firstly, Pega moves now into a new sphere of her life. Ealhswith can companion her in this. And of course Ealhswith, so lovely in her person" – and here she inclined her head to the girl's mother, as the daughter so resembled her – "and from a distinguished lineage, is deserving of a fine match. I can help her to one. With your approval of course," she hastened to add.

Here the girl's mother must again speak. "Not all maids are fitted out for a strategic union," she hazarded. Ælfwyn thought not only of her youngest, but of her eldest daughter, the lost Ashild. Perhaps neither girl was Fated to grace the high table of a hall as help-meet to its Lord; few maids were, and even fewer to serve as peace-weavers between fractious tribes.

Æthelflaed was quick in her answer. "I could not agree more, Lady Ælfwyn. And that is why I am glad to bring Ealhswith out of the Dane-law, where her chances for a match with a nobleman of Wessex or Mercia will be much the greater."

"Ealhswith as well is young for her years," her mother posited.

"An attractive quality in a bride," her guest returned.

"Ealhswith will be with you at Kilton," her mother went on, thinking of the coming visit and the challenge it might pose to the girl. "It may not be easy for her. The King proposed she wed the Lord of Kilton, but Edwin refused her. It was due to her father, Sidroc, who killed Godwin of Kilton."

So skilled was Æthelflaed at keeping her face immobile that Ælfwyn could not gauge if the Lady had known of this ill-Fated match or not. Æthelflaed gave but a slight shrug of her shoulders, suggesting it was of no consequence now. At any rate Æthelflaed had seeming answer for any objection.

"If her presence at Kilton is awkward, Ealhswith need not remain there with Pega. I will bring her to Mercia. Or send her to my mother in Witanceaster while I find a worthy match for her. She will be seen there in my father's hall, a great advantage."

Lady Æthelflaed now took another sip of the ale. Her carriage, always erect, eased as she leant forward over the small table to Hrald's mother. What she must next impart would be the final jar for her listeners.

"One thing more you must know, a fact of some import. The King and my mother stood as God-parents for

Dagmar's child. The King offered without knowing who the father was, nor what would happen in the aftermath of this boy's birth. The honour was extended due to his esteem for Guthrum." Æthelflaed's voice dropped in tone. "It is of course an honour which extends to Guthrum's daughter, as well. It was I who informed the King of the identity of the boy's father. He has always looked favourably upon the Jarls Sidroc and Hrald, and despite the upset I think was far from displeased."

Ælfwyn could only think: The King knows the way of men, and the way of the Danes.

"I will not tell Pega," Æthelflaed went on; "not yet; perhaps not ever. There is no need to cause her further hurt."

Ælfwyn looked to her husband. Raedwulf, for years in the King's company, showed no startle at this announcement.

Ælfwyn, considering these last tidings, was herself much taken by this revelation. It placed the disgraced Dagmar in new light for her, that her own King, whom she revered, held Dagmar and her babe in such regard. And despite her son's sin of adultery, that regard which Ælfred had ever shown for Hrald remained undimmed. Ælfwyn had little time to absorb this twist, for her guest spoke again.

"The Lady Dagmar," Æthelflaed went on, conferring that title of honour to Hrald's first wife, "told me the child's name. It is Hroft."

Hroft, thought Ælfwyn. The name of Sidroc's grandfather. She closed her eyes, already yearning to hold the boy. It was all confusing; Ælfwyn's mind was reeling, her heart full with love and pity for both Hrald's new child and his little daughter.

It was the latter Lady Æthelflaed spoke of in closing.

"I hope you are comforted that Pega will be welcomed at so noble a burh as Kilton. And Ælfgiva will be within your ready reach, and raised there."

And mayhap never see her father again, Ælfwyn thought. She was forced to smile, but lowered her eyes in sorrow at the fact.

⁂

That night after they had supped, Lady Æthelflaed asked Pega to come to her, and alone, in the garden bower house. Night had fallen, and a serving woman held a flaming torch for Pega as she took her there. Once within the room Pega soon learnt why.

"You are carrying no child," Æthelflaed said, in a tone demanding a truthful response.

Pega repressed her sigh. "I am certain I am not," she answered. It was not only a recent Moon-flow told her this, but the fact that in the past few months her couplings with Hrald had grown less frequent, as if he knew their marriage to be at an end.

Æthelflaed gave a decided nod. "It is vital you do not go to Kilton carrying the babe of another."

"I do not," Pega assured her. She felt an article of livestock, and must work hard to keep her voice even as she said this.

It was not until after the party had reached Weogornaceastre that Ealhswith understood their true destination. A letter awaited Æthelflaed there, confirmation of her hopes, which she speedily conveyed to Pega.

Then Ealhswith must be told. Again, this was done privately. When Ealhswith returned, pale but silent to the chamber they were sharing, Pega went to her.

"Did she tell you?"

Ealhswith nodded her head. She felt abashed in her confusion. Edwin, Lord of Kilton was to wed Pega – he who the King himself had once selected for her. Æthelflaed had delivered the news to her with neither apology nor explanation. Ealhswith had received it silently, save for a small and initial cry of surprise. But as she stood before the Lady of Mercia Ealhswith's mind had been active with her thoughts: Your father wanted him for me, and now you want him for Pega. Well, Edwin should be glad. Pega is rich beyond measure. But Ealhswith had seldom felt as small as she did at that moment. Now she would be forced to watch Pega be handed over to Edwin. The sting of this was much to bear.

"Your match will come, in time," Æthelflaed had told her.

Yes, I will be disposed of as you wish, Ealhswith thought. For the first time she saw a glimmer of why the Lady had taken her from Four Stones. It was clear she had as yet no match in mind for her. Her removal from Four Stones was yet another chastisement to her brother for having forsaken Pega, who Æthelflaed was all too willing to champion a second time, and to the man who had refused Ealhswith. No man whom she could have, wanted her.

One other thing was in her mind, that Kilton was the place Ashild would have come to, if she had agreed to wed Ceric. This thought alone shed a kind of hallowed interest to Kilton; Ealhswith could see with her own eyes what her sister had refused to look upon, while living.

Pega spoke again; she almost had no words for Ealhswith, but must try.

"I am sorry, Ealhswith. How hard this must be for you."

When Hrald had returned from that ill-Fated trip to Witanceaster, he had of course told Pega the outcome, that Edwin had refused his little sister, on grounds of her father. She had not been rejected; her lineage had.

Ealhswith, young as she was, took pity on her sister-in-law. "Do not speak of it. I hope you will find love with him."

The scarring of Pega's heart made her say the next. "I do not seek love. None of our kind should. It is enough to like the men we are married to. Love is owed to our children, for as long as they are in our keeping. And love is for God."

Something in Ealhswith rebelled at these words, as true as she feared they might be. Yet her own mother had found love, at last. Within her own breast Ealhswith harboured a tiny spark she cherished, a spark she would not surrender, though it had never been fanned to an enduring flame.

At this moment Pega placed her hand atop one of Ealhswith's and gave a squeeze. Her words were mere echo of what she had just been told, and nothing Ealhswith wished to hear again.

"Æthelflaed will pair you with someone worthy. And you will run a great hall, and do him credit."

THE ROAD SOUTH

Four Stones

HRALD walked through the gate of Four Stones into a morning dark as new-made ink. Away to the east the dawn was slowly lightening the sky to a smoky grey. The setting Moon was now obscured, slunk behind dim trees or hidden, cloud-bound, in the western sky. A mere mellow and fading glow remained, countered by the slowly growing light. The road through the village lay before him; he would take it, as established paths would get him the quicker to his goal. His folk were not entirely abed. In a few crofts some man or woman was already afoot, poking up the embers in the cooking-ring, or answering the call of a lowing cow eager to be milked. Yet if any marked Hrald, he did not see it, though he felt keenly the sting of walking from those who fed him and his hall in return for his defence of their lives. It struck him as a form of abandonment. Then he shook his head to rid the thought. He must fulfill his penance, and trust no threat to Four Stones would arise in his absence.

His shadow slowly became discernible in the creeping rays of the Sun. After he passed through the village and the confines of the outer pastures he became aware that he had been a boy the last time he reached this far on foot, on some ramble with Gunnulf or another of his friends. His thoughts fixed on Gunnulf, who wild as he was, had been so willing to fight and die for Hrald, and for Four Stones. Hrald turned his mind with some effort away from that bloody triple duel, to the unfolding dawn before him. There was dew on the grass, great beads of it quivering at the bent tips of the narrow spears, weighing them down. A blackbird, so often to greet early risers, skittered across his path, and another, still hidden, trilled from the branch where it perched.

The day came up, fresh-washed, and scented with the green smell of downy meadow fox-tail. Amongst it nodding wildflowers innocently lured bees to their nectar, offering their faces to the clambering of tiny furred legs. Insects hovered in the near distance, silvery flashes as their wings were struck by the gathering sunlight. As well as he knew this road, Hrald was aware he was seeing it differently now, and seeing more. He had always been horsed, and trotted or cantered down this way, often in converse with Jari or another of his men, scarcely noting the fields, the clumps of hazel, the stands of osiers in sodden places, glimpsing but not truly seeing a great oak or ash in solitary splendour. Now Hrald was in the middle of it all, and not above it.

He swung his walking stick in his right hand and soon fell into a gait with it, making, as the morning wore on, a new companion of the thing as he moved forward. The lifting Sun shone bright and then hot on his skin. He was alone, almost a boy again in nature. This in itself was freeing, and cleansing. Even going without spear or sword was a strange form of liberation. With nought but a knife at his side, the same size as that carried by any free man, he could forget himself in a way he had never been allowed to since boyhood. His layers of privilege began to peel away. First there was his method of travel. The simple pleasures of walking a field, or through a forest – these were things he might enjoy as Jarl for a brief time while hunting wildfowl or deer. But again, it was purposeful – flushing game, that it might be driven into the nets or spearpoints of his men so it could be killed and carried back to his hall for sustenance. This was walking with an entirely different goal. The walk itself was a vital part of the penance, if not, he reflected, the larger part of it. His arrival at a predestined point might almost be secondary. He had nothing to do but place one foot before the other and move on.

Rounding a bend, a figure came into view, heading toward him. From the distance it was hard to discern if mounted or walking, but it came at an easy pace. As Hrald neared he saw it was an older man, a worn leathern bag upon his back, and at his heels a spotted dog of the kind used for herding sheep or cows. The man too held something in his hands – a shepherd's crook. They neared, then passed each other with a nod, the dog whining his own greeting to Hrald. To where did the shepherd travel, Hrald wondered. Was he walking to some distant flock, to buy a good ram, or a few ewes or wethers? He might even be heading to the village of Four Stones; some of the crofters had fine flocks. Hrald almost wished to ask him, but allowed the man to pass after their slight acknowledgment of the other, two walkers on a long and empty road.

A few tracks met the road Hrald trod, some long over-grown and unused, others rutted from more recent passage of wains or small waggons. He was, he knew, still on his own lands, yet there were folk in these forests who had little or no congress with Four Stones. They lived not on farmsteads, however small, but in isolated huts, where those akin to her-mits dwelt. They grew nothing beyond what they consumed themselves, gathering the rest from the forest, and owed the Jarl nothing, in Hrald's eyes. Yet thinking he was passing such a hidden dwelling-place gave him a sense of satisfaction. Some man or woman or even a small family might live at the end of that track, and Hrald found himself wishing them well.

He began to look for a place to stop and rest, and in the warmth he was also aware of a growing thirst. Off to his left a patch of bright loosestrife, purple heads reaching, told him water was there. He had two water flasks, both pottery, which he had filled before he left. One was nearly empty. If he found free-flowing water he could refill it here. The loosestrife was rooted in a twisting beck, one which did not meet the road. The water was low this time of year, and mostly stagnant, and he must continue to drink from his jarred water.

But his feet felt hot, and he stopped, pulled off his low boots and stockings and waded into it. The soft mud of the bottom squished between his toes, a memory of how as a boy he had enjoyed the sensation, even though a few pokes from broken reeds might make him wince. He stepped about in the cooling shallows, looking down at the brown ripples circling his ankles, the water flecked with bits of green leaf litter. There was as well that smell of oozing mud rising to his nose, which seemed to contain the seed of life for all in the water above it.

Again he thought of Gunnulf, and then of Ceric, and the year they had spent on Gotland. The sole of his foot had met no sharp reed, but Hrald winced, thinking of his friend. There at Kilton he confessed he had spent a night with Dagmar, and laid bare his shame. Ceric had not judged him. At some point his friend would hear of the destruction of Hrald's marriage, and of how he had angered Æthelflaed, sister to his King. When he was back at Four Stones he could send a letter. It might have slight chance of reaching Kilton, but he could try. Ceric deserved nothing less.

He sat on a low rock, bare feet drying, and took a moment to study the walking stick Jari had given him. It was ash, that was clear, just as were the best spears. The leathern thong had been plaited of three narrow strips, then passed through a smoothed hole a hand's grasp from the top of it. One nimble-fingered, and not Jari, had done this part of it, he knew. At any rate Hrald was glad for both stick and securing strap. He restored stockings and boots to his feet and again set off. The road called him, south.

Though he saw none but the passing shepherd all that day, he was not quite alone. From the tall grasses and clumps of shrubby growth birds piped, not the full-throated song of nesting time, but a backdrop of repeated calls, signaling to all like-hearers where, and what kind of feathered being they were.

The more he walked, the less he thought; or rather his thoughts became more diffuse, engrossed as he was in the action of moving forward. A blue tit flitted before him, its wings twisting to show him a flash of brilliant cobalt, then a breast of buff yellow. From a low rise an old hare sat up on its great haunches to wash its pointed face with furred paws. Even the smallest bodies of water sported dragonflies, defending with vigour their patch of its glistening surface, and driving off intruders. Hrald kept a steady pace onward, deliberate and purposeful, yet had time to take in the unfolding action about him, full of quiet interest and a kind of rest to his mind.

As the Sun dropped, he looked for water and a campsite. He found it in a stream, still fast running in the heat of Summer, emerging near a copse of hawthorn. Hrald recognised it with almost a start; it was a place where he and his men had often stopped to water their horses while traveling south. He gave a shallow laugh at this; he had walked all day, and thought himself farther. As he neared the bank he saw the marks of dried and cloven hoofprints, paired with those of human feet, crumbling in the Sun. A single ox, he thought, and he who led it, long gone on their way.

He moved behind the hawthorns and claimed the place as his own, dropping his basket-pack, now hot and heavy on his back, finding three rocks flat enough to act as tripod for his iron pot, gathering twigs and dead wood to boil his grain into browis. He filled the pot with water, added handfuls of barley, and used his knife to cut a chunk from the green cabbage in his food bag, slicing it thinly to add to his grain. Salt he had, in a small stoppered piece of hollowed tree branch, and he shook some into the bubbling mix. This was his supper. When he had gathered his stores from the kitchen-yard the day before, he had taken no smoked or dried meat. Some form of flesh nearly every night was the great boon of the evening meal taken by Hrald and his warriors. Doing without was part of the effort of his penance.

Hrald had never camped alone, as either boy or man. For all the many nights he had spent roofed by stars, he had always known the companionship of others, even if what awaited them next day was battle. Sitting on the calfskin as he spooned the browis into his mouth he thought of the long ride his father had taken him on, clear across the island of Gotland. At the end of this they came face to face with his name-sake grandsire, Hrald, a connection neither Sidroc nor Hrald ever thought could be made. It was on that trip he had told his father that he had wed a daughter of Guthrum, and then been forced to put her away from him. Now Hrald walked to win her back, walked that he might be absolved and Dagmar be fully his again.

He stopped himself here. A swift yearning to see his father, and a greater one, sharp and hot, for the woman he loved rose in him, almost closing his throat with the power of his desire. He stood up in sudden motion, stretched his stiff and tired legs, and walked a few paces, gaze fixed on the reddening sky. He could not allow himself to think on Dagmar. He was making his penance, and should not lose himself in longing. Though every step took him further from her, he walked also toward her, and their son, at the same time.

Hrald was forced to think of Hroft; the babe was so winning a boy. He could not forget the way the child had reached his tiny hand toward him when discovered with his mother. He had a son, Dagmar's son. Hrald blinked the water from his eyes and readied himself for sleep.

In the morning Hrald came upon a stone cairn that marked the southern limit of his lands. This stacked pile of rock at the roadside divided his lands from those of Agmund, Guthrum's eldest son. Hrald knew he might be met by guards of some kind, though a single man on foot might occasion no alarm if spotted by those on watch within the trees. If he were stopped, he would be known, his name enough to grant him unmolested passage, though why the Jarl of Four Stones was found unattended and walking south would be another story. He could prove who he was readily enough through what he could tell the guardsmen. And if he were apprehended and detained, tell the story again to one in authority to allow him to proceed. In fact he met no one. In this time of general peace watch had been relaxed, or if he had been spied, gauged to be of no threat.

Walking alone and seeing no one suited Hrald. If he stopped to rest or drink, or to rifle in his food bag for a handful of walnuts, he would soon fall back into the trance of walking. He did not wish to be roused from that. He kept on.

When the Sun stood over his head he passed the adjoining road he had several times taken, heading south and west to Witanceaster. He looked down it a long moment. Two years ago he had discovered Dagmar there at Witanceaster, and there, a fortnight ago, Pega had angrily, and justly, ended their marriage. Hrald turned his gaze away, and to the road he must take; his task was to walk. He remained steadily on his southerly track.

He did not know these parts. He walked on through forest now, the road darkened by the overhanging trees. Many oaks grew here, hornbeams too, some in which redstarts and nuthatches sheltered; Hrald saw them flit from trunk to trunk. No trees had been felled along the edges, but at points there were clearings he could discern deeper in, rocky outcroppings, naturally devoid of cover, perhaps; plots swiddened by fire to make them more fruitful, or places where woodmen or charcoal burners may have been at work. Still, the trees hemmed him in, and the course of the road twisted, allowing no clear sight ahead beyond thirty paces.

It was cooler in the wood, yet still Hrald needed water. He found it in a spring, a rocky pool off to one side of the road, from which water burbled and collected in slight hollows of rock. There was a mound of small stones left near it, in Offering, common to folks grateful for sweet water on their way. But behind this was also a cross which had been hammered up, with cut nails, and set into the ground. It came no taller than Hrald's knee, but unexpected as it was here, formed a strong presence nonetheless. He set down walking stick and pack. Someone had dedicated this as a spring also sacred to the Christian God, or one of his Saints. He was, he knew, on Agmund's land, but here Christians practised, still. It made Hrald blink, and he found his hand lifting to his brow, to bless himself.

He found a pebble to add to the collection already left in Offering. Then he filled both water flasks by allowing his wooden bowl to fill with water, carefully pouring it into their pottery mouths.

The next day dawned grey, and thus cooler. The road cleaved more forest, then ran to mixed woodland and open meadow. When it came time to set his camp, Hrald looked in vain for flowing water. He had boiled enough browis the prior night to leave him a cold mass of it, which, settled in his iron pot, and covered with his bowl, had made the day's journey with him in the bottom of his pack basket. He need only build a fire, add a bit of water from his flask, and make do.

As he walked Hrald did not look back upon the road. His goal lay forward, and he kept eyes and thoughts upon it. And there was nothing to alert him to the approach of any fellow travellers. He kept steadily onward.

Hrald was nearly out of food; he must seek a farmstead from which to buy some. He did not find one. Instead he spotted before him a small waggon, not more than an open cart, pulled by a single ox, by the head of which walked a man. They moved slowly enough, and Hrald gained on them without over-hastening his own step. Upon the waggon bed was fastened a kid goat, tied by two lines that it might not leap out. It was young and strong and looked balefully upon Hrald as he approached. The remains of some turnips and cabbage leaves were there, scattered too far now for the animal to reach them.

The drover did not turn as Hrald neared, and he found he must give voice, and called out in greeting, alerting the man to his presence. The man turned, though the ox kept plodding forward. The drover saw a young and quite tall man there, alone, and holding a staff. Hrald's next words gave the man reassurance.

"Have you food to spare? I have silver, and am hungry," Hrald told him, in the tongue of Angle-land. His free hand went to the purse at his belt to make good on this statement, and gestured to what lay in the waggon bed.

The man strode a few steps and stopped his ox. Hrald came up to him with a fragment of silver on his palm.

"I have better than that fodder to offer you," the man told him in answer, pulling a basket from over the wheel. Within were cabbages, small but firm-looking, turnips, beetroot, and onions. "I am nearly home, and will be there by dark. Take what you need," he invited.

He spent a moment studying Hrald, then asked, "Do you make pilgrimage?"

Hrald gave a quick nod. "I do. And I thank you for this."

"Cantwaraburh is four or five days, still," the man warned him, "though you will meet others on the road as you near it. Few come from the north, as you do, but as you grow closer, many from Lundenwic to the west.

"You are a Dane," the drover now risked remarking.

"Yes," Hrald answered. "My mother is of Cirenceaster, though."

A shake of the man's head told Hrald he did not know where that was. The drover considered Hrald again and concluded, "God's blessing on you, and your way."

Hrald spoke to no one for a full day following this exchange. His life in a bustling hall could have no greater contrast than these hours spent on the road. Despite the many times he had risked his life, he saw how circumscribed that life had been. Son of the Jarl, then after his father's absence protected by his mother; guarded by the unflagging Jari, one of the best warriors of Four Stones; backed by scores of trained men – he had never been as solitary as this. Even in his duel with Thorfast, or his sequestered contest with Onund, he had had the trappings of estate and Jarldom, to back him. Now he walked alone.

Without distraction, and focused on his one end, Hrald saw much. Dawn and dusk were alike times of subtle fascination, the rising and setting Sun turning gold the tips of the trees; the warm light gradually falling downward along branch and trunk. Night jars sang in the dark, and more than once as he drifted off to sleep, tired from a long day's walk, a hooting owl awoke him, as if asking him who he was. As he passed meres, dipping water birds paddled amongst the rushes, and there he saw ruddy foxes on the prowl, or deer with shifting ears lift their heads from the water they drank, before bounding away. On soft-banked streams buntings and sedge warblers clung to trembling reeds. At the edges of clearings wagtails darted, their sharp tail feathers twitching. Wild fruit was ripening, and there were damsons and sloes ready to be picked, growing along the road.

If he smelt a cook-fire or spotted smoke and needed provender he would approach its source, to be met at times by barking dogs or children, eager for the sight of anything new, running out to greet him. He bought more barley and oats, more vegetables. At times Hrald was not far from a village, even a fortified burh created by Ælfred to shelter his folk. But if it meant turning off his southward track Hrald would not take it, unless his need for food was pressing.

The nature of Hrald's journey created its own rhythm, arising at first light, often to the chirking and chirping of nearby birds, who, finding an intruder near their wood, urged him also to rise. Then followed a simple meal of the remains of last night's browis, heated over; cold ablutions in whatever body of water he had slept near; and the striking of his camp, which took even less time than it had to set up the prior day.

One morning he awoke to drizzle. When Hrald made his camp at each dusk, he lay his calfskin ground-cover under the shelter of trees, or overarching shrubs, their branches sparing himself from some of the dew which would fall by morning. But this was true rain. He was able to warm his food, but it came steadily down. He thought of how best to keep himself from it, and sliced a long thin strip from the calfskin, and then, draping the rest of it over his head, punched two holes by his shoulders. He threaded the leathern thong through the holes, then could wear the hide, like a small cape, over his head and the top of his woven wood basket. His body still got wet, his boots and leggings sodden, but the contents of his basket remained dry.

A few times Hrald must go amongst folk. There were fording points across rivers he must cross, and he joined men, women, their offspring, and often their animals in flat bottomed boats which were punted or rowed across. Reaching the shore, these folk would disperse, to go their separate ways. Some continued on in the direction Hrald was going, and he was now sometimes in sight of those preceding him toward his goal. Cantwaraburh was a great town; its cathedral, sainted history, and royal mint lent it importance, and made it destination for many. Some folk would be heading there to trade, others on pilgrimage, or even doing penance, as was Hrald. At one such water passage, Hrald helped steady the boat so that a father and son with a half score of white-faced sheep could safely board. The boy was of some twelve Summers, and both shouldered heavy packs; the father with his crook in hand as well. Hrald was not alone amongst other passengers; there was a young couple, the woman with a babe tied upon her hip, the man burdened with their own kit; and a grizzled old man with a hand-wain rattling with tin-ware who ran the thing up the gangplank, seeking to take his goods to the other shore. When all were aboard two boatmen punted off, long poles grasped in strong hands as they pushed the boat ahead. Hrald had moved to the prow of the vessel for the short transit, the sheep crowding about him, baaing and bleating in unhappiness at the motion of the boat. The father and son in charge of them served to hem the sheep in, their hands full with the flock they shepherded, amongst them an unruly ram. This animal, tired of being bumped, tried of a sudden to scale the gunwale. Hrald was luckily there, and grasping the ram's curved horns, pulled him back. He then flung his leg over the fleecy back, straddling the ram to still him.

When they landed and the sheep were prodded off, the shepherd gave Hrald a nod of thanks, and jerked his head at the ram, now fronting the ewes. "He is the best I have, and so cannot afford to lose him."

Hrald gave a returning nod of his own, and said, "My mother always says a good ram is half the flock."

The farmer took stock of this remark, and looked Hrald up and down. "I need another hand at the farm," he offered. "If you are honest, and as handy as you just showed, you will be well fed."

Hrald almost felt the colour rise to his cheek. It was not common for an utter stranger to be offered such a place, and was, he knew, a sign of the man's guess at his worth.

"I thank you," Hrald answered. "I have work, up north." He let a moment pass before saying the next. "Just now I make pilgrimage to Cantwaraburh."

"Ah," the farmer answered. "I wish you good journeying, then."

As he walked further south, the nearness of the sea shaped the land. Coming through a gorge with a strong and prevailing current of wind, Hrald noted the trees and grasses all bent in the same direction, as if trying to hear a secret far from their reach. Crofts were now more frequent, and those who worked them. The cottars afield he passed, toiling over mattock or hoe, never failed to lift their heads to him; strangers were a source of interest, profit, or danger, and he acknowledged all with a greeting nod of his head, to be granted the same courtesy. These folk had little, but there was pride in their capacity for hard work, and the dignity of the work was theirs. There was as well the bond between the land they tilled and their own lives, the clarity of the connection, age-old. Freed from his horse, walking with so little kit and no weapons marking him as either warrior or war-lord, he met them eye-to-eye.

Hrald had taken himself off the road, so that he might rest a spell. He ate from his dwindling store of walnuts, washed them down with water, and seated on the trunk of a felled tree, stretched his legs out before him. The Sun had passed the highest point above his head, though its rays were obscured in a milky sky. He stood up, slipping the straps of his pack-basket over his shoulders, took up his walking stick, and moved forward.

There were none on the road before him, so when he heard what sounded like cries coming from the trees ahead, a sudden alertness roused him. He took a striding step, heard the cry again, certainly human, and broke into a run toward it. Finding its source, he halted.

Off the road and some way into a clearing stood an oxcart, around which moved two men brandishing spears. The screams came from a gowned figure upon the ground, no more than a girl, her hands tied. A third man bent over her, hastily binding her ankles. One of her pale feet had lost its shoe in the struggle. The girl screamed again, and her captor slapped her, hard, across her face to silence her.

A second brigand stood before a white-haired couple, the woman cowering as she clung to her husband. The old man, in a torrent of sputtering oaths answered by his assailant, tried to pull the knife from his belt. This attempt was met by the spear-man striking his resisting victim in the head with the shaft of his spear. The force of it knocked the old man flat, and out. His wife, shrieking, fell to her knees by him. The brigand followed her, reaching for the old man's belt, and what it might hold.

The third brigand was at work, riffling through the cart, ripping the tarpaulin covering it off, and away. Another figure was there, a boy of perhaps four or five Summers, still upon the waggon board, and seemingly frozen in place, though his arms reached towards those upon the ground. The ox, still in his traces, bellowed out his own distress, but was tied by a neck rope to a tree.

Hrald took this in, with a single thought: Three against one, a dead-man's odds.

He would take them.

Hrald had no time to shrug the basket from his back. He pulled his right wrist from the tether to his walking stick, and gripping it in both hands, ran forward with it, across his body. He whooped out his war-cry, a two-tone roar such as his uncle, Asberg used. He reached the man who had downed the oldster first. The attacker rose, holding his spear, but Hrald, behind him so quickly, had his stick up at chest height, and swung it at the brigand's head with far greater force than what had been used to disable the old man. The cracking of bone, either skull or spine, was audible as the attacker dropped to his knees, and then to his back. The other two brigands whirled towards Hrald, now both with weapons in hand, spear-points foremost.

This was a bind. He faced two spear-men, neither with shields, but ready to kill the man who had disturbed their plundering. With no shield of his own, Hrald could not fend off a thrown spear, but it was unlikely they would risk losing one of their weapons should he dodge it, and it fell to the ground. He had killed or greatly harmed the first brigand. Hrald's best chance to survive was now to run; he knew this. But the bound girl's screams had turned to sobs. She lay there, hog-tied, and ready to be carried off to slavery. The remaining two brigands would likely kill the old woman, just to silence her as she bent over her husband. Their terror gave clarity to Hrald's actions. He would not run.

A kind of rage overtook Hrald, one greater than his own anger at these despoiling raiders. Anything and everything that had ever raised his ire was alive and aglow in his core, rising like a gorge to choke all but his driving response to act. Their numbers were legion: Watching Godwin of Kilton try to kill his father, and the grievous cut to the thigh Sidroc had taken; his anger at Gunnulf, his friend, for being someone other than Hrald had expected; the far more pointed anger of Gunnulf's death; Hrald's wrath at the double treachery of Onund, first betraying Four Stones and then, when he had feigned surrender, trying to kill him; Haesten who had done damage beyond counting to Hrald and his kin; and through it all, a ripple of anger at himself for the missteps in his own life. He stood there, clutching his walking stick as a staff across his body, with the fury of ten men.

Both brigands came at him, the one by the cart first. This was a man in his third decade, with light brown hair and a tunic to match. The second was just behind him, yellow-haired, younger, clad in a dull red tunic. They looked at each other, and grinned. They were two able men with spears facing one holding nought but a staff. They could dispatch this lanky interloper with little effort.

They had not been trained by Asberg, one of the best spear-men to hold that formidable weapon. Hrald had. The great advantage of spear-play is in keeping distance from one's target. But these two must move in to strike, and Hrald surprised them by attacking first, running at the nearest, in brown. Caught off guard by this audacity, Brown-tunic stopped short, before raising his spear to strike. Hrald whirled, and the brigand's spear point hit the rolled calf hide on the top of his pack-basket. Brown-tunic's spear point caught there, in the heart of the roll, long enough that Hrald could pivot to his right and dive. It brought the man within range of the butt end of Hrald's staff, and he slammed it down on the brigand's forward foot, crushing it.

Brown-tunic collapsed with an agonized howl. Red-tunic was almost behind him, and was tripped up in the falling spear of his brother. He staggered, but kept his feet. He squared to come after Hrald, and before Hrald could leap

back, landed the tip of his spear-point in the fleshy underside of Hrald's left forearm. The strike was no more than a
jab, but the flat and sharp iron head of the point was telling.
It was Hrald's turn to yell, and he loosened his grip on his
staff for an awful moment before re-tightening it. He held
it up at chest height to help quell the bleeding, but in an
instant blood was running down his arm, and dripping from
his elbow.

It was then another warrior ran into the fray. He was tall,
slight, armed with both spear and shield, and wore an iron-
strapped war-cap of leather upon his head. Hrald uttered his
name through gritted teeth.

"Bork!"

He named wasted no time, and went, shield high, spear
in motion, for the second man.

Red-tunic's annoyance at being disturbed when he
had drawn blood was unconcealed. But now he was at the
disadvantage; he faced two warriors, one fully armed, the
second with proven skill with a staff. Red-tunic jumped at
the newcomer.

Behind Hrald Brown-tunic was struggling to his knees.
Hrald turned back to see the man draw his knife and ready
to throw it. Hrald was there first, and with both fists in the
centre of his staff, knocked the brigand in the head. It may
have been a killing blow, but Hrald would take no chances.
He dropped his staff, now grown slippery with his blood, and
pulled his own knife. A thrust of the blade to the heart dis-
patched him.

Bork had said nothing. No war-cry issued from his open
mouth, but the furrow between his eyes, and the strength
in his young arm behind his spear told much. He must fend

his assailant off. Bork, in true combat for the first time, and seeing his bloodied Jarl and two men lying dead or dying, thought only this. He had a shield as well as spear, changing the rules of engagement with the remaining spear-man, and he used both. He could approach as near as Red-tunic could, but with far more safety for the shield held fast in his left hand. Bork used that shield to deflect the first blows from the man, pushing the startled brigand back. Everything his sparring had drilled into him was there, that with the other youths of Four Stones, as well as the constant coaching of Kjeld and the older warriors. As he had done in all his training, Bork need make a touch to indicate a hit. His goal was to disarm his man, knock the spear from his hands. The goal of Red-tunic was to kill Bork.

Behind them Hrald had just delivered the death-blow to Brown-tunic. Bork did not see it, but the man he fought did, and it made Red-tunic redouble his efforts. He could try to break and run, but this youngster looked fast and would lob his spear into his retreating back. If he could draw blood with this one, he might be able to escape with his life.

He would need to get in closer, take a stab at the youngster's long legs. Red-tunic came fast and hard, dodging and feinting as he aimed his spear at Bork's exposed legs and feet. But the youngster had seen this before, from none other than Asberg. Bork jumped to meet him.

A shield is weapon too, not only the iron boss of it, which may be forged to a bodkin's point, but the rim, which could be slammed down on an opponent's arm, or lowered and then drawn up in sudden gesture under his chin. It was this last tactic Bork used, one he had seen played out in slow motion on the sparring ground by those with no intent to shatter a jaw. In swift action Bork tipped his shield forward under the man's chin, then jerked it upward with all the strength in his left arm.

Red-tunic's eyes bulged from the impact. His mouth had been open, and his tongue caught between his teeth as his jaws were suddenly snapped shut, nearly severing it. A rent opened under his chin, caused by the iron rim of Bork's shield, and the force behind it. The spear butt slid down the brigand's hands, and he fell, gagging on his own blood. Bork had cracked his jaw, and gashed his throat.

Red-tunic fell to his knees, spear still in one hand. His free hand reached out to grasp at nothing, but his right acted to move his spear.

"Kill him!" ordered Hrald.

Bork raised his spear and ended his man, a thrust to the heart. He hit strongly, but at the moment of impact closed his eyes. He could not look at Red-tunic's face, the lower half of it running blood. Bork turned away.

He came to Hrald, who was leaning over, hands on knees, gulping air. His staff was at his feet. The blood from his left arm was reddening his fingers and staining his leggings. Hrald straightened to meet Bork. The youth dropped his spear and shield, and flung himself, chest heaving, into his Jarl's arms.

The shock of being called into a sudden, and mortal combat was part of it, Hrald knew. And this had been Bork's first kill. He placed his hands on Bork's shoulders so that he was forced to look at him.

"It was a mercy kill, one his actions did not warrant. But you spared him from a lingering death."

All Bork could do was nod.

Behind them the girl had grown mute with terror. But Hrald's arm ran blood, and he now held the wound capped in his other hand.

This need, to be again of service, roused Bork. He had no field dressing or Simples with him, but he ripped a piece of linen towelling to bind Hrald's arm. The spear-point had caught him on the backside of the forearm, where there is most flesh.

When Bork was done, Hrald gave another command "Untie the girl, and claim your battle-gain. I will see if the old man lives."

Bork freed the girl as gently as he could, knowing she might fear him almost as much as she did their assailants. Her little brown shoe was not far off, and he handed it to her. She clutched it to her bosom and ran to her grandmother.

Hrald approached the oxcart. The boy, still on the wag-gon-board, but with his hands covering his eyes, rocked back and forth, whimpering. Hrald came up to him, lowering him to the ground so he might join his sister and grandmother. The child ran to them, wailing, and was swept into the old woman's arms with his sister. Hrald knelt on the other side of her prostrate husband, who lay unmoving. His white hair was bloodied over his ear, but farther back than the temple; a man could survive such a blow.

"Does he breathe?" he asked. He thought them folk of Angle-land, but no, they were Danes; the man himself per-haps an old warrior. He spoke again, slower, and the woman answered. "Já, he breathes."

"Do you know these parts," he next asked. "Who can help you?"

"There is a farm, not far south down the road," came the answer. "We have traded with them in the past."

Hrald nodded and turned to the oxcart. Indeed, the old man may have been a warrior. On the bed of the oxcart lay a spear, its shaft darkened with age. Its owner had not time to reach for it, and if he had, would not have lasted long before his three assailants.

Bork returned to the man he had downed. He had been told how to strip a body of booty, and these instructions sounded again in his head. First be certain the man you kneel beside is truly dead. Bork needed no proof of that; and before doing anything else, pulled his spear point through the grass to clean it. Then he knelt at the side of the dead man. Take all weapons of value; protective gear, if any; and then the belt and its purses. Check neck and wrists for silver ornaments and talismans. This one had little. His spear lay on the ground, and a workman-like knife of no special value made up his weaponry. Still, metal jingled in his purse, which Bork did not open. As he bent over the body, his hands still hovering as they reached to turn back the bloodied collar in search of silver, a wave of disgust filled him. Bork would not do it. He turned quickly aside to retch.

His belly emptied of its little contents, Bork rose. He steeled himself as best he could, and stood, his slight battle-gain in his hand. Hrald had gathered that of the two he had bested, and carried the spears, knives, and belts to the oxcart. He must use only his right arm to do so, for the pain in his left.

Bork joined him. He had dropped his shoulder pack at the entrance to the clearing, and gone back to retrieve it.

Hrald gestured that he put the knife and purse into it; the spear he had gained could ride with those Hrald picked up.

The two shared a moment looking at the bodies of the brigands, two on their back, one on his stomach.

"Who are they," Bork asked.

"From their oaths, Danes," Hrald answered, based on a few choice words issuing from the mouths of the attackers. "Likely three who were driven off from a hall, to roam, looking for easy marks."

Bork's eyes dropped swiftly down. His own father had been forced to be such a man, but Bork would not believe that he had ever acted with such viciousness.

Together they shifted the contents of the cart enough to lift the old man in. His granddaughter knelt at his side, her hand on his heart. Bork handed both the old woman and the boy up to the waggon board. The ox was heavy-laden with its added cargo, but with a shake of its great ears, seemed eager to quit the place and its smell of blood. They must go at the beast's pace, and in truth neither Hrald nor Bork felt up to more. The wound to Hrald's forearm was now throbbing, and though the blood had clotted and none leaked through the reddened linen, the need to hold it raised and before him made every step an effort.

It did not take long to reach the farmstead, sitting a short distance down the next turning. The arrival of the cart, flanked by two strange men, brought all the inhabitants out. The crofter was a widow, in perhaps her fifth decade, strong-featured, living there with a grown daughter, her husband, and a passel of active children. Rounding this out were two young men, who, judging by their looks were the brothers of the daughter's husband, so they had hands enough.

There was a second dwelling in which abided an elder pair, the crofter's parents perhaps, and a nearly equally old woman, who appeared to care for them.

They let the woman they had rescued tell the tale. She did so in a few words, pointing to the two whose arrival may have saved them all. The old man was carried into the house by the crofter's family. Hrald was glad just to be gestured to the benches near the kitchen-yard, where they might rest.

He went to their well. Bork hauled up water and filled a waiting basin. Hrald pulled off his tunic, the act of lifting his left arm over his head occasioning more pain. Bork then untied the strip of linen from Hrald's arm. He could see the wound by twisting his forearm toward him; a puncture with a ripped end.

He washed his arms and chest, and Bork scrubbed as much of the blood out of the torn sleeve as he could. Hrald's leggings were spotted with it as well, but they could not wash them now. Hrald had a single change of clothes, and must keep them for his entry into Cantwaraburh. The best he could do was wash the blood and dirt from his upper body.

When he was done Bork tore a fresh strip of linen from that which the crofter gave him, and rewrapped the wound. After doing so there was almost no fresh bleeding; it was clotting well.

Hrald pulled on his tunic, half of it soaked. They sat across from the other on the two benches. Hrald considered the youth before him, one with straight, light brown hair, a freckled nose, and eyes of greenish blue, eyes which showed something of the determination behind them. Bork was still gawky, and a bean-pole, but would fill out with time.

Hrald's thoughts went back in time, and he said, "I never saw you."

Bork lowered his chin. "Jarl, you never looked back."

This was true; Hrald had kept his attention straightforwardly ahead.

"And I walked as much as I could behind cover," Bork went on, "trailing you so that you were oftentimes scarcely in sight. A few times I lost you when you turned off the road, and looked for the mark your walking stick made."

"You are a good tracker," Hrald praised. He thought of his best friend, and of Kilton. "Ceric of Kilton has a tracker, Worr by name, who is renowned in that place. You will be his equal."

Tracking men, Bork thought. It was one thing to follow his Jarl in hope of being of use, another to think of men as game. He said nothing to this, only gave a slight shrug.

In all the action, the small silver cross Bork wore had swung out from under his tunic, and now lay atop it. Hrald recalled when his mother had given Yrling that cross, and had glimpsed it around the stableboy's neck afterwards. Bork had told Hrald how he had found it on the ground under the great beech tree behind Four Stones after his brother had flung it into the branches. Bork had generally kept the cross hidden, but now his hand went to it, closing upon it. From this day onward Hrald would not see Bork tuck it away. He knew Bork cherished it; it was from the hand of Lady Ælfwyn, and a symbol of Christian devotion.

Hrald must ask the next.

"Why did you follow me?"

It took Bork a long and considered moment to answer this. "You said you wanted me with you. When we rode to

Witanceaster, with that gold. That is what you said. And —
and I am your rear guard."

Hrald could not chide the youth.

"You likely saved my life."

Bork's eyes were filling with water at these words, but he
shook his head as if to shake off this truth, as well.

Hrald must answer with a low laugh. "I should be angry
with you for following me. But I did not order you to stay.
So you did not disobey." He reached across and laid his right
hand on Bork's shoulder, and gave it a squeeze. Bork closed
his welling eyes, tight.

"The killing, Jarl," he murmured. "The blow I gave him —
to the heart — it was horrible."

Hrald turned his own face away a moment. "Já. But none
would say it was not just. They may have killed the old man,
and would likely kill the woman, and even the boy. They were
after the girl, the ox, the cart. Instead they can take their
chances in Odin's hall."

"Or the Christian Hell," offered Bork.

"Já. However things are meted out, if justice awaits all of
us, Hell will surely be their end."

Bork was not certain what Hrald's displeasure at his
being followed truly meant, and so had to ask. "Please do not
send me back, Jarl. Let me go on, to Cantwaraburh."

He felt compelled to say why.

"There is a shrine there to St Augustine. He who brought
the Word of God back to this land. Abbess Sigewif told me of
it, during my writing practice; and Father Wilgot has spoken
of Augustine. A prayer for my father there — it will help him."

Hrald let his chin drop forward. Bork's father had been
a renegade like these three they had just killed. Yet somehow

he must have been a better man, at least to his boy, for Bork to care so much for his immortal soul.

Hrald was forced to consent. "Já. You can pray for the soul of your father there."

Nothing could seemingly convince Bork that his father, a heathen all his life, one killed as the result of a violent act, would be denied that chance of redemption and eventual entrance into the Heavenly Kingdom Bork had heard so much about from Wilgot.

Hrald gave an affirming nod to the hopeful youth. "You will come with me. But I have a task of my own there. I must seek the Archbishop, and make confession to him."

"I will not be in your way," Bork assured.

"We are very near now, one or two days only," Hrald added. "These folk will be able to tell us."

There was something more Hrald must say. Jari had been at his side since he was a boy. Yet Jari was now as old as Hrald's own father. At some point the Tyr-hand would agree to step back from his role as Hrald's shadow. Nor did Hrald need such a man; it had become Jari's habit, as Hrald was so young when his father left. Jari would always sit at Hrald's left at his table; Hrald would always want him there. But another good arm to join his larger body-guard was here, sitting before him. Bork, of proven faithfulness, would surely welcome the advancement. It was this Hrald spoke of.

"I promised you, and my brother, swords. I have not given them yet. When we are back at the hall you will receive them. And I think, soon, you might join my body-guard, and sit at the high table."

Bork's face went through a change, a shift from recounting the gruesomeness of Red-tunic's death, or his efforts to accompany Hrald, to a look of startled wonder that he might, and far sooner than any warrior his age could hope, be sitting at his Jarl's own table. He took a breath, and nodded.

Off to one side the crofter and her daughter had been active at the cooking-ring, and now one of the boys approached, summoning them to the tables between the houses.

They stood, Hrald a little unsteadily, to accept the food laid before them.

The Jarl of Four Stones could not hold his bowl. He kept it on the table before him, and lay the wrist of his left arm upon the board as well, in support of the wound. It was Bork who broke his bread for him. His attention was such that it was clear to the household who sat about them that Bork was in some kind of service to Hrald. He must let them wonder.

"Eat," Hrald urged, as Bork was neglecting his own bowl. They did eat, both of them, grateful for the bread smeared with sweet butter, heaping servings of oats over which the women poured cream, the boiled eggs, the roasted turnips and yellow carrots. There were thick slices of smoked pig as well, sizzling in its own fat. Bork was famished. Having little silver with him, he had suffered greatly from hunger on the road. And he had even less kit than Hrald.

That night, in an alcove, Hrald found little sleep. Though he felt drained in body and mind, his arm hurt. That was one part of his wakefulness, but even more was the restless circling of his thoughts.

CANTWARABURH

IN the morning Hrald and Bork readied to set off. The old man had survived the night, and the girl, a maid of twelve or so Summers, had come forward to them both and curtsied her thanks. The boy shrieked at the sight of Bork's spear, and fled to his grandmother, who, holding the child to her, uttered her thanks. From her they learned they had been on the way to their own farm, a day's travel north.

The best path was to leave them here at this welcoming croft. Hrald did not know if the old woman could care for both injured husband and the frightened young, and if the old man was to die here, she would have help with what followed. He took the old woman aside and handed her all he had taken from the two he had killed. Weaponry and silver both held value. She began to protest, looking at him, and the paucity of his goods. "But," she answered, "you have need of this."

He gave a shake of his head. "I am in need of none of it."

As a final act Hrald took two whole silver pieces from his belt, and placed them in the hand of the widowed crofter. "Care for them well," he said. She had replenished their food bags, and told them Cantwaraburh would be theirs on the morrow.

The day they walked into was over-clouded, even cool. They had had fair share of warmth and Sun upon the road, and the sky seemed to foretoken the seriousness of their nearing goal. Hrald had his left arm bound in a sling of linen, as the pain was greater if it hung down at his side. He could slip it out when needed, but when walking, it was as much a help as the stick in his right hand. As they made their way, side by side, Hrald considered the walking stick.

"Without this, I could have done nothing," he said. "It was Jari gave it me."

"I know," Bork answered, and something in his tone implied he knew more than this.

"Did you aid him?"

Bork gave a nod of his head. "I bored the hole for him, and cut and plaited the tether for your hand. He did not tell me it was for your journey, but then in the morning I watched him give it to you."

"And slipped out after me," Hrald suggested.

"The men at the gate, they let me pass," Bork admitted.

"They will not be punished," Hrald said. He felt moved to again tell the youth the difference he had made. "If you had not been there, Bork . . . "

He did not finish.

"You spared my life, Jarl," was Bork's answer. "At last I could do something for you."

They walked all day, with the knowledge that Cantwaraburh was near. They were not alone; the road they trod was travelled by tradesmen, farmers, and cattle herders, heading to or leaving the town. They passed four tonsured monks, dark-habited, resting by a stream, pilgrims to the tomb of Augustine, surely; and once a double file of well-armed warriors rode past, as escort to a small but heavy waggon, for it was pulled by four horses. The waggon bed they guarded was covered over, but Hrald could guess it might carry chests of hack-silver, destined for the mint.

They camped, and were up at dawn. Hrald washed himself as best he could, and drew on his change of clothes. Bork was possessed of none, and though his tunic and leggings were grimy, made sure his hands and face were not.

Off they walked, joining others. Cantwaraburh came in sight. The River Stour ran here, narrow but of good current, and alder trees grew in abundance along its virid banks. The walls of the town were flint and sandstone, and sat upon a raised ridge of heaped earth. Their height and round towers were further testament to the skill of those long-ago builders of the Caesars. Such was the wall's extent that it sported five gates, two of which they passed on their way to the main entry. A cattle market stood outside one of them, and the lowing of the cows and oxen as they milled about and were examined by prospective buyers filled the air.

Witanceaster was large, and the royal city, but it was of necessity a garrison town. Cantwaraburh carried about it an ancient air, a certain mellowness for all its wealth. The name meant 'Stronghold of the Kentish men,' and indeed, Kent had once been its own Kingdom, before falling in estate to become a vassal Kingdom to first Mercia and then Wessex.

Before they entered Hrald rested his walking stick against a tree. His hand went to his belt and the purse there, then extended it to Bork. "Here is silver. Feed yourself, and find lodging somewhere."

Bork could not help a grin forming. "There are always stables which need mucking," he said, ignoring the silver Hrald offered.

His Jarl shook his head at this.

"We will be here one or two nights, that I may complete my penance, and we both rest."

"Still, Jarl, I need none of your silver. There are stables everywhere. I will find work, and food here, while I wait for you."

"You will take my silver anyway," Hrald countered, and forced it upon him. "And keep your eye out for decent animals for sale. It was a condition of my penance that I walk, but I can buy horses on the way back, and we will do so."

As they passed through the gate almost the first structure they saw was a large stable, ready to welcome the mounts of visitors. Bork tilted his head at it. "I will be there, if they will have me. If not, I will tell them where I am to be found," he promised.

Bork's tunic, soiled to begin with, had blood stains upon it from when he had thrown his arms around the bleeding Hrald. "Buy yourself a fresh tunic," Hrald told him. Clothes were not bought, but made, yet in a town of this size there were often stalls in which made-up items could be had.

"And get some food into you," Hrald ended. In truth this need was nearly as great for Hrald as it was for Bork, and the provender the crofter had given them was nearly gone. He watched Bork vanish into the dusky recess of the stable.

Now here at his goal, Hrald looked about him, not certain of his next step. The town, despite its antiquity and mint, seemed dedicated to God. Even given the comings and goings of the many tradesmen, and activity of workshops, once within the walls there was a quiet prosperity about it all, the peaceful order of a convent or monastery.

Before him rose the cathedral, at the end of the road Hrald stood upon. He headed to the open door of the hallowed building, its tower of grey and yellow stone square and forthright.

He entered. No service was underway, but many were about, standing at prayer before the images of certain saints, or clustered around the shrine of Augustine himself. Hrald approached the altar, touched his knee to the stone floor, and crossed himself. He closed his eyes, giving thanks for his safe arrival.

A priest was moving about, off to one side of the altar. Hrald went to him.

"I am Hrald, Jarl of Four Stones in Lindisse," he said. "As part of my penance assigned by Wilgot, our priest, I must make confession to the Archbishop."

The priest blinked his surprise, then looked behind Hrald as if expecting a retinue of armed men.

"If you question who I am," Hrald went on, "I can tell you more."

"No, no," the priest assured him.

"Is your soul in danger?" he then asked.

Hrald had to lower his eyes a moment. If he had been killed fighting the brigands, he would have died unshriven for a mortal sin.

"I am grateful I was not killed upon the road, coming here, for then it would have been," he avowed.

This young man's seriousness made the priest hasten to aid him.

"Come, follow me. You may wait in our cloister, refresh yourself. I will see how quickly Archbishop Plegmund can see you."

The priest accompanied Hrald to a hidden garden, enclosed by the cathedral itself and three other buildings. Fruit trees, carefully pruned to keep them small, grew in the four corners, and the ground was rife with herbs, many of them in flower. Hrald sank upon a bench of carved stone, set against a wall, and leaned his head back against its cool surface. In short order the priest returned, to lead him to the study of the Archbishop.

It was a room not unlike that used by Abbess Sigewif, but of greater magnitude, and furnished with many more bound manuscripts, as well as piles of parchment leaves, closely copied over, waiting on one of the long tables. At a smaller table sat an old man, robed in a cassock, black, with red outlining around the sleeves and neck.

When the door had closed Plegmund nodded him in, but said not a word of greeting. Hrald, uncertain if he should again present himself, began to do so.

"Your Grace, I am Hrald of Four Stones."

Here Plegmund lifted his veined hand the slightest amount to stay him. He rose, and moved forward to a bench.

"I have been told, my son. And God knows who you are, and why you are here. Tell Him aloud now before me, his servant, and make a true Act of Contrition."

The Archbishop sat, ready to hear Hrald's confession.

The exhalation of breath from Hrald's lips, though not deep, was cleansing. He crossed himself and knelt off to one side.

He told the prelate all, and in more detail than had been needed with Wilgot, who was possessed of background the Archbishop could not know. Hrald named Pega of Mercia, so that her wealth and estate were clear; also the depth of insult to her protector, Æthelflaed, Lady of the Mercians, and the King's own daughter.

Plegmund had heard none of this, not yet; though he doubted not word would arrive. The loss of a devout heiress in Lindisse was just that, a loss. Such a woman was key in strengthening the faith of a people still half-heathen. But she had taken her gold and her faith, and returned to Mercia.

Plegmund had but two questions for Hrald. "To whom have you admitted this?"

"The priest of Four Stones, Wilgot, who set me this penance. And Abbess Sigewif, of the Abbey of Oundle, a woman revered in our parts."

The Archbishop made a small sound at this, a murmur, Hrald thought, of esteem for the woman mentioned. In fact, another woman rose as well to the Archbishop's mind, one he had never met, but also heard much of. This then, must be Lady Ælfwyn's son, she who had raised Oundle from rubble with her silver.

The second question Plegmund asked was the crux to forgiveness, and was voiced in its simplest form. This young Jarl would have heard plenty from both sources, and assuredly did not lack in further self-reflection upon the road here.

"Are you truly contrite, in heart, mind, and body, for your sinful act?"

"I am, Holy Father."

"Then I absolve you, in the Name of the Father, the Son, and the Holy Ghost."

As simple as it seemed, it was to Hrald both meaningful and freeing.

Hrald kept his head bowed, eyes lowered, awaiting his further penance. Plegmund assigned him none.

"You have fulfilled your penance. Keep God's law, and the laws of man, and go in peace."

He spoke in the speech of Rome now, making the sign of the cross with his hands over Hrald's head.

Both rose.

Though the bandage was hidden by Hrald's sleeve, Plegmund had not failed to note the stiffness of his petition-er's supported arm, nor the pained effort it took to move it. He offered that the Jarl might lodge with the monks, and rest, until it healed.

But Hrald, eager to be on his way, would not.

"I will stay the night, and thank you."

"We are skilled at leech-craft," Plegmund returned. "Let one of our brothers attend to that wound you are hiding, and do what he can."

Hrald could not refuse this, and after further thanks, found himself led back into the enclosed garden, thence to a work-room hung with drying herbs, and tables strewn with mortars and pestles, spoons of all sizes, and bowls. There he was placed under the care of a monk and two postulants. They unwrapped the wound, and Hrald was made to place his arm in a liquid, pink to the eye and pleasant to the nose, which yet stung badly as he lowered his elbow into it. The monk, seeing the contortion of Hrald's face, smiled. "It will do you good, and speed the healing. You will take it out and let it dry, untouched. I will make two or three stitches, at the widest part, and leave the rest open that it may weep its healing fluid. Then I will wrap it, and give you more linen for the road home."

The monk spoke to one of the postulants, rose with him to go to one of the work-tables, and returned with a cup in hand, which he passed to Hrald. "This will help, both pain and healing, for there is no healing without sleep."

It was a cup of the darkest wine Hrald had ever seen, black nearly, and though he could taste the grape, there was an undercurrent of some musky stuff.

There were three simple cots aligned against one wall, and the leech-monk gestured to one of them.

"You will lie down now, and rest for a short while."

Hrald did, and found his eyes heavy with sleep as the monk lifted his arm, and with the help of one of the postulants, went to work. Needle and thread were in hand, but the monk began by singing softly an Ave Maria to the wound, as if addressing it, and not Hrald; singing out in the tongue of Rome the pain and any evil humour which might settle there.

Hrald closed his eyes. He was safe, amongst those friendly to him, and most of all shriven. Darkness rose to cover him like a blanket.

When Hrald awoke, the light had changed; the window showed approaching dusk. A priest was sitting by his cot. Hrald sat up, his head buzzing, heavy with the herbs he had been given. A fresh strip of linen bound his wound; he felt it under his tunic sleeve. The priest was holding a large cup, and handed it to Hrald, indicating he drink it down. It was fruit-water of some kind, and Hrald was not aware of his great thirst until it touched his lips. It did much in helping his alertness.

"Archbishop Plegmund tells me you are close to Abbess Sigewif of Oundle," the priest offered. He was a well-built man of some forty-odd years, his brown hair streaked with grey, but eyes clear and of a bright blue. "She is a friend to me, one of vital importance to me as a young man. To my vocation," he added, in a quiet tone.

The priest seemed to recall himself, and went on, "Forgive me. I am Father Edfrid, one of the priests here at Augustine's cathedral. I sent my nephew, who was then considering a vocation, to Oundle, and the Abbess' oversight. He was impressed with the scriptorium there, and a certain monk, Balin, who taught him much."

Hrald of course knew Balin, and nodded his head at this. "Sigewif has said Balin has one of the best hands she has seen, and as her own writing is so fine, this is true praise."

Father Edfrid gave a nod. "I felt Oundle would suit my nephew. It was a short period while he thought over if he had a calling or not." The priest gave a mild laugh, and then a shrug. "Apparently not; he came back without warning, and distracted. But he would not speak of it to me. Nor I think to anyone. I only assume that there he had a revelation that a life of religious dedication was not appropriate."

Edfrid reflected a moment on what he just said about the boy, and then went on.

"If you might indulge both uncle and nephew, I know Congar would enjoy speaking with you, for that is his name. My brother is a King's thegn; his hall is not far. They would welcome you for the evening meal."

Hrald could only accept this courtesy. He could find lodging for the night here at the cathedral, but accepting a meal with this kind priest's kin was the least he could do to repay the service Cantwaraburh had tendered.

Bork entered the stable at the town's main gate and was brought almost face-to-face with the man who owned it. He bobbed his head in respect and asked if he could work a day or two in exchange for food and a pile of straw to sleep on. The stableman, seeing the weaponry Bork carried, remarked, "You are more than a stable-boy. I keep mounts to hire and buy, not far outside the walls, with two men always on watch. You could join them."

"I am here but one or two days," Bork countered. "But I am good with horses, even those frightened, or fierce. I can mend bridles and build saddle frames for pack, as well."

"I can use you," the man decided. "There is an empty feed bin in the back; put your kit there."

Bork put himself to immediate use, side by side with the man at the work bench, cutting leathern strips for a new bridle, and pulling off and re-fitting the bronze mounts and buckles from one worn to create a new. After this he turned out the horses still in their stalls into the adjoining paddock, and addressed himself to shovel and hay-fork.

At the end of the day Bork sat down with the other stable-hands and the family, to sup. After taking part in their meal, Bork spoke.

"The man I serve has need of two horses, and has the silver to buy them. If I go to your herd outside the walls I might find those he will like."

The stableman was not sure what to make of this, but a sale is a sale, and others had sent agents to select beasts for them in the past. At any rate Bork had worked manfully all day, and deserved nothing less than seeing the animals on offer.

"Go out at first light and look them over. If you find two or three to suit, have one of my men bring them here, so we might ready them for a buyer to judge."

Bork did so, arising at dawn and making the short walk to the pasture. It was fenced round, and a hut stood at the gate, where the men who watched over the beasts slept. There was indeed some good horse-flesh amongst those kept there, and animals seemingly for every need; heavy dray horses, broad of breast, strong of rump, for the pulling of waggons weighted with goods; sturdy and patient animals suited for pack; riding animals of many sizes, including even a pony or two. Bork, after walking amongst them and prompting several to some speed so he might gauge their action, selected two. These he had led aside, and after checking their teeth, and running his hands down their legs, asked that they might be led back to the stable. Both handsome beasts, all they lacked was a good grooming to show to advantage. One was a light chestnut gelding, well-muscled, the second a roan mare, with a delicate muzzle and small ears. Both seemed willing animals, and Bork looked forward to presenting them to Hrald. The Jarl might value the mare in particular; she was one of the best horses on offer, and besides being a worthy saddle horse could be a good breeding animal at Four Stones.

Father Edfrid's nephew was summoned to the Abbey, and arrived in short order. To Hrald's eyes he looked a keen enough lad, slight of stature, beardless, of medium height or slightly below, and with a mouth which seemed cast in an enduring smile, as it was slightly crooked on his face. He was as finely dressed as a thegn's son should be, and bore a seax of value on his belt.

"Jarl Hrald, this is my nephew Congar, of Cantwaraburh," said Edfrid.

The priest went on. "The Jarl is a great patron of Oundle."

Congar's mouth opened in surprise. The confused emotions on his face shown too briefly for Hrald to fix on any one of them, but it was clear a greater story lay there. The two took leave of Father Edfrid and began to walk, first skirting the enclosed garden, then through the cathedral and out into the road. Now dusk, the lanes were nearly empty. Congar seemed so ill at ease that Hrald was forced to speak.

"Father Edfrid said your father is a thegn."

"That is correct, Jarl Hrald, as are my three brothers. And now, me."

The youth paused before going on in near-apology. "I have seen no fighting; I am posted here, assigned to the mint and its protection." Here a playful nature took over, and Congar acted a moment as if he held a spear in his hands, lifting it in a kind of salute before him, and lowering it to his side.

"A needful duty," Hrald answered. "There are brigands on the road. A leech-monk of the monastery dressed my wound for me."

It was clear that the young man would like to hear more, but equally clear the Jarl was disinclined to tell it. All Congar could do was to pick up on the prior comment.

"Yes, a needful duty. Yet there are many of us to stand and watch. And no way for me to distinguish myself."

"Your uncle said you were at Oundle, and Brother Balin taught you much."

"He did; he was generous with his training, not only in the formation of letters, but the preparation of both parchment and vellum, the pounding of minerals to make pigments for paints, and even on forays into field and forest for the collection of certain tree galls, walnuts, and like plant-life, so that our inks could be mixed in different colours."

Congar's face had become transformed during this telling, brightening as he recounted these experiences with the writing master of Oundle. He ended on a more sober note.

"I continue my practice in the scribal arts as I can, at the scriptorium here. I have a great love of the work, as little good as it does me as thegn."

Hrald gave thought. "It sounds perhaps you should have stayed there, at Oundle."

Congar gave a kind of start. "I could not. And – I am not truly fitted for the life of a monk."

All Hrald could do was nod. There was a long silence, then Hrald spoke again.

"It is a rare gift to be in the presence of a woman such as Abbess Sigewif."

"It is, indeed."

"What did you do there?"

"I came in the spirit of discovery," Congar answered, aware of the hesitancy in his voice. "I performed all the labours a postulant would do. My favourite was to aid Brother Balin in the scriptorium."

"You are a scholar," Hrald observed.

Congar shook this praise off; his cheek even coloured under such words. "Books, and learning, and the keeping of records; there is little more important than this."

Hrald gave a nod of agreement.

There had been more than one remarkable female Congar had met at the Abbey, but he dared not mention her name. Hrald startled him by naming her.

"I wonder when your visit there fell. My sister Ealhswith, after being away from Four Stones for a while, spent some time at Oundle. Your time together did not cross, did it?"

Here Congar stopped fully, and turned to Hrald. The change in the young man's countenance was so pronounced that any denial falling from his lips would be seen through for the lie it was.

How he answered sealed the matter. "Do you then know of Ealhswith and me?"

Hrald did not, his face told Congar this, but Congar had revealed the secret. The rest must come out.

"What is there to know," Hrald asked, with enough seriousness that Congar flinched.

"I did meet Lady Ealhswith. I found her a young woman of unusual comeliness. And attraction."

Hrald thought a moment. He had learnt from Father Edfrid that Congar had removed from Oundle with some suddenness. When Ealhswith returned to Four Stones from her second stay at Oundle she was changed.

"Will you tell me more?" It was more quiet demand than question, but voiced in a way to give confidence to the youth. After all Hrald had gone through, and was still going through, he sought the simple truth.

Congar's mind was racing even faster than his heart was thumping in his breast. Yet he knew fear. He could not endanger so sweet a maid as was this Jarl's sister. And if his next words gave offence, he was uncertain how the Jarl would take them. The man had his arm in a sling and wore only a knife at his side, but paired with the staff, was more than enough weaponry to take a life.

"If you would speak of her, speak fully," Hrald prompted.

Congar's throat had tightened in uncertainty of what to say.

Hrald tried to help. "Is it just to say you liked each other?"

Congar was forced to swallow.

"It is."

"Did any act occur, in word or deed, to bind you two together?"

"In deed, no. Nothing. And this I swear by the sanctity of the Holy Virgin. I did no more than hold her hand. Not a single kiss did we share.

"In word, also. She was modest, awaiting a promise of my own. I was rash, foolish beyond belief, and mayhap beyond forgiveness. I wanted to take her to Rome with me, that we might start a life."

Hrald's head tilted back as he lifted his eyes to the sky.

"Yet you did not."

"We were discovered. Or rather, our packs were, where I had hidden them, in the barn."

"And the Abbess sent you home."

"She did. Ealhswith is blameless, blameless and untouched. She did nothing. It was all me."

Hrald voiced the next with care. Congar was clearly alarmed, and he did not wish to frighten him into a false statement.

"She was willing to run off with you. Was there other proof of her devotion?"

"Only the tears she wept when we were parted," Congar conceded.

And her own hidden sorrow when back at Four Stones, Hrald thought.

Here their converse must end, as they neared a timber house.

The tidy and orderly hall of Congar's family sat not far from one of the round watch towers, fitting for the domain of a King's thegn entrusted with the protection of the place. Hrald was presented to Congar's parents, and warmly welcomed. Of the four brothers only Congar lived at home, the others at their respective posts.

Hrald's plainness of dress, lack of weaponry, or backing warriors did not give his hosts pause. They had seen even Kings in sack-cloth before, and Cantwaraburh drew such to it. All humbled themselves before God, to receive His forgiveness, and benediction.

The meal, though the average for the household, felt a feast to Hrald. First of all, there was ale, which he had not tasted the length of his pilgrimage. It was of such savour that he must comment on it, and Congar's mother, with a becoming smile, admitted it to be her handiwork. Hrald slipped his left arm from its sling and again rested his wrist on the table, but other than that ate unimpeded, if more slowly than his appetite demanded.

Congar's father, having been told upon meeting his guest that Hrald was Jarl of Four Stones in Lindisse, had done little but nod his respect. Now, as they finished their meal he observed, "You are Sidroc's son, and Yrling would have been your great-uncle."

Hrald must avow these truths. He could see the man considering. Yrling had done great damage to the countryside of Lindisse, and his actions would have been known in Wessex as well. Hrald's father, in contrast, worked largely to safeguard and consolidate what Yrling had won. Congar's uncle was a priest and interested in Four Stones' support of Oundle. Congar's father was a warrior, and agent of the successive Kings of Wessex, with a lengthy memory of past predations. The two men approached Hrald's kin from different points of reference.

"My father and I have long worked for peace," is how Hrald answered this.

"Indeed," came the response. "Four Stones has stayed a stalwart force in upholding that which Ælfred and Guthrum forged."

Hrald had not expected to hear Dagmar's father named here. The man had been dead nearly a decade, yet his greatness was still recalled. Hrald murmured a word of thanks, but thought: And my son is of Guthrum's blood.

The meal came to its end, and Hrald took grateful leave of the hall. Congar would walk their guest back to the Abbey, and once outside and alone with Hrald he turned to him with a look of eager expectation.

It was Hrald spoke first.

"Would you wed her if you could make offer?"

The abruptness of this did not put the young man off.

"Of course, if she would have me." Congar did not have time to tell the Jarl that there was no way he could assemble a worthy bride-price for his sister.

"What would they say of your taking Ealhswith to wife," was what Hrald now asked, with a tilt of his chin at the hall they had just quitted. They had moved no more than a few steps away, and the torch burning outside the door gave light so Hrald might study Congar's face as he questioned him.

Congar gave something akin to a laugh. "That I should wed a Jarl's sister?" he repeated. "They would hardly believe that I, no more than a cumberworld, had turned to such good account, when all my life they have expected little. And received little," he added, in justice. "But I would do anything to wed Ealhswith, undertake any service."

Hrald must share the truth, and its pressing urgency. "Ealhswith is now under the care of Lady Æthelflaed of Mercia." These were the words he spoke, while the truth circling in his mind was simply, Æthelflaed has taken her from me, as punishment.

Nonetheless Hrald went on. "The Lady means to wed her to further her goal of strengthening bonds between the great halls of Mercia, and Wessex."

Congar's face fell, and with a struggle attempted to show he must accept this was a worthy end, but his brow was still furrowed.

A sense of resolve filled Hrald, resolve to help Congar and his little sister wed, if that was what Ealhswith wanted. He felt certain their mother would be happy for Ealhswith to find happiness with a young thegn and remain in Wessex. Yet this was a far more modest end then that which Lady Æthelflaed sought for Ealhswith, and Hrald's mother and the Bailiff, knowing the King himself had once singled out Ealhswith to be Lady of Kilton, must themselves have higher hopes for her than this slight young man with his love of learning. Congar's father was a thegn of moderate means. There was nothing Hrald could do to elevate him to higher estate; only the King or Prince of Wessex could do so. But the young man himself – he could be placed in a position of real, and rising, importance. Hrald sized him up.

"What are your years?" he asked.

"Close to twenty now."

Even if he gained muscle, with his stature Congar was no real candidate for the shield wall. If his arm was good enough and his aim true, he could wield a throwing spear, joining others flinging them to soften up the enemy lines before the larger warriors met shield-to-shield. Hrald had seen boys slinging stones who were not much smaller than he. He understood why this final son had been set apart, designated hopefully for the Church. The fact that, now a thegn, Congar served as guard to the heavily-protected mint underscored this. Despite his desire to distinguish himself, there was much about the young man which did not suggest warring. Congar would be wasted in battle. His talent lay elsewhere, and he would prove far more valuable at a writing table.

Hrald went on to tell him so.

"You are skilled with pen, and could act as scribe at a high level. If you were attached to Prince Eadward, you could serve as scribe to him in Witanceaster, and on his campaigns."

Congar was so taken aback it took a moment to respond. "That would be a posting beyond anything I could dream of."

"The Bailiff of Defenas is Ealhswith's step-father. Mine as well," Hrald said. "You have only to convince him of your worth. Lady Ælfwyn, our mother, wishes her happiness, and has told her so. Raedwulf has the ear of King Ælfred. My best friend, Ceric of Kilton, has fought for years at the side of Prince Eadward, who will soon be King. The Bailiff's word, together with that of Ceric, will go a long way in securing you a place amongst Eadward's companions."

Congar, listening open-mouthed, was stunned. Working with the monks in the scriptorium at Cantwaraburh he had been perfecting his hand, but to what end he knew not. He excelled at this work, and saw it also as a kind of service, one which also recalled him to Ealhswith and to his time at Oundle. Congar assumed he would never see her again, and suddenly Hrald was before him, saying that if he proved himself worthy of his sister by winning an appointment to Prince Eadward, she could be his wife.

"But you are her closest male relation. And I have so little as bride-price, to offer . . . "

Here Hrald ruefully recalled that this lack had been no impediment to his running off with his sister. He would not remind Congar of this lapse; he seemed deeply ashamed of the incident.

"I do not need your silver, Congar. My father and his uncle before him won enough, and I have won more. But for Ealhswith to be wed to a good and upright man, one whom she loves, that is nearly bride-price in itself."

All Congar could do was nod his head in hopeful silence.

Hrald realised he must think, and quickly. His sister could be led into another union without knowing one with Congar was possible. If he wrote to Ealhswith himself, he feared his letter might be intercepted and read by Æthelflaed. Congar could not write directly, either; an unexpected missive carried from Cantwaraburh would rouse curiosity. But if they both wrote to Ealhswith, Hrald with a promise of help should Congar prove worthy, and Congar, with a declaration of intent, Hrald could carry both letters to Oundle. Abbess Sigewif could enclose them in a letter of her own, directly to Ealhswith, and Lady Æthelflaed would not think to open such a packet.

"We need parchment and ink," Hrald declared.

"The scriptorium," Congar answered. "Some monk will still be there at work, and will grant us such."

They hastened ahead to the Abbey, and once there to the long room in which books were made, and copied. Sure enough, two monks worked there by candle-light, and gave Congar and his guest no more than a benevolent nod as they searched through quire trimmings on which to write their letters.

Hrald penned a few quick lines:

EALTHSWITH
– I have met Congar of Cantwaraburh. If you will have him to husband, I will help. HRALD.

"Tuck this within your own," he told Congar. "I will leave you now, to write your own letter. Bring it, unsealed, to me here at the Abbey, in the morning. I will not read it, but Abbess Sigewif must. It will be she who determines whether she sends our letters on to my sister."

Congar's face whitened at this, but he must nod agreement.

"After that, your suit will be in the hands of my sister," Hrald summed.

"But your mother – and the Bailiff," Congar protested.

"They seek Ealhswith's safety and happiness. You will have time to convince them that you are the man to bring her that."

Hrald left him then, to make his way back to the cot awaiting him in the leech-room. The day had demanded much, and Hrald had never considered that here he might do something to help his little sister to her own happiness. Sigewif had protected both Ealhswith and Congar, never telling Hrald of their meeting, nor how close they came to disgrace. If she forwarded the missives that would be approval enough of Congar.

The leech-monk had left a small cup of the black wine on a stool by his cot. Hrald drank it down, grateful for coming sleep.

In the morning, after Hrald had broken his fast with the monks, the Archbishop summoned him to his study before he left. Plegmund looked up from his writing table and uttered a single word of opening.

"Ashild," he said.

His sister's name came so unexpectedly from the prelate's mouth that Hrald was caught off guard.

"She is beknown to me," Plegmund went on. "Word of her has come to my ears from sources both clerical and secular."

Hrald was not sure from his tone if the Archbishop sanctioned Ashild's renown, but he was moved to speak on her behalf.

"She rode like a man in defence of Oundle and killed an enemy Dane. Later she was herself killed by mistake on another field of battle, trying to aid me." Sudden water smarted Hrald's eyes, which he blinked away.

"Of these facts I am aware, my son," Plegmund granted.

"Sigewif claimed her body," Hrald went on. "It was surrendered with honour."

"As Ashild of Four Stones deserved," the Archbishop murmured. "I know her tomb has drawn visitors, and spurred devotion."

Here Hrald lowered his eyes a moment. Did Plegmund also know his sister died with a hammer of Thor about her neck, he wondered. It had made no difference to Sigewif; at least, seemingly not.

The Archbishop was speaking again. "There could be no better chronicler for Ashild's life, than Abbess Sigewif," he conceded.

Plegmund studied Hrald's face. A long pause followed before the Archbishop said the last. "Nor for her after-life."

Hrald bowed his head at this tacit approval, and being granted the Archbishop's blessing, took his leave.

Once in the cloister, Hrald came upon Congar, the youth flushed with hurrying to the Abbey with his missive. He wordlessly passed Hrald a flat linen pouch; the thinness of which told Hrald that Congar's letter was no more than a single leaf. If Abbess Sigewif approved, and Ealhswith wanted him, that would be enough.

They walked together, retracing their steps of last night through the garden and into the cathedral. They stopped at the shrine of St Augustine, already at this early hour clustered with pilgrims praying before his tomb. Hrald turned and took in the length and breadth of the church a final time, then crossed himself before the altar. By the western door was a stout oaken poor-box, upright and time-worn, the mouth of which he fed with a handful of silver coins.

He and Congar parted; Hrald with the promise that he would receive word. Sigewif would endorse his suit, or not; Congar would learn either way.

Walking stick in hand, basket-pack over his shoulders, Hrald made for the stable where he had left Bork. He saw him almost at once, rubbing down a chestnut horse, while a second, a dappled roan mare, was tied nearby. Bork had washed both animals, finger-combed their manes and tails with true attention, and was readying to fit them with saddles. He had insisted on doing all this himself, refusing the help of another stable-hand, for it was a quick and sure way to make himself known to the animals, to gain their trust, and learn about them. As Hrald neared, the owner of beasts and stable was only too glad to see his prospective buyer approach, and in short order they had struck a satisfactory deal for both horses and tack.

Hrald's arm was held in its sling, keeping it from unwanted jarring. Bork led the chestnut gelding, which was the larger of the two animals, to a mounting block so Hrald would not stress his arm while gaining the saddle. Hrald was well pleased with the two mounts Bork had chosen, and as for Bork himself, he had never sat a horse as fine as the mare beneath him.

They set off on their northerly course. After so many days afoot, eye to eye with ploughmen and shepherds, Hrald was once again horsed, and looking down on those who laboured on the earth. Their eyes rose to him just the same, but now he rode with a man armed with spear and shield. Hrald was the first to nod in greeting, and though that nod was returned, it was one of respect, and not the simple bond of brotherhood he had met with from such folk on his walk down.

They moved their horses smartly and made good time. At the widowed crofter's holding they stopped briefly to learn that the old couple had removed to their own farm, the man still abed but alive. Bork had stayed astride his own horse the whole time, and listened to this report from Hrald as they went on their way. Passing the clearing which had seen the attack, Bork could not look towards it. Hrald did. The bodies had been removed; burnt perhaps, though there was no near sign of fire. He said as much, aloud, but Bork had no answer.

As they rode on, Bork still in silence, Hrald asked, "Did you seek confession, there at Cantwaraburh?"

Bork shook his head. "I could not. I prayed for my father, that is all. The cathedral – it was so grand."

Hrald murmured a word of assent. The importance of the cathedral and the tomb and relics it housed made it almost forbidding.

"I will tell Wilgot," Bork went on.

"Já, do that, it will help."

Bork seemed lost in thought, and Hrald returned, "These are good animals you found. Let us put them to the test a while, to bring us the faster to Four Stones."

THE SEA-GIRT BURH

Kilton

EDWIN had given thought as to how best receive visitors so august as were the Ladies Æthelflaed and Pega. In the past all the family of Kilton would assemble to greet the arrivals, either outside the palisade, if the approaching party were of some size, or just within, before the hall, its door left open in welcome.

"When the advance guard arrives, telling us they are near, send eight of your men back with him, as escort," Ceric suggested. He was sitting with his brother and Dwynwen in the hall, at the high table. It was mid-day and few were about in the warm weather, for most spinning and child-play had moved out into the forecourt. A few weavers stood at their wall looms by the open doors, from which sunlight streamed in.

Edwin would not have thought of this, and was silently grateful for the good impression such display would make.

Dwynwen spoke now, with real thought behind her words. "Lady Æthelflaed is daughter to your King, and nearly the Queen of Mercia in her own right. When she crosses over the border of Kilton, be there awaiting her, Edwin, on your horse, and ride to her. You are very fine on your horse," she suggested.

Again, Edwin had not considered this. "Should I not be here at the gate, to welcome them?"

"Lady Pega will be eager to see you, and as courtesy it shows you place her arrival, and the arrival of Lady Æthelflaed, over your own pride in your hall." The Welsh girl said this with such simple discernment that Edwin must admit the truth of it.

"I see," he agreed. "I see this . . . "

He must consider acting on her words; she had knowledge of the ways of young women of high estate. And Edwin was quietly flattered at Dwynwen telling him how fine he looked mounted.

The young Lord of Kilton determined to do so; he would ride out fronting a troop of eight thegns, led by Alwin and Wystan, pennons flying from their saddle cantles. The rest of the household would assemble by the gates to greet the arrivals, but he himself would serve as escort.

Edwin was thankful for the counsel of both brother and his wife, but unable to say so. As the days passed and he awaited the visiting party he was in fact in the act of nerving himself for the ordeal. He reminded himself that he need not accept her; the match was not assured; Pega might not find him to her liking; or upon seeing her closely, he might find an objection, a fault, impossible to overlook. These thoughts were as fleeting as they were likely fruitless, but as he waited they helped soothe him for what was to come.

As the convoy of riders and waggons neared Kilton, Pega sat with Mealla and Ælfgiva in the small covered waggon, that sporting the tarpaulin of brightly painted lozenges of red, blue, and yellow. Ealhswith was perched in the rear of the waggon, looking out at the waggon following them, and the verdant landscape flanking them. At one point Pega found herself lifting her eyes to the painted cloth over their heads, and at the ghost of the colours to be seen where the thick paint had seeped through. This was her marriage-waggon, that Lady Æthelflaed had sent her off in when she wed Hrald. It had been repurposed, just as she had, for a new man, a new union.

The sounding of a horn turned all faces ahead and to the right. Ealhswith clambered forward from the rear to crouch behind Ælfgiva, so she too could see. Ahead of them rolled the wagon of Lady Æthelflaed, which slowed in response. A small troop of men on horseback neared, and off to one side rode the Mercian thegn who had been sent ahead to Kilton to tell of their coming. A second horseman, riding alone and fronting the doubled line behind him, pressed ahead, urging his horse to a canter in seeming eagerness to greet them. This was Edwin, Lord of Kilton.

He reined his horse in by the first waggon, that holding Lady Æthelflaed and her women, and Edwin bowed his head to them. A priest also sat with them, Edwin could see that much. The Lady raised her hand in acknowledgment, a smile on her lips. Then Edwin stayed his horse for the second waggon in line, one so gaily decorated he knew it must hold his potential bride. Indeed, he saw two women on the board, one with raven hair, the other the tawny-haired Pega. Again, Edwin bowed his head, his horse dancing beneath him. It was his best animal, a true golden chestnut with flaxen mane and tail, and he hoped the effect was as impressive as the Welsh girl had promised.

But now Edwin faced a small dilemma. Should he ride forward to accompany Lady Æthelflaed more directly, or keep pace with the painted waggon wherein Lady Pega sat? His intended had smiled at his approach, but now seemed to keep her gaze modestly averted. Perhaps it was indication he should ride forward with the Lady of Mercia, who had arranged this meeting, and this match. He did so, leaving the painted waggon with a respectful nod.

Edwin was glad when the walls of Kilton came into view. The convoy slowed as it neared the village, not only for the safety of loose beasts and gawking children, but for the benefit of Kilton's cottars, out in force along the road to welcome the daughter of their King. Only a few kenned the identity of those in the second waggon and why they were here; those who had kin working within that hall and knew a prospective bride would be soon entertained. At any rate, those ahorse and those in the waggons were met by glad cries of acclaim, raised hands, and wide smiles.

The gates were fully open, but the train stopped without the walls where the family of Kilton awaited them. There in a line stood Ceric, dressed in dark green, belted with his sword and seax; at his right Worr, the horse-thegn of the place, similarly armed, and in his customary brown; and at the left of Ceric his wife, Dwynwen, a child-like figure in red. Dunnere the priest stood next, in his black cassock, and by his side Edgyth, Lady of Kilton, in a gown of dove grey. She was in many ways most expectant of all, yearning as she had for a fitting wife for Edwin. Behind her awaited both the steward of the hall and the under-steward. Garrulf, the scop of Kilton was there as well, revered singer of songs. If a new verse was to be written in Kilton's history, he must be there to witness its players first hand so he could tell of it later.

The waggons halted. Edwin swung down from his horse and went to where Lady Æthelflaed, in a plum-coloured gown, awaited. Edwin wore a tunic of deep blue, over darker blue leggings, setting off to advantage both his dark coppery hair and his sword and seax. He handed Æthelflaed down, bowed again, and went to the second waggon. Ceric had joined him there, to aid the descent of not two but three young women. As Edwin murmured "Lady Pega" to his intended, Ceric aided the dark-haired woman and the child in her arms. A moment later Edwin was brought face to face with the Jarl of Four Stones' sister, Ealhswith. Neither spoke, but Ealhswith, knowing she would see Edwin, at least did not suffer the momentary startle he did.

Ceric spotted her as well, and at once went to his brother's aid, offering his hand to Ealhswith, to bring her forward to where Edgyth awaited. He then returned to Dwynwen's side, and despite his own surprise was able to lower his head and tell her, "This is Hrald's young sister, with them."

Lady Edgyth welcomed the Ladies Æthelflaed and Pega. The latter, aware that she was likely meeting her soon to be mother-in-law, could only hope she would be welcoming, despite the haste with which the marriage had been brokered. Pega was in fact met with the warmest of smiles by Edgyth, who, extending her hand to the young woman, clasped it in her own. Edwin then made formal greeting to each Lady. Curtseys were dropped, bows offered. The priest, named Willehad, was welcomed by Dunnere, who was glad of his presence. The union was of importance enough to demand that the Mass following it be celebrated by clergy from both families.

Ælfgiva, still in Mealla's arms was named, and Edwin presented Ceric, to whom Æthelflaed made flattering reference from her brother Eadward.

Then Dwynwen, splendidly attired in the red silk gown she had worn to wed Ceric, the golden fillet he had given her around her brow, broke from the line, and came forward with quick steps to Pega.

Hrald had told Pega of the pretty child Ceric had wed, but still she must wonder at the girl's youth and stature.

"Princess," Pega murmured. She bowed her head and made the deepest of curtseys.

When she lifted her head she saw Dwynwen smile, before giving her short but merry laugh.

"I am Dwynwen," she corrected. "And now we shall be as sisters."

Her sudden words, both decisive and cheering, felt as if she had sealed the Fate of the two who had come together here. Even those used to Dwynwen's forthrightness were surprised at this, but Edwin was taken aback. This sprite – it was as if she had uttered a decree, naming Pega as sister to her, and thus already wife to Edwin. Blurting this out was another prediction, another way in which Dwynwen overstepped herself. It was grating that she did so with such charm that most who watched her were at once won over. Indeed she was now standing before Lady Pega's companion, smiling at Ælfgiva and making much of the little girl.

Edwin must hide his discomfiture, for now two great coursing hounds appeared from the back of a rear waggon,

brought round by one of Æthelflaed's men, who held both
on short leads. The man stopped behind Pega. One of the
hounds gave an open-mouthed whine, eager to be brought
forward to the side of his mistress. The man holding them
loosened the grasp on his lead, allowing the hound to come
up to her side. Pega placed her hand on the animal's sleek
head, then rested it on his shoulder. The dog wore a wide
collar of blued leather, studded with gems.

"This is Frost, my true companion," Pega explained, "and
his son, whom I have named Snow." They were fitting names
for both hounds, the sire, dark grey yet frosted with silver,
the younger dog whose short coat was dark at the skin, but
so heavily tipped with white to look mantled with snow.

Edwin, confronted with these imposing beasts, was
honestly pleased, gesturing them toward the open door of
the hall. But Pega, mindful of her hosts, and with a nod at
the man who held them, bid the hounds stay without and be
allowed to stretch their long legs.

The men and waggons of the escort must be dealt with,
and it was Worr who took command. That waggon which held
Pega's dowry was quick to espy, for the four thegns marking
each corner of it. It was pulled into the smaller mare's stable,
easy to secure. But beasts and men must be offered food and
drink, the horses set loose in paddocks, the men to rest and
eat at long tables in the kitchen yard.

Now the welcome ale awaited the Lady of Mercia and
her party. All moved forward to the great oaken door, swung
wide, its heavy hinges of iron glowing dully in the sunlight.
The hall's casements were open to admit the day, and the
lime-washed brightness of the place shown to advantage.
The quantity of light enhanced the carving of vines, leaves,

twining animals, and birds in flight embellishing every post and cross-beam. Picked out in colour as these were the hall, even with few folk, seemed alive with movement. Bright as it was, tapers flared, already lit upon the high table to welcome those being ushered in. The trestle table of prodigious length was set upon a dais of the same pale stone from which the floor had been pieced. It formed an impressive backdrop and destination to all as they stepped over the threshold.

Just within a staff of six awaited, three serving men, neatly attired, holding basins of warm and scented water, and three women in new aprons bearing linen towels. Hands were rinsed and dried, and neither Ceric nor Edwin could recall any event in which guests were received with such prompt ceremony, save those few visits from the King himself.

They processed to the high table, Edwin escorting the Lady Æthelflaed as was proper to his rank as Lord, and Edgyth at the side of Lady Pega. The two priests, Dunnere and the guest Willehad came next. Mealla followed, a squirming Ælfgiva in her arms. Ealhswith was just behind, and Dwynwen was happy to accompany her, flanking her with Ceric.

Lady Edgyth had ready a beaker of clear Rhenish glass, beaded round with dots of green glass. From this she poured golden mead into cups of silver for her guests. Edwin offered words of welcome, and the priest Willehad thanks to God for safe travelling. Then with all seated, pleasantries could be exchanged, each to each, an altogether more challenging task for the Lord of Kilton.

Placed as he was between Æthelflaed and Pega, Edwin was torn as to whom to give his attention to, but he was able to steal a few glances at the young woman who had been carried here. Lady Æthelflaed saw his efforts, and with a smile turned her own head to Lady Edgyth so that Edwin might fully gaze upon her ward. She was much as he recalled her at the cathedral of Gleaweceaster, of mid-height, with a fall of honey-coloured hair. Now that she was so near he could move beyond that first, and distant impression. With such hair Edwin expected blue eyes, but they were a blue of smoky hue, near to grey, and deep set under her fair brows. The eyes, both in colouring and depth, gave her a solemn expression in repose. A small mole sat upon her upper lip, in no way marring her attraction. Her movements were measured, her manner reserved. She could not be thought stately; she lacked the bearing and height for that, but the quiet womanliness about her marked her as from an estimable family. He knew she was in her twenty-first year, yet seemed in her composure older than this. But then she had been wed, and was a mother.

Still, Edwin must admit that the fair young woman before him had lost none of her attractions. If anything she had perhaps gained in them. Her apparent steadiness and maturity was something Kilton would need in its coming Lady.

Pega had heard nought of Edwin's person. Æthelflaed had briefly met him, but told Pega nothing, just as she had left the Jarl of Four Stones undescribed when he came to court her. The Lady wished Pega to form her opinion uncoloured by her own. And in fact, Edwin could scarcely be more different from the dark and tall man Æthelflaed had allowed to meet her at Weogornaceastre. The Lord of Kilton was slightly above mid-height for a man, with striking colouring. His hair, a dark ruddy shade touched with golden strands, made him stand out. He was as well-formed in his person as any young warrior could be, the fair skin on his face showed a dusting of freckles, fading under the effects of much sunlight. The eyes, she saw, were more green than blue, an admixture perhaps of both. In all he was both alike and dissimilar to his older brother. The hair of Ceric was lighter, the eyes a truer green, and though she had been told there was but four years between them Ceric seemed a decade older. There was something deep in his eyes, and also in his manner, which Edwin had yet to gain. Both were handsome, uncommonly so, to Pega's eyes, and for a moment her thoughts strayed to how fair a child would be, fathered by Edwin.

He she considered must inquire how went the journey. Pega answered, expressing her pleasure in again seeing Mercia. It made Edwin wonder if missing her home had proved an impediment to her happiness in Anglia. He dare not ask that; at any rate here at Kilton she would be in reach of Æthelflaed within a short journey. He hardly knew what to ask, and Pega kept lowering her eyes, as if looking upon him were an effort.

A fidgeting Ælfgiva, having been handed a small cake, was placed on the floor, and Mealla rose. Dwynwen did so as well, and as the child had scampered behind her on her way toward the open door, reached her first, dropping down to speak to her in some unknown tongue. The words were uttered so softly Mealla did not think any at the table could hear, at least not distinctly.

"Is that Welsh," Mealla asked, more demand than query.

Dwynwen smiled up at her. "Nay. It is rather the language I think of sometimes, one I think babes come from Heaven knowing. But they lose, once we force our own tongues upon them. I recall some of it at times, and thought I would see if she liked it."

Ælfgiva did seem to have liked it, for she had stayed her action to the door, and now placed her free hand on Dwynwen's lips, as if to pat them. But the maid of Éireann would have none of it, and took the child's hand and drew Ælfgiva to her. With a small squawk of protest the child turned to look back at Dwynwen, who straightened up. Ælfgiva's attention was now drawn to the firepit, in Summer cold and empty, but the large round rocks surrounding it were a lure for any child, and Ælfgiva sat down on one of them. Dwynwen laughed, though Mealla shot a disapproving look her way, and scooped the child back up into her arms.

It was Edgyth who rose now, in offer to show their guests the features of grounds and gardens. The hall itself was on trial here; it and all of Kilton, and before Edwin and Pega made decision about each other, his prospective bride must be won over by the place. Out they went, through the forecourt, to view stables, cattle barn, and workshops, granary, and brew-house. These formed a broad array of wooden buildings with planked roofs, mossed over, or thick thatch crowning them, all in fine repair. They saw where waggon-wrights and coopers laboured, and the deep saw-pit with its growing stack of sawn wood, ready for building repair. The kitchen yard with its springhouses and fowl pens was visited, and cooks and bakers lined up in their aprons to bow before their guests, pleased that in the midst of their work for the coming meal they could look upon those they cooked for. They walked amongst a score of outbuildings, Edgyth enumerating what was stored in each. She pointed out the two wells, which had never run dry. The Lady of the place did not speak of it directly, but between ground water and grain held in reserve, it became clear Kilton could withstand a long siege. At the sparring ground Edwin spoke of his men, both his and those of Ceric, and also the ceorls of the village who took training here with bow and throwing spear. Dunnere opened the door of the church and welcomed all in, to stand silently amidst painted statues and the glister of silver upon the altar. Last came the pleasure garden, and the sea-side cliff and its views over a tossing ocean.

The rush of impressions upon Pega was great. Raised in two ancient cities of the Caesars, no timber burh could truly compare, but next to Four Stones both hall and out-buildings could be remarked upon. And the abundance and quality of light – perched on a sea-side cliff as Kilton was, all was brighter, more luminous than any burh or keep she had lived in, or visited. The sound and scent of the sea was added attraction. There was as well something Pega had yearned for, the stone church. There was no better proof of the devout nature of those who had built it. Kilton's priest was of Cymru, just as Ælfred's was; such clerics were renowned for their learning. The way in which Willehad and Dunnere had fallen into steady discourse told Pega of the former's approval.

It was in the garden that the group separated, as Edgyth answered a question Willehad posed about a quince tree. Ceric and Dwynwen walked with Pega and Lady Æthelflaed as the latter questioned him about her father's visits to the burh. As the others drifted off, Ealhswith moved closer to the edge of the cliff, so she might peer down at the beach. She kept a safe distance from the drop, and stood, seemingly lost in thought, looking out at the curling waves, narrow lines of white coming from afar to melt into rippled foam on the shingle below. Edwin moved closer, and she turned and saw him. Her slight intake of air at his nearness was nearly a gasp, and she could not speak.

Edwin found himself just looking at her.

"I am sorry," he said.

Her hand rose slightly, and she gave a small shake of her head; he need not explain.

A moment passed, his eyes still fixed upon her.

"You are very pretty," he told her, and meant it.

Ealhswith remained silent, unable to answer this, though it held great meaning to her. It truly had been her father, and not any lack in her person, which had stopped Edwin from choosing her. She lowered her eyes, glad to have heard it.

Edwin finally released her from his gaze. Behind him he could hear the voices of Æthelflaed and Pega. Prettier than she who I will wed, he told himself.

The meal that evening began with drink Kilton was justly proud of. Ale was poured out, the famed recipe perfected by Lady Modwynn and adhered to ever since, though grain crop and seasonal potency of herbs lent variation each year. The men of Kilton held it unequaled, anywhere. Cups were raised filled with this amber liquid, the first of which was poured out by Lady Edgyth, a smile on her pale but welcoming face.

Edgyth had given great thought to this first meal, which must be a fitting display of Kilton's late Summer bounty. Yet, both mindful and hopeful that a nuptial feast would also be soon called for, she would reserve special dishes for that event. The highlight of the welcome feast was extravagant enough, a fowl and mushroom stew in sage-flavoured cream sauce. Early mushrooms were foraged, and many more, dried from last year's forest floors, were soaked in broth to tender plumpness. The precious jar of black pepper corns Dwynwen had presented Edgyth with was pried open, and a spoonful measured out, pounded to dusky powder in mortar and pestle by the head cook herself, and sprinkled liberally upon the pale sauce shrouding the jointed fowl meat. The fragrant result, black-flecked and redolent of the pleasing heat of the costly pepper berries, was remarked upon by all.

Pega did not sit next Edwin; despite Dwynwen's pronouncement, it would not be fitting to place her where she would sit should she become his wife. Instead, rank-to-rank, Edwin sat between Æthelflaed and his mother Edgyth. Pega was to the right of the Lady of Mercia, and then sat the priest, Willehad. Still, there was new weight and importance at that board, what with Ælfred's daughter and the woman she had brought to wed Edwin.

Ealhswith had been placed next to Dwynwen, and though the Princess was several years younger it was she who befriended the maid of Four Stones, placing her hand in her guest's in warm reassurance and welcome. Though Ealhswith had met and even travelled with Prince Eadward, she had never any congress with a Princess, and was entranced by Dwynwen's lilting speech and child-like charm. And Dwynwen was so at ease. When the Princess turned to speak to Ceric, Ealhswith was left with her own thoughts, too shy to intrude on the conversation the guests on her left enjoyed. It gave her time to merely look over the hall, at its many tables and the men and women filling them. She let her eyes flit as well down the length of that board she had been led to, to see all sitting here, engaged both with their salvers and each other. As much as she liked the Princess of Ceredigion, Ealhswith came to sudden, and chilling, realisation. Now

here at Kilton, she could not have fulfilled the role of Lady.
The whole of Kilton frightened her. The burh was too large,
too fine. Its imagined history, the vaunted military prowess
of its Lords and refinement of its Ladies, their long commit-
ment to learning and to Christianity, the efficient and just
marshalling of the hall staff and village, carried over generations now, was a burden too weighty for her narrow shoulders to assume. Ealhswith had not time before her trip to
Witanceaster to meet Edwin to consider all this, the vastness
of the role and what would be expected of her, nor could she
then conceive it. She faced now the enormity of the charge
the King had laid upon her, that she wed Edwin, and take
over the management of all from his adopted mother. She
saw it here in action. Her own mother had run Four Stones,
and run it well, for years; she knew this, and Pega, a few scant
years older than she, had assumed those tasks after her. But
Ealhswith knew she could not, not at a burh like Kilton; it
was beyond her.

Garrulf the scop sang; he was one of the attractions of
the hall, and Edgyth, remembering so well how her father-
in-law Godwulf valued the man, was proud of his ability. The
scop did not disappoint. Well aware of who he would play for,
Garrulf chose to tell of King Offa of Mercia, an effort greeted
by surprised delight by the Lady thereof. This was matched
only by Dwynwen's barely repressed glee; it was Ceric wore
that great monarch's sword now. Garrulf sung of Offa as the
minter of gold coins, and King who had his wife Cynethryth
also emblazoned on his coinage. This seemed good omen to
those who listened.

Before all parted after the meal, Æthelflaed turned to
Edwin and with lowered voice addressed him. "Tomorrow

Pega's dowry will be displayed. You will wish to have an advisor, some counsel, with you. And it is my desire that our conversation be so witnessed."

Edwin knew this was coming, yet was at a loss. There was no one save Ceric, or Dunnere. He would ask them both.

At night's close, guests were led to their beds. Edgyth had prepared a bower house for each Lady of Mercia, well equipped to accommodate four. There must as well be additional lodging for those Æthelflaed travelled with, including the serving women who followed her everywhere, and these must be housed. The priest Willehad could stay with Dunnere, so Edgyth need only make sure additional bedding be delivered to his house.

The Lady Pega was granted a bower with Mealla and Ælfgiva, and after Mealla snuffed out the cresset left burning on the table, all three were now in their respective alcoves. As Pega lay on her back in the dark, a trickle of silent tears escaped the tail of her eyes. These were followed by quaking sobs. She turned over, her face above her pillow, and let her tears run down. Mealla, in the next alcove, stirred, then rose and hastened to her side. She slipped into her bed and held Pega as she wept.

"You need not do this, you need not," the maid of Éireann told her.

Pega shook her head. "I am so angry."

Mealla, no stranger to the heat of ire, did not know how to follow this declaration. In the past when Mealla had reviled Hrald, Pega had hastily silenced her.

"You have cause to be angry," Mealla pressed. "You were betrayed."

"Yes. I was betrayed by Hrald. And then discarded him at once. I need do that for my own sake. And now I am here."

Pega had severed her union with Hrald in an instant, but Æthelflaed did not understand it had been an instant of searing pain. Like an inflamed wound gone green to which a flaming iron is held, the injury was still sore. The Lady had her welfare at heart, and felt the distraction of a new husband in a new hall to serve both their interests best.

"You were right to do so," her friend insisted.

Fresh anger rose in the breast of the maid of Éireann, that Pega had been so cruelly used. Returning to Four Stones to collect her goods was a torment to her. She had done all Pega had asked, and gone beyond. When she discovered the red silk pouch holding the elaborate body chain, she had not merely left it behind. She had broken it into a hundred pieces. The righteous outrage she had felt doing so, pulling the delicate links asunder, rose in her memory. Of all gifts this was, to Mealla, most hurtful, as Pega had confided to her that she had worn it upon her naked skin to please the giver.

"It was all a lie!" Mealla proclaimed.

"Not a lie," Pega answered, with more gentleness than her companion thought possible. "He believed our life possible. He wished to believe it . . . "

Mealla gave thought to the men of Kilton. "Will it be hard for you, to live with he who is so close to the Jarl?"

Pega knew she spoke of Ceric, Hrald's boyhood friend, and also knew Mealla could not bring herself to voice either name. She took care in her response.

"It must not be hard," Pega told her. "I have little choice. The Lady wants this for me, and for Wessex."

A longer pause allowed Pega to share another truth. "At least it brings my treasure back from the Dane-law. That must hold meaning to Æthelflaed as well. I was sent as peace-weaver, and spurned for a Danish woman. No one knows what the next years will bring, as far as a return to war."

Mealla took a breath and turned her thoughts to the young Lord of Kilton. "Edwin – he is a handsome man, and I have watched him look at you. He values your person."

"And my gold. We have no choice, he and I. I will do my best. Ælfgiva is what matters; a father for her, a home such as this."

Mealla murmured her approval of such talk, and risked saying more. "And those children you will bring to Edwin – his sons."

Pega nodded her weary head at this, and buried her head in Mealla's shoulder.

MERCIAN GOLD

P EGA'S dowry had been carried into the hall, and from thence to Edwin's private chamber. Lady Æthelflaed asked that it be taken there. As a room it was most secure in the entire burh, and the larger message of displaying it within could not be missed: Pega's wealth is here, and awaits only formalities to remain so.

It came in small chests and sealed casks shouldered by Æthelflaed's thegns, and when they had opened them for the Lady of Mercia, she went to work alone, drawing forth pieces and setting them upon the table, propping them up on chairs, and resting them on the tops of the several chests near the broad bed. She had done this before, in her own chamber, awaiting Hrald of Four Stones. She must offer silent thanks Pega's gold and silver objects remained intact and in her possession. Pega had spent silver coinage to build the timber church for her former hall, but had sufficient supply so that she need use none of those items which made up her family's ancient treasure.

When she was satisfied Lady Æthelflaed opened the door. Edwin was just without, standing with his brother, and with the priest of Kilton. The Lady gestured them in with a nod.

She had lit two wax tapers to further illuminate the treasure, and their flickering light danced over the surfaces of the gleaming metal. If the Lady's goal was to astound, she had entirely achieved it. A small iron casket sat, lid open, on one of the chairs, holding gemstones in every hue set in gold and silver mounts, and raw stones awaiting the ministrations of the gem-cutter. Upon another chair seat sat a bronze urn of heroic size, cunningly adorned with bronze serpents, and so wide of mouth that many of the smaller items before it might have been stored within. An array of silver and gold spoons lay there on the board, along with small dishes and bowls of these metals. Cups in silver, some gold-rimmed, stood, arranged in size and shape, stemmed and straight sided, embossed or plain metal, ready for the hands of a skilled smith to further adorn them. One large footed bowl of silver was brim-full of silver coins, whole, uncut, and proclaiming their worth. Around its base lay a circle of larger golden coins, teasing the eye as they vanished around the back of the vessel. Most surprising of all was the array of figures, as large as a man's hand, and fashioned in pure gold, which ran along the front edge of the table. These were beasts, and men with beasts, of a make Edwin and Ceric had never before seen. Two golden horses trotted, one bare-backed, the second cast with a man, arms upheld in the air as if in joy, astride its gleaming back. There was a golden ox, with another figure upon its back, as if vaulting, and a cockerel in gold, just the same size as the bull, and several cats, sitting or standing, sly-eyed and satisfied in their golden glory.

It was Dunnere who spoke, and of these figures, for the priest had been to Rome and there seen much. "They are from a southern island, Crete by name, and old beyond reckoning."

There was more, but Æthelflaed now lifted something of gold from the top of one of Edwin's clothes chests. It had been laid upon a fabric pouch of deep blue shot with golden thread, a fitting enclosure for what the Lady held before them.

Edwin's mouth opened, and he gave a small inhale of surprise. It was a neck-ring, one of gold, but sized for a giant. If it were placed over the head it would span across the chest from nearly shoulder to shoulder. In the front of it were two large terminal knobs of gold, touching each other. The knobs were crusted over with tiny beads of gold, adding to the glittering effect.

Edwin could not help but look to his brother. This immense treasure was what the Jarl of Four Stones had forfeited. What woman was Dagmar, daughter of Guthrum, for a man to turn his back on this? Edwin must curb this thought before it grew.

The Lord of Kilton must rouse himself to speak, and with a bow to she who presented this bounty uttered his approval.

Æthelflaed answered with a brisk nod, yet gave them no hint as to what was expected in return.

She went on to stress that there must be no cause for the marriage to be sundered. She assumed the highest degree of rectitude from Edwin, and hoped he understood and agreed to Pega's stringent moral standards. Edwin could but reassure her he found both Lady Pega and her dower to surpass his expectation, and voiced the hope that his character would never be a cause of disappointment to either Pega or her noble guardian.

Æthelflaed went on, and in most decided tone. "Pega is a healthy young woman, one who has brought forth a robust child. There should be no cause for her to fail to provide you with sons."

With that, the interview seemed to draw to its close, for the Lady placed her hand upon one of the dazzling gold ornaments, and lifted it into a strong box to nestle amongst the folds of cloth within.

"You may speak to Pega today," she advised. "I will send her to your garden pavilion."

Edwin had his own view of this, and offered it now.

"I would do so here, my Lady," Edwin replied. She looked over to him, and he added, "It is the one room of importance Lady Pega has yet to see."

"As you wish," she conceded.

Ceric would speak now. He had never bargained for any woman's hand, yet knew he must act on behalf of his brother. The bride-price should be plainly stated, and then objections raised, where needed. None of this had happened. "My Lady, Lady Pega does indeed bring a dower without match. Please tell us your demands."

"Pega shall tell you herself," Æthelflaed replied, and gave a nod of dismissal.

With respectful bows the three men left the chamber. A few steps outside the door Dunnere turned to the brothers. "I was not here when Lady Modwynn arrived with her dower. But what the Lady Pega carries must be every bit as rich in Earthly treasure as Lord Godwulf was granted by his bride. Godwulf answered by giving her great tracts of fruitful land."

It was all the priest could add, but gave some guidance.

Ceric led Edwin outside, and to the garden. After such a display of wealth, they needed sea air to clear their heads. Indeed, his younger brother could scarcely speak; he was cudgeling his brain for a worthy response to this staggering dowry.

As they passed through the beech hedge they saw Dwynwen emerging up the stone steps from the beach. A basket was clutched to her chest, one still dripping with wet. She had again been at the wrack-line, choosing her own treasure. She smiled at them, but as she searched their faces, her smile faded to a look of question.

"Lady Æthelflaed has just shown Edwin Lady Pega's dowry," Ceric told her. "It is more gold than we have ever seen."

"Ah," she answered, and nodded. She walked to the table, and they followed.

"I can speak to Pega now," Edwin said. "But the Lady gave no hint of what will be asked from me in return."

"I can tell you," she said.

Dwynwen stood there in her simple day-gown, a plain linen smock worn over it, the bodice stained with sand and sea-water. She looked almost a child removed from her tidal-pool play. She smiled at Edwin and began.

"Gold is like the Sun," Dwynwen told him. "It can dazzle the eyes, and make it hard to see what else is there before us.

"What you say to Pega of Mercia is only this: 'I offer you my home.'"

Here the Welsh Princess paused. It allowed the simplicity, the directness of these few words the importance they deserved.

Edwin had cocked his head in seeming disbelief.

"In Ceredigion you told me of Kilton," she recounted. "Of its sea-side cliffs, and the waves beyond. Of the goodness of its land, and the folk who people your village. You told me of the books kept here, your priest of Cymru, your stone church, of a kind woman ready to greet me, Lady Edgyth.

"Pega has seen all this for herself. She need not imagine it, she is sitting in your hall, and walking your land. Tell her only, I offer you my home. That is what she will crave, for herself and her daughter. And that is what you can give."

"That is all?"

"That is everything." She blinked, and the small pointed chin rose in the air a moment, remembering the huge wine jug King Elidon demanded be filled with silver coins for her own hand. She went on. "Oh – if you must, you can present as well a quantity of gems, or a sack of silver; Ælfred's daughter may need to see such things. But Pega needs only to be wanted, to hear that she will have a home in your hall. And in your heart."

"I offer you my home," Edwin repeated.

"Yes," Dwynwen breathed, in response, her smile bright. "All you have here, you offer to your Lady."

Edwin only nodded, perhaps just as stunned by Dwynwen's words as he was by Pega's treasure. He excused himself, walking off along the cliff edge where he might think.

※※※※※※※※※

Just after the noon hour the Lord of Kilton sat at the high table awaiting Lady Pega. She appeared with her favoured hound, and Mealla at her side. Whatever their own tasks, a kind of expectant hush fell over the remaining family of Kilton, knowing this was taking place.

Ceric had recourse to his copy of Boetius in the bower house. He would sometimes open the volume at random, to see what message the great and doomed philosopher could supply. Today he held the book without opening it, his eyes tracing the austere line work incised into the leathern boards which protected the parchment leaves within. He laid it down, and headed to the garden and its sea cliff, needing greater diversion.

Lady Edgyth was there, near where he entered, a basket looped over her wrist, cutting late roses. She saw Ceric approach and smiled. She would not speak of the task at hand for Edwin; it was best not to, though her hopes ran high. She and Ceric moved to another rose, and with her shears Edgyth snipped off spent flowers and selected those unfurling to join those already in her basket. The day was warm, the sea calm beyond the cliffs, and of deepest blue above a paler sky.

They heard faint laughter, and a few notes of song, and turned their heads to see the maid Tegwedd, visible above the tall wooden trellis supporting the roses backing the pavilion. Ceric paused and realised he was seeing the top of Dwynwen's head as well; her long brown hair looped up in a ribband of white linen. They must be standing on the table to have gained such height. He rounded the trellis work. Both girls had a cloud of fluffy wool roving upon their shoulders. They stood back-to-back to keep the table balanced, each close to one edge of it. The extra height such position afforded allowed their spindles to drop a much further distance before needing to be drawn up as they spun.

Edgyth, alarmed at seeing them up there, suppressed a small cry of concern at their safety. But Ceric could not help but laugh at this playful inventiveness.

Tegwedd was abashed to be found standing upon the table with her mistress, and squatted down so she might return to the ground. She jumped down with a little grunt of impact. Ceric was near enough now to reach out and wrap his arm around Dwynwen and lower her to the gravel at his feet.

Tegwedd's face flamed in embarrassment, but Edgyth, looking on Dwynwen, could not chide the serving girl. Dwynwen had her own ideas of deportment.

"You must not fall, from such a height," Edgyth tried to caution.

"Ah, Lady, I would only float," Dwynwen returned, with twinkling eyes.

"But," Edgyth added, "I see the advantage. The draw of thread is much the longer standing up there."

"Amongst the clouds," Dwynwen laughed.

Lady Edgyth must smile as well; it was Dwynwen's gift to make others lighter in heart. The girls ran off, spindles and roving in hands, chanting a song in the tongue of the Cymry.

Edgyth, looking after them, said, "I do believe Dwynwen would only float."

Ceric made a sound of acknowledgment. The way she skimmed over the surface of the garden paths and descended the stone steps to the beach, it was almost as if she flew, so lightly did her feet touch the ground.

Now alone, Ceric turned his head back in the direction of the hall, where they knew Edwin and Pega spoke.

"Lady Pega – are you pleased with her?" he asked. She seemed to Ceric to possess every attribute demanded by the role of Lady of the hall, and was in addition comely in her person.

"More than pleased," Edgyth answered. "I sorrow for the circumstance which brought her here, but if Edwin and she agree . . . I think her ideal. Hers will be a steadying hand for Edwin, and for Kilton. And her little daughter is a delight, a happy harbinger of other babes to come."

The child Hrald has lost, Ceric thought. Yet it forced Ceric to speak of she he himself had wed. There was no one to whom he could confide this to but Edgyth, and he must speak of it.

"Dwynwen . . . she and I have been much together, as man and wife. Yet she has not conceived."

He saw Edgyth's lips begin to open in answer, but he stayed her with a small lifting of his hand as he went on.

"I have been almost fearful of her doing so, in that her body is so small. Yet how is it that she does not, if she is truly . . . woman."

He could not yet admit – even to one so trusted as his aunt – his wondering if Dwynwen was even fully mortal. This was the fear which had taken root in his heart.

Edgyth nodded her head in gentle understanding. "I told her the day of your pledging that I wish she could have waited a year." A smile played at Edgyth's pale lips. "It was clear she could not."

Ceric had no smile in return. There was a note of suppressed anguish, one near to despair, in his voice as he answered this, as if he were revealing a long-held secret too difficult to further conceal.

"She has not grown, Lady. She has not grown."

"Are you certain?"

He gave a hopeless shake of his head. "She promised she would grow. When she stands next to others, to you, or certainly Tegwedd, I see she is no taller."

Lady Edgyth had not changed in stature, but certainly Tegwedd, the serving girl, had sprouted. She and Dwynwen had been nearly the same size when they came from Wales. Now Tegwedd was both taller and more womanly in her form.

"She told me she would grow."

So plaintive was his tone that Edgyth placed her hand on his forearm. "She will in time, I am sure," was Edgyth's consoling response.

But in fact, she thought Dwynwen had not grown, and might not ever.

"I asked once about her birth mother," Edgyth went on. "Dwynwen told me she was of quite small stature. Perhaps Dwynwen is destined to be the same."

"I think her Lady-mother, her birth-mother, was fey," Ceric murmured. "She speaks at times of her as if she were fey; or some part. And Dwynwen too."

Edgyth would have crossed herself, yet the distress of the young man before her placed his welfare above her own salvation. And, though it be nearly an instinctive act, blessing herself might lend credence to his fears.

"Ceric. There are things we cannot know. It is true the workings of the world and the Heavens are mysterious. But I believe Dwynwen to be under God's protection. Were her kin from the land of Faery? I cannot judge. Her child-like wonder – she is a child, and part of her will always remain so." There was more Edgyth could have said; the uncanny way the girl had with herbs; the surprising things she said.

And perhaps, Edgyth thought, but would not risk saying, Dwynwen grows old more slowly than us.

Ceric too was silent a moment, as he recalled all the many predictions his child-wife had made, which seemed to come true. And then there were her drawings – not just designs, he thought, but some secret tongue she shared with Lady Luned. He gave his head a clearing shake. That Lady was his grandmother; if she too were fey that blood might run in him. Perhaps that was why he attracted Elf-shot; his true nature was seen and known by those who lived in the other-world . . .

Lady Edgyth was speaking again. "Her body may not have grown, I grant you this. But she has grown in other ways; grown in experience, perhaps even in wisdom." They both knew the Welsh Princess possessed a rare knowing, an insight into others, into their futures, which was uncanny and strange.

Edgyth went on. "And Dwynwen has not a single bone of ill-will in her body, small as it may be. Nor, I believe, a single particle of evil."

Ceric nodded; he believed this with his whole heart. Dwynwen's powers must be the power of good. His child-wife had overcome the act of an Elfin Queen to heal him of lingering madness.

Yet mention of Dwynwen's person spurred another thought, a realisation of not long ago. He had never seen a single bruise on her arms or legs, nary a scratch or scrape. He could not share this, so unnatural it seemed. He tried to reassure himself with the fact that she was possessed of grace in her person, was lithe and light on her feet. More than once she had in her surefootedness reminded him of a cat. He wished to turn to Edgyth's belief, adopt it wholly, but instead found himself questioning it. His voice, tight with fear, was barely distinct to Edgyth's ear.

"I have heard that faeries, if they dwell with men, must leave at the end of seven years. Is this true?"

Edgyth closed her eyes before answering. "We have no way of knowing."

She felt Ceric near to wandering a path hurtful to his own health, and spoke of this. "Ceric, you must guard your thoughts."

Edgyth did not wish to think of Dwynwen as anything less than a mortal child, one blest with a cheerful spirit and at times discernment far beyond her years. To consider her anything less – or more – was not a track Edgyth wished to follow, not when the Princess had done so much good in restoring Ceric.

"I would trust her wisdom," Edgyth found herself saying, though she could not keep the briefest of smiles from crossing her lips, ascribing so great an attribute to the girl. Yet this was the second time this word had crossed her lips in reference to Dwynwen. There was such freedom in the girl's utter confidence. Edgyth went on, with answer to her claim, and tenderness in her words. "She knows how to be happy. She knows how to give happiness."

The young man before her gave a shake of his head. He must be fully honest with Edgyth and tell her of his fear.

"When I first saw Dwynwen I thought her fey. She knows much of such folk, and told me a woman of the Faery cannot bear the babe of a man."

He could go no further with this.

Edgyth countered this with as much firmness as her gentle nature allowed. "When I first saw her, I thought of the blessed Saints, and how in their own girlhood, they would look like her.

"I still think this, Ceric. Dwynwen was sent from Heaven to you, and to Kilton."

Ceric nodded, grateful for her words. He ended with what he knew was true.

"Dwynwen gives me great joy. I would like to have a child with her, but would never risk her life or health, that she might do so."

Edgyth recalled how Godwin, in despair at all their lost babes, and the cost to her, refrained from their love-making, though she begged him to try again. He was so fearful of her death, and indeed she grew weaker with every loss.

"Perhaps Dwynwen cannot bear a child. I could not bear one to my Lord Godwin.

"But – you have a son. One by a woman of great vigour, Ashild. I think it time you bring him here. Cerd will be quite the boy now, able to speak and understand. And he will be eager to explore Kilton, with his father."

※※※※※※※※※

When Lady Pega arrived with Mealla in the hall, Edwin rose to greet them. Pega had her great hound Frost at her side. The dog might be protector, but Mealla must act as chaperone. It was sufficient that she wait in the body of the hall, near the opened door of the treasure room. Edwin unlocked the door and gestured Pega and her dog in. Frost was held by a short lead, and Edwin further gestured that she might release the animal to explore on his own. Pega did so, and the dog moved off, sniffing, his plumed tail in movement. Edwin and Pega stood together, side by side, as Pega took the measure of the place.

It was a fine room, large, high ceilinged, lime-washed as was the rest of the hall. His bed was there, hewn of some sturdy wood now dark with age. The dull sheen spoke of beeswax well rubbed in, a warm glow shared by the table and four chairs. A wall loom, unwarped and unworked, stood against one wall; the others were stacked with casks and chests containing she knew, small armaments, silver, bronze, and whatever else the family of Kilton held as treasure. On the wall opposite the bed were ranged a quantity of spears, stored upright between iron arms, carefully sorted as to size. Despite the quantity of goods within the room, there was a barracks-like spareness to it, the chamber of a young man. Off to one side, and not far from the table, Pega recognised her own property, the chests and casks which held her dowery.

They were alone for the first time, and his showing her this held meaning. Now brought face to face with him, she must ask what he knew of her past.

"Have you been told how my marriage ended?"

Though her voice was low, her frankness surprised him. "I have not." Yet Edwin knew something, and must in candor share it. "Ceric suggested it had to do with Guthrum's daughter."

The tawny head dropped a moment before lifting. "Yes. Dagmar. As you must know, she was Hrald's first wife. She disgraced herself in front of Hrald with a visiting warrior, a Dane. I do not know the details, but she was cast from the hall that day.

"Yet, it was not over. After we had wed, and our daughter had been born, Hrald was called to Witanceaster on behalf of Ealhswith." Pega paused; this was delicate ground she trod upon, but say it she must. "We understood why you could not accept her. But once there, Hrald was again brought into contact with that woman.

"He left Witanceaster. When Hrald and I went there this Summer at the invitation of Æthelflaed and the King, they saw each other again. When he had left Witanceaster the first time, he left Dagmar with a coming son. I chanced upon the three of them and ended my union then and there.

"My natural recourse was my guardian, Lady Æthelflaed, who took me in. She told me then that you had seen me earlier, and inquired after me. This was all she could say."

Edwin was startled by the details, yet he should not be. Hrald was half-Dane, and therefore waywardness was to be expected. Pega had spoken with steady directness and with no attempt to win sympathy for the upset in her life. He must admire her for how she had handled herself. "I thank you for this," he told her. He added something more.

"As your former union was annulled, it is as if it never occurred."

"That is what I have been told," Pega answered. "It is an odd status for the children thereof; they are legitimate, though the union that produced them was not."

Edwin's eyes lowered for a moment. "The innocent must not suffer. Just as you, Lady Pega, were innocent."

She turned her face a little away; telling him he should not have said this, to remind her of the ordeal she had been put through. Pega stood on the threshold of a new marriage, one with him; he should keep to that, only.

They spent a moment in silence as he considered her. As Pega was so open about the end of her first union, Edwin thought to speak of his own attempt to wed.

"Lady Pega, there is something you should know about Dwynwen."

"The Princess," Pega said.

Edwin must nod. "The Princess. She was meant to be my wife. I travelled to Ceredigion, to court her. She wished to come to Kilton, and make decision. While here – and within very little time – she saw Ceric. And became his wife. I tell you this as you will learn it sooner or later, from some serving woman, and I would have you know from me that it is true."

She was not alone; Edwin had been spurned, had felt the sting of rejection. And taking thought of the wider circle, young Ealhswith had been refused by Edwin.

Pega's answer was a nod, and in a low tone addressed this. "I thank you for telling me." She was forced to give thought to the young Princess, who, seemingly destined for one brother, and the Lord, had instead determined her own Fate. It was an utterly untoward act, but Pega must admire the Welsh girl for choosing he whom she wanted.

Edwin spoke now, turning fully to her. "Lady Pega, you please me greatly. If you will have me, I would wed you."

He must slow before he said the next.

"I offer you my home."

He almost recoiled at the spareness of the words, but was able to speak them with the warmth he felt.

Pega's head rose, and the grave eyes were turned on Edwin's face.

"Did Lady Æthelflaed tell you what is demanded for my hand?"

"She did not."

"I asked her not to. Nothing is demanded."

"Nothing?" It could not be; for a Lady like Pega a high bride-price would be asked.

"I will not be bought with swords or silver," Pega answered. "The royal houses of Wessex and Mercia have already profited from my first marriage. As the bride-price was forfeited by the giver, we will neither demand nor accept another. This is my decision. And Lady Æthelflaed agreed; she did not wish to be seen as profiting unduly from the new union. Kilton nearly borders Mercia, and Kilton is powerful and rich. Our marriage means greater security for Mercia. And my family's gold is brought out of the Dane-law and back into the sphere of Æthelflaed's kin. Her brother will be King of Wessex. You will be at his side. That is what matters to her."

"And to you?" he must ask.

"I seek a home, one for myself and my daughter. You have offered me a fine one."

Edwin was struck; the Welsh girl had been right. It stunned him into silence for a long moment as he stood looking at Pega.

Pega's next words seemed to signal her acceptance. "This is then our sleeping chamber."

Our sleeping chamber. Edwin's voice as he answered reflected his uncertainty, and his eagerness.

"Yes – yes, it will be."

"I will wed you, Edwin."

The hall was told that night that the Lord of Kilton and Lady Pega of Mercia would wed; Edwin himself announced it. Toasts were offered, health was drunk, and Garrulf, at the meal's end, regaled all with a song of how King Offa of Mercia had, generations ago, wed a woman of Wessex, and how this happy coupling was reflected in the coming marriage. Pega knew her face flamed more than once at table. She had arrived as prospective bride and now would be Lady of Kilton, and felt with some keenness the sense that all were considering this.

That night in their bower house, Ceric must embrace Dwynwen in the act of love. Warmed by wine, gladdened and hopeful that his brother had finally found a fitting wife, Ceric caressed his own young wife. He did so with great tenderness, and yet, real need. As he held her to his body he whispered, "You must not leave me, Dwynwen. Not in seven years. Not ever."

Dwynwen's eyes shifted of a sudden to the left, and back to his troubled face. Then, understanding, she whispered back, and hands about his neck, pulled his face closer to her own.

"I will not leave you. I will never leave you, Ceric." This was echo of the vow she had made to him when she first appeared at his door to give herself to him, and claim him as her husband. Now she repeated it, her voice as soft as a murmured prayer, but with much resolve behind it.

In the morning Ceric awoke at first light. Dwynwen was sitting by the casement, a piece of linen in her hands. He watched her from under his lowered eyelids, not sure if she knew he was awake.

"Oh," she cried, and jumped up. He lifted his head.

Dwynwen laughed. "It is nothing. I pricked my finger with the needle, that is all."

She came to him, holding the finger, a tiny drop of bright red blood resting at its tip.

He was greatly relieved to see this, and could not voice it. But there it was, a drop of blood, seeming proof she was made of the same stuff he was.

"See, it is nothing," she said, with a smile. Ceric took her wrist and pulled her to him, and kissed the ruby drop away.

The wedding of Edwin and Pega would take place on this, the third day of her arriving at Kilton. It was a vast and needful preparation, reflecting the importance of those joining hands, and their respective houses. From the hour Edgyth had been told that Pega would journey to meet Edwin, she had given thought to what a coming nuptial feast must comprise. It was late Summer, and the best offerings of field and farmyard there for the taking. The kitchen yard cooks would make the most of it. Pigs, nearing their fattest, were roasted whole, and rosemary and sage leaves stuffed under their skin for scent and flavour. Young bullocks were ready to be culled. Their meat, stewed with apples and raisins, would form a dish of unusual savour. Hundreds of small loaves were being baked with which to soak up the resulting gravy. Cabbages, carrots, and onions would be shredded, steamed, and then simmered in cream. Honeycombs had been washed for mead-making, and plenty sat by, jugged, and ready to be poured into pitchers and ewers for the tables.

It must not only be a meal of distinction for those within the hall, it must be uncommonly abundant, for all of Kilton would partake of some special fare. A browis enriched with meat and long-simmered bone marrow would be trundled out to the village crofters, as well as ale, a kind of early Harvest Home for Edwin's folk.

The door of the small church at Kilton would be the setting. Pega neither wanted nor needed another grand cathedral setting. Two priests would celebrate the Mass following the hand-fast, Dunnere of Kilton and Willehad, brought by Æthelflaed.

Pega did not don a pale gown, as that of butter yellow she had worn for her earlier wedding. She was as simply dressed as she had been splendidly so for her first union. She wore instead bellflower blue, with but a cross of silver about her neck. She did not place her golden crown of delicate wrought leaves and gemmed fruit upon her brow; that was laid away, and she might never again do so. Her hair was covered by a thinly-woven veil of silver-grey, which she fastened with the two golden hound-head pins Lady Æthelflaed had given her. It all lent distinction to her prettiness; she looked the heiress she was.

The family of Kilton gathered, and given the small party of the bride, they joined as well in the walk to the stone church where Edwin awaited with the priests. Mealla was at Pega's side, tending Ælfgiva, the child by turns excited and shy. Ealhswith appeared wearing the horse pin Pega had given her, on the latter's first day at Four Stones. Ealhswith had ever favoured it, as it was gift from her new sister-in-law, and for the memory of Ashild, who so loved horses. But seeing it brought tears to Pega's eyes, remembering the hopefulness of her arrival there. Ealhswith, abashed, placed her hand over Pega's. "I am sorry. I should not have worn it."

"No. I thank you for doing so, for the reminder of a happy day."

Dwynwen also wore a special ornament, a pearl necklace, which all the women remarked over. "It was gift of King Ælfred to Lady Luned, my step-mother; and Luned gave it me," she explained.

Æthelflaed knew nothing of this necklace, but then her father's coffers were deep. It stood as clear sign of the King's regard for this Welsh Princess, and her kin. One of the Lady's companions had already learnt the story of Edwin's courting of the girl, giving Æthelflaed further reason to celebrate her success in so pairing Pega. She would have been forced to look further afield if the Lord of Kilton had wed this odd child.

The actual fastening of hands took place before the church door. Edwin stood there upon the step, his captains Alwyn and Wystan near him. On the other side of the portal stood both priests, Dunnere in his chasuble of brilliant green, signifying hope and new life. Æthelflaed's cleric was also gowned in green, but one encrusted with a pectoral cross of sewn gemstones on his chest. Edwin was dressed in as much splendour as he possessed. Edgyth helped him choose, and he awaited Pega dressed in a tunic of rich mallard green enhancing his eyes and setting off his dark coppery hair. He wore the sword and baldric given by Ælfred, and it was the hilt of this he placed into Pega's hand as he made his promise to protect her and her children. It was Æthelflaed who bound their hands, laying a ribband of cream-coloured silk over them. They spoke their simple vows, were blest by both priests, and entering the church, stood side by side for the celebration of the Holy Mass.

It seemed unreal to Edwin; he had met Pega three days past and now they were wed. But it was often such for those of high estate, and if he could have brought himself to think on Ceredigion, he would have remembered that he wished to wed the Princess thereof then and there. Now he sat at his table, Pega at his side, as they lifted mead in silver cups before his cheering folk. All seemed happy; Lady Æthelflaed had even offered him her hand and clasped it warmly. He pressed drink upon his new wife, who accepted, and he drank rather more than he might have himself, until Ceric caught his eye and he put down his cup. Course after course of rich foods filled their salvers, and for the first time, Edwin shared a salver with his wife. Both priests spoke, Garrulf played and sang, and then Edgyth and Æthelflaed rose. Pega did as well, and the two great hounds who had been lying behind the high table stood and shook themselves. It was time.

Mealla had been seated at the women's table with Ælfgiva, and she now left Ealhswith, seated next them, in charge of the girl. The women gathered by the door of the treasure room. Lady Edgyth unlocked the room. and with a smile said to Pega, "In the morning this key shall be yours, dear Pega." The hall had quieted for a short while as the women rose, and as they vanished, cheers and whistles erupted.

A serving woman joined them with a basin of warm water, for Pega to wash herself. Once settled into bed, Lady Æthelflaed slipped out to call in the priests for their further blessing. This act was summons as well for Edwin, who having been all too aware of the absence of his wife, must

stand now, take his leave of his men and hall amidst their
cheering hoots, and join with his bride.

Pega was sitting up in bed, patently naked under the sheet
pulled up and tucked under her bare arms. Her eyes were cast
down, but those of all else in the room were upon Edwin, the
women smiling in encouragement, and he thought, happiness as well; it was surely that upon his Lady-mother's face.
He came to stand at the head of the bed near Pega, and the
air before them was sliced by the Sign of the Cross made by
first Dunnere and then Willehad. Each of the women came
and kissed Pega, Mealla last. The two dogs remained, sniffing about in the corners of the room. The room was lit by a
pair of wax tapers upon the table, as well a cresset on a stool
near the bed. Also on the table was a beaker, holding drink
of some sort, and a jar of flowers, roses it looked, which had
not been there when Edwin had dressed.

He took off his clothing with some care, even making
an attempt to fold them on the lid of the chest he laid them
upon. He left the tapers burning, but snuffed out the near
cresset. Then he lifted the coverlet and slipped into the bed
next Pega. She made no move towards him, no welcoming
gesture, but then, she was not Begu, and paid to do so. He
twisted so he could bring his face near her own. He touched
his lips to hers, a gentle kiss which he hoped would lead to
more.

Her hand rose, and she placed it on his chest, over his
heart. He leant nearer.

"I give you my home, Pega. I hope you will be happy
here," he whispered.

REDEMPTION

Four Stones

HRALD and Bork rode through the palisade gates of Four Stones, unable to keep a few young and rowdy escorts assigned to various checkpoints from following them. The speculation about the Jarl's absence had been such that Kjeld had reinstated the watch along the southerly road, in reassurance to the body of Hrald's men, who had been told little. Thus Hrald's arrival back on his lands had been witnessed, and a few stationed along the way must accompany him back to the hall, in hope of learning the whole story.

What was known from the day Hrald left was that Bork must have followed him. The youth was nowhere to be found. Jari knew it first, after seeing Hrald off. Returning to his house and the still-sleeping Inga he did not fail to see that despite Bork's effort to pull the wadmal curtain fronting his alcove closed, it was enough parted that Jari must go to it and find the truth. He said nothing though, and even Yrling failed to comment on Bork's absence until he was missing at table in the hall when they broke their fast. As soon as the meal was done Yrling went to Jari in complaint, wanting the Tyr-hand to confess that somehow Bork had been allowed to follow Hrald. Yrling received no satisfaction. Jari, though he claimed upset at Bork, was secretly glad Hrald was not wholly alone on the road. But what that slip of a boy could do to aid him should they get into a scrape was beyond Jari's ken.

When the two rode in, Hrald, amid the general tumult of his unexpected arrival, had time to turn to Bork. "Care well for your mare," is what Hrald told him.

Bork was too astonished to give answer. When escorting the Jarl he was of course issued a horse, but now Hrald was giving him this fine mare, a far better animal than he had ever been granted.

Hrald answered Bork's silence with a grin; there was no time for more, as now Jari, Kjeld and many others were come to meet them, and Mul and one of his sons ready to take their horses.

Still in his saddle, Hrald had his walking stick upright in his hand, as if it were a spear. As Jari neared, Hrald tossed it to him. Jari caught it, with a laugh. Then Hrald swung down to the ground. He no longer used the sling for his hurt arm, and as Jari embraced him in welcome he grasped both of Hrald's forearms. Hrald gave such a start that Jari knew at once he had touched some hurt to him; the grimace on Hrald's face told its own story. Hrald recovered himself as quickly as he could, and only muttered, "I will tell you later."

Yrling meanwhile was glaring at Bork, who despite looking tired and filthy was being surrounded in warm greeting by Mul and his boys. Yrling heard just enough to tell him that the roan mare Bork had ridden in on was now his very own.

Mul was making much over the animal, a further sting to Yrling, for she truly was a good mount.

Hrald and Bork must bathe; after this the Jarl wanted Jari, Kjeld, and Yrling to join him in the treasure room.

An hour later the three invited stood outside the treasure room door. It was ajar; two serving women had entered with refreshment and were setting up cups and jugs. Hrald was within, and much to Yrling's dismay, Bork too. Yrling's vexation was only to grow as Hrald told the tale.

The drink Hrald had asked for was no less than wine. Jari took charge of the jug and measured out goodly portions of water into the cups he filled with the stuff, and then passed to Yrling and Bork. He took his own first cup unwatered, as did Hrald and Kjeld.

Hrald told of his walk, and how he thought he travelled alone. It might have seemed an idyll, a lark to some listeners, but none gathered there at that table felt it so. Even given the beauty of the landscape Hrald traversed, all, including Yrling after his foray up to Jorvik, knew danger might lurk in the most peaceful of settings. Hrald's discovery of the brigands was told with the direct precision of his actions then. He described hearing distant screams, and running to discover three spear-bearing miscreants at work. He spoke of overcoming the first with a blow of his walking stick to the head, and then facing two more. The calf-skin roll topping his back-pack served him, catching the spear-point of the first attacker long enough for Hrald to dive, and drive the butt of his stick onto the man's foot. The next brigand was right behind, though, and his spear did not miss Hrald.

"I had already been hit when Bork ran in. He took on the third man, driving him back."

Hrald looked to Bork, encouraging him to go on, and tell his own story. Bork swallowed, but did so. "I kept my spear moving. He tried to get in close and hit my legs. I used my shield, under his chin. He fell. Then . . . "

The youth's pause was so long Hrald must speak.

"I ordered Bork to kill him, a mercy kill to one undeserving of such."

Bork had lowered his head and only nodded. "I had to kill him," he murmured.

"It was lucky for me that you did," Hrald answered. "Once I got hit, I might not have lasted long."

Bork had told the merest outline of his actions, and Hrald filled in the spare account, so that the boy would get his just due. He described Bork's skillful use of both shield and spear, driving the aggressor back, and then felling him.

All during this Bork's eyes were steadfastly cast down, and into the cup he clasped in both hands.

Hrald was careful not to say that Bork had saved his life. He did not wish to lay so heavy a charge upon the youth's head, for he had seen how such could change a friendship. It could be burden indeed on the one so named, and burden too to he who was beholden. And he recalled his own father telling him that though Asberg and others ascribed their survival to some act of Sidroc's, he had insisted that no man could truly save the life of another; the Shield-maidens chose you or not. And Bork was troubled enough by his own actions that Hrald repeating he had ordered the kill was some help, he hoped.

Now Hrald pushed back his tunic sleeve. There was still a light dressing of linen over his forearm, freshly laid on, which he unraveled. He held up his arm to show the wound.

The animal sinew the leech-monk had used to stitch was now darkened from the blood it had met, but given its strength had held firmly. Only the widest part of the wound had been sewn, the rest, purpled now, left to drain, and join as best it could. The skin was puckered around each needle puncture from the tightening of the flesh as the wound healed.

Jari had viewed many a spear-wound in his day, and this one spoke of the spear-point entering, sliding up through the flesh, and then being ripped away as Hrald withdrew his arm. What remained was a slice rapidly widening to a broad gash. It was an ugly wound, but the leech had done well in setting it to rights.

It was in fact the Tyr-hand who was the first to speak. "You kept hold of your stick, with that?"

Hrald gave a nod. "It was the weapon I had." Their eyes met, and Jari saw the thanks in them.

Jari's eyes shifted from Hrald to Bork, and he shook his great head in admiration of them both.

As for Kjeld, sitting nearest to Bork, he reached his arm out and set his hand upon Bork's shoulder, and gave it a squeeze.

The rest was told in a few short lines, but all listened with care. Hrald's confession had been heard by the Archbishop himself, and even Yrling understood this was the most powerful churchman in all Angle-land. Hrald found himself saying the next.

"Plegmund – he knew of Ashild." It was all he said, but it held meaning to those who recalled her.

Now Hrald stood in dismissal, and looked at the two youths. "In the morning we will have your sword-bearing. Return here after we have broken our fast."

Yrling jumped up as if speed would bring the morning faster. Yet he remembered to pick up his cup and gulp down the last of the watered wine.

Bork stood, and with a bow of his head, withdrew. Jari followed, but Hrald had gestured Kjeld to stay.

"Kjeld," he began. "You may tell the men, but only as Bork and I have told it."

His second in command could not stifle his laugh. "Ah! There will be embellishment enough, once word spreads. And Bork will be roundly chaffed for his boldness, and envied by many."

Hrald could not join in this mirth. "You – and Jari – you must look after him. Bork trusts you both."

Kjeld nodded; he had brought Bork as a frightened boy here to Four Stones, walking side by side with him, leading the horses carrying the bodies of Bork's father Aslak, and Hrald's man Kolb. Both men had been killed in a futile attack of which Bork was the sole surviving aggressor.

Hrald was speaking again. "In the morning you will ride to Oundle, and tell the Abbess I will wed Dagmar on the aftermorrow. I will bring but few men with me; she need do nothing for us."

Kjeld was forced to smile. "Then you will bring your Lady back, right after the hand-fast."

Hrald nodded.

Kjeld had more to say, for he had given thought to Hrald's return with Dagmar. "And you will find the kitchen-yard has been readying for a feast, storing up eggs, pressing more cheeses, and brewing much ale. Now you can tell them when that feast will be."

Hrald had to grin; Kjeld had thought to warn the cooks that when he returned, they would soon be called upon for a meal to celebrate.

∞∞∞∞∞∞∞∞∞

Bork finally opened the leathern purse of Red-Tunic. He took the belt from where he had stowed it under his box bed, and walked quickly toward the busy kitchen-yard and out the iron-strapped door behind it. He headed down the slope past the beech tree and to the small mound covering his father. There, kneeling at the edge of his father's resting place, he opened his battle-gain. It was a fat fistful of hack-silver, and a few coins. There was also a small number of tiny but well-wrought iron keys, to be worn or carried for luck, or used in charm-making. It was thus a not inconsiderable amount of booty, and likely more than his father had ever possessed. He did not know how to speak to his dead father about this, but felt he must share the opening this way. After a while he knew what he would do.

Half he carried to Mul and his wife. Their house was snug against the other side of the biggest stable, and first he found Mul and asked him to follow him to it. Mul's wife was in the act of coming outside to gather the clothing she had hung up along a line to dry. Without a word of warning Bork began speaking, looking to her first. "You fed and clothed me, and took me in your arms when I was scared," he recounted. He looked to Mul. "You taught me all about horses. Now I have something real to give back, and I thank you."

He held out his hand so that Mul must extend his own beneath it. A heavy shower of hack and coin fragments fell into the stable-man's calloused palm.

Bork could not wait for their thanks; he felt his eyes brim and he needed all his strength for what would come next. But as he strode away their voices followed him, in thanks.

He went next to Wilgot's house. He passed the new wooden church on his way but could not even nod toward it, not when his soul bore so much. The door to the house was open and the priest within. Bork stepped in so white of face Wilgot feared he might faint.

Instead Bork dropped down on his knees quickly enough that the priest himself must rise from his table and close the door. Wilgot took his accustomed seat on the bench for those seeking to be shriven, and uttered his blessing, signal for the penitent to begin.

Wilgot knew Bork must have followed Hrald, just as all at Four Stones did, but now he heard what that had entailed. The story came out, in confused and disordered style, Bork at times gasping as if for air. Though Wilgot had his face turned away he must at times look at the youth when Bork fell into silence. Bork's head was bent so low over his chest that the priest's checking went unnoticed.

He told Wilgot all, even Bork's grinding hunger upon the road, and how he had prayed to remain strong and fleet for his Jarl's sake. He spared no detail of the attack he had run into, so that Wilgot was forced also to see the terrified, bound girl on the ground, the bloodied old man over whom an equally old woman bent, the flattened body of another man near them, his head cracked open, a cowering small boy witnessing this, and worst of all, his own Jarl, Hrald, bleeding and fending off attack with nothing more than a stick in his hand.

"If I had not been there, he could have died then and there, alone, and at the hands of those brigands . . .

"The power of life and death was in my hands. I was forced to take the life of a man, to spare that of the Jarl. They were bad men, but it was horrible, horrible."

Bork rocked back and forth upon his knees as he recounted this. His eyes were shut tight, which did not keep the tears from running from them.

Wilgot was now aware that the harsh penance he had imposed on Hrald had cast him into far greater danger than he had imagined. And this youth, a lad of fifteen or sixteen years, and far tenderer than any had thought, had killed to save Hrald. It was true, the two of them had stopped a potentially great harm, for the brigands might have killed the couple, and into what harm the children would have been taken could only be imagined.

Bork could not go on, and Wilgot was much shaken. The penitential pilgrimage he had imposed had veered close to disaster.

The priest composed himself, and with quiet words absolved the youth before him. Wilgot had no special penance to assign. "The prayers that you utter, those which bring you most comfort, say those," he told Bork. "That is all." He made the Sign of the Cross in the air over Bork's head, who rose, and with a nod, mumbled his thanks.

Bork then reached his hand to his belt and pulled out a small pouch of fabric. "This is for the poor. I have been hungry, and near to death, as a boy. If this will help another . . . " Bork's words ended, and he merely held out the pouch to the priest.

Wilgot walked the boy the few steps to his door. When it had closed behind Bork, the priest turned to face the table. It served as writing and reading table, and before the church was built, even as altar. He dropped down before it now, heavily, and on his knees. "My Lord and my God," he uttered. "Forgive me my gross sin of pride, my sin of resentment, which led to endangering Hrald and this poor boy."

⚬⚬⚬⚬⚬⚬⚬⚬⚬⚬

By the time all gathered in the hall that night, the nature of the Jarl's journey was known. He had in honour of the Christian God walked to Cantwaraburh, thinking himself alone, but finding brigands at work, had in turn been aided by Bork, who had secretly followed. They had killed three men, two the Jarl had downed, the last killed by Bork. No one spoke openly of it, not yet, but all knew. One day and soon it would be sung of in this hall, but for now the knowing was enough.

The priest Wilgot was the last at the high table to arrive. He glanced at Hrald, who fixed his eye and gave a nod. Hrald had indeed sought and received absolution from Archbishop Plegmund. For the first time Wilgot realised that Plegmund might know it was he, Wilgot, who had sent the young Jarl almost to his death. The thought caught him unaware; beyond the sin of pride and resentment which Wilgot knew himself to be stained with, the Archbishop might think him guilty of utmost recklessness. The priest lowered his head, and began to sit down. He could not do so before Jari also caught his eye. There was no mistaking the glare in Jari's eyes, nor the set of his strong teeth in a seeming snarl; both were meant for him.

Wilgot found himself looking down and blessing his salver.

Bork, who sat at the table with the youngest warriors, was also late to it. He took his place next to Yrling, who did not turn his head in greeting. Yrling held his filled spoon, but a knot of anger and envy had tightened his throat, making it hard to swallow. Bork had been brave enough and caring enough to follow Hrald, and then took part in a real skirmish and fought at his side. And Bork had made his first kill.

Bork uttered Yrling's name, and again was ignored. He could hardly bear this cut, and whispered, "Do not be angry, Yrling. I must follow the Jarl; he spared my life. I must be of service to him, if I can. And I did not know you had been ordered not to follow."

Yrling must relent. His hunched shoulders slackened. "Well," he offered, "Hrald gave me a job to do, and I must do it, stay with Kjeld." Yrling spent a long time looking down at his browis, then spoke again. "I am glad you were there." Yrling had another thought. "You must tell Asberg when he next comes. He will hoot in glory when he hears how you used your shield."

Bork nodded his head. "Já, I will do that," he agreed, then added, "You are better at stories than me. I will let you tell it."

This made Yrling blink. Was he thought a liar? It seemed suggestion that he was not always truthful in his telling, or at least was known to embroider the tale with details not part of the original event.

But Bork had lowered his head over his bowl, so Yrling did not ask further.

In the morning Hrald and Jari stood in the treasure room before the same five swords Yrling and Bork had before seen. It was the final chance to assess the blades and choose amongst them. All five were wrought with equal or near-equal skill, pattern-welded, well-balanced to serve any warrior admirably. All had been polished to a dazzling brightness. They were of slightly different lengths, and their hilts fashioned with more or less interest in catching the eye. Hrald was quick to choose that for Yrling, and lay it aside.

"For Bork . . . " he said next, looking down at the blades. Jari made a grunt, and with his good hand pushed the hilts of two forward, indicating that Hrald choose between them. He did so. It was in fact the soberest of all the weapons, and for all that seemed the more deadly.

Kjeld came in with the two, Yrling noticeably freshly washed and wearing his best tunic. The Thor's hammer Aszur Gold-Tooth had given him, that shaped almost like an anchor, lay upon that tunic. As he had readied himself Yrling had given thought to the dwarf, imagining appearing before him next time wearing a sword, and how Aszur would laugh with delight at this, his gold tooth shining as he did. Bork too was bright of eye, though neither Hrald nor Jari was sure if the glimmer there was water forming or mere excitement.

This then would be their sword-bearings, no one present but Hrald, the two youths receiving their weapons, Jari, and Kjeld. It was not a formal symbol as Ceric had received, at which the recipient of the sword pledged to use it to protect the body and goods of the giver. A blessing was then given, and vows of loyalty unto death sworn, before ale was passed. Hrald recalled being struck with awe when, as boys, Ceric had told him of this. His own sword-bearing had been of the

simplest, with only his sister Ashild to attest to his worthi-
ness, by touching the blade to his brow, and voicing aloud
the hope that he never fail the weapon. At least this witnessing by the men most vital to Four Stones added weight to the
giving, and Hrald hoped, the bearing of the weapons.

Of the five weapons upon that table, two had been singled
out, by being pulled forward, grip toward the viewers. The
eyes of both youths were fastened upon that table, just as they
had been the first time they had seen the blades so arrayed.
There were as well two scabbards of worked leather, in which
to carry the swords, both freshly waxed, and new-lined with
sheep-skin, as the wool-wax would keep the steel from rust.

Yrling must come first; he was Hrald's kin, and Hrald,
having seen his brother's face when Bork rode in at his side,
knew he must not rub salt in the wound. Hrald wished there
were some special words he could recite, some ritual to mark
the giving, but must fall back on merely speaking Yrling's
name. He did so.

Yrling stepped forward, and Hrald reached for one of
the swords. He had selected the one with the showier hilt
for Yrling, one of figured horn, with a guard sporting coils of
silver wire hammered into it, and a pommel equally graced.
The fuller of the blade, that hollow ground down the centre
to give lightness to the weapon, had been marked by the
smith in a line of spidery runes. He passed it to his brother's
extended hand. "A bit of flash suits you," he told him, and
smiled. It was in fact the sword Yrling had most coveted, and
now he held the blade extended before him, admiring it. He
squinted at the runes.

"What does it say?" Yrling asked, looking up at his
brother. "Ster-kari?"

Hrald had studied the blade and nodded. "Já. I think it means to say, Sterkari. Stronger."

"Stronger!" Yrling repeated. "Then it will be stronger than any sword. Sterkari," he said again.

Hrald turned his attention to the next weapon, and he who was to receive it.

"Bork." He named stepped forward, and Hrald picked up the dark-hilted weapon. But at this, the final moment, Bork refused to take it, though it was from Hrald's hand.

"I – I do not want it. I cannot," he stammered.

The eyes of Jari and Kjeld shifted; no one had ever spurned a sword, most prized of all weapons. Not least one given from the hand of their Jarl. It took Yrling, so involved in his new weapon, a moment longer to react. His lips had been parted in wonder at the blade in his hand. Now they opened wider, gaping at Bork's refusal.

Hrald gave a nod, releasing the tension of the moment. "No need to take it now," he murmured. He set the blade back down.

A few words were exchanged, with which Jari and Kjeld made much of Yrling's weapon, pleasing him the more. He was so eager to be off in the hall and yard, showing off his sword, that he nearly forgot to thank his brother. It was a sharp look from Jari which reminded him.

"Uh – thank you Hrald. My Jarl."

Hrald nodded, barely suppressing his smile. Yrling made for the door. Hrald nodded at Jari and Kjeld, a kind of signal that they keep his brother from any immediate sparring with it.

Bork had stood off to one side, turning slightly away from the iron on the table. He too began to move off.

"Stay, Bork," Hrald told him.

When the heavy door had closed Hrald told him why.

"Will you come to Oundle with me? I will go on the aftermorrow. There will be a wedding there; a small one. You can stay a while, with the monks, and Abbess Sigewif. The Abbess – you may wish to speak with her.

"You are," he added, in attempt to make Bork smile, "a favourite with her."

Bork did not smile, but he did agree, and readily. "Já, I will come. I thank you, Jarl."

Hrald looked down at the untouched sword. "There is no shame in refusing it. I have seen your courage. The sword will be here, waiting for you, should you want it."

There was one more Hrald must invite on this trip to Oundle. He followed faint and unanswered taunts through the hall yards and found Yrling, sword extended, sparring with his shadow against the Sun-lit western wall of one of the fowl houses. Disgruntled hens fluttered and squawked in protest as he thrust and slashed so near them. As Hrald appeared, a kitchen-woman came at Yrling, apron flapping in her fists, shooing him off, and warning there would be no eggs in the morning for the fright he was giving the poor birds.

Yrling turned to see Hrald behind him, and red-faced, reached for the scabbard hanging from his belt. He had no actual sword belt yet, and had in haste slid the belt opening of the scabbard on that carrying his tinder pouch and purse. A clumsy groping followed before Yrling could secure the scabbard and slide his new sword safely within.

Hrald did his best not to further embarrass his brother, and moved at once to the reason he had sought him.

"In two days I ride to Oundle and wed Dagmar. Jari will come with me, and Bork as well. You may stay here with Kjeld and keep Four Stones, or ride with us."

He paused before he went on. "You are my brother. I would like you with me."

"Then I will come," Yrling was quick to say. He had been given the choice, an honour in itself. He would wear his new sword. And in truth he was eager to see the woman who Hrald had discarded so much for. She had better be as beautiful as Freyja, he told himself. She had certainly cost his brother a lot.

Next morning Kjeld rode for Oundle to speak to Abbess Sigewif. He must wait until prayers at the hour of Sext were finished, but Hrald had left a score of Four Stones' men here. As soon as the gates were opened to admit him most of them had gathered to learn that Hrald himself would arrive on the morrow, and all would ride back to the hall together. Serving men brought ale, taken outside the stable block, giving Kjeld a chance to rest both his horse, and his eyes on the monk's garden, as the men told him of their eagerness to return home. Though a number of the monks at Oundle were old warriors of Lindisse, the peace and beauty of the place held little allure for the young warriors Hrald had stationed here. What was more, few had seen more than a glimpse of the Lady Dagmar. So quiet was she in her movements she had kept strictly to the nuns' garden, the sisters' cells, and to the nuns' hall, away from where they had been billeted with the monks.

The Abbess must have been told Kjeld awaited, for presently he was summoned by a young monk who escorted him to her. They stood outside the main door of the nun's hall, and Sigewif, after greeting Kjeld, heard his message from Hrald.

"The Jarl will arrive on the morrow, and the wedding held post-haste," she summed. "I will tell the Lady Dagmar at once. There will be joy in the hearts of both of them."

Kjeld gave a nod, and looked to where his horse stood tied. The animal had been watered, and he could take his leave now. But the Abbess seemed to hold him in her gaze.

"Kjeld – you have not wed," she offered, more statement than inquiry.

"I have not, my Lady Abbess," he answered, not quite certain how to address her. He had might as well go on and tell her all. "Lady Pega had a companion, but . . . "

Here Sigewif nodded her head in encouragement.

"She did not return my . . . "

"Your interest," the Abbess helpfully supplied.

"Já. My interest."

Sigewif took stock of him, a good and loyal man disappointed in his quest to better himself through the sacred bonds of matrimony. Joining her hands before her, the Abbess tucked them into her wide sleeves.

"I will remember you in my prayers, Kjeld," Sigewif promised, "that a faithful help-mate, one worthy of you, should appear."

The Jarl of Four Stones arrived at Oundle before mid-morning. He had been seen from afar, a horn from the ramparts sounded in welcome, and the gates opened to admit him. His party, unencumbered by any waggon, was small enough to allow him to ride in haste. Hrald needed this, needed to feel his horse work under him, needed to feel his own breath as he neared. As companions he took only Jari, Yrling, and Bork, thus the oldest and the youngest of his men. Twenty more awaited at the Abbey to escort his wife and boy back to Four Stones.

Dagmar was there in the forecourt, Hroft's head nestled under her chin, as Hrald cantered in. He was off his horse in an instant, and had pulled both woman and son into his arms. He pressed his mouth near her ear.

"I am free," he breathed.

A moment later he had drawn both within the open doors of the stable. There in the dimness, out of sight of others, he drove himself against Dagmar's body, forcing her against the wall, and kissed her. No words could express the longing in that kiss. He had not meant to use such strength, but his body felt hardly in his control. His second kiss left her almost without breath, such was his want.

Hroft, in her arm, though laughing, was kicking his little legs, and flailing his free arm. Hrald pulled back enough to loosen him, and to allow his hands to go to his own belt. He unbuckled the clasp, and his hand moved along the underside of the leather. He held something to Dagmar. It was a ribband of dark red, one she had not seen for years.

"The morning after I sent you away I found this under your pillow . . . "

She was shaking her head in wonder, and he went on. "I have worn it here, at my waist, since our night at Witanceaster. It was one way to have you with me."

That night had ended with his ordering her to wed, to go to Paris and wed. Her answer had been that she would live under no man's protection but Ælfred's, or his own.

She was too moved to speak; the pain they had both suffered too great for words. Dagmar took the ribband, and clutched it in her hand.

Then Hrald took their son into his own arms. Even in this dusky stable light, the boy's eyes, blue and wide, shone bright. Hrald kissed his soft brown hair, and holding him, rested his gaze upon she who was his mother. Dagmar smiled; she must for happiness, though tears too welled from the tails of her eyes.

So glad was Hrald to see her face that it took him a while to realise she was again dressed as a woman of the Danes. Her shift was worn underneath a sleeve-less over-gown, set with shoulder straps. These were fastened, as he had ever seen, with the bronze, silver, and pearl-set brooches her father had given her, while King. Strung between them were the double strands of round rock crystals mounted in silver. She looked as she had the day he had first laid eyes on her, the day his life had utterly changed.

His face told Dagmar some of what he was thinking. Her answer was low and measured. "Your men are Danes. Many of them recall my father, and all have heard of him. I will own my heritage, here in the Dane-law."

She lowered her eyes a moment, before again raising them to him.

"Should I be granted grace to again see Ælfred or his Lady, I will dress as I did at Witanceaster, out of respect for what they did for me."

Hrald nodded, and lifting her hand, kissed it. The son she had given him had the blood of many Kings coursing in his small body; that of his grand-sire, Guthrum, and of Guthrum's uncle, King Horick of Dane-mark, and of Horick's own kin, Kings before him. His boy was almost wholly Dane, but would be raised here as a true Christian, and one day, Hrald could hope, become as he was, a Christian Jarl of Lindisse. Here was the needed bridge to span the gap between the largely heathen Dane-law and Christian Angle-land.

The shifting of the light outside the open doors told Hrald those he had ridden with, and the men he had left here, were waiting.

They moved out, the three of them, into the bright sun-light, Hroft now in Hrald's arms. Bork was there, a look of hope upon his face, holding the reins of Hrald's horse. Yrling stood next him, wide-eyed, but grinning. The rest stood looking back at their Jarl. No one need prompt the cheer that came forth from the throats of his men.

Next they were greeted by the Prioress Mildgyth, and just behind her, Sigewif herself. Hrald and Dagmar then made confession to a priest of Oundle, in the private chamber of the Abbess. Nothing they confessed differed from what they would have told Wilgot, the priest of Four Stones, but as they began their new marriage, the nature of the hearer mattered, and the nearness of the confessor, in time and space, to the joining of their hands. For Hrald it was confession to the needful taking of life amongst the brigands, for this he had not mentioned to Archbishop Plegmund. For Dagmar, the sin of having lain with a man no longer her legally-bound husband. This was the final act of redemption for her, that and the fact that she would soon be again wed to him. She would, Dagmar thought, never match Hrald in his devotion to the Church; it had come to her too late. But she would try hard to adopt its precepts, and if she could not match her stride to his, remain near to him in her efforts.

Hrald's men, wide grins on their faces, were waiting for them outside the church door when they emerged. The rest of the forecourt was nearly empty, but any serving folk of the Abbey also stood and watched with rapt attention. The couple walked side by side, and in a gesture never to be forgotten by Dagmar, Abbess Sigewif took Hroft from her arms and carried the child herself. This act of benediction was lost on none.

Nearest the stone step stood Hrald's chosen men to witness, Jari, Yrling, and Bork. Dagmar had no supporter, but her boy in the arms of the Abbess felt of greater meaning than any ten kinsfolk could have shed upon her.

They mounted the step and turned and faced the other. They did not touch, but merely gazed upon the face they loved, had lost, and won again. Hrald spoke.

"I, Hrald of Four Stones, Jarl in East Lindisse, take you Dagmar, daughter of Guthrum, King of the Danes in Angleland, to wife. Here at Oundle, before my friends, I swear to protect your body with my own." His eyes moved to Sigewif and to Hroft, in her arms. "God in his graciousness has granted us a child, who I swear to defend and protect with my life.

"I choose you above all women."

This last line was that which he had spoken when he had the first time taken Dagmar to wife. Hrald had lived the truth of it. On that day he had also sworn to preserve ever the bond so created. It had proven unbreakable.

Dagmar now spoke. She had been living in a heightened state for weeks; and the rush of emotion she battled at her first hand-fasting, that admixture of fear, shame, and doubt, had been burnt away by two years of certainty. She had been granted a single night with Hrald, to confess her love for him, and been left with the gift of his babe. It would have been enough to sustain her through her entire life. But she had been given a second chance to make Hrald happy, as well as the chance to live in wholeness and happiness with him.

She faced the man she loved and told him the truth.

"I, Dagmar, daughter of Guthrum, take you Jarl Hrald, to husband. I will make fast my hand to yours. I will make fast my heart to yours. They will not be sundered."

Now she pulled from her sleeve the red ribband he had given her. Hrald extended his hand, and she clasped it. He lay his other atop hers. She draped the red ribband over their joined hands, then laid her own above. "I bind myself to you, Hrald."

"I bind myself to you, Dagmar. Only death will part us."

Their lips met a moment over those clasped hands. Then they turned and faced Hrald's cheering men.

Dagmar tucked the ribband away in her sleeve. To Hrald this homely scrap of cloth had been as a relic of their first life together, and now for Dagmar took the greater role of near-sacred artifact of their new hand-fast.

The priest opened the door. A Mass would now be said as thank-offering, to honour the pair. When Hrald and Dagmar entered, they found the church not empty, but filled with the community of Oundle, there to bless and welcome them in their new estate. Nuns and serving women awaited on the left, monks and serving men on the right. Off to one side of the altar, and not far from a spear which stood bolted upright to the wall, a cluster of flowers lay upon the floor, tribute to Ashild.

And you, Ashild, Hrald thought. You are with me always.

No Mass had greater meaning for Hrald than this one. The first time standing here with Dagmar he had been in a near-delirium of joy and expectation, unable to absorb the sacred ritual. The Mass following his marriage to Pega, though solemn, was shadowed by the sense that he must wed this sweet young woman, for the sake of Four Stones. Now he felt the true sacrament for what it was, a celebration of Christ's sacrifice and triumph.

As they filed from the church, Sister Bova moved forward from the last rows of the nuns, to hand a bouquet of herbs and flowers to Dagmar. It was bound by a strand of twining ivy, ready to be set into water and take root. It was one of many gestures of kindness Guthrum's daughter had been met with here at Oundle.

A male postulant was banging a brass gong, inviting all to the tables set by the monk's garden, where jugs of Bova's good ale stood in greeting. But Hrald and Dagmar followed the abbess to her writing chamber, where the final task awaited. Hroft had been passed to a young nun, who privileged with the slight burden of the Jarl's child, trailed behind them.

The register of the Abbey church had been prepared and lay open upon Sigewif's small table, a bound volume containing many filled sheets of parchment, and many still blank, for the recording of births, weddings, and deaths to come. The Abbess had already begun the new entry, writing in the names and estate of the two who had joined today. She wrote without looking back to that record when these two had before stood upon the stone step of Oundle's church.

They signed anew, and this time no drop of ink fell to blot Dagmar's name. In fact, her hand was noticeably more assured, for during her time at Witanceaster she had taken some practice with a nun, one of those who served Ælfred's wife when she had need of a scribe.

Sigewif, with a smile of satisfaction at the new entries, then turned to the long writing table. There stood a salver, holding something covered with a linen cloth. The Abbess lifted the cloth to reveal three cups, and an ewer. One of them was Dagmar's silver cup, that which Hrald had wished to crush the morning he awoke without her, but then brought here, asking Sigewif to melt it down for the poor. Hrald had seen this cup, whole and intact, in Sigewif's treasure-box, and now watched the Abbess take hold of it.

"This, I think, is yours, Lady Dagmar," she told her. "I have been holding it in trust for you."

Dagmar did not understand, but was content not to. The Abbess was again speaking.

"Wine our Sister Bova has made," she invited. It was neither red nor white, but a rosy hue between, a kind of blush fitting to the sweetness of the moment.

Sigewif filled her cup, and then one for Hrald, and a third for herself.

"I drink your health, and that of your son," she told them. "Be whole, and hearty."

They drank, and for the first time, Hrald and Dagmar again laughed together as married folk.

The happiness Hrald knew led to the hope of happiness for his little sister. He drew from under his belt a flat wallet of parchment, and placed it before the Abbess.

"This is for you, Reverend Mother, to read in private. It concerns two known to you, and you alone will decide if the letters are sent on. When you have made decision, let me know, and I will send word to Cantwaraburh, either way."

The Abbess paused, considering, but then her furrowed brow relaxed. She could guess this might concern Ealhswith, and one Congar of Cantwaraburh. Sigewif tilted her head benignly, and with the faintest upturning of the corners of her mouth, said, "I will give the matter due consideration."

Hrald had another to speak of, one troubled, and did so now. "And I have brought Bork with me, as you have seen. I would he might stay with you awhile. He will tell you why."

The Abbess clasped her large hands together in approval. "Bork is welcome now, and will always be welcome at Oundle." In fact, the youth had sought her out following the Mass, and already asked if he might remain.

Out in the forecourt of the Abbey ale and oat cakes had been enjoyed by Hrald's men, and now they began to ready themselves for the ride home. Yrling, having spent some time with a few of the men who had been stationed there since Lady Dagmar's arrival, now drifted toward the stable block. He saw Bork's new roan mare nosing about a pile of hay in the paddock, unsaddled and loose. All the other horses were ready for the ride back. Bork himself was standing at the head of Hrald's stallion, waiting for the Jarl to reappear. Yrling came to him.

"Your mare – did she go lame?"

"Nej. She is sound," Bork answered. "But I am staying here with the monks for a time."

Yrling looked around. All the men from Four Stones were tightening girth straps or pulling themselves up on their horses, eager for the ride back, not only for the waiting feast, but for the tedium of being here.

"Why?" Yrling asked. "Nothing happens here."

Bork's eyes rose to the palisade, one he had been told, Sigewif herself had stood atop. "There was a battle here, a few years back," he said. "The Jarl's sister Ashild fought, and killed a man here. Kjeld fought here. The Jarl's father was there, too – your father."

Yrling had heard this from some of the men, including Asberg himself, during one of his many stays at Turcesig. Ashild had ridden at Asberg's side, and Asberg told how his father Sidroc had claimed the bodies of the slain Danes. The men of Four Stones had hauled them into the trees at the limits of Oundle's grounds in warning to others attempting the same predation. Kjeld had killed two men, and took part in this himself. Hrald had not been here at the battle for Oundle; he must remain at Four Stones to guard it from attack. It had been some action, with the forces of Four Stones springing from the gates, and Yrling thought Hrald must have been sorry to miss it.

"Well," Yrling conceded, "maybe something happens, once in a while."

The two stood there, side by side, Yrling with an anchor-shaped hammer of Thor about his neck, Bork with the small silver cross, once Yrling's, resting upon his own tunic. They gave each other sidelong glances, but rarely facing the other.

Yrling did not know what to say to Bork's remaining here, but then another objection rose to his lips. "But we are training the hounds," Yrling reminded.

They were doing so together, working with Myrkri, Frost's former mate, and her pups, the mother teaching her young her coursing skills in the field. Bork again found answer.

"And between Myrkri and your animal, you will be running down stags this Winter."

Yrling gave a small grunt of agreement. The two spent a while watching the rest of the men, now bantering and laughing as they readied to ride.

"You will miss the feast," Yrling warned Bork.

Bork gave a nod, and a slight smile. "You will eat and drink for me. Right now the Abbess has placed me in charge of the Abbey's horses."

It was work Bork was happy to return to, and the few beasts kept by the foundation would benefit from his care.

They watched Hrald and his new wife come out from the nuns' main hall, and walk towards the stone church.

"He will want to greet Ashild," Bork said in a low tone.

Yrling, fidgeting as he stood there, could do nothing but nod; he had never met that warrior-woman.

"So," Yrling said, a note of finality. "I am riding rear guard. Without you," he added.

"You will do well at it," Bork answered.

Yrling had no reply other than his nod. He must leave his friend behind.

Hrald had told Dagmar that before they left he must again enter the church. She paused a moment on the stone step which had so lately seen their hand-fast, uncertain if she should not allow him a moment alone. He made the slightest gesture of his head, as if inviting her in, and she followed him. This time the sanctuary was empty, yet the cool and silent atmosphere seemed to ring with an echo of the shaken bells and chanting of their Mass.

Hrald crossed himself and moved to the right of the altar, and from thence to the broad white ledger stone, and the flowers upon the name ASHILD OF FOUR STONES. He stood in silence above it, thinking of his lost sister, and then of the Archbishop, who knew her name and repute. Dagmar moved nearer and stood behind him, off to one side.

Hrald spoke.

"It was her father won Four Stones. And mine that kept it," he added. He looked to she now again his wife. "And yours, King over us all, who struck peace with Ælfred so we Danes could stay."

THE BLOOD OF KINGS

THE village of Four Stones stood watching the waggon holding Dagmar roll down the pounded clay road. Ten men on horseback fronted the waggon, and ten men trailed behind. The Jarl rode next the waggon, his big bay stallion reined in to keep steady with the slow pace of the dray horses. Jari and the Jarl's young brother Yrling rode just behind the waggon. It was in all a most imposing entry, but one which left the crofters bewildered. Lady Pega was gone, they knew that; and now here was proof of what had been bruited about, that Guthrum's daughter would soon arrive. They had scarcely known her; there for half a year, then cast out, it had been said, for harlotry. Now she was back, and with a child. Some lifted their hands in greeting, uncertain smiles on their faces. Many did not know what to do, and merely gaped up at her. Dagmar sat seemingly composed, at a distance from them and their wondering. But little Hroft, alert and wide eyed, made to stand up in his mother's lap, as if to see, and be seen. She held him there, her hands underneath his waving arms as he chortled out his own welcome to the folk of Four Stones. There was one thing certain, the sharp-eyed older women thought, seeing the boy and his likeness to the man pacing by him: This was the Jarl's true son.

The Jarl himself looked quietly pleased; he looked down upon his folk, nodding at them as they looked from the two figures on the waggon board, up to him, and then back for another glimpse of his wife and child. Hrald had never thought such a scene possible until last month. Now he lived it.

On they came, the gates of the palisade opened in welcome, gates that Dagmar, the last time she rode through them, thought never to see again. Today they yawned wide, men stationed on either side. There was the stone preaching cross, of which Dagmar had strong memory of standing at with Hrald and his mother as they prayed, while she studied the thin boy shifting from foot to foot across from them, staring at Hrald and Lady Ælfwyn in adoration. Today she had seen Bork, now a young man with a shield and spear, but with the same quiet reverence in his eyes when they turned to Hrald. Bork had stayed behind at Oundle, and it was clear the Abbess was glad to have him.

Now the waggon had rolled through. Jari's wife Inga was there, her plump, good-natured self, a broad smile on her face. Asberg was there as well, with his wife Æthelthryth. Dagmar had not expected this. Asberg, she felt, had ever been wary of her, and her disgrace must have given credence to his doubts. Æthelthryth had always treated her well, but then, she was even-handed by nature, Dagmar thought, and their interactions had been few.

The waggon pulled up, the horsemen halted. Hrald lowered himself from his horse and came to her, helping her from the waggon board. He then turned to greet his uncle,

Asberg, and his aunt, Æthelthryth. Dagmar smiled and nodded at both, but as soon as Hrald had finished greeting them, Yrling was in front of Asberg. Rising up and down on his toes in excitement, he began telling of Hrald's adventure, and how Bork had used his shield to down a man.

Past the stable Dagmar saw the church, a small timber building, but one fashioned with care. Hrald had told her of it, and that it had been Pega who had built it. She could not look long, but Dagmar knew it might be one of many changes wrought by Pega's hand.

Æthelthryth greeted Dagmar with the same warm common sense which was her manner. Like all, she had ever been aware of Hrald's attachment to Guthrum's daughter, and like many, had been utterly surprised at the abrupt ending of his marriage to Pega. Yet here Dagmar was again, and tasked with the running of a large hall. Both Æthelthryth and Inga made much of Hroft, easing the way for Dagmar.

"Inga will be a help to you," Æthelthryth told her in reassurance.

This praise brought the pink into Inga's round cheeks. "Já, já, long as I have been here now, I have seen how all ought to happen."

When Dagmar had been Lady the first time, she had not only Hrald's mother Ælfwyn to aid her in learning and carrying out the many required duties, but the redoubtable Burginde. There had also been Ashild. Dagmar's final memory of her was Ashild shrieking insults at her as she was driven off into the cold. But Ashild had been her own model for Dagmar. The ordinary stuff of a Lady's concerns was village and hall, with their diverse needs and wants and contributions to all being fed and housed. It had seemed to

Dagmar that Ashild looked beyond this, to a larger whole comprised of folk, cropland, forest, the wealth held in their horses, silver, and weaponry, and the value of the relations, frosty or warm, with neighbouring halls, and neighbouring Kings. Ashild considered all this just as a man might, and Dagmar had seen it. Hasty and hotheaded as Hrald's sister could be, these things had concerned Ashild, just as they did Hrald. Dagmar had admired her for this.

"I have found a serving girl for you," Inga was saying, "from the village. Wite is her name. She will be good to mind your boy, for she is the oldest of many young. She is well-mannered and clean. Also Christian, and says her prayers."

This last was important to Inga, as she had years ago whole-heartedly accepted the new faith, preferring its hope for an eternity spent in light and love to the shady after-world she would certainly be confined to if she still worshipped the Old Gods. Not for her, mists and drear, when the men-folk were carousing in Odin's or Freyja's halls.

Inga looked behind her and made gesture. A maid came forward, perhaps of fourteen or fifteen Summers, and dropped a curtsey before both Dagmar and Inga.

"And she is a good spinner," Inga added, before addressing Wite directly. "You will live in the hall now, up in the weaving room, and do for the Lady Dagmar what must be done, and taking great care of the boy. He will be Jarl one day."

These wants had always been small, but a trustworthy watcher for Hroft was more needful than any serving help for Dagmar. The new Lady of Four Stones was grateful to find an immediate friend in Inga. She had not much time to know the woman when she first lived here, but now, having seen Dane-mark and its strife, could value why Inga had agreed to forsake her homeland and follow Jari here. Dagmar knew Jari was of a prosperous family back in Dane-mark; Hrald had told her so, and Inga, as neat as a pin about her large person, was known for her good sense. Dagmar said a few words in Norse to thank her.

"Ah, you speak Norse well now," Inga praised.

"I had to, when I lived at Viborg," came Dagmar's quiet answer. "No one spoke the tongue of Angle-land there. Only thralls."

Inga nodded. "It is only fitting, for a daughter of Guthrum," she pointed out. "You are like Hrald now, in ability with both. But with the village folk, and in most trading, we use the tongue of Angle-land, as Father Wilgot does. It is best."

Dagmar's goods were carried into the treasure room, along with Hroft's cradle. Crossing the threshold again to the room of her expulsion required her to take a deep breath. Hrald, talking with Kjeld and Jari by the high table, seemed to sense this, and appeared at her side as she entered.

The room was unchanged from her first time as Lady here, something she was thankful for. She stood just inside the door while serving men deposited her clothing chest by Hrald's own, set the cradle down, and placed her baskets and other items about. Behind her was the heavy iron bar which could be slid across the oaken door, the bar she had suggested Hrald use before their wedding so she might lay with him, proof against him dismissing her should her mother Bodil arrive and tell him she had before known a man. Hrald had resisted her tempting, telling her that because he loved her, he would stop himself from acting. The memory of his good-ness made her shut her eyes; the memory of her fear forced her to give thanks to a merciful God who had reunited them.

The hour drew near for the evening meal. The noise of the gathering folk was such that as Hrald opened the door, it swelled to a din. Then as Hrald emerged with Dagmar, Hroft in her arms, it quieted.

All were seated at the high table, and rose at their appearance. Around the tables lining the hall, men and women hastened to their benches. Kjeld, fingers to his mouth, commanded the attention of all with a shrill whistle. He then bellowed out, "Hrald, Dagmar. Guthrum's grand-son, Hroft. The blood of Kings!"

As welcome to Dagmar and the boy, Kjeld's words could not have been bettered. Hrald added to it with his next gesture, taking Hroft from his mother's arms and holding him aloft over all. The boy crowed, legs kicking, then suddenly grew shy, ducking his head. Hrald lowered him to his arms and held him. A gleeful roar arose, one only quieted by the swift action of the serving folk filling cups with mead.

Dagmar's chair awaited her. Inga had earlier pointed it out, telling her it had been in the keeping of Wilgot, and had just been returned to the hall. Small gesture as it was, it held large meaning for Dagmar. No other woman had sat in the chair Hrald had presented her with. Had there been another, carved for Pega? She did not care. Hrald had returned her own, just as he had returned her, to his side.

There at her place was the silver cup which Abbess Sigewif had just presented to her. Hrald drank from the same cup his father had, and seeing the two once again together did much to close the gap between the years of separation.

The meal was of fitting richness for a wedding feast, but neither Dagmar nor Hrald might later recall the exact efforts of the kitchen-yard. Mead and ale were amply poured, and Wilgot cleared his throat and told the tale of the miraculous changing of water into wine at Cana, making happy those wedding guests of long ago. A few men stood to sing, including Kjeld, possessed of a mellow and fine voice. He sang of the creation of all mankind from two trees, the first woman Embla from the Alder, and the first man Ask, from the Ash. It was these two who peopled the entirety of Midgard, and Odin himself who tutored their offspring. To honour a couple newly-wed, who had already brought forth a son, it seemed a most fitting tale, and Hrald tipped his golden-rimmed cup at Kjeld when he had done.

Dagmar had already laid Hroft in his cradle and soothed the tired boy to sleep. She had returned to the table when Hrald rose. His act was greeted with whistles and cheers, just as it had been the first time he had wed. He lifted his arm to all, who answered by holding up their cups in salute. Together Jarl and Dagmar moved to the treasure room door.

She had left two cressets burning, their light radiating from the table on which the oil lamps sat. The golden glow granted near things surety, and the rest of the room in a kind of indistinct and limitless border, one lost in dusky and unknowable mystery.

Hrald at Dagmar's side stood motionless, his eyes resting upon his bed and its wolfskin spread. Before he had left Dagmar in Witanceaster, he whispered to her in urgent passion that soon they would be wed, and he would bring her back to the treasure room. Now wed they were, and he turned to slide the iron bar across the door.

At last alone and together, Dagmar must speak. This was the room in which she had made the greatest mistake of her life. Her voice was husky, nearly hoarse, as if she whispered a prayer too sacred for human ears.

"I would undo what I did. And begin again."

Lives had been changed, and the good and innocent injured. There was much they must pass into the hands of Fate, or God. Much was beyond their repair. And all the wrong, all the sorrow and pain they had caused each other from their own rashness was rooted here.

Hrald had cast her out as she had knelt weeping at his mother's feet. It was his great fault, that haste in which he had condemned them both. Now he could voice it to her.

"I would give almost anything to undo what I did that day. I cannot. But I can start again, with you."

She nodded her head, the tears glistening in her eyes speaking for her. He moved to take her in his arms. Her own hand closed around his left forearm. The wince he gave at her touch brought her concern for him full upon her lovely brow.

"I have a hurt to my forearm; it is healing."

Her face told him he must say more, and he did. "It happened on the way to Cantwaraburh. Road brigands attacked an old couple, and their grandchildren. I must act, and right favoured me, as Bork had followed in secret behind me, and likely saved my life. We killed the three of them."

Bork again, she thought; he was like a guarding angel.

"But you were hit," she must say.

"A spear-point. A leech-monk at Augustine's Abbey put it to rights. But it needs more time."

Dagmar raised her lips to his, and kissed him.

"I will be mindful," she breathed. "Tonight I will be sure you need not use your arms for support. You will lie down, and . . ."

Dagmar said no more, for her mouth was covered by Hrald's own as he moved her to the wolfskin spread awaiting them.

Toward dawn Hrald awakened. He was lying on his side, holding Dagmar in his arms, her back against his chest. He whispered to her.

"I have no morgen-gyfu."

He had prepared no gift to present her on their first morning as man and wife. In the urgent press of concerns leading up to this dawn, such an offering had utterly slipped his mind.

The first time they had awakened together he had given her something choice, but of little size, a ring of twisted gold. It had been too small for her finger. She had worn it about her neck, until the day she had been cast out, and handed it to Ælfwyn. Later, in Witanceaster, she had heard from an innocent Ealhswith that Hrald had given the ring to Pega to wear. Had it belonging to her first tainted it for Pega, Dagmar now wondered.

She shook her head and turned to face him. "I have need of nothing," she murmured back.

He kissed her brow, and she lay her head closer against his shoulder. Her thoughts kept on, though, so that she asked in a quiet voice, "Have I impoverished you?"

He gave his head a short shake of negation, and she lifted her face so she could look at him in the growing light. His brow showed his puzzlement, as did his words.

"Impoverished me . . ."

It was Hrald himself who had depleted his treasury, forfeiting Pega's bride-price after it had been she who had so quickly severed their union. Yet he would not ask, nor could accept, its return, for the harm he had caused.

"I know Pega's treasure was vast," Dagmar whispered. "You surrendered it all; you returned it to her intact, and even the bride-price."

Hrald thought of how best to answer this. Pega's treasure had been so immense that this room would surely never again, he thought, house such abundance of gold. The relinquishing of the weaponry he had paid to wed Pega – yes, it was a goodly share of his own armoury, and that too of Turcesig. But he must, in act of reparation, let it go. He had excess of horses to sell or trade; these could be taken to Jorvik anytime, should he need more armaments.

"I have enough," he told her. "You have before seen into these chests and casks. There is as much silver as when we wed, the first time. You are the treasure I sought. And you have brought me your son – our son."

It was what she most wished to hear. Yet her own content could not be perfect; none was. She lowered her head a moment. "Your little daughter, Hrald – Ælfgiva. I am sorry at her loss."

He could not answer this, and just lifted his face to the darkness of the roof rafters.

"She will be safe, and well cared for," he uttered, as if he had before told himself this.

"Yes," Dagmar said, and placed her hand over his. "She will be well-loved, and cared for."

Later that morning Dagmar readied to go up to the weaving room. She had yet to greet Hrald's aunt, Eanflad, and wished to do so. The village girl Wite had spent the night there, and Dagmar thought also to make certain the girl had all she needed. After this she and Hrald would walk about the work and kitchen yards, so she might reacquaint herself with those who laboured there. Wite would walk with them, so she might see and be seen as well, and Hroft get to know and trust her.

Hrald and Yrling stood together by the fire-pit as Dagmar passed to go upstairs. Hroft tottered by his mother's side, holding on to her skirts in one tiny hand, as Dagmar clasped the other. She smiled at the brothers, and Hroft made a little whoop of greeting.

There was silence between the brothers after she began to climb the wooden stair, Hroft clambering up before her. Hrald had felt Yrling to be troubled at the danger Hrald had met on the road, and a misplaced envy too that it had been Bork at his side, and not his own kin. And then too, the swift change in the hall would take getting used to, for all. To counter this Hrald said a word about the good report he heard from Kjeld on Yrling in his absence. Yrling nodded, but his eyes still looked after the vanished Dagmar.

"Já," he conceded. "She is like Freyja. Or a Queen." He turned his face to Hrald and grinned.

Hrald looked at his younger brother, smiled, and put his hand on his shoulder.

Hrald and Dagmar walked through the whole of the keep. All had seen them together upon their arrival, and most had also viewed them in the hall, but now to greet warriors and work men and women on their own footing and at their daily tasks was a most needful act. Ælfwyn and Burginde had done this for Dagmar the first time, taken her about, but now only Hrald could shed that authority upon her as new Lady. Pega had been endearing for her goodness, her hard work, and the liberality with which she treated all from her abundant wealth. But Dagmar had been admired for her stateliness, nobility of bearing, seeming reserve, and quiet yet striking beauty. Now she was back to take up the former role she had held so briefly, and Hrald must be at her side as she greeted his men, and her folk.

The fact that little Hroft was with them, and often in Hrald's own arms, did much. The boy was the future of Four Stones, and the knowledge that he was of Guthrum's blood, that Dagmar was that King's acknowledged daughter, did much to elevate the rightness of their union. It was truly Fated, and Hroft one proof of this.

After Hrald and Dagmar had made their rounds, they neared the wooden church. Dagmar had not thought to enter, but the door, kept closed against the fore-court dust, opened. The priest Wilgot was there, framed in the opening. He bowed his head, as Dagmar did to him.

"Did you wish to see inside, my Lady?" he asked, and moved aside as if to admit them. Hroft though, now in Wite's arms, was tired, and growing fussy. Dagmar had cause to excuse herself. But Wite spoke up, proud to be of service, saying she would take the boy to the weaving room and put him down for his nap on one of the beds there. Dagmar was left with no choice but to enter. Hrald was with her; that was much, but she felt Wilgot's scrutiny, if not judgment. Pega had built this, and now she was the beneficiary of that gift.

The church was simple enough within, but with joinery as well-crafted inside as out. The altar was a broad slab of some fine stone, partly covered by a linen cloth with white embroidery, and cut-work on the wide border. "Lady Pega's hand work," Wilgot mentioned, seeing Dagmar admired it. All Dagmar could do was nod. Wilgot had more to add.

"The Lady ordered the work in timber, certain Four Stones would soon grow in faith to require a larger nave." They stood there now, in that greater space which held the congregation. Dagmar must speak, and so said, "I am sure it will."

Wilgot gave a nod and went on. "The bell on order from Lundenwic has yet to arrive. I will send message that we will do without it."

If it was challenge, it was one Dagmar could meet. She had memory of a bronze bell being rung outside the palisade of Viborg, summoning the thralls to their field work. She would hear bells again, but for a better cause.

"I have silver, and will pay for your bell, Father Wilgot," she said.

Dagmar had in fact a goodly amount of treasure carried from Dane-mark; treasure she had once thought need last her the rest of her life. Now, freed from fear of want, she could be open-handed with it for the sake of the folk of Four Stones, now again her own.

Hrald knew a bell had been ordered, but not that payment was upon its delivery. Dagmar at once taking up this charge to complete the building would place her hand upon it as well.

His wife was again addressing the priest.

"It will be the crowning touch to what Lady Pega has built here, and she will long be remembered for her act in doing so," Dagmar ended.

This was generous in deed, and in word, and Wilgot, his heart closed against Dagmar, must acknowledge it. He bowed his head. "A lavish gift, my Lady," he murmured. "She worked for the glory of God and the good of her folk," he said. "As you do here," he must add.

⚜⚜⚜⚜⚜⚜⚜

The next morning Hrald and Dagmar were late arising.

Hrald's desire for her was such that they had lingered long in bed. It was a relearning of the ways of love, each to each. It held the passion of their night together in Witanceaster with none of the grief to follow. Dagmar could give of her body with that same openness and freedom, wholly secure in herself and in Hrald's love. And as for Hrald, there seemed no limit to the delight he took in her body, and in each expression of her love, whether voiced or proven through gesture.

At last they must arise; the hall was stirring. All would be gathering soon to break their fast. The smiles with which they were greeted may have caused the colour to rise to Dagmar's cheek, but in no way could cast their own happiness in any light but the sure joy the newly-wed have in each other. Jari, Kjeld, those men who knew Hrald best, saw a new lightness in him, one not seen even during his first union with Dagmar, for now, utterly assured of her, and with the added benison of their son, his happiness was complete.

Later in the day they returned together to the room. Dagmar had yet to unpack a second chest she had brought, and asked him to join her. Hrald stood near the bed and straightened up a few items on the shelves, his comb and such, which had been left in disarray when they had quitted the room in haste that morning. Dagmar brought out a few folded linens from the chest and lay them upon the table, and then drew forth something else. Hrald turned to see a long and shrouded object, which she unwrapped.

It was a sword, in its scabbard. Hrald saw what it was, and was hit with a sickening pitch in the pit of his belly. He found himself stifling the breath his body wished to heave, to rid himself of this sudden inner turmoil. The sight of the weapon closed his throat, stunning him into silence.

Hrald voiced his question with effort, so certain he was that this weapon was that of Vigmund, the man whose appearance here had caused so much pain to them both.

"Whose – whose is this?"

Dagmar, alarmed by the tone of his voice, and the look on his face, answered at once.

"It is your son's, Hrald. This sword, and this cup," – and here she unwrapped a gold and silver cup and set it upright – "These are Hroft's baptismal gifts from his God-father and God-mother, King Ælfred and his Lady-wife. They are Hroft's God-parents."

Hrald need allow this to sink in.

"Here," she went on, unwrapping a small object, a small, oval-bowled silver spoon. "This is his baptismal spoon. I know it is a common gift amongst the high-born; they gave Hroft this, as well."

Indeed, the spoon now passed to Hrald's hand was engraved with the words Agnus Dei – Lamb of God – and a cross. Such spoons were gifts to those of noble birth upon their christening, child or adult.

Dagmar went on. "The silver cup – though large, the King told me Hroft would grow to use." It was a cup sized for a man, and worthy gift it was. Hrald's hand reached for the sword, and pulled it from its fleece-lined scabbard. It was a beautiful weapon, freshly polished, the light stream-ing from the high window making the waving bands of beaten steel dance before his eyes. The King had words for this gift as well.

"He presented this sword, that Hroft might defend the Faith, as the King said."

"The King of Wessex stood as God-father for your boy," Hrald repeated.

"Yes. It was before he knew who his father was; he was kind enough not to question me. Nor would I have told him, to protect you."

"He honoured you in this, greatly," Hrald answered.

"He did," Dagmar agreed. "But the greater honour was I think, to my own father, Guthrum, or Æthelstan, as Ælfred sometimes calls him; his Christian name." She thought a moment. "He must know now the boy is yours; his daughter Æthelflaed would have told him."

"Yes," Hrald said, then added, "You did not tell me of this."

"I told no one," she admitted. "Not even Abbess Sigewif when she asked if Hroft had been baptised. I told her he had, and at the cathedral there, but not who stood as God-parents. I could not tell anyone, until I told you. And I wished to wait until I could share with you the proofs of Ælfred's kindness to our boy."

Hrald must handle each gift, in sheer wonder of this mark of favour. He made Dagmar tell of the ceremony as he did so, that he might in some wise be part of it. His eyes then lifted again, to Dagmar's face.

"Hroft," he said, with a slight smile, "he is up in the weaving room."

"Napping; and Wite and Eanflad are with him, as is another woman from the village who spins each day with Eanflad, for company."

"Then I need you now, to lie down with me," Hrald said.

That night in the hall Hrald brought out these gifts, that he might share them with the hall. He first held up the sword, and drawing it from its scabbard, displayed it.

"My wife is greatly favoured by the King of Wessex. When our son was born Ælfred stood as his God-father, without knowing who Hroft's father was. It was honour paid to Lady Dagmar, and her father Guthrum. This is what the King of Wessex gave to Hroft, as a sign of his favour."

He then held up the silver and gold cup, and the silver spoon. Dagmar was at his side, Hroft again in her arms, as he did this, so that the glad pounding of feet, and cheers of glee washed over them.

The Jarl of Four Stones grinned back at his men. Ælfred, King of Wessex had presented Hrald with a sword as reward for felling Haesten. Now both father and small son had swords given by the hand of the King.

ONSLAUGHT

Kilton

ON the first morning Edwin of Kilton awoke as a married man, he must present his morning gift, the morgen-gyfu, to his bride. Edwin had no idea what to give a woman who possessed so much wealth in her own right. He had spoken to Ceric of this the day of the wedding, and the two sat a while in thought. There were odd treasures, and many beautiful, laid by in the chests around them, things which would not be fitting for a bride. Some of these were things which Edwin did not even wish to look upon himself, like the great spotted cat skin. He had been told Sidroc, when Jarl, had brought this to his own father as gift.

It was Ceric who spoke, about something overlooked. "There is the Frisian gold," he pointed out.

There was indeed the Frisian gold, three fingers of it, still wrapped in cylinders of tawed leather and tightly laced. One was a full ingot of the precious stuff. Edwin had worn that one about his neck, and Alwin and Wystan the other two when he ventured to Gerolf of Fresia to see if he might wed one of his daughters. Since he had come back in possession of all three golden treasures, and no wife, they lay waiting.

"Gold is gold," Ceric pointed out. Edwin must agree that objects wrought of silver or gold seemed ideal. Such appealed to women; their tidy compactness, inherent lustre and beauty made them attractive in every sense. Precious metals were as well easily transported, and concealed.

"Yes, I will give her those," Edwin agreed.

He did so, after cutting through the tight lacing binding them in their leathern casings. There was the solid ingot; a heavy and well-wrought chain, sized for a man; and a collection of golden coins, small pendants, and golden hair pins. He placed all on a cloth of red, and then of blue, judging which was the better effect, and determined the blue, for its contrast.

In the morning when he presented them, Pega was pleased and perhaps surprised as well, at the value thereof. She examined the pieces and touched each one. "This is generous, Edwin. I thank you." A moment later she had made decision. "I will set them aside for Ælfgiva."

Edwin understood. Pega might fear that being raised far from her birth father, the girl might be thought to possess but scant dowry when it was her turn to wed.

"The gold is yours, and you alone have power over it," he encouraged. She rose from the table at this and kissed his lips, the first she had initiated. It was a simple pressing of her lips to his, but it had been her act, and not his. It gave Edwin heart.

Later that day another gift was to come to Pega. Dwynwen had sent Tegwedd to her, bidding Pega come to the bower house when she might. She did so, Mealla at her side with Ælfgiva, and Frost as well. The door to the house was open and Dwynwen was alone within. Upon her table sat three bolts of silk, as thick and lustrous as could ever be wished. One was of a near scarlet red, one of moss green, and the third of richest blue.

As soon as Pega appeared at the open door Dwynwen ran to her, and taking up her hand, kissed Pega on the cheek.

"Dear sister, I have my own gift for this happy day. I have much silk my step-mother Lady Luned gave me, forty ells worth, and I would you choose which hue you like best, and sew a gown from it to enjoy."

Pega was deeply surprised, both at the beauty of the fabric, and the giving of such a noble gift. She had not time to react when the Princess piped up again, turning to Mealla.

"You as well, Mealla," she urged. "Choose which colour you like best."

The raven-haired maid spluttered. She could not wear silk. No one wore silk save Kings and Bishops and heiresses like Pega, or Lady Æthelflaed. This Welsh imp had no sense, none at all, offering her silk.

Dwynwen did not seem to see the rebuff in Mealla's turning aside, for Pega, in true gratitude and wonder, had moved forward to touch the blue silk. It lay in folds, the light falling upon it so that the peaks looked like vibrant sky, the hollows the shade of the deepest sea.

Pega asked for a length of the blue, and embraced Dwynwen in return. Mealla had been forced to place the restless Ælfgiva on the floor, and the girl, having caught full sight of the shimmering bolts of fabric, now made for the table, pointing, her arm outstretched, as if she would make her own choice. Dwynwen laughed, and at the sound Frost too, who had been nosing about near the chests of goods by the dragon bed, came to Dwynwen as well. The Princess dropped into a crouch and thus greeted both child and hound, placing a hand on both. The raven-haired Mealla swooped in and plucked Ælfgiva from amongst the swirling tail and happy whine of Frost, and the slight figure who embraced them.

Dwynwen only laughed. "I think Ælfgiva would like the red, would she not," she asked, as that was the shade the child was now reaching for. And it was in fact the colour the Princess herself so often wore, and was wearing now.

∾∾∾∾∾∾∾∾∾∾

Two days after the wedding Lady Æthelflaed left Kilton. She was satisfied in Pega's happiness, and more than satisfied in Kilton itself. Before departing she took Edwin aside.

"It is timely we have met, and timely that you are now wed to my ward. I am glad to be certain of you, Edwin, Lord of Kilton. You may be called upon to fight for Mercia. Not this year perhaps, but soon."

Edwin hid his surprise as best he could. There was no questioning the Lady, but he could only think she spoke of some coming instability at the death of her father, and her brother's assuming the crown of Wessex. Would Mercia front a usurper, he wondered. From what he had heard of Lord Æthelred his loyalty seemed assured. Æthelflaed and he had only a daughter, and Pega no close male kin. Yet others could rise, Edwin knew.

Ealhswith left that day with Æthelflaed, to return to the royal hall at Weogornaceastre in Mercia. She had been offered the choice to stay with Pega. Yet the new Lady of Kilton had no real need of Ealhswith. Lady Edgyth was there, she who had run the hall for years. And Pega had Mealla as well to aid her, and a raft of serving men and women to do her bidding. There was also the Princess Dwynwen. Ealhswith was not certain what role she played, other than being wife to Ceric, but her presence meant Pega had companions enough.

Edwin was another reason to leave. Ealhswith had been grateful for their moment together, and the reassurance it provided. The Lord of Kilton told her she was pretty. Young men said such things without thought, Ealhswith assumed, yet his graveness as he told her gave credence to his words. They could never wed, but to be so admired by a Lord – that was much for her. And like her older sister, Ealhswith did not want Kilton. Æthelflaed had claimed her for some as yet unknown role, and she could be certain it did not lie here.

The Lady of Mercia was not unduly surprised when Ealhswith asked if she might go with her, and see more of Mercia. Ealhswith had been sheltered in her upbringing, and observing her a few days at Kilton Æthelflaed had seen that she was rather out of her depth in such a hall. Sweet the girl was, compliant, perhaps, diffident certainly. But such often-times had a streak of stubbornness in them as well, the Lady knew. The girl was uncommonly pretty – to the surprise of none, as her mother was a beauty – and if Æthelflaed kept Ealhswith with her in Mercia, she would be able to show her off to advantage to the great families thereof. It was thus she readily acquiesced to Ealhswith's request that she be allowed to travel on. Bringing her to Kilton had served a purpose, though. The girl had been exposed to a family of renown, and would have better idea of what marrying into one of Mercia or Wessex would bring. Ealhswith too had been glad for the adventure, for adventure it was.

It soon became clear to Pega that the Princess of Ceredigion occupied a special place at the hall of Kilton. Firstly, she appeared to do almost no work, or that which she did was at the side of Lady Edgyth, in gathering healing herbs, or at her Simples chest. This was of course a labour of the most needful kind, yet Dwynwen was rarely to be seen at any normal task a woman of her rank should fulfill. She enjoyed spinning, this was true; and one day when Pega approached her still spindle resting upon a table, she must inwardly remark on the fineness of Dwynwen's thread. The Princess excelled at this work, but she made a game of it, almost always singing as she spun, and often in the tongue of Wales, with her serving girl. Her real work seemed to yield no such useful result, though. Every morning, whether fine, or cold and wet, Dwynwen went down the steep steps to the shingle beach. And each afternoon in fair weather, even if the air was chill, Dwynwen could be found in the pleasure garden, seated at the table there in the slight shelter of the pavilion. She would work at the designs she made, painting with the tip of a feather upon birch-bark, aligning pebbles or seashells in fanciful designs, or tracing in a shallow brazen bowl intricate paths into fine sand she had brought up from the beach and sifted. No matter when the weather grew colder; Pega had been told Dwynwen would be found there, a brazier at her feet, and another one upon the table that she might warm her hands. The spotted hens which were her pets were often about her, and one at times in the lap of the Princess.

Pega had also seen Dwynwen with the scop, Garrulf, the two at the end of the high table during quiet times within the hall. Garrulf sat on his tall stool, his harp in hand, and the Princess, holding a red-painted harp, perched on the end of the table so she might be at his same height. Tegwedd was rarely there in attendance; the women spinning or weaving in the hall, and the serving men raking out the fire-pit served as her only chaperone. The second time they were thus engaged and Pega crossed the hall to the door of the treasure room, the scop saw her, and nodded in respect. Pega could hear Dwynwen's singing voice, one unexpected, as it was warm and almost husky, not the notes of a child. Pega almost wished to grow near, but feared her presence would be gross intrusion on these two, as they sat with their harps and sang to each other.

And Pega saw that Ceric was often with Dwynwen, far more than most men might be after the first few sweet months of marriage had worn. His protectiveness toward her, his arm wrapped about her, even before his own men, was something Pega, raised with fitting decorum, had never expected to witness, and so could scarce approve. Yet it was clear his men loved Ceric. She saw that readily enough in their manner towards him, a love rooted in respect for him as man and leader. Pega understood this form of devotion, and had witnessed it from early girlhood. Pega's own father would have taken strong liking to the horse-thegn Worr, and kept him at his side, and Worr was utterly devoted to Ceric. Edwin's men were different, most of them younger, yes, but many seemingly lacked this quality of devotion, or – something Pega did not wish to consider – Edwin lacked the ability to inspire. The two captains of the Lord of Kilton's body-guard, though undoubtedly fearless fighters, seemed merely that. They had been elevated by their skill in battle, their alertness in guarding their Lord, and that was all expected of them, or they expected of themselves. There was no role as counsellor for them to grow into.

Beyond this Dwynwen confused Pega. She truly liked the Princess, and Pega felt it impossible for any with a beating heart to find fault with her. Even Edwin's grumblings about her looked petty. Dwynwen's cheerfulness, bright smile, winsome face, and quick actions entranced Pega. She was akin to a bird, one of beauty and charm, that you long to settle and stay near you. Ælfgiva, shy with strangers, had taken to her at once. Frost, trained by Pega's father to be a guardian to her, took slowly to newcomers, unless Pega took pains to show him she was safe. But both hounds, Frost and Snow, seemed to crave time with Dwynwen, coiling about her, plumed tails swishing, their bodies so big that one might expect she could ride off on the back of either one of them.

One day when Pega and Edgyth were sorting linens in the store room kept for such, Pega spoke of Dwynwen. Mealla had been working at her side, Ælfgiva at their feet playing at crumpling and attempting to fold a small piece of linen herself. After a while the girl grew restive, and Mealla took her out for a walk. It was quiet in the room, and Pega, feeling the weight of that silence, spoke aloud over her work, without turning her head towards the Lady.

"The Princess," she posed, and stopped her words at that.

Edgyth, acute as she was, understood. The Princess was noticeable in her absence at such tasks.

"Dwynwen restored Ceric to health, and mayhap, life itself," was what Edgyth said. Her hands kept on in their work of smoothing and folding the linen sheet before her. "The Princess is vital to Ceric. Ceric is vital to Kilton. As he is to Prince Eadward, and to all who love him."

It was not rebuke; her tone was far too mild for this, but rather explanation. Dwynwen must not be expected to act as other wives in her role would. Her course of work was along other lines. She trod – or danced – a different path, and did so admirably.

Within her Pega must admit to the justice of this. She herself, while young, had lost both parents to death, and lost her first marriage as well. Those we love must be cherished while they are near.

And Ceric had been deprived of his natural role in the household, that of being Lord, so there was something fitting about his young wife being an exception to every rule. Why should any expect the Welsh girl to shoulder the responsibilities that accompanied the role he was denied? Dwynwen was a Princess. It was enough for her to spin her fine thread and keep Ceric in health. The hall was amply staffed with men and women, skilled at their tasks.

"I thank you, Edgyth," Pega murmured. "I truly thank you."

The next morning Pega, Mealla, and Ælfgiva walked the pleasure garden. Mealla always kept close watch on the girl, for the steep drop of the cliff side, but the child, attracted by a bed of flowering thyme, had chosen to seat herself in it, and pull at the tiny blue flowers thereof. The day was warm this late in the season, the sky a milky blue, but the fine mist which had risen from the sea was now creeping up the cliff face and spilling over onto the shrubs and herb beds around them. The mist, thickening as it rose, rolled upon the grasses and flowers, transforming the familiar garden beds into something other-worldly. It sat in low drifts, revealing as much as it concealed, for tiny spider webs, before invisible, now stood out to the eyes, like beaded necklaces.

When Mealla lifted her head from admiring one, Ælfgiva was no longer in sight. Mealla walked with quick steps to the thyme bed, and to the taller flower bed just beyond it, where the girl might be hiding. She turned to scan the edge of the cliff; Ælfgiva was nowhere near it. The maid of Éireann walked onward, calling the girl's name, softly so as not to frighten her, but with some little insistence that she answer. Pega looked up from where she had been studying a garlanded web, to see Mealla's hastened step, and followed her.

The door to the bower house in which dwelt Ceric and Dwynwen was open for light, as it often was. Mealla made for it. There she found Ælfgiva, standing in an empty cradle, holding on to the high head board, laughing in delight as she gently rocked herself. Bending over her and whispering into the girl's ear was the Welsh creature, her very hands upon the child.

Mealla's sudden intake of breath was followed by a sharp, "So!"

Both Ælfgiva and Dwynwen turned their faces to her, the girl's still crinkled in laughter, and Dwynwen's, smiling. The briskness of Mealla's step, and the set of her face told both of her anger, and the child, taking fright, turned to Dwynwen, placing her hand upon her breast and clutching at the fabric of her gown. A moment later Ælfgiva had been plucked from her stance in the cradle with such strength that it nearly upset. Dwynwen rose, just as Pega walked over the threshold.

Mealla uttered not a word, just swept past the child's mother, the girl pressed close to her own bosom. Pega, both alarmed and then relieved, looked wonderingly after her. She turned back to Dwynwen, who gave a slight smile.

"Ælfgiva came, to play in the cradle. That is all," she said.

Pega felt abashed at Mealla's seeming rudeness, and with a helpless gesture of her hands, followed after.

Mealla was walking with such speed with the child that Pega must call after her to slow. Ceric, coming from the hall, heard Pega, and the worried tone of her voice. Not wishing to intrude, he paused by the bushy yew tree near the church, where Mealla seemed to be heading. The two kept coming, and Pega called again that Mealla need slow her step. Mealla did, a halt sudden enough to show her displeasure at being stopped. For her own part the child was fretting, and struggling to be set down.

Pega's concern was unconcealed in her words. "Mealla – what – what is this about? What did you say to the Princess?"

The raven-haired maid's answer was sheer defiance. "Nothing. I said nothing. I needed no words, I had my eyes!

"We of Éireann – we know when we see one from the other-world – we feel it. One of the hill-folk, the wee people. We know that ilk, and the danger they pose. She could make of your dear child a mere lakin, a plaything for the fey!"

Pega's face showed her bewilderment, and Mealla forged on.

"What evil lies there, in such as she – small babes can be enchanted by such, and snatched away to realms below!"

Ceric could see Pega's face, and the wonderment upon it. "The Princess? She is a child, a kind and generous one."

"A child she is not, Pega. She may be a hundred years old – a thousand! Such are able to cast a glamour upon themselves, shift their shape, work all manner of mischief."

"Mischief! That is stuff and nonsense, Mealla. The Princess is as Earthly as you or me." Pega thought how best to describe the Welsh girl. "She has charm . . . to a rare degree."

Mealla seized upon this. "Ah! Charm she has indeed, enough to enchant Edwin's brother into thinking her real!"

Ceric had been alert to every word as he listened to this outburst. Hearing this last was like a jolt to his body, felt in his very core. He rocked forward slightly against the yew branches, yet stayed concealed. The maid of Éireann was not quite done.

"They steal babes outright, and if they cannot snatch them from the cradle, will steal the affection the babe has for its God-given mother, so that the babe sickens, pining for the false and fey woman who has enchanted them. Little can save the child then! It will languish and die."

"Enough, Mealla," Pega answered.

"Not until I make the Sign of the Cross with Holy Water upon Ælfgiva's brow," she replied.

The two walked by, and into the church. Ceric remained at the yew tree, looking into the darkness of its poisoned wood.

Alone again in the bower house, Dwynwen took her most precious object from its resting place. It was the silver hand-fast cup she had filled with water and offered to Ceric the day they met. She walked with it to the nearest well in the kitchen yard, for it must know only living water. She returned, holding it with care in both hands, and set it down upon the table.

Ceric walked in. Dwynwen did not see the distress he wore upon his face, for her back was to him. Nonetheless she knew it was he.

She bent over the silver dish, and blew her breath upon its water.

"Luned packed this for me; her hands were the last which had touched it before I drew it forth and handed it to you," she recounted. She again leant forward over the bowl and breathed a small ripple into the water it held. "I am sending her my breath, so she might know we are well."

Ceric came to her, and placed his hands on her shoulders. Whatever ugliness Dwynwen had been exposed to, she was ready to release it, as he must do.

"I would breathe too, to send Lady Luned a message," he answered.

Dwynwen turned her head to him and smiled. She moved the silver dish to the side so he could do so. The breath he exhaled across its surface carried a prayer: Lady Luned, grand-mother, let no harm come to she I love.

※※※※※※※※※※

A week later, on a warm yet waning Summer day, all Kilton was roused to danger. The alarm was sounded by the watch-men secreted in the blind on the sea cliff. They did not use their horns, for fear of alerting an enemy across the water, but rather one of them ran to find Edwin.

In short order the young Lord of Kilton stood at the cliff face, flanked by the captains of his body-guard, Alwin and Wystan. Ceric and Worr stood with them. The Sun was dropping in the sky, and outlined against it stood two ships, under sail. They were far offshore, but from their profiles looked to be war-ships of the Danes. They were not driving for shore, but rather sailing, seemingly in line. The five men stared at them for long moments.

"Heading east," Worr muttered. "Two of them. If they are raiding, they could be three score men, or more. If they are trading it will be two score, and their goods."

"Who else had seen them," Ceric wondered aloud. "Has any rider come from up the coast warning us of this?"

"No word has come," Worr said, "not yet, though the coast-guard is at watch." If the ships had been before sighted, Kilton should have been alerted by now.

Edwin spoke. "They head east. From whence did they come, and where are they heading?"

Worr gave answer. "They may have sailed from the north, dropping down from Éireann, away from the watch stationed east and west. So they have not yet been seen."

Behind the men, and waiting in the garden pavilion, were Lady Edgyth, Pega, and Dwynwen, standing together and looking out toward the horizon as well. Now Ceric moved to them, and the others followed. He walked behind one of the rose trellises, and used its upright as a sight to mark the progress of the ships. A scrim of low cloud revealed and then concealed their hulls. The sails of the vessels had vanished.

"They are dropping sail for the night," Ceric posited.

The men stood, staring at the reddening sky. Kilton had no answering ship, only a few small boats which could be either oared or sailed. The warship Godwin had commissioned with his mother Lady Modwynn's silver had years ago been taken by Ælfred under urgent need.

Worr and Ceric looked at the other, and with the same realization. Though Ceric had been but a child, both had memory of the Twelfth Night attack on Kilton, when a horde of Danes, guided by the torches flaring in celebration, landed and ascended the steps from the sea to wreak havoc. It was Ceric who spoke in memory of that bloody fight.

"Light no torches. Give the order to light no torches," he said in real urgency to Edwin. "They likely have not spotted us, and we will not lead them to Kilton."

This might be true; the burh was not easy to discern from the sea. The cliffs, the garden beech hedge, and the fact that the larger buildings were set well back made this so.

Edwin nodded, and Alwin and Wystan left to make sure none were lit. As dusk came on the folk of Kilton need go about in darkness for a while.

Ceric needed more, to go out and discern what these ships truly were. He moved his eyes from the dark hulls to his brother. "I will go, with Worr, and some of my own men, in two boats. I will captain one, Worr the second. If we can grow near enough to learn who they are, it might save an action, large or small, from taking place. There will be light enough; the Moon will rise soon, and though waning, is nearly half-full."

Edwin's objection was immediate. "I, and Alwin and Wystan, have fought aboard a ship."

Ceric shook his head. "Fought at sea, yes, but not in a small boat. We are not boarding them, Edwin, just growing close enough for a guess of who they are, and what they are about. Prince Eadward must know of this, the King too. No. You must stay here, and in command."

Edwin must admit to this, his first duty, to remain to defend the burh. His eyes travelled back to the ships outlined in the setting Sun. "How do we know they have not already done their raiding?"

It was a fair question, but Ceric made simple answer to it. "If they were loaded with booty they would fear pursuit and sail through the night on their way home, or wherever their base is." Ceric studied the ships a moment longer as the Sun crimsoned the sky. "No, if they are raiding, I think they have not yet made their strike."

Ceric went on with his plan. "We will not hoist sail; it catches the eye. But two small boats, oaring, will be easy to miss in the chop of the sea." The water was still white-capped from brisk wind during the day, though the air itself had calmed.

"And if they follow you here?" Edwin posed.

"Lightly laden as we will be, they will not easily catch us."

He thought a moment longer. "If they overtake us, we will fight them there, on the beach."

Worr spoke now, and to Edwin: "You might have our archers at the ready, lined up at the cliff edge, should they follow us back."

Edwin nodded at the horse-thegn. "Yes." He was of a sudden in charge of defending Kilton, and in mind to follow the counsel of the older thegn, who had seen much action here.

Ceric too looked at Worr. "Get our strongest rowers, and have them ready the boats. Dark clothing for all. Go arm yourself; I will meet you on the beach."

All this had been spoken in front of the women, and they knew, and could see, as much as the men who acted did. Edgyth crossed herself and uttered a prayer. The hall had been nearing its evening meal. None would eat now, save the women and children, and she would go now and encourage them to do so. The men would have their hands full in readying their defence. Later, if all went well, they would be welcomed to their own meal. Pega had remained near Edgyth, silent and watching. She had not faced such a threat, and now did so within a few short weeks of becoming Lady. Dwynwen turned to both women and took their hands, giving them each a squeeze. Then she turned with Ceric and went with him to the bower house.

His fabled sword, that of Offa, hung on the wall, and she went and stood by it. She watched as Ceric pulled off his tunic and replaced it with one of dusky hue. On his bare chest glinted the small golden cross; he never took it off. He re-buckled his seax, and came to where Dwynwen stood by his sword belt. For a moment he recalled coming into this house to find her wearing it, and how, as startling as it was, it had made him smile. He reached for the belt of the weapon. A long sword was nothing if not awkward in a small boat, but he knew neither Worr nor Edwin would question his lack of a spear.

Dwynwen had remained silent, alert but not seemingly alarmed. He spoke aloud his thoughts, to reassure her.

"The King and Prince must learn of their presence in our waters, as more ships might follow. If they mean harm we will soon know.

"I must go and see, that is all."

Ceric was now buckling on his sword, an act that undercut his words. He was heading toward unknown ships, and likely into grave danger.

Dwynwen gave a slow nod of her head, and when he was done with his sword, gestured him nearer.

"Close your eyes," she whispered.

He did so, and she rose on tiptoes. Then Dwynwen gently placed the tip of each of her pointing fingers on his eyelids.

"Tonight you have the eyes of a cat," she told him.

She lifted her fingertips, and he opened his eyes. He blinked, and then his arm wrapped about her as he pulled her close and kissed her. Any blessing from her, and any wish for his safety, he could trust in.

It was their parting kiss, though she followed him back to the cliff face. Edgyth had returned, and placed her arm about Dwynwen's shoulders. Pega was not there; she may have left to speak to Mealla, who had Ælfgiva in her care. Ceric said a word or two more to Edwin, then in near-darkness made his way down the stone steps. The rock itself was light grey, and the Moon, now visible in the west as it began its own descent, shed its cool light upon the cliff face, though it was not a transit for any uncertain of the unevenness of the steps. Fourteen strong oarsmen awaited below, with Worr. They were dressed in their darkest clothing, as Ceric had ordered, and armed but lightly. The rowing would be heavy and fast, and none could be encumbered with protective gear. The men had their seaxes belted across their bellies, and their spears in hand. Worr had brought two extra to lay along the keel of each boat, should any be lost overboard. Shields were a must, to deflect arrows or other missiles that might be cast their way. The boats were stripped of their tarpaulins, oars set into iron oarlocks, and the men, eight to each boat, heaved them to the water's edge. The foam riding up upon the beach pebbles shone white as the hulls broke through it. As they pushed in time, the scraping of the keels, and grating rush and suck of the water over the stones was backdrop to their efforts. Free of the beach, they splashed through the water, scrambled in and took up their oars.

Those above strained their eyes to see them; it seemed a long time before the boats crossed into view, oaring beneath them. The final streaks of red from the setting Sun were fading, but those watching could still spot the two war-ships on the dark water.

The boats from Kilton struck out, in strong and steady rhythm. Ceric was at the starboard oar in the bow in his boat, and Worr at the final starboard oar in the stern of his. Ceric led the way, Worr's craft following in his wake. The ships they headed for had drifted further apart, and they aimed for the eastern-most one, as the current favoured them, and they must save their strength. As they neared a sound or two drifted to their ears from the ships, voices. A layer of cloud came and went over the Moon, giving them glimpses of the hulls.

The gathering dark emboldened Ceric to approach closer. Both ships were drekars, that was certain, and both of nearly the same length. Worr had been right to think them of a size to carry three score men. They pulled hard for the lead drekar, staying well in front of its bow, for the steers-man and captain would be at the stern, and be most watchful. As they neared the clouds favoured them, slipping by the Moon and allowing just enough light for them to hold fast to their target.

Ceric narrowed his eyes. The eyes of a cat, his child-wife had granted him this night. He felt again the gentle pressure of her fingertips as she said this. He blinked those eyes and set them upon the drekar. There were plenty of men moving about on the deck. As he watched the scene resolved itself. The men, a long trail of them, were lining up to receive their supper. Ceric started counting, by twos and then by fours. He could hear voices from the men aboard, Norse, certainly. The voices grew louder, the sound of rough-housing. Someone had been pushed or trod upon. A louder voice bellowed out, in attempt to quell any violence. They might be hungry, Ceric thought; far hungrier than what the ship's store could dole out.

Ceric had seen enough; he would not poke at this wasps' nest. He raised the blade of his oar out of the water, signal to the men to come about. They could head back now. An unlucky parting of the cloud covering the Moon sent a beam of light in a shaft down to the water. It caught, glinting, on the flat of the wet oar blade, almost if it had been polished metal. It caught the eye of the star-reader aboard the drekar, always vigilant to conditions of weather and water. He whistled out warning. More whistles and cries from the ship told them they had been spotted.

Aboard the drekar the captain and steers-man came forward to the bow. His second in command came after, leaning out over the gunwale. He saw the two retreating boats. "Locals," he judged. "Night fishing, I think."

"And we are hungry," answered the captain. "Let us catch these larger fish. Their nets could be full."

In fact, the two Kilton boats, laden only with the men within, fixed all effort on returning to shore.

The captain of the drekar ordered his men to their own oars; he would not lose time in hoisting sail. "Stay in sight of them," he yelled. "We will run them down, and overtake them on the beach."

Ceric had never rowed as he had that night; few of the other men, none strangers to boats, had either. They drove for shore, certain of the cove above which Kilton sat. But behind them the drekar chased in pursuit, with thirty men at the oar, and more ready with spears and war-axes. The drekar aimed for what looked a sheer cliff face; was there even beach there, the steers-man asked himself. Yet the steady cries from the men in the bow of his ship told him to drive on. They did so, their hull scraping bottom of a pebbled shore. Some of his men jumped down into the shallows soon as they shipped oars. Others remained aboard, arming themselves. There on the beach, hauled just out of the tide's pull, sat two boats, wet from surf. There were no men, nor fishing nets, full or empty to be seen. The oaths rising from the captain were lost in the sudden war-cries of his bow-men. All was not lost – there were steps, carved in stone, up the steep cliff face. Something would lie above.

It was true the beach looked void of men. Ceric and his troop had just time and breath enough to haul up their boats, and then make for a thick finger of rock which descended from the cliff face on the western side of the cove. It extended out into the shingle beach, its root always in water even at low tide. Any venturing around it would find a cave, hollowed through countless years of waves. It was into this Ceric and his men vanished.

The crew of the drekar made for the steps, shields on their backs, spears in hand. Edwin, waiting above with two

score archers, made command. Those invaders climbing up
the steps, and those upon the beach, were greeted by a hail
of arrows. The height from which the archers aimed gave
them perfect access, even to men still aboard the ship, a few
of whom fell headlong into the water. Each archer had a full
dozen of arrows in the quiver at his hip, and ready refills when
these were spent, for a line of youths stood behind them with
more, fully fletched, at hand.

Those who had climbed the furthest up the steps fell
first, their bodies tumbling and often taking other men down
with them. The warriors on the beach, looking up, could see
the archers, but make no return. War-cries turned to oaths
and cries of pain, death-cries as well. Shouted orders carried
above this, and some men at water's edge and on deck made
effort to free the ship and so escape. No men remained upon
the stone steps, and none tried to follow the Fated footsteps
of their fallen brethren. The archers, nocking yet another
round, turned all their attention to the ship, and let fly a sleet
of winged barbs.

A cry rising above the din brought near silence to the
beach. Their captain must be dead, or hit, for now the warriors began to throw down their weapons in surrender. They
cast them down by twos and threes, and then lifted their
arms in the air.

"Still your bows," Edwin commanded. The Moon, lower
now above the water, sent its rippled light towards the
beach. The Lord of Kilton looked down upon the carnage his
archers had wrought. Men groaned in pain, and tried to rise,
but many lay still, studded with the arrows which had found
home. Standing by the drekar were but a handful of sound
men. They had killed most of them.

From round the rock face, and splashing through the tide came Ceric and Worr and their fourteen men. Ceric had his sword drawn, and all others had their spears in hand. Their appearance was so sudden that the remaining drekar crew might have thought a band of ghost warriors had appeared. They were real enough though, and their advance upon the survivors threatening in action, as they herded the men at spear-point against the cliff, their faces to the rock.

Ceric whistled up at Edwin. The gladsome cry heard from the cliff edge was followed in short order by the scramble of Edwin's men, descending. They kept the captives pinioned against the wall while Ceric's men swarmed over the prisoners, relieving them of knives and other small weaponry; one had a truncheon-like bar of iron, akin to an ingot, to surrender. These captives were sent up the steps to those awaiting them. Next the men who rowed with Ceric and Worr went to where men lay dead, or seemingly so, and gathered their purses, amulets, and weapons as their battle-gain. Others of Edwin's men now descended, to deal with those injured. These must be helped, and even hauled up on the backs of others, but all save the dead were carried up.

Meanwhile the drekar was made fast upon the shingle, so the pull of the retreating tide could not free her. Ceric, at work with this, looked at the dark horizon. A double watch must be set tonight to make sure the second ship did not approach.

When all the injured had been sent up, and the ship secured, the crews of Kilton's boats ascended. They were met with cheers and whistles of acclaim, which they returned to the archers, standing there still at the cliff edge, where they had watched the aftermath of their handiwork.

The last men up the stone steps were Ceric, followed by Worr. Edwin came to them, flushed with the pride of victory, and pounded his brother on the back.

Dwynwen stood not far off, her arms at her side, a smile on her closed lips. Ceric gave her a nod, and then turned to Edwin. The survivors must be questioned, and the injured dealt with. Ceric, having spent such time at Four Stones, spoke to the men. They were not Danes, but Northmen, from the land of the deep fjords, whose men had founded Dubh Linn in Éireann. They would name neither intent nor destination, but they had given chase to Kilton's boats and readied to storm whatever dwellings they might have found on its cliff top.

"Keep the torches unlit," Ceric told Edwin when he had done with them. Edwin needed no explanation; the second drekar was still out there.

For her part Lady Edgyth turned to the care of the injured. They had taken arrows to their shoulders, legs, and for one, at the waist. She had them helped to the church, deeming it the most suitable place to care for them. Cots were carried in, that she, the serving woman Mindred, and Dwynwen might work on the men there. They would be kept together, and their wounds more easily dealt with. And too, the church could be readily secured, if any of them attempted escape. Pega appeared to aid them; she was untried in treating wounds, but must learn. At Four Stones the slight injuries to men while sparring or in the work yards were looked after by Inga, or the men's own wives or daughters; during her time as Lady there had been but one real battle, that when Hrald killed Haesten. Pega had been with child, and Lady Ælfwyn had insisted she herself and the other women look after the injured. Now Pega kept to the side of Edgyth, helping as she could, and trying not to sicken at the look of the wounds. Pega had never handled the body of any man she had not been wed to, so even cleansing the skin around the gashes was a trial. The men too were unwashed and reeking from their time at sea. Once or twice Pega looked over to see the Welsh Princess at work, and must wonder at, if not envy, the sure action of her hands, and her quick smile for those who groaned in pain. Dwynwen worked thus together with Mindred. The serving woman possessed good sense, and having been active in healing work amongst the hall folk, was skilled. As further help there was Tegwedd. She had seen many a bad scald and knife cut from her time in King Elidon's kitchen yard, and was there to fetch and carry as needed. The wounds, punctures all, were washed in water of earthgall, and then bound in linen.

All the men were in pain, and Dwynwen took this task on, for which Edgyth was grateful. Herbs that dulled pain could be given in such amounts, or in combinations with certain roots and berries, that even strong men fell into sleep from which they did not awaken. The Princess took cowslip, feverfew, and seeds of white poppy and pounded them into a paste, then mixed it in mead to quell the bitterness. Even with her skill, she showed Edgyth the proportions she selected, so that Lady's long experience in wort-cunning could guide her. When her potion was ready, Dwynwen went from man to man, spooning a small amount into a cup, to which she added more mead, and stirred them together. The men, some writhing in pain, drank it readily, and one or two even touched her hand in thanks. He who had taken the arrow to his waist was too weak to sit up to drink, and Mindred held his head as Dwynwen spooned in the mixture. Though some of it dribbled from the corner of his mouth, he was able to swallow most, a hopeful sign.

Ceric entered the church as the women were working. Two of Edwin's men were stationed there within the sanctuary as guards, and Ceric saw the helplessness of most of the injured at a glance. Still, those who could open their eyes watched as he entered, and saw Dwynwen go to him. They saw the two of them speak together, his head bent to hers. Whether she was wife or daughter they cared not. It was clear the two were paired, and this was the man who had captured them. They would not risk angering him, for his power over them, nor for the care they had received from the women moving amongst them, and most specially this young one who could still smile to comfort them.

Led by Worr and the other men on the boats, the bulk of the prisoners had been marched to the kitchen yard, to sit at two tables. "Feed them," Worr ordered, gladsome words for the captives, as they were indeed hungered.

It was late by the time all in the hall had been fed, and laid their heads down to welcome sleep. Edwin and Ceric had good cause to praise their young wives for their part in this. Dwynwen had Tegwedd bring a bucket of hot water to the bower house; the day had held much, and she must bathe before she slipped into bed. She stood in the shallow copper basin, and poured the water over her bare skin, scrubbing herself well with soft soap pounded with costmary. She stepped out and dried herself in a sheet of rough linen. Her ablutions were not complete though; she went to one of her small chests emblazoned with dragons to recover a vial of some oil pressed from fragrant wood, which she held to temples and wrists. Ceric, sitting up in bed and watching, welcomed her under the covers. He knew she did this to free herself from the actions of the day, and most of all the suffering of the men she had cared for. She herself could assume their pain, he feared; Edgyth had told her of this. It was a danger to all skilled healers. How much more so it might be to Dwynwen, with her deep feeling, and insight into others. He who watched her was too wearied to embrace her in love. Just to hold her naked body to his was enough that night.

The Moon set. Upon the cliff top the guardsmen at Kilton remained at their watch, yet in the inky darkness there was little to discern. Still at sea, the second drekar, sighting on the Northly Star, drove south. The captain wished to near the place where they had lost sight of their companion ship. They had not seen why it had given chase, only that its men had started rowing suddenly for shore, as if in pursuit. There must be a reason, and he would learn it.

They dropped anchor before long, fearing to run onto shoals unseen to them in the pre-dawn hours. A small boat was lowered from the drekar, and men set to row forward to see what they could. The launch grew nearer to shore, and sighted the cliff face, far lighter than the water they rowed upon. They saw the missing drekar, pulled up and heeled over on the beach. Utter silence surrounded it. No lantern was lit aboard it, and from what could be seen, no guard had been set at its hull. The strongest swimmer of them pulled off his boots and lowered himself into the water, and set out, hands to his chest, parting the water. He made not for the ship, but off to one side of it, lest there be a watch.

He did not stand up when his feet touched the beach, but instead moved himself forward on his belly, the chill water covering most of him as he strained his eyes to see more. Off to one side, and not far from him, lay a body, with two arrows sticking upright from its back. There, another body. And another. They were his brethren, he was sure, as they had no archers amongst them. Two small boats lay there as well. But none inhabited this beach now, save for the dead.

To stand could be to reveal himself and be caught in the same trap. With his hands he pushed himself around and made his way as quietly as he could back to the waiting launch. He was hauled up, to tell of what he found. Death had met their fellows upon that beach, and none left to voice their end.

At Kilton the tasks of the next morning were many. At the cliff face the guardsmen, steady through the night, made report. The Sun had dawned on an empty horizon. The second drekar, having watched its sister head toward shore and not return, was reluctant to meet the same Fate. It had sailed off.

Then came the sending of two riders west down the coast, to the keep of Arx Cynwit in Defenas. The Lord thereof, Deorwine, was also a King's Reeve, and it fell to him to act on behalf of Wessex. The ship would be forfeit to the King, but it was likely that half the goods on board would be meted out to Edwin. They must wait until the Reeve's arrival to act further, but if he were found, he would sail up the coast and be at Kilton on the morrow.

Lady Edgyth and Dwynwen returned early to the church to check on the wounded Northmen, and make sure they had been offered food and ample drink by the kitchen-yard. Dwynwen made up another batch of the cowslip potion, and administered it round. The man who had taken the arrow to his waist had his eyes open, and glassy though they shone, Dwynwen coaxed him into taking more of the enriched mead she offered.

Edwin sent a serving maid to Mealla to come to the kitchen yard where the bulk of the captives were held, a summons she did not welcome. She pursed her lips from where she sat mending a stocking in the weaving room, but laid down her needle. Mealla was already up in arms due to the demands of the evening before. Pega had only poured oil on the fire by telling her of the Welsh girl's kindness to the injured men they tended, going so far as to offer her cheering smile to them in their pain. Mealla had erupted in umbrage; they were weak and needy now, but earlier had been ready to act as rapacious raiders.

"It is only Christian charity," Pega tried to point out.

"Christian charity! To act thus she must be in secret league with them!"

Now Mealla was being forced to go and look in their filthy faces.

It was thought they were Northmen out of Éireann, and Mealla could imagine why the Lord wished her to see them; some of them might speak her native tongue. If she could learn more from them now, it could be helpful. She left Ælfgiva in the care of her mother and headed down the stair and out into the yard.

Mealla walked, as straight and unyielding as a poker, to the tables where sat the captives. Edwin was there, and the men were heavily guarded, so she need fear nothing. She glared at them, scruffy bearded and slumped on their benches. A few perked up at the sight of her, fiery-eyed and raven-haired. With an angry shake of her head she launched into the tongue of Éireann, a tirade of shrill insults, that though not understandable to those of Kilton was clear in intent. The worst of her bile was reserved for the oldest amongst them. One of them might be her father through rape, or the brother of her father, and she scorned them the more for it. In unrelenting stream she berated them, their fathers, and their forefathers before them. Then she paused, and asked a question. It was met with silence. She repeated it, and stamped her foot. Alwin and Wystan came to her side, and struck an offensive position with their spears.

One of the men spoke. Mealla nodded, listening, and asked more, which was answered. She finished, hurling what sounded like more taunts, and turned on her heel. She went to Edwin.

"They come from Éireann, aye, and Northmen they are. But they hail not from Dubh Linn, but from an outpost on the south-east of the isle, called Port Láirge. If you do not know of it, you do now. There is some trouble there, they will not say what. The chief there is one Offir, or Ottor; they speak badly and I cannot tell. His son captained the second ship, the one that left. The captain of their own was also kin, a cousin, I think. He is dead, and they will not speak of him, for fear of his anger in their Heathen paradise."

Edwin gave a grateful nod. "I thank you, Mealla. When the Reeve arrives this will add much to what we can tell him."

She gave a returning nod of her own fine head. "If I were not a Christian woman, I would march them off that cliff," she said in closing.

Now they must await the arrival of Deorwine the Reeve. As they did so, Edwin and Ceric, accompanied by Worr and a few of the men who had taken part in the action, descended the steps to the abandoned drekar. In the bright daylight they could fully see, and board her. They stepped upon the pebbled beach with caution, lest any Northmen still live amongst those lying there, or one, escaping the sleet of arrows, had hidden himself. The beach was empty of all living save the few shorebirds, who, glad of the groove dug up by the big ship's keel, stood over it, pecking through the wet stones for sea snails and other morsels.

The quantity of arrows was almost staggering. Edwin had watched volley after volley being fired from the cliff edge; he had the bow-men fire their arrows as soon as they could nock the next. The dead were bristling with them, certain men having been hit five or more times. The beach itself was littered with arrows, the feathered ends standing upright in the air from where the iron tips had lodged themselves in sand and pebbles. Others lay flat, some having shattered their shafts striking the large rocks there. The bow of the ship was pocked with them, the goose feathers of their fletching trembling slightly in the breeze. Men went about, retrieving them.

Worr took charge of the dead. He and a few of the men dragged three-and-twenty bodies to one side of the cove, and laid them shoulder to shoulder. The horse-thegn and one of the archers then went about pulling the arrows from their bodies; most were sound of shaft and could be returned to the archer's quivers. The bodies had begun to swell in the night, and the yank it took to remove some of the arrows made the bodies jerk as if still alive. Edwin watched this, seeing how pitifully young many of the dead were, no older than he himself.

Then Worr went over the bodies of the dead a second time, looking for valuables missed in the first rifling for battle-gain. He found much, especially talismans of silver hanging about necks, and a few arm-rings of the same stuff secreted under tunic sleeves. These would go into a common pool of booty and be shared amongst all the rowers.

As this was going on Ceric and Edwin had climbed aboard the empty drekar. Three bodies lay there, one fallen face down over a sea-chest, two arrows in his back, the other two on their backs, looking blankly into the clarity of the morning sky. These had each been hit with a single arrow, but telling blows, as one had struck near the heart, the second, in the belly. Two of Edwin's men hoisted the bodies up and over the side, then using a pail from the ship, dipped sea water enough to wash much of the blood away. It ran across the planking to the starboard side where the hull canted.

There was not much cargo stowed aboard, and they must not open it until the Reeve appeared. But weaponry abounded, and half should be theirs and remain at Kilton. The number of spears lashed under the gunwale far outnumbered the men the ship had carried; it must be booty from prior raids. Beyond this were shields, a few swords, war-axes, and perched on the tips of an iron anchor, two visored helmets, staring blankly out over the deck. These last were the real prizes, as few were the warriors who could afford the making of one. The ship itself, though lacking any decorative elements to make her memorable, was sound-looking, with a newly carved steering oar laying still.

As the brothers moved about they glimpsed movement from the starboard side. Something alive popped up from the stowage area under the decking, perhaps driven out by the water from the cleansing buckets.

"Rat," Edwin muttered, an easy enough answer.

When it had emerged fully they saw it for what it was, a young cat, or kitten really, orange and white. It arched its back and rose up on tip-toes, dancing sideways towards them to fend them off. Both must laugh; as ship's cat it was small, but feisty.

Ceric squatted down. At once the kitten collapsed in size. It did not near Ceric, but did allow him to come close. He reached his hand under it and picked it up.

There was little more they could do until the Reeve arrived, so leaving a few men to guard the drekar, they ascended the steps. A waggon must be readied to transport the wounded overland, amongst other tasks to be fulfilled to transfer ship and men to the Reeve's keeping. Edwin went to speak to Dunnere; they might need his scribal skills in accounting for the goods aboard.

Ceric went to the bower house, glad that Dwynwen was within. She was moving amongst her clothes chests, and greeted him with a smile. He held a bag of coarse hempen cloth against his chest, a bag that moved under the hand that held it there. He opened the bag and pulled out a half-grown kitten, one with orange and white fur.

"You granted me the eyes of a cat last night," he said. "Here is your cat," he told her, handing her the kitten.

Her delighted laughter brought them both pleasure. It was a pretty thing, white bodied, with an orange and white face, white ears, two large splotches of orange on its flanks, and a fluffy orange tail. It had paws well out of scale to its small size, and Ceric splayed one out to show it. Instead of five toes on its front paws it had seven, including two, clumped together almost like thumbs.

"Such cats carry luck, it is said," Ceric told her. "At least it has luck now, to live here with you."

Dwynwen placed the little furred one on the bed, and fairly ran to the kitchen yard, returning with a dish of whey curds, and some boiled fish spooned up from a stewing pot. The kitten jumped on the floor and tucked in at first one dish and then the other, fairly growling in happiness at this abundance.

They both stood watching the kitten at his repast. Ceric did not know what might await in the drekar's cargo, but felt this unexpected discovery meant more to Dwynwen than any battle-gain he might be awarded to give her.

He must say more of the scene below the cliff. Dwynwen went there every day, and he did not want her to do so now.

"The beach – there is blood on it."

She only nodded, then said, "As there is always, from fish and sea birds who die there. The tide will come and wash it away."

"It will," he agreed. "But do not go down until the Reeve has taken all."

"I will not," she promised. The kitten now stood before two empty dishes, and after licking both sides of its mouth with a pink tongue, began the work of washing its head.

"With such big paws he will be done in half the time," Dwynwen jested.

Next day as promised Deorwine the Reeve arrived, sailing up the coast in a broad beamed cargo ship. He was in his sixth decade, pink-skinned, with long grey moustaches to balance the balding of his head. Despite his age he moved with some vigour, an energy needed for a man entrusted with the transport of dangerous and oftentimes still-violent prisoners. Deorwine brought a number of burly men with him, for Kilton's messengers made clear that only eleven of the Northmen were hale enough to man the oars. Edwin, Ceric, and Worr were there to greet him on the beach, the captured drekar before him for his inspection, and the bodies of the dead aligned against the cliff face.

He was told the full story by both Edwin and Ceric, nodding in understanding at what they said, sometimes stopping to ask a question. At the end, satisfied, he said merely, "The King shall hear of your action. And your boldness," he added, looking to Ceric.

Dunnere the priest came down the cliff face, aided by one of Edwin's men, and was helped aboard the drekar. He had a piece of wood to serve as writing board, and a satchel holding parchment, quill, and ink.

All the cargo was opened before those from Kilton, so they might view the contents. Little of real value was there, but one cask held some fine bronze work, packed in straw. There were small pots forged of it, some lidded, and a quantity of bronze bridle and horse-harness fittings, newly cast, for none of the fine detail had been worn down through handling.

"From the east," Deorwine said, "Sassanian, mayhap."

The sea-chests of the men held more, modest amounts of amber and silver trinkets, some smaller bladed knives, and such like metal work. In the sea-chest in the stern, likely to have been that of the captain himself, they found true value. Layered amongst his clothing was walrus ivory, six long tusks of it. This treasure was accompanied by another. In a large bundle, wrapped in protective cow hides, lay the enormous skins of the beasts themselves, three of them, rolled together. The Reeve made just division of this. The walrus hides could not be cut, destroying their value for the making of walrus-skin line, which would be carefully sliced in a single piece, circling round the entire expanse of the skin to its centre. Instead he set aside four of the tusks, and one hide thereof, for Kilton, and kept two tusks, and two hides for the King. Dunnere noted all, and in two copies, and Deorwine divided up the goods and weaponry aboard, awarding half to Kilton. Deorwine examined both steel helmets, different in feature but both well-wrought. He handed one to the Lord of Kilton. Edwin uttered his thanks, and turned to his brother. Ceric had led the action, and deserved a rich gift. Here it was. Edwin also passed two of the four walrus tusks to him. Ceric bowed his head to both Edwin and the Reeve.

Beyond this were nearly empty casks of food, the remains of dried bread and smoked fish, and water. If the drekar had dropped down from Éireann it had either been caught in bad weather and delayed at sea, or had left in haste with little provender aboard. Still, the ship itself held great value, and though the sail, lying in folds on the keelson, was patched from long use, the rigging lines were new.

The disposition of the bodies remained to be dealt with. Burning this number of men upon the beach would be a tiresome labour, for all the wood must be tossed down from the cliff, the pyre built, fired, and tended. Hauling the bodies up was likewise nothing to be undertaken without considerable effort, and then they must still be buried or burnt. The Reeve walked slowly by each body, gazing upon the men as if in reflection of their lives, and deaths. He made his decision.

"We will carry them aboard the ship, and drop them at sea. It will be best."

It was determined that when the tide turned both drekar and cargo ship would sail to Arx Cynwit, with the Northmen who were sound of body at the drekar's oars. Those injured would be carried by waggon thence. The crews of the boats Ceric and Worr had captained could keep all they had taken carried by the prisoners, and theirs too the spoils of war from those dead. Edwin would reward his archers justly, and in a fitting sharing of the spoils, Worr found himself recipient of the fine helmet awarded to Ceric. Worr was father to three boys, and this gift meant the youngest of them would one day be as well-armed as his brothers.

Deorwine ordered the bodies be hauled aboard the drekar, and then with his hosts climbed the stone steps to the garden. There at the pavilion refreshment awaited in the form of bread, cheese, and ale. No stronger drink was offered, as the Reeve was in haste to be ready to catch the tide, but to sit surrounded by the garden when he had spent time viewing the dead was welcome to the man.

Soon the prisoners were brought forth, to be sent down the steps. They would once again man the oars of the drekar, but this time as captives of the King of Wessex. Some looked surly, some mournful. Their eyes moved neither right nor left, but only out to sea. Deorwine went with them; his men awaited below, but his was the charge to transport the men, and now having been handed them by Edwin, he must ensure their delivery to justice.

As the last of them vanished down the steps, the Lord of Kilton spoke.

"What will happen to them?" Edwin wondered aloud.

"They will not be hanged, not by Ælfred," Worr answered. He had learnt much of the workings of Ælfred's law from his father-in-law Raedwulf, Bailiff of Defenas. "They were not actively raiding."

Ceric, having been privy to the rough justice meted out by Ælfred's son, was not at all certain that Eadward would be so lenient. But Ælfred still lived, and the sentence, his to decree.

Worr added to his supposition. "But given the chance to raid, they took it. And lost all, and many of them, their lives as well."

"They might be held to ransom, or sent back to Éireann, to be rid of them," Ceric said. "If men of Wessex are held captive there, an exchange could be held." He and Worr had heard of many such trades of captives.

They then followed the Reeve down, to bid him Farewell, and safe voyage. The two ships must coast, and drop anchor at nightfall, but the morrow would see his return to his keep, as the tidal current would aid them.

Next were the injured. These would be carried in a waggon which had been driven to the very door of the church. Most of the men could walk, and those who could not were helped. Edgyth and Dwynwen were with them, and received a nod of thanks as the men passed by. They had not been poled with a spear while lying helpless on the beach, but rather been tended with care, washed, and fed. Dwynwen had made up a jug of her cowslip potion to go with them, and entrusted it to the care of the driver.

"If you drink it, you will fall from the waggon board and be run over," she warned. His eyes bulged at this threat, and he vowed to keep it for those who groaned with pain.

The final man to be loaded was carried on a litter. It was the Northman who had taken the arrow to his waist. His eyes were closed and he moved not.

"I do not think he will live," Dwynwen murmured to Edgyth.

"It will not be from lack of your care, or skill," Edgyth returned, in attempt to console the girl. "Still, he lived through two nights. That is much."

Dwynwen gave a shake of her head. "I looked into his eyes. They gazed to a distant shore."

Edgyth could say nothing to this, feeling now the man would surely die. She crossed herself, and then placed her arm about Dwynwen's waist in comfort.

※※※※※※※※※※

The next morning Dwynwen did go down to the empty beach. In her hand was a basket carrying fruitwood charcoal, and small bundles of dried herbs. She built up rocks in a flat spiral, laid the charcoal upon it, then a few dry herbs, and kindled fire with her flint and iron striker. The herbs smoldered, then sparked into flame, causing a thin racing line of fire to spread across the dark surface of the charcoal. It began to smoke. She placed stem after stem of the dried herbs upon it. Three-and-twenty were the men who had died here, and she added another for one she felt would soon die. The scented smoke rose, an incense sprung from the ground, plucked and dried by she who made this Offering.

GOOD WILL FOLLOW

Four Stones

HROFT became the favourite of the hall of Four
Stones. When Cerd lived there, he had been such,
and now the small nephew was replaced by the Jarl's own
son. Young as he was, it did not keep the men from carving small weapons of wood for Hroft to play with, joining
the wooden horse he bounced in his hand upon the floor,
to make it walk. He was given a toy sword with blunted tip,
emblem of that real one already presented to Hroft by the
King of Wessex.

Dagmar knew great joy with Hrald. Their happiness was
such that when alone they often found themselves laughing aloud, for sheer joy of the love they shared, and now
expanded. Watching Hrald spend time with his son was a
sweetness equal to that she had always imagined. Hroft had
taken to his father from the first, and to Dagmar, for whom
the blood-bond was so vital, it seemed proof of the child
coming as a gift to Hrald, and to his hall. The gift was of enormous price, including another child Hrald had loved, and

this knowledge must ever temper the satisfaction Dagmar took. Yet there was a deep rightness about their union, and the child it had produced. Dagmar had in secret little cause to take pride in her several brothers, all by different mothers; none had remotely approached her father Guthrum in ability or action. Here in Hroft there might arise a son worthy of that King's blood, through her, and through such a man as was Hrald.

Jari looked upon the child as a proud grand-sire might, yet as Hroft was still toddling, was more than grateful that Dagmar's care and Wite's watchful eye spared him from any real duties about the boy. The Tyr-hand, watching the child one day, gave thought to Bork. He was away at Oundle, and they had heard no report, good or ill, from him. Surely, Jari hoped, he would not be there long. After the youth's trailing Hrald, and his telling action on the road to Cantwaraburh, Jari felt Bork might one day become the child's special protector, as he himself had been to Hrald when he was a boy.

Even Yrling took interest in Hroft, bringing the hound Myrkri to him, and laughing with Hroft as she licked the boy's face. Hroft stood up on unsteady feet and clung to the dog, only laughing the more when the plumed tail swished in his face. As big as she was, Hroft showed no fear of her, and Yrling was glad that Dagmar also liked the hound, who was well-mannered and gentle.

Dagmar took true pleasure in the fact that her boy was so valued. Returning with Hrald's son cast her return in a new and favourable light, one she was grateful for. Yet she was left with doubts about how she herself was regarded. Pega had served as Lady for nearly three years. Her leaving upended all at Four Stones, and Dagmar had been the cause of it. Dagmar did not, she knew, project the natural warmth of a woman like her mother-in-law, Ælfwyn. She had not known that kind of warmth from her own mother, and thus had no one on which to model her own actions. She feared that while Hroft was welcomed and loved, there were those who resented her. It was true that Hrald had taken her about the work yards on her return. These were the folk who had once served her, but the way in which some of them looked at her, their heads cocked slightly to one side, felt as if they were considering her anew, and in light of she who had pre-ceded her.

The changes to Four Stones were marked, in ways small and large. At her wedding feast there had been squares of linen set at each place at the high table. Dagmar watched others lay these as coverings over their laps, and knew this must have been the custom of Pega, a custom brought to Four Stones by her. The church Pega had built was the great-est reminder of her presence, and now, Dagmar thought, her absence. The bronze bell arrived, with two men to hang it, for they must fashion the headstock of timber to hold the bell, and then suspend the iron clapper within it. It gave a pure and clear sound, one never heard over Four Stones. The first time it was rung for Mass the priest Wilgot did not fail to mention it had been gift of the Lady of the hall, and then, after a pause, expanded on this by naming Dagmar.

Wite had proven worthy of her selection by Inga as Hroft's nursemaid, and was young enough to play with him in a way that delighted the boy. Inga too was a help, espe-cially about the work yards, but she had never been privy to much beyond. Dagmar remembered all she could about the numbering of the bronze cups each night, the keeping of

tallies, where spare salvers were stored, and when to order
the repair or replacement of such things from the metal
workers in the yard. But there was much she thought she
had forgotten, or never learnt in her short time here. Most
of all Dagmar felt keenly the absence of her mother-in-law, a
feeling always followed on its heels by how Hrald must have
fallen from grace by returning to her. It was a thought that
made Dagmar close her eyes.

The presence most with her though, was that of Ashild,
Hrald's older sister. Her loss was everywhere felt, Dagmar
knew, though her name was not often spoken. Hrald had
not only loved but admired his sister, and trusted her utterly.
Ashild had disobeyed a single order, and been killed. And
Hrald, Dagmar felt, secretly bore the brunt of the guilt, for
allowing her upon the battlefield.

Dagmar knew, or felt, that Ashild had disliked her,
though when she and Hrald had first met at the hall of her
cousin Haward, and rode to Four Stones together, he had
told her Ashild would like her. Dagmar had seen scant proof
of that. She could not free herself from hearing the scorn-
ful oaths she had been driven out with; Ashild's voice had
been the last she had heard, damning her for the way she had
harmed Hrald and all of Four Stones. It felt indelible, a stain
on her memory, one that not even her talk with the Abbess
had removed, for she had been too ashamed to mention how
deep ran this hurt.

Beyond the scores within the hall work-yards, there
were the village folk. Dagmar had clear memory of Ælfwyn
taking her about the crofts there, so that she might greet each
family. She should, Dagmar knew, do this again, yet thinking of it caused her throat to tighten. She would ask Inga to

accompany her, Inga who knew all in the village, and most important of all, Dagmar felt, bring Wite with her, holding Hroft so that all might see the Jarl's son.

The three of them did so, choosing a fine if cool day. They made stop at every croft, greeting women at their washtubs and men with their ards and rakes, and many young, caring for those even younger than they, or going about the work of weeding, cutting or picking vegetables from croft gardens, shooing hens or geese out from the open doors of cottages they had wandered into, and for the females, the endless task of spinning wool thread. These were the folk who would come to Dagmar with their worries and complaints, and now by showing herself to them, they might know she would help them as she could.

Dagmar's goal was to say a kind word to all, and in this she was greatly helped by Inga, who could inquire of each family how they fared, if they had known recent sickness or trouble. Inga too could point out which of the women supplied the hall with spun thread and even woven cloth; these Dagmar must have personal dealings with. Having Hroft with her made all, man and woman, smile. To Dagmar this was nothing less than another reminder of how vital the boy was to their acceptance of her. One of the villagers seemed proof of this. She was an old and toothless woman, sitting outside her cottage, winding wool. The ball in her withered hands was quite small, but she snapped the yarn and tied it off. Then with trembling fingers she handed it to Hroft as a ball to play with.

There was also a wider sphere Dagmar must enter. At Witanceaster she had lived the quietest of lives, that of a guest, yes, but one on the edge of the royal family and its concerns. When Hroft was born her life, already narrow, contracted further, as she devoted herself to him. Now Dagmar must not only head the running of a large, active, and demanding hall, but take her place as Lady to those looking on.

Within the first fortnight of her return, Hrald told her they would take a few men and make a call on her cousin Haward. His was the closest hall to Four Stones, and he was Dagmar's only near kin. It was there Hrald had first seen Dagmar, and it was Haward who had brokered the union. Haward could not offer much to augment Dagmar's scant dowry; his cousin's wealth consisted of the jewellery she wore, and her bloodline. Asberg and Hrald had gone to see Haward to discuss the bride-price, and Asberg took charge of the bargaining. When Haward named arms as the bride-price, Asberg offered five swords and twenty spear-points. Haward had studied both men, but shook his head. Hrald spoke up, doubling the number of swords to ten. It did not please his uncle, but it did Haward, who readily agreed. All the bride-price had been returned to Hrald when Dagmar had been forced out, leaving Haward lucky, he thought, to have escaped with his life, for Asberg had so threatened him over the perceived deception of her past.

This time Hrald was already wed to Dagmar, and had no intention of doing more than bringing her to Haward's hall so she might meet his own wife. There was a hall dependent upon Four Stones for its defence, yet free beyond a yearly tithing of grain, Geornaham by name. Its steward was Tillbert, and his daughter, Werburgh. The small keep had been attacked and overrun by none less than Haesten, and Hrald, aided by Haward, had given chase. Haward had been attempting to court Werburgh at the time, but been refused. His action in the chase, and subsequent gift of a full score of young pigs to replace those plundered by Haesten, had gone a long way to placing Haward in better light. Not long after he renewed his suit of Werburgh, and was accepted.

Hrald and Dagmar had not visited Haward after their first marriage. It was thus a social visit of some importance, and for Hrald, one imbued with strong memory of first seeing Dagmar here as she stepped through a line of drying laundry. That day he had been subject to an ambush attempt, and lost a good man. He then, after speaking with Haward and meeting Dagmar, must ride on to Turcesig, the great garrison of Dagmar's father, to address the warriors there, many of whom had been provoked by lies about Hrald's behaviour. It was a day marked in memory on many fronts.

Hrald and Jari, along with an escort of eight, rode alongside a waggon bearing Dagmar and Hroft, with Wite to tend to the child. It was important to show the boy, and Hrald was glad to do so. They were received more than cordially by their hosts. Haward only held his hall by the grace of Hrald, and to his credit did not allow himself to forget this. Werburgh, comely enough with rosy cheeks, a ready smile, and curling brown hair, extended every courtesy; Hrald was Jarl and this, his new Lady, though Werburgh had never met Dagmar.

Another was called to join them for the welcome ale. A maid of some ten or so Summers came to the table. It was Siggerith, Haward's niece. Dagmar marked her at once; this was her cousin Thorfast's orphan. Hrald had been forced to kill Thorfast in a duel over whether they would join Haesten's forces or not.

Dagmar greeted the girl with a smile, but Siggerith had seemingly forgotten the weeks she and Inkera, Dagmar's half-sister, had spent here with her, or had turned her back on any happy memory thereof. Perhaps seeing Dagmar in the company of the man who had killed her father blunted her response.

The girl was largely silent, though Dagmar, in attempt to draw her out, asked of her pony. The corners of Siggerith's mouth curled upward, if briefly. Haward offered that she was growing tall for the little animal, and he would give her another soon.

"Let us send you one, Siggerith," Dagmar countered. "The Jarl has many fine mounts." Dagmar voiced this with care; with her father's death the girl had been deprived of all her belongings, and it had been Dagmar asking Hrald if she might have her pony returned that had made Hrald realise this, and restore it to her.

At this Siggerith pressed her lips together, and shook her head with some vehemence. It made Werburgh speak sharply to the girl, who then arose and asked to be allowed to return to her sewing work.

Hrald watched Siggerith walk away, head high but with shoulders slack as if burdened. He could not blame Siggerith's act, nor feelings.

Dagmar must inquire of another Haward had sheltered here. "Have you news of Inkera?" she asked.

Dagmar had no contact with her half-sister since before she had left Four Stones on that cold Spring day. Nor had she attempted to send message to Headleage upon her arriving Witanceaster; the shame of her dismissal by Hrald was too strong upon her. Inkera must have learnt of it through some means; their cousin Haward, Dagmar imagined, should he and Inkera be in contact. Perhaps Inkera had been back to Haward's hall, and had learnt of her disgrace there.

Haward shook his head. "I have seen her but once, when she stopped here. She is at Headleage, as far as I know, living with one of our kin."

All Dagmar could do was nod; Haward had greater concerns than her sister.

Later Dagmar and Werburgh went into the work yard so Hroft, with a piece of bread clutched in his hand, could scamper about with Wite. Hrald walked through the same yard with Haward. The latter scarcely knew what to say about Hrald's new marriage, save that he must congratulate him on his fine son. They spoke of the last of the harvest, and such like things. They had neared the stable and its paddock, and Hrald was put in mind of the maid who had left them at table. He uttered her name.

"Siggerith," he opened. "In a few years she will be of an age to wed."

Haward, more than aware of the girl's orphanhood, as he had witnessed it, drew a deep breath. "That may be true. But she has nothing to her name, save a few gems left her by her mother."

"If she finds a worthy man, that will be enough," Hrald suggested.

Haward gave a short shake of his head. "She has spoken of going to Dane-mark. At Turcesig she has heard much of it."

Dane-mark, Hrald thought. She was young to think of this, but Siggerith might hold the same hope Dagmar had held once, that it was her true home. If she were to go, she might find nothing but strife. Hrald just nodded his head. If in future the girl was serious about leaving, Dagmar could speak to her of what she had found there.

The visit to Haward's hall left Dagmar feeling no less alone at Four Stones. It was partly the memory of her time there with Inkera, and Dagmar's memory of Inkera's cheer. She and her sister had been close as girls. If Inkera were not now wed, she might come to Four Stones, and help her. Even if she were wed, she, husband, and any babes would be more than welcome, should her husband be able to leave.

Dagmar broached this topic to Hrald next day. They were dressing in the treasure room, readying to join the hall in breaking their fast. His wife's slow and thoughtful manner of speaking told him her thoughts concerned her.

"I would like to see Inkera, to invite her here . . . Could you send a man to Headleage, to see if she can join me?"

It was the first request Dagmar had made of him. And it was reminder to Hrald of how alone Dagmar was. He did not need to consider who he would send on such a task. Kjeld, so often confined to Four Stones, always relished a chance to ride out. The journey to Headleage, and from there perhaps on to other halls, would be welcome diversion for him.

"I will send Kjeld, with another man, to carry her back should she wish to come," he answered without pause.

Dagmar's face showed her gratitude. Inkera's safety was such that he would send his second in command after her.

Kjeld knew the route, having once travelled to Headleage to deliver a gift of silver to the woman Bodil, Dagmar's mother. He had found her a drink-addled harridan. Now he could return, and for the young sister, Inkera. Kjeld had met her when Dagmar and Inkera came to Four Stones for their first visit. Unless some mishap had befallen the girl, Kjeld should find her far more pleasant to approach, and invite.

Dagmar would write a letter to her sister, bidding her come, and also as proof it was she who asked. Inkera might not recall Kjeld, and she must feel safe travelling with him. Only one at Four Stones made, and kept parchment here, and Dagmar need apply to him. She found him in his house, as was his wont. She voiced her request as respectfully as she could.

"Father Wilgot, may I have a piece of parchment. I would write to my sister Inkera at Headleage."

Wilgot's lips pursed in surprise.

Dagmar could write but little, and Inkera even less, but her sister knew the look of both their names, and Dagmar would make sure that Kjeld's message was accompanied by her own greeting to her.

"A small piece will do," Dagmar went on. She knew how costly parchment was, and also did not wish to make the priest expect she would pen a long missive.

Wilgot studied the woman before him. Here was a temptress, a Jezebel if he had ever met one, asking for his help. She, after all, was the root of Hrald's penance. The priest gave his head a slight shake, attempting to drive his own misstep in that matter from his mind. He had lost the fine carved chair that had stood against his wall, not that he had ever sat in it, but it had been an admirable resting place for important objects. Now it was back into the service Hrald had it made for, Dagmar's chair at the high table. A smaller one took its place, that the Lady Pega had occupied. These earthly concerns ran through the priest's mind in rapid sequence, and then he squared his shoulders. He overcame his inner judgement, hard as it was against this daughter of Guthrum. She had supplied the bell, that was true. Wilgot gave a slight inclination of his head.

"Of course, Lady Dagmar," he answered, and turned to the table where he wrote and read. There were a few larger trimmings from the squaring of quires, and one with a rounded portion from where the lambskin reached up the back of the animal's neck. He took knife and ruler and scored through this, squaring it for her. It was no larger than the palm of her hand.

He held it to her. "That is fine," she answered. All writing was difficult, but writing in smaller letters even more so. Dagmar would make do with what he had given her.

"Would you sit here, Lady, and compose your message?"

She had no choice, as his were the quills and ink. Dagmar nodded and pulled the bench closer to the table. She seated herself as he brought forth a small dish of ink and a selection of quills. He made a clean point on one, for which she was glad, as she did not wish to spoil one with poor cuts to form her tip.

Dagmar's letter was the briefest:

INKERA Please Come. DAGMAR

She added the rune Gyfu, gift X after her name, that Inkera would know her coming would be a gift to Dagmar, and that good awaited her. Then too, there would be added message in the silver Kjeld would pass to Inkera. It was as much as Dagmar could do.

Kjeld prepared to set off next day from Four Stones to find Dagmar's sister. The Lady thereof had given Kjeld her letter, the smallest Kjeld had ever seen. Nonetheless Dagmar stitched up a sleeve of linen for the little square, that it might not get soiled in transit. She also gave Kjeld a leathern purse with three score silver coins in it, to give to her sister.

Hrald too had supplied Kjeld with silver, so if he found Inkera he might buy a waggon for her and her goods. Kjeld would need a second man to drive the waggon, and Hrald told him to select he most fitting. Kjeld mentioned this to Yrling, who at once offered himself. Kjeld only laughed. Yrling may have driven a horse-drawn waggon at some point on Gotland, but here at Four Stones only the most skilled handlers of teams would be allowed to do so. Such a waggon was a prime target for brigands, and the driver must be ready to urge the horses to a frenzied pace. Keeping control of the animals under such stress, understanding how much could be asked, not only of the beasts but the waggon they pulled, was knowledge gained through long experience.

"Well," Yrling offered, "you will need a rear guard, whether you have a waggon or not. Let me ride with you, Kjeld."

Kjeld just shook his head. Yrling was nothing if not persistent, and went on.

"Hrald always tells me to shadow you. I have, and have learnt much you have shown me. This is but another chance to learn from you."

Here Kjeld had to laugh. Yrling did have a point, even if he would not admit it to the youth.

"And you will bring Lady Dagmar's sister. She is a Lady, deserving of the Jarl's brother to greet, and escort her."

Kjeld must pause at this reasoning. It was impossible not to admire the cleverness of the boy. The brightness of Yrling's eyes as he smiled at Kjeld said as much. Yrling's wheedling had worked, and Kjeld put up his hands in surrender.

"If the Jarl consents, you will come," he conceded. "And as my rear guard. I will ask one good with driving horses for my true second."

On their horses the ride down to Headleage should take three or four days, assuming good weather and no mud. If they returned with a waggon and the young woman Kjeld sought, the trip back might be twice as long. Yrling had wanted to wear his new sword, that called Stronger in the Norse tongue, but Kjeld shook his head and told him he would carry a spear. The showy weapon would attract unwanted attention, and Yrling scarcely knew how to use it to advantage.

They set off with Kjeld riding side by side with Orri, a man well-skilled in driving. Kjeld made certain Orri's mount was heavy enough to pull a small waggon, should they find Dagmar's sister. Yrling trailed behind. There should in fact be little need for a rear guard on this route, but Kjeld, having survived many an ambush, was ever cautious, and he was in command of these two men, and the younger of them the Jarl's own brother. At times Orri switched positions with Yrling, giving the youngster plenty of time to talk with Kjeld, who of Hrald's full-fledged warriors was much Yrling's favourite. Kjeld, as second at Four Stones, commanded great respect throughout the hall; only Jari, for his age and experience, was more admired than Kjeld. As Hrald's kin it was natural to Yrling that he be oftentimes in Kjeld's company, especially as his brother had often assigned him to be so. If it led Yrling to take certain liberties, Kjeld himself was quick to correct him.

At the open palisade gates of Headleage Kjeld announced he was sent from Dagmar, Lady of Four Stones, to find her sister, Inkera. They were rough from camping, but now arrived, Kjeld felt the need to see her at once, if she were here. The three passed through quickly enough, and were told to seek out a timber building topped with a ship's wind-vane down the main road of the settlement. They scanned the rooflines and found it easily; the vane must have come from a long-ago war-ship. The hall had its own wattle fence surrounding it, and the quantity of ducks and hens within spoke to the need for this. There was a woman working amongst them, scattering grain from a pan balanced on her hip, who when asked, shrilled out Inkera's name. In short order a yellow-haired woman came out from the hall, brushing her hands together to free them of the dust of what she had been handling.

Kjeld knew her at once as Inkera, and had the slip of parchment which was Dagmar's letter in his hand. Yrling, at his side, had not expected her to be so pretty, nor so young. As sister to Dagmar, she might be older than she, and this he had assumed.

Yrling opened his mouth to speak, but Kjeld cut him off.

"I am Kjeld, from Four Stones. I am second there; you might remember me from your visit with your sister Dagmar. She is once again Lady."

Inkera's astonishment caused her lips to part. She had heard that Dagmar had been cast out, and over her old lover, Vigmund, and then vanished. Now she was back.

Kjeld went on with the story. "Hrald had wed again, to a Lady of Mercia. That marriage was dissolved. Hrald brought Dagmar back to Four Stones, and with their son. He and Dagmar were once again wed, at Oundle, some two months ago."

This was much to take in, but of greatest moment was that Dagmar was not only alive and well, but had been restored to her former estate.

"If you can, Dagmar would have you come to Four Stones," Kjeld went on. "She has written you a letter, so you know this is true." He handed her the linen-covered square of parchment. Inkera pulled it free from its sleeve. There was her own name, and Dagmar's, and the rune Gyfu. Good will follow.

"Já, I can," Inkera said. Her ready answer, the first words she had spoken, seemed to indicate her own estate. If Inkera had wed, her husband would have a role here at Headleage, and they must at least discuss this offer.

"Good," Kjeld answered, glad that she would come. Now he would present the youth at his side. "This is Hrald's brother, Yrling. He was born and raised on Gotland, but has been living with us at Four Stones for some time."

Yrling could finally speak. "It is only right that I should escort you to my brother's hall," he said.

Inkera smiled at the youth. "That is kind, and I thank you, Yrling."

Yrling was trying to think of some flattering thing to add, but Kjeld spoke again.

"Can you make a start, tomorrow? We are five or six days from Four Stones. I will buy a waggon to carry you and your goods." Kjeld gestured to a third man now. "Orri is a good driver, so you will be well escorted."

Inkera was nodding her head.

"Dagmar has sent you silver, so you might buy what you need for the journey, to furnish the waggon." Kjeld did not forget the second part of Dagmar's instruction. "And to settle any debts you might have."

Here he handed her a small pouch from his belt.

Inkera bit her lip, to keep it from quivering. Dagmar knew too well how meagre might be her resources. Inkera had scant silver to buy what was needful for the journey, or for her leave-taking.

"I will be ready at daybreak," she promised. "This is the hall of Steinn, one of my brothers. You can stay here tonight, that we might all leave the quicker."

"My men and I will go find a waggon," Kjeld ended.

Yrling lingered as Kjeld began to turn away, and finally spoke. "Do you need help packing, my Lady?"

Inkera gave a small laugh. "I have but my clothes, and a few small items. But I thank you for the offer."

"Yrling. We need your help," Kjeld reminded. He might have laughed at Yrling's attempts with her, save that the pool of young maids at Four Stones was limited.

Kjeld could well understand Inkera's willingness to leave Headleage. Her brother Steinn, wary-eyed and surly, could not conceal his envy that his sister had been so summoned, and came close to taunting both Inkera and Kjeld over the supposed riches of Four Stones, and the admiration of the King of Wessex for its young Jarl. Steinn had supported Haesten in his efforts to overrun Wessex, and though he escaped with his life, had lost both silver and land. Their reception was so cold that even Yrling took note when Kjeld did not name him as Hrald's brother, for fear of the youth being seized and held to ransom. None from Four Stones rested easy in their alcoves that night, and were more than glad to be up and on their way.

Orri was already at the waggon, easing his horse between the shafts. Inkera for her part had been busy the prior day buying bedding and other necessaries required for the journey, and guiding Kjeld in the procuring of grain, eggs, and cheese for the journey. Kjeld looked upon what she had assembled for the waggon with admiration, and no little surprise. This was a woman who had been much on the road. This morning she came forth from some other dwelling wherein she slept, carrying a large basket, and at last Yrling was put into service for her. He walked back to where her chest of goods awaited. She made one final stop at the kitchen-yard for some ready provender with which to break their fast, as none wished to linger.

They set out into the cool morning, heading north, and west. On the trip back to Four Stones, Yrling's sole position was as rear guard, trailing the waggon holding Inkera. Orri served as driver, and Kjeld rode as lead. Denied of company, it gave Yrling time to think. He had been away from Gotland now for three years. At times he missed the island, small as it now seemed. He remembered his mother, for she could make him laugh, and she was just when he and Eirian had teasing fights when they were younger. Tindr was often in Yrling's mind, and he wished he had spent more time with him, but he had been careful to keep up his bow-work and fully planned to take a deer of his own this Winter. Now that he had his sword Sterkari, being an archer no longer held the same allure, but every group of warriors needed men good at it. And no one could hunt a deer with a sword, he knew.

Most of all Yrling missed his father. Once he came to Four Stones and saw all it held, he could not understand how his father turned his back on it. But then as much as Yrling admired his father, there were many things he did not understand about him. His father had deep faith in the Gods, yet often times laughed at their ways. No one who accepted the Christian God laughed at him, Yrling saw that right away. Though Lady Ælfwyn had made him get baptised, it did not take, but Yrling knew he did not believe in the Gods as his father did. Here his brother Hrald was Christian, and there was no one with whom Yrling could observe the feasts and sacrifices they held at Tyrsborg. Even at Blót, that blood-festival just before the onset of Winter, there were no added sacrifices to the Gods or to God, just late harvest feasting as animals who could not be kept over were killed and their meat roasted, smoked, or dried. It was only at Turcesig sacrifices were made, and Asberg said, by fewer men every year. Here at Four Stones Yrling had no one to join him at the Place of Offering when he took a cock from the fowl-houses and Offered it there. Alone, the act lost its savour, and almost its meaning. He had such strong memories of his family on Gotland, joined by Tindr and Rannveig, doing this, and then walking back to a fine meal.

Sidroc had shown and told Yrling many more things as well. His father had taught him and Eirian about their family-spirit, their fylgia, and how they must train themselves to hear, and then listen to her voice. It had never meant much to Yrling until he had hidden from the slavers on the road to Jorvik. His heart was pounding out of his chest, but he felt he heard his fylgia tell him when to make a run for it.

Riding behind the waggon, seeing the landscape of trees and marshland pass, Yrling thought these things, and more. He could not be Jarl here; Hrald was Jarl, and now had a son, and Four Stones would be his one day. And Hrald was young and should live a long time, at least Yrling hoped he would. And Yrling could not be Jarl because he was not a Christian, and Hrald said that all must be believers now. He would learn what he could from Kjeld and Hrald and when he was older return to Jorvik and seek Aszur Gold Tooth, and together they would go find silk and spices. Yrling had better win some silver before then. He found himself shrugging his shoulders in his saddle. His mother had told Yrling his was a restless nature, and he guessed now she might be right. He looked at the back of the waggon he trailed. It was lonely riding rear guard, without Bork.

SECOND IN COMMAND

INKERA arrived in a deluge. The rain had begun when they were still a two-day journey from Four Stones. The light waggon Kjeld had purchased, suitable to be drawn by a single horse, was little more than a jog cart, and open. As the rain came pelting down they had the fortune to spot the grey smoke of a cook-fire rising amongst the trees, and followed it. The croft there sheltered them, and the folk thereof had cow hides with which to hammer up a shelter over the waggon bed. This took a day, giving them time to dry out by the fire. Then they were off again, in more rain. The riders got wet, but Inkera, if she stayed off the waggon board and deeper into the body of the cart, was kept mainly dry.

The rain did not relent when they reached the gates of Four Stones. So it was, damp, bedraggled, but with a smile, she was helped down by Kjeld. From there, Inkera ran to the arms of her waiting sister.

Dagmar must laugh. "To arrive in rain, they say, brings abundance."

"Well, I am here now," Inkera laughed back, "and wet, in abundance."

Her things were carried up to the weaving room; she would sleep there, as did Eanflad and Wite. But now Dagmar was as eager to be alone with her sister as Inkera was.

"Let us go to the bower house, and speak there," Dagmar decided. "Hroft is asleep in the weaving room, with his nurse-maid, Wite, and Eanflad. You will soon meet him."

They held light cloaks above their heads to spare them-selves from the worst of the rain. Once inside a serving woman came and brought them ale in a ewer, with cups which had collected a few raindrops on the way. It made both sisters laugh as they tapped the water out. The woman had also brought a wooden box, which revealed small seeded cakes, thankfully dry. It would keep them both until the hall was called for supper.

They spent some time just gazing at the other, as those who have been parted do. To Dagmar's eyes Inkera had changed not a whit. She was surprised to hear her say nearly the same about her.

"You are as beautiful as ever," Inkera told her. Her ready smile seemed to underscore that, but Dagmar gave a slight laugh.

"You were always kind, Inkera. I feel ten years have passed since we came here together. But I am happy now, and that does much."

Inkera nodded, but then bit her lip. She must not delay the telling of the most important news.

"Bodil is dead," she murmured.

Dagmar turned her face away. Her mother was dead. Bodil, the drunken slattern whose gross advances Vigmund rebuffed. Then, in a fit of jealous rage over her daughter,

Bodil went to Guthrum and had Vigmund outlawed, and thus hopelessly parted from Dagmar.

Now both Vigmund and Bodil were dead. The same numbness she had always felt when she recalled her mother spread through her.

"I was not there," Inkera went on, "but at our brother Agmund's hall."

This brother, from yet another wife to the Danish King, was more than a score of years older than either Inkera or Dagmar, and had been Guthrum's chief heir.

"When I returned to Headleage I asked about her. Bodil was even then dying. She had not been seen for some days. At last men broke down her door — she had it barred — to find her lying within. She was alive, but barely. Her body was swollen, and her skin, yellow. The herb-women did what they could for her, but she died that same day.

"I looked about her place to see if there was anything I could save, lest I see you again. It was bare. There was nothing left."

Dagmar could answer this. "She had sold anything of value, to pay for drink."

Inkera nodded. "Yes, that; and to stay alive. There was little food in the place."

Dagmar closed her eyes. The house had become a near-hovel long before she had left it. She recalled how she had pleaded with Ælfwyn not to send Bodil silver, as she would only drink it up. Silver had been sent, nonetheless. Whether it prolonged her life or hastened her death Dagmar would never know.

"Where . . . where was she buried?"

"Not by our father. Guthrum rests in consecrated ground. But she is not far off."

Inkera thought a moment, then looked back to her sister. "The silver you sent – I needed it, Dagmar. Thank you. I did in fact have debts. And it allowed me to give small sums to a few who were kind to me. If I return to Headleage to live, their good will might serve me. But much silver remains; I will give it back to you."

Dagmar gave a single, decided shake of her head. "It is yours, to keep."

Inkera murmured her thanks, and a moment passed in silence. Then she asked a quiet question.

"Why do you think father left us nothing? He was kind to us in life."

Dagmar breathed a sigh. "I have thought much on it. That it was purposeful there was no doubt. I think he wanted us to be desired for our own sakes, and for his bloodline, and not for any treasure we brought. Perhaps he even did us a favour in this; spared us men vying for us, when they only wanted silver and land."

Inkera looked down, but gave a nod. "How glad I am that you now have silver."

It was Dagmar's turn to pause. "All silver is won at the cost of blood."

They were both quiet, until Dagmar spoke again.

"How is your own mother?"

"Inger is well; she made a good match at last, though there is not much left over for the likes of me. She has his four younger boys to feed and clothe."

Dagmar touched her hand. "You have a home here, as long as you like, Inkera."

In the days following Inkera's arrival, Kjeld found himself looking at her. He did this often enough that at times Inkera noticed, and looked back. Her expression was not easy to read. She was one who smiled easily, but her look was closer to that of inquiry, Kjeld thought. When she caught him staring, he would give a quick nod, and look away.

Kjeld was not alone in his looking. So few young women ever came to Four Stones that Inkera's presence was noted by all. It was true that girlish maids about the hall, or those living out by the valley of horses, could transform into young woman with surprising speed, and turn heads. Inkera did this, and more. She was not only Dagmar's kin, but it was thought she was meaning to remain.

One who was attracted was the youngest who had gone to fetch her from Headleage. Yrling knew Inkera was several years his elder, and it mattered not. She had impressed him, and he worked to impress her in return. He made show of bringing the hounds to her in the stable-yard, both Myrkri and her daughter, which Hrald had given him. Yrling had named the dog Ör, arrow, and well named she was, for she was as sleek as a fletched arrow in action, long legs extended nearly straight out as she ran. Inkera was happy to pet and stroke the dogs, leading Yrling to invite her to go hunting with him. Inkera laughed, but not unkindly. As this was going on Kjeld walked by. He saw Yrling, holding the collars of both animals, as he tried to draw nearer to the fair-haired Inkera. Kjeld wished he had some sudden task to call Yrling to; he did not, but found himself smiling at the boy's efforts.

As the days and nights went on, Kjeld could not help but think more on Inkera. Though to sup she sat with the widows and unwed maids at the women's table, she was much about the hall, and in Dagmar's company as she went about the tasks demanded of a Lady. Wite was oftentimes in charge of Hroft, but sometimes Inkera took him, a scene with its own appeal, as she took delight in the boy. Beyond this Kjeld found Inkera quite pretty, and even approachable. He allowed himself to wonder about this amiable, yellow-haired maid. Kjeld did not know what it was to be wanted. Mealla had rebuffed his advances so long that Kjeld found the prospect of being himself desired a sensation unexpected, but welcome. He had courted Mealla fruitlessly, if courtship it could be called, and as he looked at Inkera he felt himself nearly coiled like a spring to act.

There was much to tempt his eye. There was a sweet plumpness to Inkera's form, adding to the contrast with Mealla's angularity, and Kjeld thought, temperament. And she knew how to laugh; she had a smile upon her pretty lips more often than not. Kjeld liked her; if she did not possess the striking looks of the lost maid of Éireann, Inkera had a fair comeliness that most men would find greatly pleasing. Mealla had been as slender and straight as rod, and, Kjeld had learnt, just as unbending. Inkera was shorter, and with a softness to face and form to make her a welcome armful.

Yet Kjeld must hesitate. He felt he might commit a grave overstep if he declared himself, either to Hrald or Inkera directly. Then he would correct himself. Indeed, the other men might look, but could do little more than that. She was the Jarl's sister-in-law, after all, and in her own right a daughter of Guthrum. Kjeld bethought himself of who else other than the second in command of Four Stones might be worthy of such a woman. No one here, he thought; but then recalled Ulf and Abi, Asberg's two sons, strapping young men, and neither wed yet, or pledged to any. Inkera might be a few years older than they, but this had never proved impediment when a man wanted to wed, especially if his family wished the union. For that matter, there was even Yrling to consider, though he had so often spoken of the travelling he hoped to do. Even so, Kjeld began to think he must move soon, if he wished to win her. If he did not marry now, and to such a fine woman as Inkera, then elsewhen? It might be never.

He found himself speaking to Hrald. Kjeld waited until they had cause to ride out to the valley of horses; he did not feel he could broach the subject at the hall. They had dismounted and were looking over a few animals which might be sold. After discussing the merits of several, Kjeld changed the subject.

"Inkera. She is your wife's sister."

"Já," Hrald agreed, though he was sure Kjeld knew her history. "From a younger wife; I think she who Guthrum wed after Bodil, Dagmar's mother."

Yet the women were close to each other, with no seeming rivalry nor enmity, despite the mother of Inkera having replaced Dagmar's mother in the affections of their father.

Kjeld went ahead and said it. "I would like to . . . know Inkera more."

It took Hrald a moment to ken the deeper import. "Já," he affirmed. He began to smile, but was forced to add a caution. "But if what Haward told me is true, she owns little."

It mattered not if Inkera had no silver. Mealla had owned little or nothing, just the good-will and affection of Lady Pega. Kjeld felt that Inkera had the same from Lady Dagmar.

Hrald went on. "Inkera is also a daughter of Guthrum. Her blood cannot be bettered."

Kjeld was aware of this parentage, but was struck anew at this truth. His own father had been born one of several sons in a struggling farm family in Dane-mark. He had come with many other hopeful young Danes to Angle-land, seeking a modicum of treasure, but especially land on which to farm. To win treasure one must join a war-band. Kjeld's father did so, with a war-chief whose success did not meet his boasts. But he had met a woman then, and Kjeld had resulted. Kjeld was not certain if his mother had been a Dane, or of Angle-land, his memory of her was so slight. All he truly recalled was sitting on the saddle before his father as the two of them made their way north, looking for a war-band in which his father's services as warrior could be put to use. It brought them to Four Stones, and he won a place in Sidroc's ranks. Kjeld had truly come from nothing. Now there was a chance to wed a daughter of the man who in Kjeld's boyhood had been named King of all the Danes in Angle-land. He thought of his father, long-dead, and what he would have said at such a prospect.

Kjeld said the next. "She is as pretty as a man could hope."

Hrald had his own memory of the first time seeing Inkera, and how he had been forced to smile at her fresh loveliness. A moment later Dagmar had appeared.

Hrald made what offer he could. "I will speak to Dagmar about her, if you like." It might save Kjeld from a painful rejection, which Hrald knew was all Mealla had ever served him with.

But his second in command preferred to be accepted on his own merits, few as they might appear, to a daughter of Guthrum.

"Nej," he answered. Kjeld had a fat bag of silver, good weaponry, and three horses. More than that, he had won Hrald's trust, and that of Hrald's men. It gave him confidence to say the next.

"I will speak to Inkera myself," he answered. He would learn at once if she would countenance such a match, and not allow himself to be toyed with as had the maid of Éireann.

Hrald nodded. The fact remained that Inkera must now be above twenty years, and still not wed. She may have had few choices, or perhaps had held out in hope for a richer match, or had simply not found a man who valued her as she hoped to be valued.

"Try your hand with her." Hrald looked at the men moving about the horses. "Also – there are many men at Four Stones."

Kjeld gave a short laugh. "Já. Time to get my oar in the water."

It took a day for Kjeld to act. He knew that each late morning, Inkera and Dagmar spent time at the bower house, either in the garden, mending or spinning in the good light, or inside the little house itself. In such a setting he would be able to speak to her away from any other men. None but Hrald, or the rare guest such as the Bailiff of Defenas, was ever permitted within its confines. Kjeld put on a clean tunic and combed his hair. Then he made for the bower house.

Inkera was there, sitting at the garden table with both Dagmar and Wite. Hroft stood on the ground, prattling happily, walking from chair to chair, holding on to the legs as he toddled around them. The three women sat absorbed over their hand-work, with Kjeld at the gate, his eyes boring at Inkera's lowered head. Kjeld cleared his throat, rather louder than was necessary. Inkera raised that yellow-crowned head, and saw him, as did Dagmar. So clear was Kjeld's intent to catch Inkera's eye, even from this distance, that the Lady of Four Stones rose. "Wite," she proposed. "We will take Hroft inside now; he will be wanting his nap soon."

So it was that Inkera stood, and leaving her sewing behind, came to the gate. She approached with that same look of mild inquiry she had worn when she had before caught Kjeld staring. His eyes were fixed on her as she neared; he could not help it. Kjeld swallowed. He felt himself at a gaming table, ready to disclose all, and see which way the dice fell.

"I am Kjeld," he began, a fact which Inkera well knew. She gave a slight smile at this.

"Hrald made me second in command, and I have been so for four years. My father was from Jutland, as many of our fathers were. I am not sure from where; a place with shifting sand which filled the fields and caused folk to go hungry. It could not have been far from the coast, I think. He went for a warrior, came here to Angle-land, and served with two or three chiefs before he came to Four Stones, and Sidroc accepted him into the ranks. I was a boy then, and lived in the village. I think I am pure Dane, but I do not know.

"I have amassed a good store of silver, several weapons of worth, and three horses, all fine beasts. Saddles too," he remembered. He thought of what else might recommend him to such a maid. "I game but little. I do not get drunk, not even at feasts; I am second here and cannot do so."

Inkera nodded. It was true; some must keep a clear head, even when the chief himself might be riotous with drink. The hall would be in Kjeld's keeping during such occasions, even when Hrald was not away.

Now came the most difficult portion of Kjeld's disclosure.

"After Dagmar left, Hrald wed another Lady, named Pega, one of Mercia. She came with her companion, a maid of Éireann. I fastened upon this maid, but she would not have me. I had hoped over time she would soften; she did not." Kjeld looked down. "She did not like Danes . . .

"When Lady Pega broke the union, this maid returned here to pack up Pega's goods, and said Fare-well to me."

The finality in this was unmistakable.

"That is all I can tell you. I have had no wife. And I want one."

Inkera had to blink at this. Direct it was, but the gravity behind his words could not be discounted. It was, she knew, no time for coy rejoinders.

"I am Dagmar's youngest sister, with a different mother. I have never been wed. You will know that our father, as open-handed as he was to us in life, left us nothing in death. I have the gems and silver I wear, and little else. Because of this, few men would look at us with anything other than lust. I have my own pride. If I were to wed, it must be a man who thought not on a single night with me, but of a lifetime spent together. It is true I have shifted from hall to hall; those of cousins, half-brothers, any who would shelter me."

She was as frank with him as he had been to her. Kjeld gave a nod of encouragement. "And now you are with Dagmar, your half-sister."

She nodded. "Dagmar is different. We were always close. I admired her. Who could not? I grieved at her fall from this place. Now she has returned, and called for me to keep her company. And I am more than happy to do so."

Inkera considered Kjeld. He was not perhaps a man a maid would turn around to look at; but if she had, the effort would have been rewarded. There was a forthright manliness in face and bearing, enough to compensate for any lack of outright handsomeness. His hair was thick and light brown, his eyes framed with darker lashes which seemed to underscore their earnestness. Kjeld had about him a quiet authority, an ease with which he moved amongst the men. Inkera, as daughter of Guthrum, had seen much of swagger in her father's halls. Kjeld had none of that. And Dagmar liked, and trusted Kjeld.

Kjeld took a breath. "Would you then be happy to remain here at Four Stones, and wed one of its men?" He paused but a moment before going on. "One who is second in command?"

Inkera's pause was only a moment longer. "If you speak of the man Kjeld, I would be happy to remain here, and be his wife."

They were still parted by the low gate between them, but he reached for and took her hand. He held it first tentatively, then with a grasp warm and strong.

"I Kjeld, make fast my hand with yours, Inkera, daughter of Guthrum."

"I Inkera, daughter of Guthrum, make fast my hand with yours. Kjeld, son . . . "

"Son of Njal," he supplied.

"Son of Njal," she finished.

He leant over the gate and kissed her. Inkera kissed him back, even placing her free hand on his face as she did so. "You will not regret this, Inkera, daughter of Guthrum," Kjeld whispered, when he could again speak.

It took a moment for Inkera to collect herself. She opened the gate and stepped out to his side.

"I will tell the Jarl," Kjeld said. "Then we can go to the door of the church, and the priest will bless us." This would be important to Hrald, Kjeld knew, which is why he suggested it.

"Yes. That will be fine," Inkera answered, and smiled.

They did so, but not alone. Joining the new couple at the door of the timber church were Hrald and Dagmar, Wite and Hroft, and Jari, all there to witness and add their good wishes. Yrling, catching wind of something afoot, appeared, and though his cheek coloured when Kjeld told him what was about to occur, offered his own respects, and stood at Jari's side. As the priest spoke, Kjeld remembered the promise of the Abbess, that she would pray that a worthy woman appear in his life. Now that woman stood next him.

After the blessing the party walked to the hall, to take mead in the treasure room. Dagmar and Inkera walked arm-in-arm, smiling together as they made their way. Hrald fell into step with Kjeld. The Jarl was not unaware of his good fortune in having such a warrior as Kjeld to serve as second, not only in his worth as a fighting man, but in his sound judgement. Hrald knew from Jari and Asberg that when his grand-uncle Yrling was Jarl, and his own father Sidroc as well, good men stayed with their war-chief only as long as was needed to acquire weapons and silver of their own. Then, more often than not, they struck out on their own. It was true that there was little left to be claimed these days, but the repute of good men was known amongst others, who could lure them away to other halls with promise of greater reward. Hrald must do justice to Kjeld, and spoke.

"Inkera is sister to Dagmar, and thus kin to me. I will add to her dowry with a good mare, and a good stallion from the valley of horses, any you choose."

Kjeld blinked at his open-handedness. He had never expected this. "But the bride-price – I have offered you nothing for her . . . "

Hrald made answer. "That is in your service to me, Kjeld."

FATHER AND SON

Gotland

W ORD of his father came to Sidroc from a fishing boat, come round from the tip of the island to land in the cove above which stood Tyrsborg. The man who helmed her enquired at Rannveig's brew house where he might find Sidroc the Dane, and was directed up the hill. The dog Flekkr was the first to greet him, with a happy bark and a swishing of his curled tail, followed by yips into the air to alert others of the arrival of a visitor. Ceridwen was just inside the open door at her loom, and stepped outside, blinking in the still-bright Sun. Sidroc was outside stacking wood for the coming cold, and strode from around the back of the hall to meet the newcomer by the gable end.

"I see you are Sidroc," were the man's first words. He was perhaps in his sixth decade, grey-bearded, and slightly winded from the climb, despite the weathered toughness of his face, and wiry fitness of his form. "Your father is my friend, and I fish not far from his farm. My name is Lifrid."

"Is he well," Sidroc asked, his worry clear upon his brow.

"Hrald is well," the fisherman told him, lifting his hand to stay this concern. "It is Stenhild, his wife. She is failing. Her heart has been weak a long time, and her skin takes on a blue cast. She cannot rise from her bed. Hrald will not leave her, so I offered to sail. You can return with me, if you like."

A glance down the hill told Sidroc the small broad-bottomed fishing boat tied up at the pier must be that Lifrid had sailed. Sidroc turned back to the man, but shook his head. He could ride across the island in less time than it could sail such a distance.

"I will leave now, overland, and take two horses, so that one keeps fresh. I will be there by tomorrow night." He recalled himself and added, "I thank you for coming. Our cook will feed you, and Rannveig down the hill will give you ale." In fact Gunnvor had appeared from the kitchen yard, and gestured to the man to follow.

Ceridwen, listening, felt words rise to her lips. Her first instinct was to go with her husband. The couple Ottar and Runa who also lived with Hrald would have their hands full, and she could be of service nursing Stenhild, or merely helping in their daily chores. She might give comfort to Sidroc's father, and Sidroc himself, for the old man was sure to be in great distress. Yet that meant leaving Eirian and Rodiaud with Rannveig, and Helga and Gunnvor alone here. Tindr would come each day to tend to their animals, but even so . . . Ceridwen's thoughts reached their own end. She would slow Sidroc down, she knew this. She must dismiss the idea.

"I would I could come," is what she said.

"I know," he answered, with a nod. Yet if he took any with him it would be Tindr, way-finder as he was. But too many here depended on Tindr. There was his wife Ŝeará, their two children, and his mother Rannveig. And Tindr took care of all Tyrsborg's animals, a daytime presence which lent assurance to those times when Sidroc himself must be away.

"But the girls, the hall . . . " He gave a shake of his head. "I will go alone."

He readied his black stallion, and Yrling's gelding for pack. Helga and Gunnvor both helped with camping kit and provisions, while Ceridwen gathered a fresh set of clothes, towelling, and two blankets for his bedroll. Sidroc had made this trip before, both on horseback and driving a waggon, when he had brought his father and his wife to Tyrsborg to visit. Now he would travel in as much haste as his animals would allow.

He bid the fisherman Lifrid Fare-well, and again gave the man his thanks. It meant something that the elder Hrald had a friend who would trouble himself to bring such tidings, and Sidroc took his hand and wished him fair sailing, and that he see him soon at Hrald's farm.

A hug from Eirian and Rodiaud, a kiss from his wife, and he was off. It was not much past noon, and he could still make a good start until dusk halted his progress. He must pick through forestland thick with pine, lindens, and hornbeams, and skirt expanses of marshland, noisy with waterfowl resting during their flight south. Yet trails could be found, crisscrossing or edging both mere and woodland, and losing themselves over the lichen-dotted barrens of white limestone, to appear again in the scrub growth.

As Sidroc travelled north he thought of his own son, the younger Hrald. They had crossed the island together, to the south, to go to Paviken. Hrald had come to Gotland to tell

Sidroc and his shield-maiden that Ashild had been killed by a spear thrown by Ceric. After such sorrowful news the trip, alone and together between father and son, meant much. It was on this ride that Hrald told his father that he had been wed but briefly, to a daughter of Guthrum. Sidroc spent long thinking on these things. He had not dreamt again of his son, or his son's distress. He must trust that their shared guardian spirit, their fylgia, was guiding Hrald, as he could not. Now he could only help his aged father. He pressed on.

He rode until near-darkness halted him, guided by the Northly Star. He need find water for the horses and for he himself. It was almost meadowland he camped in, with grass thick enough to feed his animals, and a beck of trilling water edged by osiers. Sidroc need build no fire. Gunnvor had packed plenty of bread, cheese, and smoked meat. Then he unrolled his bedding, lay down on his back, and gazed up at stars, steadily brightening in the dark heavens. He did not want Stenhild to die before he reached his father.

Birds awakened him, the honking cries of wild geese on the wing. He sat up, recollecting where he was and why. He stood, blinking at the double trail of geese as they pulled through the dawn sky, strong wings rowing like oars. He ate more, readied the horses, and was off.

The smell of the sea came to him before the sight of it. He must travel a bit up the coast from where the oxcart track leading him on left him. It was not a day of strong Sun, and a chilling breeze off the water foretokened cold to come. He brought the horses down to the beach, as the walking was easier there. He again recalled his son Hrald, and the approach they had made to his father's farm the day they found him.

When that homestead came in sight, a curl of grey smoke rose above it, a welcome sign of habitation. As Sidroc rode up, the man Ottar appeared from the barn to greet him.

Ottar's wife Runa was within the house, in the act of urging Sidroc's father to eat what was in the bowl she offered him. Hrald saw his son bend his head to enter through the door. Then the old man rose from where he sat at the side of an alcove. Sidroc opened his arms to him, and the two embraced. The elder Hrald seemed almost beyond speech, but Sidroc just nodded his head, and gestured he return to the stool where he had been keeping mournful watch. Stenhild yet lived, and Sidroc was only glad he had arrived while she did. He stood behind his father and looked down on her as she lay. She was as pale as one might expect, and her lips did indeed have a bluish cast. Her breath came shallowly, and her eyes, for the time that Sidroc watched her, never fluttered open. The thin hands were already laid one upon another across her body. Stenhild looked at peace, anchored to this world by only the finest of threads. She was not ready to surrender it yet.

Runa told Sidroc that Hrald had scarce left Stenhild's side for a week. It made the son urge his father to join him outside. Fresh air in his lungs and a look at the animals would do him good, Sidroc felt certain. The old man protested, yet let Runa swathe him in a mantle, and he pulled on a woollen cap when Sidroc handed it to him. They stepped out into a fading afternoon. There was the barn, and in fact, Ottar was bringing in the three cows. Sidroc watched his father's face as he viewed them, hips swaying, as they walked in a line to be milked. The work of the farm and the needs of its animals went on, reassurance to all men who know trouble. They turned to face the gusts off the sea. The water was tipped with white-caps from the ever-freshening wind, lines of curling foam that took on an added brightness in the lowering light. The two men had hardly moved, but what they viewed had.

Finally Hrald shifted his gaze, out past the vegetable plots, now largely bedded save for dark forms of cabbages which lay huddled there.

He spoke to his son. "Sidroc. I have begun digging Stenhild's grave. She did not like fire, and wished to rest in the soil we farmed."

His son had to lower his head at this thought, of a man digging the grave of his beloved wife while she still lived.

"I did not finish it," Hrald went on. "I want to. And then when she is there, I will build a mound over her."

"Ottar and I will finish it, father. Now you need to stay with her, talk to her, so she knows you are still with her, and she, with you."

They walked back to the house together so Hrald could do just that.

The next morning Stenhild's daughter arrived, with her eldest girl, so there were hands enough to see to the needs of the farm, and the care of the ailing. Stenhild was more still than ever, and her daughter wept over her. Then she wiped her face in her apron and went about the task of laundry, for Runa had been hard pressed to do all.

Lifrid arrived, beaching his boat in the shingle of the beach. He had brought fish with him, a welcome and needful gift, as the living must eat.

Sidroc and Ottar finished digging Stenhild's grave. It was on a natural rise beyond the vegetable plots, and thus overlooked the sea. It was not easy digging. Beneath the thin layer of soil lay sand, then increasingly large pieces of limestone. They must use a pick to free and move some of them, but to sweat as they dug under the open sky was its own kind of cold comfort. When they at last were finished they looked down at the void. One did not think of a grave as being fine or well-made, yet there was a fitness even in this, that these two men had squared the corners, and dug to an even depth across the length of the space to receive the body. This task was for the living, and they had fulfilled it well. It was worthy of Hrald and his love for the woman who would rest here.

Stenhild died that night. She made a kind of gasp, as if in surprise. Then she quieted again, so that as her breath ebbed the further, none could tell which was her last. Hrald sat by the bed, his hand over hers. His head sunk down, almost chin to chest. Sidroc draped his arm around his father's shoulders. The old man raised his head to look at him, face running with silent tears.

In the morning the women washed and dressed the body. Of grave goods there would be few. Stenhild had not much she wished to take with her; when she began to sicken she had awarded her prized belongings to her daughter, and to Runa. A few items Hrald had given her she wished to wear, or be laid with, her spindle for one, for her hands were rarely still. Sidroc and Ottar lifted her and placed her on a broad plank. Together with Lifrid they led the way to the grave they had dug. Hrald followed with Stenhild's daughter on one side, and Runa on the other. The girl had gone off to gather greenery to lay upon her grandmother's chest, and after the men lowered the body in she dropped a small pine bough, ever-green, down upon her.

After Lifrid and the women took Hrald back to the house Sidroc and Ottar began filling the grave. Shovel after shovel they lifted, of sand, soil, and small stones. They began at the feet and worked forward, the earth raining down on her boots, and then her gown, and the living green of the needled pine. The face must be the last covered, so the dead knew where to sight in the afterlife. When it was time for the first shovelful to cover it, Sidroc lifted his eyes to the Heavens and spoke aloud.

"Frigg, here is your daughter, Stenhild. She was a good wife, and good mother. Take her to your side now."

Ottar made a sound, an acknowledgment of loss. The men kept on in their work.

That night there was a meal, as rich as Runa could make. Stenhild's daughter filled their cups. Hrald lifted his and said, "Stenhild made this mead." He began to weep, but he drank to celebrate she whom he grieved.

In the morning Sidroc again persuaded his father to come outdoors with him.

It was a clear day, crisp, and with promise of true warmth, as the Sun already shone strongly. Sidroc watched his father's eyes sweep about him, as if seeing all new.

He touched Hrald's arm and spoke. "Father, come home with me, to Tyrsborg."

The old man's eyes again grew bright with tears. He gestured across to the fresh mound. "And leave Stenhild behind?" His voice wavered as he uttered this.

"It is the farm you built together," Sidroc answered. "The land she loved. She asked to be buried here."

His father must nod; this all was true. Yet Sidroc could see his father's mouth work, in protest.

He moved so he faced his father, blocking his view of the mound.

"When I was a boy and you sundered your union with Ingirith, you told me that soon you and I would live together, and in peace."

It was the day Hrald's wife had caught up the young Sidroc for breaking a bowl, and holding him fast by his ear lobe, thrashed him with a rug beater, so that she ripped the base of his ear as he tried to turn away from her blows. The blood from his torn ear had run down his neck as he twisted to escape the forked tines lashing his legs and back.

Hrald needed no reminder of what had followed. After his angry dismissal of Ingirith he had comforted his son with that promise. He and Sidroc would live there at his farm, together with Hrald's young brother, Yrling, free from wasp-ish chiding and cruelty. Hrald needed first to be alone. What followed was the Fate-ful act of going out in his boat, which had changed the course of his life.

Sidroc stood before him, staring into his father's eyes. "We never had that home. We can have it now, at Tyrsborg."

Hrald hung his head. His boy, who had been denied so much, and yet prospered in life beyond all reckoning, was asking of him one boon. Hrald must grant it. Blear-eyed from grief at what he had just lost, he nodded his head.

"Já, Já, I will do that . . . "

Hrald and Stenhild had always planned to leave the farm to Runa and Ottar. Now there was no need for the faithful couple to wait until Hrald followed his wife in death. Sidroc had the two horses, but neither had been trained for driving. Nor would Hrald take the single small cart belonging to the farm; Ottar needed that. It was the fisherman Lifrid who again was of service, offering to ferry the two men and horses around the tip of the island and to the cove where sat Tyrsborg. If they caught the turning of the early tide they would be there in two days, for they must stop at night and beach; the horses would grow restless aboard so small a vessel.

Hrald packed the kit he had used in the past to go to the Althing in Roma, a bedroll and simple cookware, that they might warm their food when they made camp at night. He had also his clothing, spare as it was. Most important were a few tools he wished to keep, things he had wrought himself over the years to work the land or repair his buildings. As the old man sorted through these, Sidroc stopped to admire a heavy hammer. "You forged this," he said.

His father nodded.

"Our smith is named Berse," Sidroc told him. "An old warrior – one my age," he added, with a laugh. "He is gone right now, but when he returns we will go to his forge. He is a bladesmith, as well as skilled in the making of all manner of iron tools, and casting bronze."

Berse's broad form and bearded face rose in Sidroc's mind. He trusted the smith would return with Runulv and Eskil and all the rest who had gone after spice. That would be no sooner than Spring. Right now he would get his father to Tyrsborg, away from this farm and its recent sorrow.

Fare-wells were made. Hrald made a final walk to the new mound, to stand over it. Grass will grow and make for you a gown of green, he whispered. His hand rose to his eye, his knuckle pressing the single tear away from his cheek.

The boat was made ready. Lifrid had a smaller sail and changed to that, so there might be room for all. The horses were tied by two lines each, on port and starboard sides. The island's stiff winds served them in their transit, even carrying less sail. Still, when they beached that night near the southern tip of the island all were ready to stretch their legs upon the sand.

Tyrsborg came into view late the next afternoon. Tindr, having brought some jarred honey to his mother, was standing with Rannveig in her brewing shed, and they were the first to spot them. Tindr made a honking noise and strode out to the pier. His eyes had told him the truth; Scar's black horse was aboard, and Scar himself, with his son's animal too. He was ready to catch the line Scar flung to him, and as the captain of the little vessel pulled his steering oar up, Tindr hauled the boat to the wooden planking.

Rannveig was there to add her welcome. On past visits the elder Hrald and his wife had come several nights to the brew house to drink and game. The old man smiled at her now, in memory of that. Now he was alone, and the brewster thought, come to stay. She would send up a small cask of ale with Tindr, so they might spend this first night alone at Tyrsborg.

Ceridwen, alerted by Eirian's happy cries, came out to look down the hill. Flekker ran down toward the figures ascending to the steeply gabled hall. There was Sidroc, walking towards her, and leading the two horses he had left with. His father Hrald was at his side. She and Helga had prepared for this, and had an alcove ready for the old man. At this distance Ceridwen saw how thin was her father-in-law. All the men of Sidroc's line were lean, but Hrald was truly gaunt, and in need of feeding. Gunnvor's cookery would restore some of his lost flesh.

Perhaps the best welcome of all was that from Eirian. She threw her arms about Hrald, and planted a kiss upon his stubbled cheek.

"I have missed you, grandfather. Now I will not miss you again."

Hrald settled in well at Tyrsborg. His body, bowed from a lifetime of hard labour, seemed to straighten a bit. On this eastern side of the island it was sunrises and not sunsets he gazed at, a hopeful rising of the glowing orb fitting for his young granddaughters Eirian and little Rodiaud. Now free from many onerous duties, he still wished to keep his hand in the work of the farm. He was skilled with his small knife, and used it to whittle useful items, and those for pleasure as well. For Gunnvor and her cast iron pans Hrald shaped secure wooden handles to slide over those of iron, so that she might lift the lid without the use of a cloth to protect her hand. For little Rodiaud and Jaské, Tindr and Ŝeará's daughter, he shaped wooden horses and dogs to play with. And he spent time with the deaf hunter. Hrald liked Tindr, a feeling returned by the bow-hunter, for the old man was content to watch Tindr as he moved amongst the animals, but was ready to lend a hand where warranted. The milking was now done twice as quickly; Hrald took one of the cows, Tindr another. Hrald would laugh at the way the skogkatts would sit under the udder Tindr worked, and beg for warm milk to be squirted into their open mouths. This took practice, and after a few attempts Hrald made use of a shallow dish to collect a squirt, so that the cats did not end up soaking from the milk he directed their way. As day followed day Hrald became part and parcel of the larger family of Tyrsborg. When Sidroc and Tindr stacked firewood, Hrald stood nearby, splitting kindling, sometimes with Tindr's boy Juoksa doing the same.

Of greatest savour for the old man was spending time with Sidroc, sometimes talking of the past, other times in that silent companionship that brings two nearer in thought. It was not easy for either to speak about Sidroc's boyhood; he had been so abused by Ingirith that Hrald must close his eyes in shame to recall her ill-treatment of his son. But the times father and son had been alone and together were things they could return to. Even that day Sidroc had fallen overboard and nearly drowned could be recounted with satisfaction for what it had led to, the pleasure and freedom of Hrald teaching his son to swim. Most of the time the elder Hrald just wished to learn more of Sidroc's life, and that of his own younger brother, Yrling, as well as his nephew, Toki, scamp though he had been as a boy. For Sidroc to revisit those days, whether good or ill, with the distance gained through age, allowed him to see all with greater understanding.

He told of Ashild as well, that daughter of Yrling named after his, and his father's own mother. Sidroc had once compared Ashild to an eagle, and she had soared. None who witnessed her action in the defence of Oundle could gainsay this. Sidroc had missed years of her growing up, as he had for his son Hrald and daughter Ealhswith. Father and son were paired in this, missing during key stages of their offsprings' growth. The sober fact was there, not often directly spoken of, but a link bridging the two: what had been lost.

Hrald went often to Rannveig's brew house, both with his son and daughter-in-law, and with Sidroc alone. Soon Hrald began walking down the hill nearly every night to play a game of tæfel with a few other elders who haunted the place. They were the same men who gathered at the mouth of the pier in trading season, watching for ships, and catching the thrown lines for traders coming to land. These were old fishermen, all, and many were the tales they could tell of nets filled to bursting with herring and cod. Now that Hrald had met them he could join their gathering at the pier's end, when the weather warmed.

Perhaps most vital to the elder Hrald's growing content was the sense of again being part of a true home. He had always regarded Ceridwen with a kind of reverence, and not only for her coming from the folk dwelling in the distant western lands from which, as a young man, he had traded for the salt which first brought him to Gotland. It was also her manner and person. That she was high-born he had no doubt; she had a beauty allied in his mind with riches. Seeing what Sidroc had made of himself, it was only fitting he had won such a prize as she. The welcoming kindness she had at once extended to him and Stenhild only deepened as he settled in to the life of the hall.

One evening as Hrald sat watching Ceridwen rise from the table to replenish their ale, he murmured to his son, words of loving lament.

"You must die before she does, and spare yourself."

Sidroc took a quiet breath. Then he reached his hand and placed it on top of his father's.

ALL THE SPLENDOURS
OF THE EAST

Miklagårdr

O PEN water had never looked so welcoming to Runulv. Gazing upon it he and Eskil and their men could not help but whoop in sheer relief to find themselves at the mouth of the Black Sea. Their trading party now numbered nine-and-thirty men, total, for two Gotlanders and one Svear had been lost along the treacherous route they had just completed. For transport they had Sidroc's drekar, Dauðadagr, and five of the six smaller boats they received from the Princes Karlen and Demyan. One of the flat bottomed karvs had been destroyed in portage over the Aeifur falls, and the other four boats were basic yet sturdy dugouts. One look at the waves curling towards the shore told them now was the time to surrender these for a larger vessel.

They had their pick. Flanking either side of the River Dnieper as it spilled into this sea were no fewer than three ship-wrights, ready to repair, sell, or rent boats for the onward journey to Miklagårdr. This late in the season there were few others approaching the great trading centre from the north, and though their guide Brani did not understand their speech, the ship-wrights, eager to strike a bargain, made it easy to do so. Gestures and a show of silver were all that was needed. Heading south Runulv and Eskil could hew to the western coast of the sea, and thus save themselves much of the danger of the swift currents and sudden high winds Brani told tale of from other traders inside the great city they neared.

Eskil rented a knorr, broad-beamed and well able to carry all the cargo from the remaining karv and the dugouts. These would remain at the ship-wright's, and in his care, until they returned to claim them. The knorr was not as long as the Svear's drekar Sharp Tooth, but its breadth more than made up for this lack. She came with a good sail and ten pair of oars, and after they had hauled the goods from the karv and dugouts on her decking all they need do was prepare for the morning. From the ship-wright and his wife they laid in a supply of bread and smoked fish, and refilled their water casks. The men divided into two crews, twenty on Eskil's knorr, and nineteen on Death-day. The weather was fair, if cold, and though snow blanketed the hills in the distance, none fell from the sky. They bedded down aboard the respective ships, needing rest from the labour of unlading the small boats, lading the knorr, and making all fast aboard both ships.

Striking out at dawn gave the adventurers a thrill of expectancy rarely equalled by the attainment of any goal. Up went Dauðadagr's ochre and white interlaced sail, and up the broad billowing ruddy brown sail of the knorr. These acts, simple as they be, were greeted by cheers. To hoist sail knowing this transit was the final to attain their goal was a freeing from much of their past hardship.

Brani told them that barring trouble they would be at Miklagårdr in four or five days. He sailed aboard the knorr captained by Eskil, and it was agreed that as the Svear had been the spark to the entire venture, the knorr should precede the drekar in their progress down the coast. The blade-smith Berse remained with Runulv, and though every man of them bore hope of profit, Berse was perhaps most eager of all to see what his trade goods would yield, as the spear points, knives, and swords he carried had been wrought by his own hands, and those of his sons.

The sea beneath them to the east was vast, its waters nearly as dark as its name suggested. To starboard they sailed past coves of sandy beaches flanked by rock cliffs and hills, much of which were heavily forested. The leafed trees stood bare now, but grew thickly where they stood, and their barren branches were enlivened by the ever-green pines amongst them. There was Moon enough to sail steadily southward through much of the night; only when it set did they run to shallow water and drop anchor for a few hours. Awake and underweigh again at first light, all were aware that the wind which filled their sails was milder. As they followed the coastline down the next three days the breeze tempered from cold to brisk. They were passing from Winter's cold to a Spring-like freshness as they drove south.

Late the fourth day Runulv sighted Miklagårdr without knowing what it was. He stood as ever on the starboard side of the stern, steering oar in hand. A whistle from Eskil's knorr made him shift his eyes from the coastline he passed to an indistinct mass ahead. Brani, on the knorr, had Eskil drop sail so he could ride up on the yard for a better look. He had not yet been hoisted to the top of the mast when he began waving wildly. Once up he hung on and bellowed so that even those aboard Death-day could hear him. All stared at what he gestured toward. A sheer cliff of grey rock lay in the distance. But as Runulv narrowed his eyes toward it he saw domes above the cliff top, many domes. Brani had told him these were of the great temples of the Christian Gods. The cliff face was not solid rock, but a vast wall. As they neared, all saw the surface of the wall was broken by countless defence towers, formed into it and rising slightly above.

Daylight was dwindling as they pulled beneath that wall, but lanterns hung along a string of piers awaited, as did a seeming crowd of men. The height of the stone enclosure was such that none but Brani could keep from gaping. Both ships were summoned forward, their thrown lines caught and made fast to the wooden pilings of the pier. They joined at least a score of other vessels, mostly unmanned, tied there. The men who stood upon that pier sported closely trimmed beards, and tunics and short mantles trimmed with tablet weaving in bright hues, some of which were enlivened with silver thread which caught the lantern light and gleamed as they moved towards the ships.

The men, officials of some kind, barked out questions. "It is Greek," Brani muttered to Eskil, "but he will understand from the look of Dauðadagr, and what I name, where we are from." Brani answered in a few words. "Svear" and "Gotland" were two of them, and at these one of the men nodded his head. A short wait ensued while another official approached, and stood on the pier to address captains and crew. He wore a red sash across his chest from right shoulder to waist, the sign, they would learn, of an agent empowered to witness the buying and selling of valuable goods.

The man spoke tolerable Norse, a great relief for those aboard.

"You enter the royal city of Constantinople, Imperial seat of the most high Emperor of Byzantium, Leo. Your first act is the payment of entry duties for the privilege of buying and selling here. These will be assessed when we inspect your goods. All customs duties, taxes, interest and exchange rates, and wages are set by the Emperor's Prefect, the Eparch. His alone is the authority over all trade and manufacture.

"The Eparch grants you thirty days in which to do your trading. After that you must leave the city precincts. If the weather is inclement – as it is likely to be – you will find lodging along the coast until you can make your return home."

It had been both Brani and young Prince Karlen who had told them they would have but a month to trade at Miklagårdr, but much else they were hearing was news to them. The list of proscriptions was long.

"You will be lodged in a dedicated hall, and will sleep no place else. Leave your spears and shields here. You are allowed no weapons within the walls; those of you who bear swords must stow them at your lodging.

"All your dealings will be witnessed by one of the agents of the Eparch; you will know them by their sashes of red." Here he touched that crossing his own chest. "There is no trading without one present. None will cheat you. The scales used to weigh your silver or gold are those of the Eparch, and true weight. Our agents are everywhere, and those who try to gouge our guests are severely dealt with.

"Likewise, do not bargain. All prices are fixed by order of the Eparch, installed in his role by the most high Emperor Leo, and any attempt to bargain is thus insult to both. As it would be to the craftsman or merchant whose goods you desire. You will pay what is demanded, or not buy."

Well, Runulv muttered to himself, that will save time. Bargaining could take hours, if not days, of returning to the same seller to obtain what was sought. The deciding question would rather be which merchant or artisan offered the most desirable goods, in the eyes of the buyer.

"Our coinage standard is the gold solidus. A healthy slave boy costs six solidi, a good she-ass five and a third solidi, a common concubine to take away with you, five. We trade also in silver and bronze coins, and in metal of the same. For everyday wants bronze coinage is required. These you will need in taverns and at food stalls. You can change silver here for bronze coins, and at money-changing stalls in the streets. At taverns a cup of wine costs two bronze coins, as does a full-weight loaf of bread. These will never cost more, nor less, than this amount.

"When you are not trading you are free to wander. But take care, there are many rogues willing to part you from your silver, or goods.

"You will be taken to your lodging now. Your ships and goods are impounded until the morning. An agent of the Eparch will then bring you here to retrieve what you wish to trade first. So it will be every day. At night, bring what you have won in trading to your ship. In the morning, take what you will to trade."

The men were allowed to shoulder their sea chests, so they might avail themselves of clean clothes and all else needful for a strange lodging, and made to follow their guide. He struck out for an opening in the wall, a wide gate not of wood, but of figured bronze. Berse must reach and touch it with a free hand, so amazed was he to see such a weight of metal. The hinges alone were a full ell's length, and the door hung from three of them. Such a door could only hang from a wall of stone as thick as this they passed through.

The party had no sooner crossed through the gateway then another marvel awaited. The road was paved with stone, and lined with buildings of the same. It teemed with folk walking, riding horses, perched on the backs of asses, and driving small carts drawn by oxen. Rising above these were two men upon huge beasts, long of neck and shaggy of coat. The heads of the men were swathed in fabric, covering their hair, and the beasts they rode were guided by simple bridles from which brightly hued tassels fell. The animals themselves had long faces, large eyes framed by feathery lashes, and nostrils which flared and narrowed with every breath. The second of these riders led a third camel, unencumbered by saddle or packs, so the new arrivals could view fully the strangeness of its shape. It had a great hump, far larger than a whither bump, marking its back. The mounted riders guided the beasts with a short stick held in one hand, and barely needed to touch the animal's flanks, so well trained were they. They moved in ungainly fashion, with a rolling, even pitching, gait, as both legs on a side moved as one. With such long legs every step took them forward a surprising distance none the less.

"Camels," hissed Brani, turning back from where he walked at Eskil's side to alert his fellows. Brani had promised they would see these animals, and here they were. They had little time to ogle, as their guide led them relentlessly onward.

Their lodging hall sat on a street with many others. It was built of stone, and for the Gotlanders and most of Eskil's men it was the first time they had set foot in a building not of hewn timber. Not every lodging was of such noble stuff, but this was a hall reserved for Rus traders and others from the far north. Such was their repute that a lodging hall above the common was set aside for them. It was of two floors, both high-ceilinged. The first was a large common space where meals could be taken, with tables, benches, and a few alcoves in which private conversations could be held. A wooden stair led to the next floor, pocketed with sleeping alcoves, and a row of cots running down the centre. Behind was a kitchen yard, staffed by cooks and serving folk, all men. Meals could be taken at the lodging or not, but the low price of the provender served there, a sum paid weekly, made it wise to do so.

Most of the alcoves above the main hall lay unclaimed. The bed frames were of wood, strung with hempen line to support the mattress. These were stuffed with handfuls of straw bundled and tied lengthwise, and covered in heavy linen. Each was rolled to the foot of the bed, awaiting the sleeper. The party each claimed an alcove, stowing their sea chest beneath. As they had been ordered, those who carried swords, numbering only Eskil and Berse, left them there as well. Later that evening when the other lodgers returned, they found them to be a mixed lot of nine Kyiivan Rus, who, returning from points even further east, would in a few days depart for the lands of the Polanie.

A bathing shed was part of the accommodation, one greatly needed by the arriving crews. There was a conspicuous neatness about nearly every man they had seen upon entering the great city, as if expectations were higher for all living under the protection of Emperor Leo. There were as well great public baths, they would learn, set aside for all classes of men, some of which were also frequented by lewd women. Women of respectable backgrounds gathered in their own bathing halls.

The men washed themselves, and then were served their supper. It was the first of many surprising meals, and though simple, proved to be of lasting impress upon the hungry voyagers. Bowls of a golden grain were ladled out, over which was poured an even more golden oil. Grains of salt were then sprinkled over this. Roasted flat fish followed, a single whole fish for each man, the flaking flesh compensation for the staring eye which seemed to fix upon the diner. Alongside were dishes of oval fruit, some green and some dark, the same size as the grapes of Gotland. Grapes they were not, and Brani named them at once.

"Olives," he grinned. "and this oil they swim in, like the oil on the grain, is their own oil, pressed through heavy stone wheels." Every man was eager to try them, but Brani was late to warn that each small fruit contained a hard pip, so that Berse nearly broke a tooth. At any rate the loaves of bread which accompanied them, flat as griddle cakes but imbued with the sharpness of rosemary needles, made a fine way to mop up the glistening oil. There were also bowls of figs, a delight in the mouth. Their unequaled sweetness was much remarked upon, until Brani promised that even sweeter fruit could be found, borne by the caravans of the huge camels from the deserts of Serkland. "They are called dates, and their stickiness is akin to honey, but their flavour is their own. You will find them at food stalls, and they are worth your bronze coinage." He looked at Berse. "I warn you now that unlike these tender figs, they have large pips."

Now replete, they decided to strike out into the streets. The weather was mild enough here that it truly did feel like Spring, though back home the Winter's Nights feasting had not yet begun. The sky above them had grown dark; trading stalls would be closed, but taverns where wine was sold beckoned, as did the play of acrobats, jugglers, fortune-tellers and all other manner of diversions to be enjoyed. A sally to acquaint themselves with some of this would be a satisfying end to the long day. First came a caution.

"There are bells of bronze throughout Miklagårdr," Brani told them, and indeed they had already heard the deep tolling of one nearby. He then reminded all of a rule the official meeting them had stated. "We must be back to our lodging before the bells strike eleven." Failure to do so meant the loss of the following day trading. Brani built on this by adding, "Any left in the brew-houses or taverns will likely also need to hew to this same curfew, so do not get lost in your cup. Make sure you leave when others do."

This agreed, the men split up in groups of three or four, and set out into the night. On the way to their lodging they had spotted men gaming in taverns, throwing dice, moving counters, and sitting at other games as yet unknown to the newcomers. Some of the arrivals, wishing to increase their own store of silver, struck out to try their luck. If their hamingja was with them they would have the more to buy with in the morning.

Runulv, Eskil, Brani, and Berse formed one group, as they had in nearly all their dealings throughout the journey. The street upon which sat their lodging was fairly quiet, but as soon as they turned onto a larger thoroughfare they saw the folk and visitors of Miklagårdr were far from done for the day. As this was the quarter where foreign traders were lodged, there were many kitchens dishing out foods, both pungent and savory-smelling, to those hungry after a day of buying and selling. Brew-houses were many, but rather than stop they wished to wander further, and explore. It was inviting to do so. Torches flared everywhere, jutting from walls, standing in fire-pots upon the ground, adding their light to oil lamps hanging from eaves.

Brani acquainted them with names for those things new to them. The twisted length of fabric upon the heads of some swarthy men were known as turbans. The men in grey robes standing and talking to any who would listen were of a special class who spent their days disputing with others. Brani could not recall the long Greek word for their trade, but as they were often asked questions of others and readily provided answers, he called them Thinkers. Those men who sported a large open eye in thread-work on their cloaks were fortune-tellers, and were paid a few coins to predict the futures of those who would pay them. Brani recalled too certain quarters and what they were known for, special areas set aside for the buyers and sellers of all goods known on Midgard. And some too known only in Asgard, Runulv thought as well. They would visit all during their allotted month.

As they walked about, Runulv gave thought to the next day and how they would begin their trading. Upon Death-day and the knorr they carried the finest stock Sidroc and the rest of them could amass. The goal now for Runulv and Eskil was to rid their ships of all the bulky trade goods they had carried down with so much effort, and to return with those small, precious, and difficult to obtain. Runulv recounted what he wished to sell.

They had crates holding sacksful of down, scooped from the nests of eider ducks. These had come from the furthest north, from Osku, Tindr's Sámi father-in-law, and been stockpiled by Sidroc for some rich trading post. From Tindr they had not only kegs of Gotland forest honey, but masses of beeswax, formed into blocks. Sidroc had paired this with coils of finely braided linen wicking ready for dipping in the melted wax to make tapers. These too were of Gotland make, by a woman from the trading road. Also from Osku were chests of furs, sealskins, walrus hides and tusks. There were as well bundles of the shorn fleece of good Gotlandic lamm, prized for its curl and softness. Soft wool was everywhere valued, and went for a good price, and Runulv trusted that would be the case here. Then there was as much red and yellow amber, worked and unworked, as Sidroc could buy from the amber sellers he knew. This formed a full hundred weight, and both Sidroc and Runulv hoped here, so far from its home waters, it would be prized. For adornment, there lay bags of glass beads, whole-coloured and swirled, which Runulv had traded for at the Baltic trading posts of the Polanie and Pomeranie.

The Dane had entrusted his captain with something more. Beyond these goods to trade was something only Runulv knew of, a small but heavy cask, the size of one of Rannveig's mead casks, filled with silver. With it Runulv was charged to buy those things which he thought would return the greatest profit at Paris, or any other trading town he might in future sail to.

There were other goods Sidroc could have sent, things still awaiting in the treasure room of Tyrsborg. They carried no Rhenish glasswork; even packed in straw and then crated it was not likely to survive the journey. They had focused instead on that which could not break.

On his own account Runulv had a few choice pieces of Frankish jewellery, too gaudy for Gyda's taste but a pleasure to the eye, for they were necklaces of slender golden chain, with trailing strands holding coloured gemstones, which dripped down upon the bosom. The main ornament on each necklace was a cross, and here in Miklagårdr Runulv would see many of them, scratched on walls, rising above domed buildings, and hung around the necks of devout men and women. This would make them all the more desirable, he hoped. He had as well a good store of silver, to turn this into wares to sell at handsome profit on future trading runs.

Berse had a heavy chest with his metal work, shears, spear-points, knives, ten swords, and diverse other objects in bronze and iron. And all the crew had whatever goods they could spare from home, be they sheepskins or fleece, amber beads or some rare coin they might trade for.

In the morning they would begin. Now the bells were tolling ten; the return to their lodging was nigh.

Their first step next morning was to appear before the officials where their ships were tied, for once their goods were inspected, they must pay the duty required for the privilege to sell them within the great walls. Runulv and Eskil went alone for this. They were met by three men, two finely dressed in tunics trimmed with golden thread, and the third, a younger man, with a kind of tablet in which he made notation in wax of what the elder two said. In the company of all three Runulv and Eskil were made to open every cask, chest, and bundled stack of goods. The two officials looked at all, and touched most, gauging the quality

of the furs, the varying colour of the amber, the softness
and staple of the fleece. They spoke to each other in Greek,
and the younger man scratched marks in his tablet. When
Runulv was gestured to pry open the chests holding the
eider down, this changed. The down had been packed in
waxed linen sacks, and then placed within the chests, and
had made the journey in perfect form. One of the officials
dipped his hand into a sack, slipping it into its depth up to
his wrist, and then moved it to restore the loft of the fine
feathers. The faces of both officials proclaimed to the two
captains that here was a prized trading good.

"This," one said, turning to Runulv, "goes to the Palace."
It was the first Norse the man had uttered, but spoke it he
did. Runulv was not sure what this meant; was the down
being seized? His face must have shown this concern, for
both officials grinned.

"The Eparch himself will purchase from you," one
assured him. "All the finest goods are destined for the
palace. Eight crates of northern down will send you home
a happy man."

There was in fact no duty to be paid on the down, for
it was to go at once into royal ownership. For the rest of the
goods they had brought, they must pay the equivalent of
seven gold solidi. Six solidi was, Runulv well recalled, the
price of a healthy young male slave, and thus seemed a good
deal. The scales were set up right there on the pier, over a
table on which Runulv could place his silver as he scooped
out measure after measure. When he was done, and the
silver swept into a locked chest, one of the officials laughed.
"Whatever you buy here in Constantinople will return at
least ten-fold, wherever you sell it."

This was much the same as what Brani had promised back on Gotland, and Runulv must believe it. The stakes here were so much the greater, though.

They were not asked to wait to learn what the eider down would bring, as the crates were loaded at once onto an ox cart, that it might be valued by the Eparch. One of the officials called for a red-sashed agent to escort them for this first transaction. The three set off on foot flanking the ox, which was guided by a boy walking at its head.

Runulv and Eskil could scarce believe their good fortune. Not only had they brought something of superior worth, an item desired by the Emperor himself, but they would be admitted into the palace grounds. The walk was not a long one, but the early morning streets were so crowded that making their way was truly at the pace of the ox they followed. It gave both captains ample time to take note of the city.

Runulv had made several trips to stone-paved Paris, with its equally solid buildings, but that rich royal seat, hemmed in by the River Seine, seemed magnified here a thousandfold. This great city of the Greeks had pools as large as small lakes, holding water to feed the fountains which sat in every square, fountains for beasts and for folk. The water flowed both above ground, carried at a height by arcaded stone bridges, and under the earth in pipes. There were stone streets, stone gutters carrying away waste water, stone buildings rising up three, four, and more floors into the air. This was marvel enough, but to see the multitudes of differing tribes thronging the squares was beyond all expectation. Never had Runulv heard so many tongues, seen so many garbed in odd and outlandish dress, or certainly gazed upon such delights as filled the trading stalls. Intermingled through the folk on streets and byways they saw red-sashed agents of the Eparch, escorting traders, or walking alone to some errand; there were at any time scores to be seen in every busy trading quarter.

Everything was heightened in Miklagårdr; the size of the buildings, quantity of stone work, the vivid striped awnings projecting out over the goods on offer. Surely this was worth the hardship, even loss, of attainment. The task now was to make good on those sacrifices, and being called to the palace seemed a good start.

In the light of day they saw many more women than they had last night, for most of the trading stalls were held by couples, and as both captains had seen at other trading towns, women stood at street corners with baskets and bushels of fruit, boiled eggs, or flat loaves of bread. The women at work with their trading were dressed in long-sleeved gowns of bright hue, and their heads were draped with fabric in contrasting colour, making fine show. On other corners men offered trinkets, and even tiny song birds in cages. Their chirping could only be heard when one neared, for the clamour of merchants calling out their wares, folk talking in unknown tongues, and the winding of horns to allow well-dressed horsemen through. These were mounted on horses such as neither captain had ever seen, small of head, delicate of bone, and with tails set high on the hindquarters. All about them were other animals being ridden, driven, or led; dray horses, asses, goats, sheep, cattle, swine, and best of all, camels. For the first time Runulv saw men with truly black skin, riding these beasts. The riders were richly garbed in robes shot through with golden thread, and had upon their heads lengths of twisted fabric, each set with a gem above the forehead. They made such show that

Eskil must turn to Runulv with his supposition. "They are Kings and Princes in their own country," he thought aloud. There were four of them, leading a string of camels packed with wooden chests. They could not gawk, as suddenly an inner wall stood before them.

The gate in the wall was a doubled door of thick wood sheathed over in iron, and closed against them. Spear-bearing sentries at either side made haste to give command that it open at the approach of the official who led them.

Unseen means from within pulled wide the doors, to a view wholly unexpected. Before them lay a broad road, again paved in stone, skirting an expanse of greenery. Trees, pruned in fanciful shapes stood there, casting dappled shade upon an intricate network of garden paths, planted with herbs, low shrubs, and a profusion of bright flowers. A low structure of carved stone arose in the centre of this, a small pool of water which bubbled over into one larger. As Runulv and Eskil gaped, a shriek akin to a murderous cry sounded from the pathways. A large bird with a brilliant glossy blue breast appeared, strutting towards them. A moment later a great arc of long feathers arose over its head, forming a circle above it, each feather so tipped with colour it looked an hundred staring eyes encircling the beast. Then the bird shook these feathers, giving off a harsh rattle, before it let out another piercing scream.

There was no time to stop and admire, as the cart rolled onward, to pause at a building with a tall colonnade of white stone. A row of four steps led up to the floor of this. Several men stood upon these steps, or at the floor level above. Another oxcart was stopped just before them, and those baskets it had brought in lay upon the floor, where other men lifted them off into the recesses of the building. The contents remained unseen, but the man now walking off with the red-sashed agent who had accompanied him seemed well pleased.

Their own agent now gestured that they unload the eight chests of down, and Runulv and Eskil carried them up the steps to the floor. This was of some rare stone, shot through with veining in pink and grey, and one glance told them this stone flooring extended throughout this upper level. They laid the chests in a single line, as the man gestured, and pulled off the lids and laid them beside each chest. Then they re-opened the waxed sacks so the pureness of the fluffy white down was readily apparent.

Their agent then vanished up the steps, and out of sight. The two captains stood on the paving below, awaiting his return. In short order two guards armed with spears approached, flanking a man in a long tunic of silk in deepest blue. The hem, collar and sleeves of this gown were trimmed with narrow bands of dark yellow silk, stitched over with what looked like thread of golden filaments. His headdress was a stiff cap with a double peak, fore and aft, covered also with silk, of a deep red. This then was the Eparch, in charge of all trade, dressed as Runulv imagined the Emperor himself might be.

Runulv lost no time in bowing to the man. From the tail of his eye he saw Eskil still upright, and muttered his name in a low hiss. Eskil recovered himself and gave a deep bow. When they straightened the Eparch lifted his hand to them in acknowledgement. He studied the two for a long moment, then shifted his gaze to the chests of down before him. The official, with a low bow of his own, said a few words in the tongue of the Greeks to the Eparch, at which the dignitary nodded.

The Eparch turned and gestured into the dimness behind him. Two men pushed forward a scale, mounted on a rolling platform. It was the largest scale set either Runulv or Eskil had ever seen, the kind to gauge the weight of bronze goods. The men went about lifting the linen sacks from their chests, lashed them together at their mouths with cord, and then, removing the second dish of the scale, tied them to that arm. A cart the size of a hand wain was now rolled forward. The Eparch turned to it and selected one of many lead weights. He laid it on the dish, and the down rose off the veined stone floor and into the air. Two more small weights were added by the Eparch, until the two arms balanced. The Eparch turned to the agent and spoke, which prompted the man to tell the traders their good fortune.

"Ten gold solidi," they heard.

Almost as soon as this was sounded, two men came forward side by side, one with a small casket with a domed lid. He turned smartly to the second man and presented the casket. Ten solidi were counted out, and Runulv and Eskil gestured forward. The coins were newly minted, embellished with the portrait of a man, and of brilliant gold. They were large enough so that Runulv's thumb just covered one, and thick as well. Runulv and Eskil could not help grinning at each other as they held them. They had agreed that with the profit of the trading goods supplied by Sidroc, they would each carry half, to guard against loss or mishap. So it was that Runulv accepted five solidi, and Eskil five. The satisfaction with which they palmed these may have been the greatest of their trading careers. They had ventured to Miklagårdr in hope of gold, and on their very first trade, they had won it. In addition, by unwittingly carrying something highly valued by the Emperor, they need pay no duty on it. The seven solidi worth they had surrendered to trade here had been more than repaid.

They both bowed deeply to the Eparch, who raised his hand to them, and nodded.

They were granted the empty wooden chests; these were sure to be useful for the return. They loaded them back onto the cart to retrace their steps to the pier. "Who lives here?' Eskil asked the agent as they passed through the iron-covered gate. "The most high Emperor Leo and his family," he told them. "The Emperor's mother, Eudokia, was half Svear," he added, looking meaningfully to Eskil, who squared his shoulders at this news.

The agent went on enumerating those resident on the palace grounds. "The Eparch and his family. Many hundreds to serve them, from scribes to stableboys. There are special workshops for the creation of goods for the Imperial family. These items are never released for sale, but sometimes are given as gifts to Kings and Queens."

They looked down the wall at the distance the palace enclosed. A domed temple rose next it, singular in breadth and height. "That is Hagia Sophia," the agent murmured. "The Church of Holy Wisdom."

"Can we go there?" Eskil asked.

"All are welcome," they were told.

For now they must return to the ships and reload the empty chests onto their decks. Having done this, Eskil joined Runulv on Dauðadagr. They sat together by the shipped steering oar and took the gold solidi from their purses, just to admire. The Eparch's coins were indeed choice, and rich reward for their efforts.

"Soon we will be as rich as Ladja," Runulv proclaimed. That near-Queen of Staraya Ladoga, draped with gold, was the standard they aspired to.

"The Gods have favoured us," Eskil was forced to admit.

Runulv must give a laugh. "Do you only see it now, with gold on your palm? We have been brought here alive to see this place, when good men died."

The Gotlander's words put both captains in mind of the men they must trade on behalf of. They agreed the best tactic was to first scout all the likely stalls so they could take the most silver back to those who would grieve their absence.

It was now past noon, and flush with this first victory, refreshment seemed called for. Their purses felt far heavier, just knowing gold sat within. To lift a cup would be fitting. They returned to the quarter in which they lodged, where both taverns and brew-houses abounded. Some were merely booths dispensing drink by the ladleful into cups one carried; others open structures with tables, benches, cooking rings, and broad counters at which food and drink could be served. They chose one with gaily striped awnings sheltering those who sat. Last night they had seen small lanterns hanging from the awning supports, a cheering effect in the dark.

Just as they took their seat at the tavern, Berse the blade-smith appeared, grinning from ear to ear. Brani was with him, also looking well pleased. Berse swung the leathern pack from his shoulder and opened it for them.

"Look what I traded for, sword for sword," he told them.

He pulled out a narrow scabbard, opulently covered in stitched and tooled white leather. The scabbard was decidedly curved, almost like the face of a young Moon. When Berse closed his meaty fist around the grip, which looked to be of walrus ivory, he drew forth a blade echoing that curve, and of dazzling brightness. The edge was so finely ground, so sharp, that Runulv almost grimaced to look at it.

Berse told more. "It is a scimitar, favoured by horsemen in these parts."

"Or a razor for a giant," Runulv offered, unable to take his eyes off the telling edge of the blade.

Eskil spoke. "As for us, we have redeemed our docking duty, and on the first day trading." They went on to tell him of how the official at the ships, upon discovering the crates of eider down, had taken them directly to the palace.

A celebration was in order, and a jug of ale summoned. The four each took a long draw on the pottery cups in their hands. All the ale they had so far sampled was distinct, from tavern to brew-house, as one might expect.

"It is malted from barley, as is much of our own ale," Berse decided. "But the herbs are different. The water too," he added, as they had all drunk from the public fountains.

The chiming of a bell made them turn their eyes toward the crowded road. "That is not the only thing different," Eskil proclaimed.

The bell they heard was held by a brown-skinned boy, of some ten or twelve years, wearing a soft hat flourished with a large white feather. His ringing served to alert others to make way for those he led.

Eskil stood up to see better. Behind the bell-ringing boy came an odd procession. Four large men followed the boy, bearing a chair in a kind of litter suspended from poles which they bore on their shoulders. "Look at what wonders

Sleipner bears," Eskil said, referring to Odin's eight-legged steed.

There was some truth in the Svear's claim, for the four men together did possess eight legs. They walked together in rhythm, in slow and measured step, which gave very little jostle to the chair they bore. The legs of the chair extended up over it to support a roof, from which filmy curtains of some thin stuff fell. They could just see the figure of a woman seated within.

The bearers were in themselves arresting to look at, large, well-formed, long-haired, bare-chested, and clothed only in loincloths. Their bare chests, arms, and legs were gleaming, as if they had been slicked with oil. It made them all the more eye-catching. Each bore a broad leathern belt across their chests, which ran to that at their waists, and their wrists were also wrapped in the same smooth brown leather. The brass fittings of belts and wrist wrappings were polished, well-wrought, and as alike as they nearly were. On their feet were strapped, open-toed shoes. Despite their brawn they had no hair on their chests. They did not appear to be slaves; at least they looked well-fed, and their bodies glistened not from their current labour, but from the oil rubbed upon their skin.

"Eunuchs," Brani hissed.

"Eunuchs?" repeated Runulv, in a low tone.

"Gelded men," came Brani's answer. "There are many thousands of them here."

"Gelded," echoed Eskil, in some wonder. "Out of punishment?"

"Nej. So that they serve better to protect the women of the Greeks from assault."

"Or unfaithfulness," Eskil offered. There would be no secret couplings with such men, that was sure.

Eskil's eyes shifted to she they carried in the chair borne on their shoulders. He glimpsed a woman past her first youth, but handsome indeed; richly dressed in green, and with a diadem upon her brow. She could be viewed more fully when the breeze parted the flowing curtains hung about her.

The curtain wafted slightly, enough to show all of her face. Eskil smiled broadly at her. She returned his look, with a cool downcast of her eyes. Then she drew the curtain more closely to her to shield herself from his eyes.

Brani went on about the bearers as the litter passed. "Such as these, tall and good looking, are often times given as gifts, to brides when they wed."

"So they are thralls," Berse posed.

"Já, but of the highest order," said Brani. "All other slaves envy them, as they live with the household, partake of the same food as does the Lord and Lady, at least to sample it for poison, and are trusted with many secrets. They are allowed the run of the women's quarters, and become valued companions to them, and even advisors to the men."

To see and hear of the eunuchs was surprising enough that his three listeners could only look at each other.

"It is, from what I have heard, not a bad life," Brani mused.

Eskil looked at Berse, then canted his head, and rolled his eyes skyward.

JADE FOR
CONTENTMENT

BELLS tolled ceaselessly the next morning. The Rus traders in their lodging told them that today was a holy day, one of seven of every week, and there would be no trading. All believers in the Christian God would crowd the domed temples in worship. Runulv thought this might be the chance to enter the great temple, Hagia Sophia, and asked this of the Rus.

"All can enter, and of any estate," one told them.

Brani had crossed the threshold of the huge church on a prior visit to Miklagårdr, but never during any ritual. If they were allowed, it seemed a good time to go. He looked at the others and nodded. "When I came here last, after Hedin our captain died, we spent much of our time in drink, in taverns. I did not see Miklagårdr as I should have." The mournful note of Brani's telling gave impetus to the other three, and they signalled their eagerness to go.

The Rus went on. "Be sure to stand with the men, to the right, and do not look at any woman, but only at those gowned men moving at the altar, in front. They will hold up gold worth the looking. There will be the tinkling of bells, and the smell of incense. And also song."

"And dancing?" Berse asked, ever hopeful to spy some whirling young women, as Prince Efim had presented them with.

"Nej. No dancing. It is song in honour of their God."

As their lodging was not far from the palace precincts, all they need do was join the throngs heading there, as the great edifice was fast by the palace. There was a sense of purpose to the men and women they walked with, and as they neared the open doors those they walked with grew silent. Couples who had walked together parted once through that yawning door, men to the right, women to the left. Runulv, Eskil, Berse, and Brani stepped off to one side, and remained in the back. One look told them why the worshippers had quieted. The utter vastness of the space they entered would have stilled any idle chatter. And it was flooded with light. Both Runulv and Eskil had seen glass casements on their travels, but this was unlike anything they had imagined. The enormous dome above the central space seemed to hover over a narrow band of pure light, as the windows wrapped in continuous circle beneath it. The sunlight streaming in hit the walls and floor, illuminating the expanse of the interior with a pale golden glow.

Everywhere was the sensation of movement, as well. The floor was made of stone in different colours, pieced together in star-shapes and waves and squares that branched off and ran long distances as borders. Most amazing of all were the brilliant images of men and women adorning the walls, formed, they could see, from countless small shining cubes of colour. The entire effect was one of splendour, and light.

"This truly must be the home of their God," Eskil wondered aloud.

"It is one of them," Brani said. "There is another, in Rome, even more holy. But I have not been there." He gave thought. "But as the Christian priests will tell you, He visits all churches, no matter how small."

"The pictures," Runulv said.

They were no crude drawings, scratched into wood or stone, but real men and women, clothed in sumptuous gowns, and holding their hands in ways to express wonder, or display a child in their care, or a scroll held in their grip. Their eyes were large and searching, and looking at them, one felt they almost looked back.

Runulv could not take his own eyes from the largest, set in a dome, of a dark-clad woman holding a boy-child on her lap.

"Mosaics. They are made from pieces of glass," Brani told them. "Those that look gold, have real gold in them, a layer set down between the glass as it was poured."

Such was the dazzling background of the piece Runulv gazed at, a golden backdrop for the woman and child.

They all knew glass, as bead makers were many in the better trading posts, and rare beakers of glass from Frankland had long been valued. But these tiny squares and oblongs joined together to form huge pictures were beyond any use of the material they had seen.

The crowd seemed to settle, and bells were chimed. A number of gowned men appeared on the raised platform at one end, upon which sat a table of stone. The men were variously arrayed in long gowns of red, white, and black, with several moving before the altar table, their backs to those watching.

They moved forward along the margin of the worshippers for a closer look. As the Rus had told them, a silver
pot on a long chain was swung about the air, smoking with
incense. The smell was such as to inspire dreams of other
lands, or deep sleep. They stayed until the chanting of the
priests and chiming of the small bells grew louder, and saw
the gold the Rus traders had promised; a large cup of gold,
held aloft over the head of one of the priests, and a small dish
of the same precious stuff, held by another. The singing and
chanting and bell-ringing came to a peak. It was then Brani
edged them toward a stair running up the wall.

"We can watch from above, if we are willing to climb,"
he promised. Many steps later they emerged. They were near
the base of the great dome, not far from the glass casements
ringing it, and through which the morning sunlight poured.
Looking down they could see much if not all of the great floor
space, the worshippers standing, men to the right, women to
the left, watching and sometimes speaking in unison to the
actions of the gowned priests pacing on the raised platform.
Their words were all in a tongue unknown to the visitors.

There were other folk wandering below along the edges
of the gathered, moving into and out of the side alcoves,
where many more images and smaller altars were displayed.
These alcoves were half or quarter domes, and their roofs
themselves taller than the tallest hall back on Gotland.

The four made a circuit of the dome, looking up, down,
and across as they did so. The height was such that Berse,
who feared no man or beast, was quick to keep his eyes
straight ahead. Looking down caused his head to swim, as
if his balance were of a sudden faulty. As they made their
way around they came across a man crouching by one of

the stone supports of the dome. His knife was in his hand, which he withdrew as they neared him. He stood with some abruptness, and made off toward the staircase. It was easy to guess he had been marking the stone as proof of his visit.

"That will likely be the only reminder he was ever here," Eskil scoffed, and in truth the fellow looked far from prosperous.

They neared and looked at his handiwork. There in jagged runes he had spelt his name, Halfdan.

"Half Dane, and half what?" Runulv posed, which made Eskil laugh.

The four made their own way down. The ceremony was not over, but all had seen enough, and the blue smoke of the incense, rising into the dome, made Berse feel even more unsteady. There would be no trading today, but with fine weather it was a day to explore further. Many days here in Miklagårdr were mild as Spring, and the Sun beat hot and pure upon them. It made the white stone of buildings the brighter, dazzling even, and the shadows cast by the columns and roofs the deeper. At night it cooled, but rarely to more than a slight chill.

Brani recalled a great square they should see, and after some doubling back, found his way to it. The square was fully paved and set with stone buildings on all four sides, and though a single glance told them that on a trading day, stalls with wares to display would sit at their base, today these were shut. A great well with a flowing fountain sat in the middle of the paving, and off to one side rose a single tall column of stone. One look at its top made them all stop, and indeed, they were not alone, for a small crowd of folk stood below it. Nearer the far corner of the square sat a second column. But it was the nearest one their eyes returned to.

The stone column before them rose the height of at least four men. It had seemingly never been a part of any building, and bore no weight, save for that of an old man standing at the top of the column. His grey hair and beard were of such length that it was hard to see the colour of his tunic, or even if he were clothed in anything other than his own hair. Surrounding the top of the column was a kind of framework that he might not fall; it was hard to make out if it was a large basket or wicker-work of some kind, but it enclosed the old man from the waist down.

Runulv, Eskil, and Berse gawked wordlessly up at the man.

"This is a stylite, a holy man of the Christian God, but revered by all faiths," Brani explained. "There were three of them about the squares when I was last here. Folk gather to hear them preach once or twice a day."

"How do they live," Runulv asked.

"They are passed food and water in a basket each day. But their wants are small."

"When do they come down?" Berse asked.

"From what I have heard, never. Once they ascend the column they remain until they die. They stay in all weathers, day and night, winter and Summer. That is why they are called holy men, that, and the preaching. Every faith that comes here, honours them."

Runulv, who was skilled at gauging any kind of distance, studied the top of the column. A man could not even lie down and stretch out his legs; he must sleep curled. To straighten them, he would need stand.

As they stood considering all this, more folk were approaching the base of the column, as if awaiting some event. A nearby bell began to clang, and as soon as its echo died, the holy man raised his arms and began to declaim to all below.

"It is likely the speech of the Greeks," Brani told them, and they could ken none of it. "And not all who gather here can understand, either. But they will listen nonetheless."

The holy man went on with his discourse, moving his arms to the Heavens, spreading them outward to the folk below him, raising and lowering his voice. Fear, anger, and seeming exultation was in his message. The four could not help but study the faces around them as the listeners looked upward to him. They attended a while and then moved on, shaking their heads in wonder.

They spent much of the afternoon watching the antics of street jugglers and acrobats as they meandered, stopping to sample as many different ales as they could hold, and even sipping some date wine at a tavern near their lodging. This latter was more potent than they expected, for the sweetness of the sticky dates, which they had by this time all enjoyed, was transformed into a drink as dark and full-bodied as were the fruit it had been made from. After so much ale, one cup was enough, save for Berse, whose ability to drink was making him the subject of good-humoured chaffing. But the bladesmith reasoned to himself that he would never pass this way again, and therefore ought to enjoy himself to the fullest.

The next day was spent in merely walking the streets of Miklagårdr. Both crews wished to see the full breadth of what wares they might buy or trade for, so they would miss no chance to sell at a profit once home. In truth it was hard for Runulv not to express the excitement he felt at all the goods offered in the great city. He took in its size and countless wonders as if in some kind of fever; all the men did. Many of his crew had been with him to Paris, but this – nothing had prepared them for such splendour and wealth. Even Brani, who had seen it all before, stood awe-struck.

"Paris," Runulv muttered, when he could not keep the name from passing his lips. That would be the destination for so much of what he wished to buy here. Silk dyed with kermes: Paris. Rock crystal, both long faceted fingers of it, and carefully shaped into spheres: Paris. And there was a sphere, already formed, which they had promised to Oleg, King of Kyiv, who had helped them on their way. They bought it, then and there. At a tavern kitchen they watched a cook at work grating a nutmeg to powder, the smell of which was yet another kind of incense. And his wife Gyda deserved at least ten prickly cloves; Runulv's mouth was already beginning to water at the egg custards she could make, boiling a single clove in milk and cream to flavour it. When they visited the spice sellers he would buy these for her, along with much more to sell on at Paris.

When morning came a different task awaited. After picking up an agent to accompany them, the two captains went together to trade on behalf of their lost men. This took longer than they had anticipated, as the gravity of their deed was with them. The pleasure of seeing Miklagårdr, to walk its stone-paved streets and savour its food and drink, began to weigh on them, and now that they had a better feel for the goods on offer they did not wish to delay this task any longer.

Runulv had lost two, Arni and Farulf, and Eskil, one of his Svear brethren. Arni had a younger brother, Emund, who had taken his purse and could trade for him, but Farulf left a mother behind. Runulv wished to make good on the hopes of her son, and would trade on his account. In addition to what was in his purse, Farulf had brought three sheepskins. Runulv would add these to his own, and thus be able to sell the better to the dealers here, and pay out Farulf's share from his own gain.

As for all goods they sought to buy, they wished to carry back something which would bring greater value when traded onward. Considering the rigours they had suffered, they also sought items that were small in size and difficult to break. Eskil let Runulv take the lead in this, and as they wandered they found themselves in the quadrant of smiths and tinkers and sundry metal-workers. They walked slowly past these, turning their heads from side to side to take in as much as they could from those items crowding the counters, or hung from the edges of awnings. Runulv stopped.

"Here," he said.

They stood before a maker of metal-work, one of several. Runulv gestured Eskil aside. Runulv had a second purse at his waist, and he looked at what it held to trade on behalf of Farulf. It was scant as a trading stake, a few pieces of hack-silver and nine drilled amber beads. He found himself reaching to his own purse, and adding a whole piece of silver to it. He said nothing to Eskil as he did so, but it was spur enough. Eskil had pride and did not like to see himself bettered in such things. He too went to the leathern belt at his waist and added a whole piece of silver for Sigtrygg, drowned in the rapids.

The metal worker they approached enriched his copperware with powdered minerals and then fired them to hard enamel, making fast the minerals to the metal below. Such wares were striking to the eye as well as impervious to water, and if Runulv could find a piece at reasonable cost, he would buy it for the lost Farulf. His mother could do with it as she liked, or if she wished, he could carry it to Paris on her behalf on his next trip, in hopes of returning with much silver. Runulv's eye was drawn to small and squat lidded pots, glossy to the eye and pleasant in the hand. They were no larger than his clenched fist, but full of interest in the designs of flowering branches and tiny birds, set against a background of almost midnight blue.

"They are for unguents, or ointments," their agent told him.

"They are fine enough to store gold in," Runulv answered, and indeed the polished copper interior suggested that precious metal.

The agent smiled. "Some unguents are nearly as costly as gold, those compounded with spikenard, attar of rose, or powdered ivory."

Runulv had seen this in Paris, and nodded his head in agreement.

"Brides are given these pots as wedding gifts, as well," the agent went on, a fact that made Runulv think he could indeed command a high price for one in Paris if he took it for the grieving mother.

He chose one, which the metalsmith set aside. His scale set was there at hand, and in one dish he placed a small cube of lead. It was Runulv's task to balance it with silver. He dropped the hack piece by piece into the second dish, making that holding the weight shudder and then lift into the air. It neared balancing, but even the addition of Runulv's whole coin did not make them do so. It was clear from the smith's face he wished the sale, but under the watchful eyes of the agent all he could do was shrug. Runulv picked out the nine amber beads and lay them on the countertop. The smith picked up one, and the agent another. Holding them close to their eyes they studied each of the yellow beads, checking that the drilled hole was centred, and the beads adequately polished. The smith nodded his acceptance, as did, to Runulv's relief, the agent.

Eskil gestured that Runulv choose for him, as the Gotlander knew what might bring the greatest return for the family of Sigtrygg. The dead Svear had left more silver, and Runulv able to thus choose a slightly larger lidded pot, which Eskil bought. This task accomplished, the two captains felt the freer. Runulv marked well where the deals had been struck; he might wish to return and buy more enameled pots from the fellow.

They wished also to visit the sellers of spice, but they must return to their ships, where they had asked Berse to await them. The agent dutifully led them back. On the way they passed into a small square which had guards at every point of entry. They soon saw why. This was a place in which slaves were exhibited and sold. A wooden platform stood there, and a crowd of men before it. On the platform young women, undraped to the hips and thus bare-breasted, were on display. There were seven of them, standing shoulder to shoulder, and they were made to turn so those viewing could see their backs. Two were dusky of skin, the others fair, and all possessed uncommon loveliness. Their agent meant to lead them past this display, along the edges of those gathered to buy, so as not to slow their progress to the pier.

Eskil slowed, and then stopped, his eyes large. It cost nothing to look and many were doing so.

Runulv had no patience with this ogling. "Eskil, come," he said, in near-order.

Eskil did, grudgingly, his head turned over his shoulder as he walked away. "You had better find me a beauty, amongst your wife's kin, for me to wed. I am counting on it."

"I will," Runulv shot back. "And unlike these women, one who will not only withstand our Winters, but relish them."

They walked on a few steps. "But any Gotland maid you wed is likely to put you in your place," Runulv added under his breath.

As promised, Berse sat waiting by the tied up Dauðadagr. Only the two captains themselves were allowed on the ships, but Berse had whiled away the time studying the massive bronze door they had first passed through, and then lost himself in thought as to how it had been made. He stood when Runulv and Eskil came into view, eager to learn why they had asked him there.

"We go in search of spice," Eskil told him. "To buy we need the Dane's cask of silver. You will be our beast of burden."

Berse bristled at this, until Eskil went on. "It is only just, as you are strongest amongst us." His feelings assuaged, the blade-smith shouldered the cask after he and Runulv rolled it forward from its holding place in the stern. It was indeed heavy, and luckily Berse was both strong and surefooted, as he must make the gangplank with it resting on one shoulder.

"Do not drop it," Runulv said, as they approached the gate, imagining the riotous scene if it should fall and shatter open, filling the street with silver coins.

"It will be as if I carried one of my own sons on my shoulder, when he was a boy," Berse vowed.

Over their own shoulders both Runulv and Eskil carried empty leathern packs, in which to carry back the spices they hoped to buy. They followed the agent, threading their way through narrow lanes, until they stopped at a roofed building, the sides of which were entirely open. As they had seen before, a line of stone pillars formed a colonnade, holding up the tiled roof, and these columns were set throughout the interior as well. This too was a place well-guarded, for sentries armed with spears stood at every corner, and at intervals along its length and breadth. Housed within were the individual booths of the spice sellers. Climbing the few steps up and entering within placed them amongst untold riches, laid before them in pots, bronze trays, and arrayed on tables.

Berse set the silver cask down on an empty table, and Runulv pried open the lid. To see the heaped coins laying within gave pleasure to the eye, and knowing they would soon be exchanged for rarities such as surrounded them gave Runulv a thrill of anticipation. Both men filled their purses, leaving Berse to guard the cask, to which they would soon, and often return.

Runulv had sold Ceridwen's sticks of cinnamon to a high holy man in Paris. He knew these were ground and eaten as remedy for several maladies, and also used to flavour food at the table of the King. He would buy as many sticks as he could, and balance these also with round nutmegs, prickly cloves, highly scented cardamom pods, and long strands of peppercorns, dry but still on their vines. Runulv had seen black peppercorns in Paris; here he saw also those nearly white, with but a faint greenish tint, and also those of rose red. Surely these too would be prized in Paris.

The buying of spices was exacting. The two captains would point out what they wanted, then were offered a minute fragment to taste or smell. Eskil had a limited past with such things, and soon waived this testing wholly over to Runulv. Those spices selected were weighed out on a small hanging scale under the eye of the agent, who studied them to ascertain they were of sufficient quality. The agent and spice-seller would converse as to the grade and value of each spice, which was then set aside on a tray of polished copper. The seller placed the proper cube weights onto the empty scale dish, and with a bow of his head, gestured that Runulv balance it with silver in the opposing dish. This done, the spice was theirs.

What was lacking was the satisfaction of securing the best price. Both Runulv and Eskil, as seasoned traders, took pride in their ability to strike a bargain, one agreed upon by both sides. Here their skills must go untested. All was carried out under the eye of the agent designated for that day. It felt almost like a hunt in which the animals, fine beasts though they might be, were consigned to a small paddock, thus assuring success to the hunter.

Still, Runulv took pride that the silver coins he offered were of interest to those he bought from, for each seller plucked out a few from the pile they accepted and examined them with care. They were a mixed lot, dirhams with lettering like thread-work, large coins from Frankland, and even some bearing the image of King Ælfred of Wessex. Runulv had journeyed twice to Angle-land, both times in the service of Sidroc, and knew of this King's repute. Ceridwen had many of his coins, for Rannveig always saved any she took in at the brew-house for her. Sidroc had told him she wanted to send some along, for luck.

By the time they stepped down into the street, many hours had passed, and the packs upon their shoulders were full to bulging. Every vendor had one or more helpers to package what was sold, filling small leathern pouches, lashing together the cinnamon bark and rolling them in linen cloth, or dropping such as cloves, nutmegs, or peppercorns in small water-tight pottery jars. The best part was the silver cask had not been lightened by even a third. The value of what they carried on their shoulders would return in Paris many times over what they had surrendered for it here.

Having this much silver in reserve gave Runulv confidence. They had sold the bulkiest of their goods straight off, the eight chests of eider down. Next they would select from their furs, and try their luck. Three large bundles awaited them, two on the knorr, and one on Death-day. All had been those brought down from Sámi country by Ŝeará's father, Osku, and purchased by Sidroc, and comprised of the pelts of several brown mink, pine marten, two of beaver, two of black fox, three of fox in their Winter-white fur, five seal skins, and two entire walrus hides and their four tusks. They determined that all silver won from their sale would go into the buying of silk. Eskil took the lead on this, as he had done much dealing in furs at Birka. They must take some of their men with them, for the carrying of the furs demanded it.

Eskil divided the furs and skins into three lots, leaving two behind on the ships, and with Runulv by his side and three men carrying what he wished to sell, set out.

The quarter housing the buyers and sellers of furs and hides was nearly at the furthest reaches from their lodging, allowing the agent to guide them through streets and squares yet undiscovered by the traders. One larger square held a set of stocks, three in number. None were prisoned there, but the very look of them caused their agent to speak.

"Any who attempts to cheat our visiting traders, who disturbs our peace, or are caught stealing will spend time here, awaiting their punishment." It was succinct enough, and the fact that the stocks were that day empty gave little reassurance, for the wear on the wood around neck and wrist locks told of much use.

They moved on until they reached the dedicated street of fur and skin sellers. All were prepared for a lavish display of pelts, but reaching the stalls, hung with numberless furs of every type and hue, did not fail to impress. Some, such as fox and wolf, still had their heads attached, adding to the sense that jaws might snap as they neared. After making a careful survey of the goods, and noting which sellers eyed what his men bore in their arms, Eskil went to work. Not all furs of the same animal could be of identical quality, but northern furs were so desired that even the least amongst the offerings, those of the marten, brought three times as much as Eskil could have sold them at Birka. The pelts of the white fox commanded four times the silver, here.

This trek was repeated next day, with the second lot of furs. The furriers were all in alertness at their return, with several gesturing wildly at them as they turned into the street. Eskil found himself waved over to the man to whom he had sold the three white fox. The Svear himself was carrying the pelts of mink he had to offer, and these had at once captured the furrier's eye. At the same time Runulv, heading the men who carried the rest of the furs they wished to sell that day, was almost instantly engaged by the two dealers in a neighbouring stall, who signaled they wished to look at the beaver skins.

The agent's attention thus divided, Eskil found himself being offered a cup of some refreshment by the furrier who had waved him over. The fellow had readily purchased the Winter-white fox, at a sum Eskil could never command back home, and was eager for the mink. These pelts had been taken at their most lustrous, thick, dark brown, and of the softness of a rabbit. Eskil set the mink down on the counter so the man might turn them over for flaws in the hide, as well as measure their length and breadth. But first they hoisted the tiny cups of ruddy-brown liquid the man offered from a pottery flask. Eskil looked the man in the eye, correct form for all who shared drink in northern lands, and the fellow met his look. The drink was as pungent as any Eskil had ever tasted, and the burn in the back of his throat told him of its strength; no man could drink much of this and keep his head. The offering of this was mere distraction though, for as Eskil lowered the cup the furrier placed a small green object near the tail of the mink nearest him. Eskil's eyes dropped to it, and saw it for what it was. Jade.

Eskil had seen jade only twice on offer at Birka, tiny figurines of it, one of a fanciful beast, the other of a man standing in a long gown. This one was also a man, one seated cross-legged, eyes closed, with the suggestion of an elaborate headdress on his head. It was clearly a bribe, that he sell the mink to him. Eskil considered the piece, then covered the small jade with his palm. A moment later it was secreted in one of the pouches at his belt. The furrier smiled, and Eskil did as well. They both raised their arms to wave the agent over, that he might witness the exchange of furs for silver.

Later that day as Eskil sat with Runulv at the brew-house they favoured, he brought forth the little figure and held it on his palm. Both men were flushed with the success of another day of good trading, and Eskil could not hide his grin as he showed Runulv what he had gained.

"Jade. From Cathay."

"Cathay," Runulv repeated. This was unimaginably distant; making the journey they had undertaken here small by comparison.

"I might keep it," Eskil said. His thoughtful tone was not usual with him.

"You might have ended up in those stocks for accepting it," Runulv could not help but point out.

"Já," the Svear conceded. "And the furrier next to me, for offering it." He gave a short laugh, but returned his gaze to the tiny figure. "He looks like he has known good fortune," he went on, studying the serene face of the figure. The tiny mouth did indeed bear the suggestion of a smile, and the roundness of the figure's belly seemed proof of a life lived without lack.

"I would say he has found contentment," Runulv agreed.

UFFA

WITH the plenteous silver gained from the sale of the furs, they were ready to hunt for silk. Neither trader was surprised to learn that this precious fabric was sold near the palace; they had already learnt that the compound had its own silk works for production of the finest grade. They would be permitted to purchase a lesser grade, only. Like all for sale in the great city it was strictly controlled, but what they were allowed to look at was pleasing beyond limit. Eskil had handled silk a few times in his trading and raiding life, most painfully allowing a long length of red fabric to fall to the Dane in a dice game. Still, he wished to see the merchants, though Runulv, destined to carry it on to Paris, would do the buying.

Their agent led them to a single building fast by the palace walls. It was guarded by pairs of dedicated sentries, as were the sellers of spice. Within were tables set with folded pieces of silk in a spectrum of colours, from subtle to eye-popping. They were not the shimmering bolts of plain stuff, however brilliantly hued, that both men had seen in the past. The fabric lengths were long and fairly narrow, an ell, the length of a man's arm from fingertips to elbow, but were figured in their weaving, and done so with unsurpassed skill. Interwoven amongst the silk warp was a riot of designs, subtle if the same colour of silk thread had been used as the weft, and a riot of colour if contrasting shades were chosen. These panels were woven with figures of birds, trees, animals, flowers, and even folk who appeared to be dancing. There was a story in every length for those who took the time to admire, and imagine. The birds flew to other shapes that could be ships on a distant sea; the people moved with each other, though facing the viewer, and the animals pranced or ran, legs outstretched.

Runulv had seen such strips of fabric adorning the dress of the ladies and noblemen of the court of Paris, and knew there he would find ready buyers. He bought the longest lengths he could, enough to encircle the hem of a woman's gown, or enrich the bottom of the vestments worn by the priests he had seen in the King's company. Such were sewn upon the linen or wool of the piece, as embellishment. He chose some in bright hues, others sombre, to appeal to all buyers. When he was done with selecting those for Paris, he gathered up two shorter panels, single-coloured but with interwoven designs. Each was enough to serve sewn on as a panel running down the front of a gown, or worn as a trailing head-wrap. These he meant as gifts, a blue length for Gyda, and a green for Ceridwen. Runulv knew of no woman or man who wore or owned silk on Gotland. For the parting of what seemed modest silver he could correct that for two who had invested much in this undertaking.

The shifting of the remaining goods they carried lay ahead. The seal skins and walrus hides were the most valuable of these. The seal was prized for the making of water-proof mantles; the walrus hide, cut into a continuous long strip, was of matchless worth as ship's line. For these their agent led them to the outfitters, just up the coast from the impound piers holding the ships of visiting merchants. None needed water-shedding cloaks more than those who lived on ships, open to all weather, and the seal skins sold at once. The two enormous walrus hides took longer, merely because few of the outfitters could afford to buy. They were sold to two different line-makers, and happy they were to have them. Runulv had been told it was the women of the Sámi who undertook the scraping of the inner side of the hide. Their goal was to pre-serve every bit of precious fat for burning in their oil cressets, and, working gently with bone and smooth stone implements, to leave the skin of even and unblemished thickness. The respect with which they had treated their work was repaid in the sums paid for the finished hides.

The beeswax and honey, both products of Tindr's bees and his own industry, were dealt next, and sold in different quarters. The many shallow wooden boxes into which Tindr had poured the beeswax were trundled in a wheeled hand-wain the agent brought forth for their use. He led them to one of the smaller churches in Miklagårdr, but one possessed of a cloister behind which teemed with workshops. It was here monks rendered raw beeswax into tapers to grace the altars for every sanctuary in the great city. Runulv brought along the lengths of linen wicking cord as well, rightly assuming any who dipped tapers might also be interested. Two dark-clad monks came out to speak to the agent and see what these northerners had brought. The slight aroma of honey rose to their noses as they inspected the golden wax, and the benign smiles on their faces told the traders they were well pleased.

Runulv sold both wax and wicking there, and not without thinking how far the product of Tindr's hives had travelled.

The agent further advised they take the jars of honey first to the compounders of medicants, as honey was used in healing salves, and philtres to be drunk. Another ready buyer would be the countless food stalls. In northern lands honey was the only sweetener. Here they had also the sticky dates, boiled into a syrup. This was a liquid which imparted both intense sweetness and distinct flavour to what it was added to, or poured over. Tindr's amber-gold honey came from the forest, the product of his bees foraging over woodland flowers, tree blossoms, clovers, and any other plants offering them nectar. Its flavour was gentle, its sweetness more subtle. The agent did not care which group they sold to, cooks or the compounders of cures, so they visited both, to see which valued the honey more. They sold it all to a woman who ran the largest of the stalls selling to healers, and those who prepared ointments to soften and soothe the skin. She was the first woman they had dealt with for an important sale, and Runulv looked forward to telling Tindr's mother Rannveig this, for like the brewster, she was a good woman of business, careful in her inspection and decisive in her offering to purchase all they had wheeled in.

They had a quantity of amber to offer, both beads and raw lumps, and of different hues, and the agent assigned to accompany them that day made swift pronouncement.

"The red amber," the agent advised. "Do not sell it to a bead maker, or the workers of amber ornaments. They will welcome your yellow amber. For the red, sell to one of the incense makers. It will be grated, blended with other resins and raw woods, and used for incense in their mixtures. Also the compounders of medicants desire red amber, for their potions. Both will pay well for your ruddy amber."

They thus began with the yellow, taking it to bead makers and the carvers of talismans. This tree-gold, as it was often called, had been mostly gathered from the shores of the Baltic by the Polanie. As with all trade goods, the further from the source anything was carried, the more likely it was to be valued. Beads and tawny lumps both would be sold on further south, where amber was a rarity.

Their agent next advised on the selling of the red. "All perfumes and incense are sold by the terrace gate of the palace; the compounders and sellers of such are stationed there by royal decree, that their sweet fragrances may float into the living quarters of the royal family. Your red amber will sell to those who make incense."

Runulv was more than ready for this, as one precious item he sought was that he had a personal stake in. Sidroc had asked that he bring back a vial of rose oil intended for Ceridwen. Knowing the red amber could be sold on the same visit added zeal to Runulv's efforts with the perfumers. Besides the rose oil, he sought to obtain those essences widely coveted by those who wished to give rich gifts to the churches of the Christian God in Paris: oil of spikenard, oil of myrrh, resin of frankincense, and oil of sandalwood. When trading with nobles there he had been asked more than once if he had these amongst his wares. Such vied to present the richest gifts they could for the glory of their God. Now he could answer that indeed he did.

First they changed much silver into gold solidi, for the oils they sought would be costly enough to demand these, and gold pieces were far more compact.

The walk to the perfumer's district recalled them to their first trading day here, when they were led to the palace with the eider down to sell to the Eparch himself. The stalls and booths of the perfumers and incense makers were of a higher class from those from which more common goods were sold. They found the wooden structures themselves more solid, the awnings above them more colorful, and the tables upon which the wares were set laid with fine cloth, fringed at the hem, and swaying in the breezes.

Beyond these stalls stood another palace gate, and above this, a garden green with small, tightly trimmed trees. This garden, being elevated on its terrace, lay open to the eye. Behind the trees they saw buildings of white stone, with peaked roofs and open colonnades of the same stone. They hoped to see folk moving about, but none save guards were in view.

The stalls of the incense makers before them did not disappoint. Their noses led them on, for it seemed each stall featured a smoking censer, from which the maker's compounds wafted. Here men and women stood or sat, at work grinding, pounding, and chipping away at those fragrant elements from which they created their blends. Some were oils, some resins, some fats, some roots, and some even woods, for both slats of pungent camphorwood and mellow sandalwood were offered to them to smell. They focused their attention on those makers who displayed red amber, for there might be a ready buyer for a fresh supply. In the end they traded all the ruddy amber they had with them for three small metal boxes of frankincense.

"Paris," Runulv could not help but mutter as he placed the boxes with their costly chunks of resin into his pack. Even the King of Paris himself had once asked Runulv for frankincense. He traded here for amber; he would sell in Paris for gold.

Now for the perfumed oils. Vials of simple, single oils could be bought, as well as scented goods for the making of perfumes and soaps: agarwood, bergamot, and from the bitter orange tree two prized products, neroli oil from its blossoms, and petitgrain from its leaves; these gave a green scent.

They must use gold to buy two generous vials of spikenard, and two of oil of myrrh. This last, Runulv had been told, was used for the anointing of the esteemed dead. It smelt ill to Eskil, as did much he was forced to sniff, but he only shrugged and let Runulv get on with his trading.

Last was the rose oil Sidroc had asked for. Their agent pointed them to several stalls near the palace wall for them to browse, but then, seeing another agent several stalls down accompanying a trader, told them he would return shortly. A slight delay was no hardship to Runulv, who did not wish to be rushed in his selection. He and Eskil approached the first of the stalls, talking amongst themselves of the array of tiny stoppered pottery jars and coloured glass vials laid out upon the counters.

Watching them was a man leaning against a nearby wall. His beard was brown, well streaked with grey. A pale turban rested on his head, and he wore a dark cloak which crossed over his chest to rest over his right shoulder. On the fabric, and positioned in the middle of his chest, was embroidered a human eye, one powerfully open and alert, for small lines radiated from it, as if it were all-seeing. He was then a teller of fortunes.

The fortune-teller was staring at them, and with a look in his eyes that suggested he knew of what they spoke. As he neared they saw those eyes were blue, and not the brown of many of his brethren, though his face, weathered by Sun and wind, was bronzed enough.

He straightened up and came to them.

"You are Gotlanders," he declared.

Eskil was taken aback at this guess; both men were.

"We are, one of us," Runulv replied. It was startling, yet welcome, to be greeted thus. Runulv gestured toward Eskil. "And one of us is Svear."

The fortune-teller gave a nod at the yellow-haired Svear, but returned his eyes to Runulv.

"But you, my friend, are of Gotland."

Runulv was quick to grin back. This stranger also spoke that tongue distinct to his home island, both in his word choice and accent.

"You wear the sign of a fortune-teller; at least we were told an open eye meant this."

The stranger laughed. "And lucky for you, and for your own fortunes," he answered. "Your hamingja is strong today to have run into me.

"I am Uffa, born and bred on Fårö." He who claimed this had a wide grin on his face, as if proud to proclaim this heritage to one who would find it meaningful.

"Fårö," Runulv repeated, and with no little wonder. This was a small island at the very northern tip of Gotland, a place of few folk, many sheep, and towering limestone rauks reaching as if to Asgard. One must row or sail across to reach it, and the channel between great and small island, though not broad, was fraught with high winds and swift currents.

Uffa gave a deep nod. "My folk have farmed and fished there since it rose from the sea." This was no idle boast, as those few families who dwelt there seemed to have done so forever.

Uffa looked pleased to have been able to share this with the Gotlander, and spoke again.

"If you wish to follow me to wine, dismiss your agent after you have made your purchases. I will be here, waiting for you."

"Right now we go after rose oil," Runulv answered. "I have already spikenard and myrrh oil for Paris," he added, with a tilt of his head toward the sellers of these rarities.

Uffa nodded, his face showing no surprise at this. He looked down the line of booths and spoke a few words of advice.

"As it is rose oil you seek, go to the fourth seller. He has large land holdings, and his own folk grow roses there. He is justly proud of them, but sells other oils and essences as well.

"You must praise his wares," Uffa instructed. "All merchants in Miklagårdr are vain, and these, more so. They have won the right to trade here in the shadow of the palace, and are persuaded that no goods can be finer than those offered here. A wise man will allow them to boast. Listen as he extolls his wares, and nod your head.

"Likewise, do not wrinkle your nose at anything he allows you to smell; some of these are tinctures, parts of greater fragrances and perfumes, and he will expect that you will know this, even if it smells foul. You must nod your head in approval at all. If you like, I will come and speak for you. Say what you like, he will understand nothing, but your face, he will."

"And the reaching for my purse," answered Runulv.

Uffa must smile, for there was no more decisive gesture than this.

"Tell him that even along the stone streets of Paris you have smelt no sweeter fragrances, nor bought from scent-sellers more skillful than he," Uffa went on.

"He will try to press many other oils upon you, for fear you will not part with the gold the rose oil commands. After this I will ask him to bring out his finest examples of rose in order of delicacy. The first will be the most costly, for the nose dulls after sniffing too many scents, and he means for you to choose that first. But insist on the second, it will have a richness of scent nearly as great, and at less cost.

"Your agent is back," Uffa noted, for the man had left the agent he was speaking to. "He will not mind if I speak for you, and will witness your dealings just as always."

Runulv gestured that Uffa join them, and the fortune-teller, with a respectful greeting to the agent in the tongue of the Greeks, did so. In short order both Runulv and Eskil were being plied with requests to sniff the opened vials of many scents, and only Uffa's firmness that the rose oil be offered deterred the man. Runulv made his speech praising the fragrance of the oils, which Uffa not only rendered into Greek but must have embellished, as he went on at far more length than Runulv had.

The rose was indeed like the concentrated aroma of an entire field of blossoms, and a single drop was enough to perfume the person who applied it. Runulv selected the oil Uffa had advised, for he could tell no difference between the first two offered. Next Runulv chose amongst the glass vials displayed, and had the seller funnel that chosen into a vial enlivened with green and blue swirls. It was no small vial, but longer than a man's pointing finger, and twice as thick. Ceridwen, Runulv thought, would long have the pleasure of this scent. The oil now within the glass, a wooden stopper was firmly pressed in, and then dipped into a small pot of molten wax to further secure it. After the seller set it upright, he took off a gold ring from his right hand and pressed it into the warm wax, impressing it with his seal. The vial was then folded in linen, and laid into a small wooden box cushioned with wads of linen tow. The box lid was placed upon it, wrapped round with a ribband of blue, and tightly tied. One more step awaited, as the seller dripped a spoonful of molten wax over the ribband, and again impressed it with his ring.

The rose oil was the most costly of all the oils Runulv bought that day, and this care was justified. As Runulv readied to pass over gold for it, Uffa nodded, and tilted his head to the wall where they had first seen him, suggesting he would await them there.

"You have done us a service," Runulv told him.

The fortune-teller grinned and touched his finger to the embroidered eye on his chest. "Your hamingja brought you to me," he answered.

When they returned to where he stood, Uffa threw his cloak over the other shoulder, obscuring the thread-work eye. It was clear he was done with fortune-telling for the day. As they joined him he repeated his offer.

"I would hear of Gotland, if not my home island. I have wine, and better than what many taverns pour."

The two had been warned about dealing with rogues and rascals. But Runulv, a canny judge of men as all good traders must be, had made up his mind to follow Uffa; he was of Gotland.

Eskil had a simple test, though.

"Who dealt shrewdly with the King at Uppsala, and bargained that he be ready to defend Gotland if needed?"

The Svear had been told this story, and in great detail by Berse, and figured it to be as good as any test of those claiming to be a Gotlander.

"Why, Avair Strabain," Uffa fired back. He followed this up by saying, "Let me tell you the tale of how the bandy-legged one brought the King at Uppsala to heel . . . "

Eskil raised his hands in surrender. "Nej, nej. I know it too well, thanks to our friend Berse, who journeys with us."

As the three began walking Runulv asked a question of his fellow islander.

"How long have you been here?"

Uffa cocked his head to one side and bit his lip.

"Eight, ten years," he guessed.

"Ten years," repeated Runulv, in real wonder. "And you have not been home to the island?"

"Nai. And I begin to miss it."

Runulv glanced at Eskil. They were three men short, but it was not wise to be hasty in such vital matters as taking on another man.

Uffa led them north, away from the palace, and almost to the edge of the wall fronting the sea. Large squares and stone buildings gave way to smaller structures of brick, and many of timber. Here folk cooked at street corners on open braziers, selling food for a few bronze coins to those returning home from a day's labour at ware-houses or the near ship-works. The streets reeked of frying fish and the boiled offal of cattle, and dogs growled for the scraps thrown to them.

Then Uffa turned down a narrow passage of stone, roofed over with more stone. It was a point of control; a sentry stood there, one known to Uffa as they gave a nod to each other.

"I live with the common whores," Uffa told them as they walked on. He followed this with a short laugh. "Lodging is cheap, and the women, mostly kind."

Eskil and Runulv wondered why they had not been asked to pay a fee as they entered, but perhaps this only occurred when a man had chosen a woman. At any rate they followed their guide down the passageway.

They soon arrived at his lodgings, a timber building of ancient make, sturdy enough, but with a cant to the ridge of the gable roof. The house was divided into rooms around a small courtyard, in which a cooking fire was being tended by two older women. Uffa produced a key from his belt and turned it in an iron lock upon his door, one dark with age. It opened to a single room, but fitted out with sleeping alcove, a table, and two benches. A large brass brazier, unlit today, sat on the floor upon a slab of stone. Uffa went out to the cookfire and returned carrying a few burning straws, and with these lit two oil lamps. The sudden light allowed him to close the door partway, for the room had no window. He then set his hands to his head and pulled off his turban, revealing his hair, light brown, and grey only at the temples. He might have seen two score years, perhaps less; with his weather-browned face it was hard to tell. Like many Gotlandic men, he was well-knit, with a breadth of shoulders to suggest they would lend both strength and stamina to all his efforts.

A jug was produced from a chest, and three pottery cups. Uffa poured out a wine so pale as to resemble water, which despite its delicate hue, was as potent as any mead.

Both Runulv and Eskil remarked on it, for it was in fact the finest they had tasted here.

They had so far seen no likely women since they had passed through the covered passageway, and Eskil wished to return to the subject.

"You mentioned women," he prompted, and leant slightly forward over the table towards their host. Uffa laughed.

"I can point out which establishments are known to be the best," he offered. "But they are simple girls."

Eskil's face seemed to indicate that a simple girl would be fine by him. Nonetheless, Uffa, with a rapt audience of two, went on in his telling.

"If you want a better sort of woman you should go to the main bath-houses, and to the halls where men and women perform. One who can dance, sing, play cymbals or pipe or harp will cost more. Services of all kinds can be purchased from them." Uffa lifted his arm to gesture about them, though they could see nothing but his four walls. "These whores are country girls, rounded up, sold by their parents most of them, to serve here for a few years. They are strictly controlled, as all else is, in Miklagårdr. Once their earnings fall off they will be dismissed, and handed some fragment of what men have paid for them. Also, any gifts they have been given are theirs; trinkets and odd silver and such."

"What happens to them," Eskil wished to know.

Uffa thought a moment. "Some remain here in Miklagårdr, becoming serving women in the households of families. Others work in taverns and brew-houses. Others return home, I am told. I have also heard some go to live together in the great halls of women which the Christians keep. Convents, they are called."

The thoughtful look on the Svear's face suggested he had never before considered the Fate of such women. He gave a slow nod, listening to all this.

Runulv was ready to move on to other subjects.

"How have you lived here, for so many years," he wished to know.

"I left Fårö and went adventuring with some Svear. I came with a crew of them from Birka. We had fair sailing; it was Summer and we made good time. But we lost nearly half our men to the Pechenegs once we ran out of water to sail on. Some of us gave up and stayed at Kyiv, content to trade there and then make it back with other traders. A few of us pressed on. I was one.

"Miklagårdr did not disappoint me. Birka was the largest trading town I had seen, then to come here . . . " He raised his hand as if to gesture at the greatness of the city. The eyes of his listeners shifted, recalling the modest structures surrounding them, but they nodded just the same.

"First I worked in the boat yard, and still do at times when they need me. Your ship is at the impound pier, I think," he guessed. When they nodded at the truth of this he went on. "Further down the coast, there are several ship-wrights. I worked at repairing and fitting ships, most of which for the Black Sea trade. I do all kinds of ship joinery. I can sew sails, as well. In Winter, with fewer ships, there is little of this work to be had.

"In the past I have sometimes acted as guide to special merchants who arrive with vast amounts of wares, two score camels loaded with goods from Samarkand and beyond. I would advise them how to most profitably offer what they carry, so as not to weaken the price of any one type of good through a surplus."

"We were told the Eparch manages the valuation of all goods," Eskil pointed out.

"That is true. But first his agents must see what is carried in. A large caravan of camels can remain outside the walls, and the goods be brought in chest by chest, over days and even weeks to meet demand. The traders from the eastern reaches are not limited to a mere month of trading time, as you are.

"But such can be a dangerous business. More and more I stay within the walls. I serve as courier for several families of note, who wish to invite certain visiting dignitaries to Miklagårdr to view their goods. I am not Greek and so am trusted to have no greater interest than that of the family who pays me."

It was easy to believe Uffa had acted as advisor to buyers and sellers; he had done so today, and for them.

"And you tell fortunes," Eskil posed.

"When times are lean, I will do what it takes to fill my bowl with grain, and my cup with wine," he answered. "As a wise man would," he added, reaching for the jug to refill those of his guests. Eskil had to grin as he accepted another cup.

The afternoon wore on, whiled away most pleasantly with wine and talk. Uffa wished to know everything of recent note from Gotland, and his naming of a number of places known to Runulv lent credence to his interest. As the shadows began to darken the courtyard outside, his guests began to stir; they must take their leave.

Uffa stood with them and made a second offer.

"Tomorrow there are games at the Hippodrome, the long and tall structure along the western wall of the palace. If you have not been, you might have heard shouts and cheers from it if you are near. There will be horse races; men in small standing carts, called chariots. Each man drives a team of four horses."

"Four, for a single man?" asked Eskil.

Uffa gave a nod. "Já. They go at speeds none of us have ever travelled." He laughed, then added. "It is free to enter and watch, a gift of the imperial city. Men can wager on their favourite driver, but a wise man would not," he added, for the Svear's benefit, for he seemed keen to hear this, "without good knowledge of the fitness of driver and team on that day. But watching is fine sport."

It was an offer both wished to take up, and Runulv and Eskil nodded their heads in agreement.

"You are at the lodging of the Rus," Uffa went on. "I will come for you in the morning, and we will set off."

After they had broken their fast Uffa did appear, in different guise. He had no turban on his head, nor did he sport his fortune-telling cloak, and looked more than ever like the Gotlander he truly was.

As soon as they neared the palace precincts it was clear a festival of some sort was underway, by the numbers of those streaming towards the massive arcaded structure which loomed ahead. They heard unseen trumpets ring out, barely muffled by the distance, and then the growing rumble of voices shouting in excitement. Uffa walked them past several arched openings which led in, choosing the one he favoured. Once inside they were in a kind of narrow forecourt, roofed over, and with stone steps leading up. It was the floor that first caught the eyes of his guests, though, for they were covered in mosaic-work. These were not the large-eyed folk whose sober personages lined the domed ceilings and arched walls of Hagia Sophia. Instead they walked upon a riot of animals, all depicted in tiny pieces of stone. Marching camels were there, great cats with spotted coats, mighty horned oxen, crowing cocks, and the big blue-breasted bird with the fanning tail they had spotted in the palace garden. Most fantastical of all was the stone picture of a bull-like animal with a huge head, flapping ears, a tapering snout longer than its legs, with long tusks, worked in white pieces of stone, protruding from its mouth. Despite the men moving around them, both Runulv and Eskil must stop in wonderment and stare at this image. They saw the beast was of giant size, for at its side stood a human figure, made puny by the beast's height and girth.

"An elephant," Uffa told them. "They are larger even than that; I have seen two, here in the city, ridden by Princes. The tusks are ivory, such as walrus, but these can grow as long as a man's leg."

The two traders just looked at each other, shaking their heads. The noise urged them onward; a race was underway, and they climbed the stone steps behind Uffa. Though they were not yet fully inside, and still under the arched passage-way leading in, they must stop and watch, open-mouthed. The vastness of the arena was before them, one holding countless men sitting upon the tiers of stone lining the interior. Below them lay the long oval of the track, with a tight turn at each end. Horses in teams of four thundered by, pulling the wheeled chariots, which looked no larger than a hand-wain, just large enough for the man driving the horses to stand in. One team reached the point almost directly opposite where they stood, and the crowd erupted in wild shouts and whistles.

"I want to do this," Eskil muttered.

Uffa, standing next him, laughed. "The men who do so, train for years. Their teams of horses, also. First they race a single pair of horses, and only after mastering that are they allowed to drive four. Rich families sponsor them, and they compete for their honour, and status. Many of the drivers of four-horse teams do not live long, though while they live, they have gold and women in plenty."

Eskil had one thought: Such a life was akin to being a body-guard to the King at Uppsala. It might be a short life, but it was a good one.

But Uffa was going on. "Men die. Horses too. Drivers are thrown from their chariots, and trampled by horses, and run over by the wheels of others'. The chariots weaken and break apart under the stress, or they collide. Also, the long whips. They are not used on the horses only, but other drivers. Drivers have been blinded by a lash across the face."

It was a sport full of fascination, but full of fearsome awe as well, for the speed and danger of it.

An interval ensued, in which men ran out into the course, retrieving pieces of chariots or harness trappings from the hard sand. The crowd quieted as this happened, only to have the air pierced by the shrill sounding of many horns. At one end, and high up the stands so they might be heard by all, a rank of trumpeters stood, long brass horns to their mouths. They blew out in unison a fanfare, which to the ears of Runulv was greatly pleasing, and also fitting to the pageantry of the contest, and its setting.

They found seats, and Uffa pointed over to an elevated platform in the walled-off centre of the track. This was an island to itself, adorned with tall shafts of stone, and set about with life-size bronze statues of horses and their drivers; great racers, Uffa told them, who lived on in memory. Men there were at work in this island, setting large oval objects into supporting cups. Runulv squinted at them; they looked almost like gigantic eggs.

"Eggs they are, from the birds kept by the Emperor," Uffa told them. "The birds do not fly, but run faster than a horse. They are taller than a man, with long legs and necks. Ostrich, they are called. Their eggs are set here to show how many circuits are left to run, and they remove one egg after the lead driver passes them during the race."

"That . . . is an egg," Eskil repeated. It was one more thing about the Hippodrome to astonish.

As they awaited the start of the next race, men and boys with baskets roamed the rising steps on which they sat, selling pouches of walnuts, bread loaves stuffed with soft cheese and the flesh of olives, and fruit.

They bought a selection, treating their host, and settled back to scan the interior. Runulv realised, with almost a start, that amongst the many thousands watching, he saw no women, none at all.

"Are women forbidden?" he asked Uffa.

"There is no law, but it is custom, followed by all. Though in the private viewing areas it is known that powerful men bring courtesans, that they might have the pleasure of watching from a couch of silk, while playing other sport." He pointed out a few stone pavilions, which jutted out from the general seating areas, and which were largely screened by flowing draperies.

Uffa pointed to a particularly large stone colonnade. "That is the Imperial viewing stand. If the Emperor were here, flags would be flying from its corners, and guards stationed about it." Above this structure stood four horses in shining metal, as if they raced abreast to honour he who made these races free for all men. With their thick arched necks and proudly lifted hooves they were of uncommonly noble design, and so life-like as to make the viewer wonder at such skill.

A race began, six teams of horses starting abreast, and nearly filling the width of the track. Two went awry before the first turn, colliding as each attempted to cross over to near the inner stone wall of the track. One chariot lost a wheel and overturned, spilling its driver upon the packed sand, luckily free from the hooves of a chariot behind him. The second driver lost his reins, his chariot veering off course after his horses had been bumped. The other four chariots raced on, while men stationed at the side of the track ran out to capture horses and drag the injured driver to safety.

The noise was deafening; Uffa and his guests had almost to shout at each other to be heard. One by one as the remaining drivers circled, an ostrich egg was removed from its holder, that all might know how many circuits remain. A third chariot broke down while rounding the tight turn, forced into the inner wall when the draught pole separated from the team harnessed to it. The horses ran off, kicking their hind legs and tossing their heads, but the driver was pitched over the low stone wall. With only three chariots left the lead team gained distance and crossed the mark, causing the trumpeters to add to the clamorous acclaim of the watching crowd. Most of the men in the arena stood the entire race, whistling, cheering, and pumping their arms in support.

The winning driver brought his lathered horses forward, and received a green and leafy wreath which was laid upon his head, and a small pouch, a purse of some kind.

"Will it be gold?" Eskil asked Uffa.

The Gotlander nodded. Eskil, considering that at least two drivers were hurt and one mayhap dead, must re-think his wish to join the action.

Uffa went on. "Such a race with six teams is the most perilous, and so gold is awarded. The winners also receive payment from those who sponsor them, to keep them racing here in Miklagårdr."

Eskil must ask the next. "There are other places to race like this?"

Uffa smiled. "All throughout Byzantium. Any place where Rome or the Greeks built a city, there is a Hippodrome. It is a favoured sport, then and now."

That night lying on the narrow bed in his alcove, Runulv let his thoughts run to his wife, Gyda. Each day here was a crush of impressions, sights, scents, and sounds. Today they had met Uffa, from their own small island, and thought of this brought home even stronger to mind, and heart. To think of Gyda and their boys snug and at their farm was a respite. Despite the many wonders he had seen, and those rare goods he had been able to acquire, the noise and crowds of Miklagårdr were beginning to wear on him. Though Gyda could not know it, he had reached his goal. He was safe, but had lost two men, and Eskil a third. He could only trust that all was well on Gotland. Gyda's nephews were with her in his absence, and Sidroc and Ceridwen but less than an hour's ride away. More trading awaited, but Runulv felt the call for home, and felt it strongly.

WISE MEN

FROM that day onward Uffa became part of almost every day for Runulv and Eskil. His presence also enlarged the pastimes of their men as well. The next time races were to be held at the Hippodrome, Uffa came to the lodging house as the crews broke their fast, and escorted as many who wished to see the spectacle to the arena, which was in fact every man of them. As far as trading, he gave advice to those who wished to hear it; many of the men had already sold what goods they had carried with them, and Uffa could encourage that with the silver earned they might buy something more valuable for trade in northern lands. If they had traded their goods for others, he gave suggestion that they might trade again to best advantage, for the men were ever visiting merchant stalls and workshops and discovering new and more desirable articles. Some men who had sheepskins or fleece to sell were happy just to accept the silver, and go home with that, for the dense, soft, and curly wool of the Gotland sheep was greatly appreciated here. Others traded them for such diverse goods as copper ware, intricately designed locks and keys, or small branches of pink coral from warmer waters than they had ever known.

There was now less than a fortnight left in the thirty days they were granted to trade in Miklagårdr. In counting their gains Runulv and Eskil were indeed satisfied. Of valuable items they sought to procure, gemstones and dyes and colourants were those they had yet to pursue. As was the case for the makers of incense and the perfumers, these two groups of artisans were placed almost next each other, for many of the costly pigments were in fact ground from prized gemstones and other minerals. Other dyes were made from insects, such as the red kermes Runulv hoped to acquire. The most prized of all animal dyes was one not permitted to leave the imperial city in the hands of foreign traders. This was the purple dye rendered from the sea mollusk. This, like the finest silk, was restricted to royal use, though Uffa told them the Emperor would send shipments to royal courts and religious leaders throughout Byzantium, and beyond.

Miklagårdr had provided a lavishness of colour in nearly every trading quarter they visited, but only the silk-sellers matched the makers of pigments and dyes in astonishing the eye. The booths and stalls of sellers were laid with both raw material and result, for side by side to a heap of brownish grains or wrinkled grey roots would be laid a strip of cloth dyed from the humble base material. Thus it was easy to seek the mineral or root desired, by the result shown. Runulv sought both dyestuffs for fabric, and pigments out of which paints could be made. Certain colours in the small pictures in the holy books of the Christians could only be made from ground gemstones or minerals.

One of their first stops was at a table upon which ran narrow lengths of brilliant fabric. Uffa greeted the seller, while Runulv's gaze moved from a series of lighter to more intense golden shades of wool, laid out as example.

"He says this is arsenikon, and gives this range of yellow. It comes from the hills of Anatolia," Uffa related, gesturing to the pale lumps of chalky mineral.

"And these are from a nearby mine to the first, and is called sandaraca. It will be pounded into that orange-red, like unto the sunset." The fabric he gestured to was indeed the hue of a flaming Sun upon its descent. The next he related was what Runulv most wished to learn. "Dyes for fabric, and paint for sculptures and pictures on parchment are made from these lumps."

Uffa listened the longer, as the man grew more animated in his telling. "Care must be taken in the pounding of them, that one does not breathe in over-much of the dust." The seller was now miming a man gone mad, akin to a dog with a frothing mouth. They watched, eyes widening, and Uffa continued after the man resumed his natural countenance.

"Only criminals mine these; it is their death sentence to chip away in the holes they are found in."

Eskil had been reaching to handle one of the dusky lumps, and now withdrew his hand.

Thus cautioned, Runulv answered with some resolve. "I will sell it intact to the court of Paris." He took generous supply of both, watching as the seller used tongs to move the lumps into linen bags, and then into small boxes. Even the dust thereof would be valuable, Runulv knew, and worth capturing in the linen pouches it was shipped in.

Their next purchase was from a gem seller, and one who Runulv was glad to see, for the display set upon his blue-dyed tablecloth.

"Lapis," he observed aloud. There it was, chunks of blue veined lapis lazuli, ready to be cut into gemstones or pounded into paint for the tiny images in the prayer books made in Paris. He bought enough to fill his cupped hands, happy to part with gold to carry this back with him.

They were not done searching for blue, and their agent led them to the sellers of indicum. Blue-yielding indigo plants were pressed into blocks under such pressure that the finished product looked stone, and not vegetal. Clothing of deep blue was much prized in Paris, and Runulv bought ten blocks of the indicum.

Kermes was there, heaps of tiny dried insects from which a scarlet-red dye could be drawn, richer and brighter than any madder. These were so painstaking to collect that they were shown under a thin veil of gauze, so none might be blown off in a passing breeze. Runulv had strong memory of seeing fabric woven from kermes-red, and indigo-blue wool, the two competing for the eye as he looked upon it. Such contrast in a single garment would be prized by the nobles of Paris. He bought as much kermes as he could, trusting the greater the risk, the greater the reward.

It was Uffa who stopped them in front of a table, one with no display of the colour the chunks of dull and dried clay would yield. "Alum," he told them. "It is the best mordant, used to fix these dyes to fabric. You must buy a cask of it; it will reward you when you sell the indicum or kermes, to offer it." And so they did. Their agent wrote out a short script to give the seller's boy, who would deliver it to the impound pier on their behalf.

From the gem sellers they bought jasper in browns, reds, and greens: opals grey and cloudy as smoke; and red and white striped sardonyx. All these were carried as talismans and carved into amulets in Frankland, Runulv knew, and Uffa, after speaking at some length with the dealer, suggested that in Paris they be shown as well to the compounders of medicants, as each of these stones held healing powers.

At the end of this day Runulv and Eskil took Uffa out to the best tavern they had found, and ordered food and drink in happy abundance. It was no surprise that Uffa was known here, as it was a place frequented by foreign traders, and he must have had many dealings with those he had aided over the years. Runulv and Eskil's task was to come back with as little silver coin or hack-silver as they could, investing nearly all in rare goods to be sold at profit upon their return. In this they had more than done their part, and Uffa had aided them.

Their crews were also well pleased with the result of their trading. Berse in particular had little need for more silver; as a blade-smith he was one of the more prosperous men on all of Gotland. He had taken delight in trading the swords and spear-points he had wrought for objects which held interest, such as the curved scimitar he had traded for on his first day. Having travelled some as a young man, he had a taste for the exotic, and was bringing back a large brass pot, ornately decorated, with a separate chamber to hold dried leaves which would steep in hot water. He had sampled the result and must hide his distaste for the drink. But as an object of fascination it excelled, with an ebony-wood handle at the top, curved legs to hold it over a fire, and a spout to pour out the brew. The metal of it was beautifully worked with stamped designs of oddly roofed buildings; the sort of thing that gave pleasure merely to look at. He had also traded for gemstones, especially red garnets and carnelian. One day his boys would wed, and these would come in handy as the bride-price for the maids they chose.

The following few days were spent in procuring the final items Runulv and Eskil sought. Runulv returned to the maker of enamel ware, and bought more lidded pots. These would sell well in any trading town, whether those of the Polonie, or at Birka, Aros, or Ribe. Berse was with him on this occasion, browsing amongst the fashioners of enamel work, and allowed his eye to run over those objects displayed. Berse had lately purchased the gem stones for the future brides of his sons, and this task put him in mind of another woman. He was moved to look for a special gift amongst the gaily coloured copper work, one as unexpected as she the blade-smith considered. He found a striking and distinctive example of their art, and was glad to lay down silver for it.

The many taverns and food stalls gave inspiration as to what to buy, as well. Runulv tasted rice for the first time, often times tinted yellow by various spices. He liked it; it was unlike any other foodstuff he had known, the grains still firm in the mouth yet yielding readily to the teeth. It was a common staple throughout much of Byzantium, and a great portion of the eastern lands beyond, he was told. He must make decision: should he buy a large cask or two, and run the risk of none at his ports of call buying, for its strangeness? In the end he shook his head at this, while continuing to enjoy the eating of it whenever he found it ready cooked. Runulv did invest in a few jugs of the golden oil pressed from the olives, but these he intended as gifts for those at home, rather than future trade items.

Only the walrus ivory threatened to disappoint, for here at Miklagårdr the tusks of the elephant could be had. Still, Eskil set off with the four tusks they had, and returned with a single tusk from the larger beast. It was not the longest they had spotted, but was impressive enough, and Runulv agreed was a good trade.

Eskil, out on his own one day, entered into the guarded workshop of a gold-smith to see what he might. The Dane had staked him, and his own gain depended wholly on that percentage Sidroc had agreed to grant him on their return. Gold was plentiful in Miklagårdr, and Eskil let his eyes run over the array of coins from foreign Kings, delicate filigree necklaces with gem-stone drops, and even entire spoons cast of gold. He saw nothing he was moved to ask about, but gazing on so much precious metal, the Svear thought with regret of the tiny golden idol he had been forced to render to the Pechenegs. Then he laughed aloud, startling the smith. Doing so had likely saved all their lives, or so he had thought until Prince Karlen revealed his own secret gold piece. It would all be a good story told at Rannveig's brew-house, at any rate. And – he had the tiny figure of jade. Eskil liked holding it, and hoped he would not be forced to surrender it as he had that of gold.

The two captains returned to the impound pier, Brani and Berse with them. They wished to review all they pur-chased and traded for. As they had carried their newly-ac-quired goods on to Dauðadagr and the knorr, they secured them in turn, and used the empty wooden chests which had held the eider down to house the small goods, such as spices and oils. The silk fabric Runulv had taken special care of. Silk could be wet, and then dry, satisfactorily. But what Runulv had bought was extravagant in its beauty, and he wanted it to arrive in the same pristine condition in which it had been purchased, with no water-stain upon it. He had shared this concern with Uffa, who led him to a woman who made waxed linen as proof against water, and Runulv bought enough to wrap the silk lengths. Everything they examined looked secure, and ready for travel.

After this the four of them stood at the foot of the pier, admiring or deriding the various ships tied there, for lesser craft lay next to those of real size and value. Dauðadagr stood her ground against these; small as she was for a drekar, her lines were graceful and told of her speed. Runulv's eyes rested on her, and he looked to Berse. They had broken her down to ribs and planking to reach here, and feared they would need do so again.

For his part, Eskil was looking at the knorr he had rented from the ship-wright where the mouth of the Dnieper poured into the Black Sea.

"First, up the coast to that ship-works to return the knorr," he said aloud, for that would be the first leg of the journey home. "Then reloading its contents to the karv, and the dugouts."

The rest of them nodded at this; this labour was ahead of them. Right now it was enough to feel confident they had remaining silver from Sidroc's cask to pay for any wants along the way.

As they were walking back through the great bronze door they spotted Uffa. He was seated at the base of a fountain in his fortune-telling guise, turban upon his head, engaged with a man who looked to be hanging on every word. Uffa's hands rose and fell. He spoke in the tongue of the Greeks, they knew; the man seemed enthralled at what he heard. The four paused, and Uffa caught sight of them, lifting an eyebrow as if to stay them. He ended his story-telling, and as the man stood and passed a few coins over, Uffa bowed his head in thanks.

Uffa rose and joined them where they waited.

"What does Fate hold for him?" Eskil asked with a grin.

"Oh, good trading, of course. His fingers were black from buckthorn leaves; this told me he is likely a maker of ink. Yet he was surprised I knew this, and listened the more to all I told him. I advised him to go to the same cloister where you sold the beeswax, for they have constant need of dark ink, and cannot make all they use."

Uffa glanced down the narrow way into which the man had vanished. "And I told him his wife is faithful in his absence. That pleased him. Men worry, and worry the more when they are sporting with the whores here."

Eskil gave a laugh, but Runulv, the only married man amongst them, understood. He had no fear of Gyda's fidelity, only her well-being. Soon, he thought to himself, soon.

"We have been to the ships," is what he said. "Other than provisioning, and a few random gifts to buy, we are done with our trading. I think we should move off as soon as we can."

The fortune-telling Gotlander spent a moment looking at the four of them in turn.

"You did not ask for your own fortunes, but I give them to you," he said.

Runulv turned to Eskil, but it was the Svear that spoke.

"And a wise man would listen," he offered.

Uffa laughed back. "Let us talk over ale." He flung his cloak-end over his left shoulder, obscuring the thread-work eye on his chest. His stint as fortune-teller was finished.

Once with brimming cups in hand, Runulv repeated his decision.

"We must leave for home."

Uffa took a deep draught of his ale. "I will take you."

"You will take us?" This was Brani.

"Já." Uffa set down his cup.

"I will take you, but we must not leave so soon. We head overland; ice and snow will speed us." It had indeed grown cooler during their stay, and one morning a few flakes of snow were seen blowing through the air, though it melted as soon as it touched the stone streets.

"In two weeks the marshes will freeze," Uffa went on. "The rivers north of them are already hard. It is ice we need.

"Your ships are here, at the impound pier. Transfer all the goods you have stowed on them to the official of the Eparch there; he will keep them under lock and key. We will take both vessels to the ship-wrights, and have them fitted out for cradles and skis. We will use our oars to push the ships along, to help spare the horses."

They all knew that for a Winter return they must count on skidding the boats along, at least part way. Uffa seemed to know much of this, and even more.

"Horses," Runulv repeated.

"Já. That farm, the last you came to before you met the Black Sea – they have horses. They are broken to harness, for they are used mainly for logging. We will buy horses from them to pull the two ships. They are strong and hearty beasts, but to make the best time we must help them. The crews will stand in the hull at their rowing stations, and push along the ice and snow with the oars."

"Two ships," Eskil questioned. "Once I return the knorr, we will have a karv, and four dugouts. And Dauðadagr, the drekar Runulv sails."

Uffa looked at Eskil, with a twinkle in his eye. "A wise man would make a trade with the ship-wright at the mouth of the Dnieper: the boats you left with him, and the silver he demands, for the knorr you hired. We will go far faster in two large ships than in many smaller ones. And when we reach the Princes who sold you the boats, they will not be sorry to have the knorr in exchange."

"But the falls."

This was from Berse, who had so lately been thinking of the labour and loss suffered there.

Uffa shook his large head.

"We travel nowhere near the falls. We will speed over frozen marshland, which in Spring and Summer only a duck could be happy on. We will be home in far less time."

"Between us and the farm, is that final run of rough water," Runulv remembered. Those rapids were of short duration, but marked the final drop of land as the River Dnieper lowered itself to flow into the Black Sea.

Uffa nodded his head. "And for that stretch we will need cradles and skis. We will haul the ships out onto them, and get our sea – or snow legs – with our tamped oars. And use our backs," he must add, as they would as yet have no horses.

None he addressed had forgotten they had hauled both ships overland, at times through rain and mud.

Runulv gave thought. "We are nine-and-thirty," he muttered, gauging the effort required for that last run of rapids.

They had needed to unload all their small craft and haul them, coming down.

"Two score men, if I am with you," Uffa added. He spent a moment looking from face to face, as all three men considered starting out with two larger ships, and no karv or dug outs.

"It will be two days, for each ship, for us to pass the rocks," Uffa posited. "Then back in water, and on to the farm."

"How do you know all this," Eskil asked. He could not help but grin as he said the next. "And do not tell me what a wise man would know."

"Because my best sailing is not on water," Uffa replied. He smiled, though his answer seemed that kind of riddle skalds made to see if those who listened could solve.

"Not on water," Eskil repeated.

"I have sailed twice to Kyiv from Miklagårdr, and once I was past the Black Sea and those final rocks, the boat I guided never touched water."

"Thus the skis," Runulv answered.

Uffa nodded.

"How will you know where to head?" Brani asked. He knew how transformed was the Winter landscape.

"I will know. I will sight on mountains by day, and stars at night. And the rivers, frozen as they are, are always there, outlined by forest or by their flow-lines in the steppe. I will know."

Uffa spoke with such surety that he must be believed. It was his turn to ask a question.

"Did you buy wolfskin suits?"

Runulv nodded. "From Vermund, who calls himself King of Novgorod. We all have them."

"Then you have little to fear. I have worn one both times I have made this journey."

"How far will you take us," Runulv wished to know.

"Home, to Gotland and Fårö," Uffa answered. "I have done much of what any man can do in this place, and now yearn for my island home. You are the first I have met here, who returns there. It seems a sign, and a wise man will heed such a sign.

"That is the fortune I give to you. Take me as guide, and I will bring you to Staraya Ladoga in such speed that we will return to Gotland for the second Spring planting."

Uffa let this rest in the air. Runulv shot a look at Eskil, and then to Berse and Brani. It was Runulv's to decide, and as no objection was raised, he gave a nod. Runulv extended his hand over the table. Uffa took it, in that clasp from fore-arm to fore-arm. Uffa would guide them home.

The following days were a flurry of activity. After entrusting their goods to the officials at the import pier, they moved the empty ships up the coast to a ship-wright well known to Uffa, that the craft might be fitted with cradles and skis. Once they had snow beneath them, each ship would be set in two cradles, one forward and one aft, with short legs extending to the skis. These would be of prodigious length, to spread the weight of the loaded ships over any ice prone to breaking. And longer skis gave better stability over snow.

"To the blade end of your oars we will wedge a block of wood to use as a tamp. Aboard ship we will use these to push; also for guidance. But the horses will do much of the work."

He folded his lip in thought.

"Of the horses, we will need three at least to pull each ship, and three as spare. With skis over snow or ice it is far easier for an animal to pull heavy weights."

"My drekar Sharp Tooth is larger than Death-day, half again as long," Eskil said.

"But she is a drekar, and slender and light," Uffa answered. "She will speed over the packed snow, nearly as fast as you wished to ride in that chariot you envied."

"And without breaking our necks," Eskil posed.

"That is in the hands of the Gods," Uffa answered. "But should you make sufficient sacrifice before we set out, I think the ocean God Njord will hear you. Also his wife, Skadi, as she lived her life on skis."

This marriage did not work out, and Skadi left Njord's watery depths to return to her snowy mountains. Still, Eskil considered this. He did not always have the luck other men seemed to enjoy. "If we return to Gotland with all our treasure, I will wed the first woman I see on skis," he promised.

"Harnesses," Uffa said one morning as they met to consider their next step.

"Many returning merchants surrender their waggons once they reach here; we can find good trappings, used, and at favourable price. The saddlers and waggon-makers are near the horse markets."

They set out, again with Berse and Brani, and with plenty of silver. Harnesses for six horses were both bulky and heavy, and they need ask for a waggon to deliver all to their ships, still at the ship-wrights where the cradles and skis were being fashioned. They took care to buy additional brass fittings, such as buckles, as well as more sets of reins. The collars were largest of all, and six of them stacked, three each in the stern of both Dauðadagr and the knorr, took up a great deal of space. But once they procured the horses the sterns would be free for goods again.

The cradles were built, and as the ship-wright had to haul both ships out to fit them properly, the captains could see themselves how securely they held the hulls. The skis were of course broader and longer than any had seen before, yet both ship-wright and Uffa nodded in approval. "The folk further east use such each Winter, crossing plains to reach open water."

This was not the only work accomplished by the ship-wright. Blocks were affixed to the decking of both ships, from amidships to stern, each almost like a small mast-lock. Upright posts could be set into them, like unto tent poles. These would be used to string tarpaulins at an angle, to shed the wet and snow at night while the men slept, huddled together beneath them.

Then there was the provisioning of the ships. They must first sail the entirety of the western coast of the Black Sea, without replenishing their stores, and then, after leaving the farm, would be weeks on snow and ice. They bought bag after bag of wheat, which boiled up quickly; the grains were large and filling, and as much was grown in these southern climes it was abundant in the food stalls. Uffa obtained other cereals as well, much split-faced barley, tiny beads of millet, and oblong grains of spelt. They assembled casks of dried meat, of both cattle and pig, and plenty of salt. Bushels of cabbages, leeks, and carrots were carried on, good keepers all. They bought boxes of dried fruits, apples, pears, cherries, and plums, including those of the sticky dates, to grant new energy to flagging muscles. And they bought a cask of fresh red-cheeked apples, as well. Looking over this Runulv and Eskil could only wish they had been so well provisioned on the way down.

Uffa had been clear about the reason for this.

"We must take food enough to make it all the way to King Oleg," he told them. "We will stop only three places to re-provision. The first will be the run to Kyiv. There we will replenish our stores and rest. Then we must go to reclaim your ship," and here he looked at Eskil. "The Princes will be glad to have the knorr in trade for the karv and dug-outs. From there we go on, straight to Staraya Ladoga."

They would camp each night upon their ships, under the stars, and other than the two stops Uffa named, speed as quickly as they might to the hall of Ladja, Mistress of Staraya Ladoga.

As they would cross the marsh and river courses in the depth of Winter cold, Uffa made sure they had twice as many pottery flasks as there were men, with a few extras. They must melt snow to make drinking water for the day. At night the flasks could be filled with boiling water and be snugged against the feet as they bedded down, for it was ever feet which were most vulnerable to frostbite.

Both ships had now been returned to the impound pier, and all their provisions and supplies were aboard. They had a fair lot of fire-wood and tinder for cooking aboard, and would get more at the farm. The day before they meant to leave, Uffa joined Runulv and Eskil as they checked that all was secure. Standing on the pier, Runulv noticed a red-sashed agent there, one who had served them on several days of their trading. He felt moved to take something from his purse and present it to the man, in thanks. Uffa read the gesture and stopped him.

"You must not. Agents are forbidden to accept any gift from those they escort. They are well rewarded, for the training needed to serve the Eparch is years long. If you offer silver, it will insult them."

Runulv nodded his head in understanding, and conveyed his thanks in words only. The agent, whose name was Belos, was more than amiable, and had a blessing for them.

"You have made good trades. May God in his three guises, Father, Son, and Holy Ghost, guide your return home."

Far-travelling traders were grateful for blessings from every God, and Runulv accepted this with a nod. And it would need to serve for now, for Uffa had warned them that in this great city of the Christians, casting the body of a cock into the sea while invoking Freyr or any other patron would be looked at askance. They would wait until they reached the farm up the Dnieper, where they had made their last Offering. At any rate, the carved figure of Odin with his single quartz eye was looking over them from the stern of Dauðadagr, and Runulv and all his men were well used to touching it for luck.

That night both crews met at a tavern for a feast, hosted by Runulv and Eskil, and much food and drink passed the lips of all. During their month here they had seen other crews at their final revelling; now was their turn to celebrate their gains before they faced the hardships and uncertainties of their return.

Runulv, Eskil, Brani, and Berse were early to the ships, having quitted their lodging the day before they sailed, and spending the night aboard. Now in the dawn light they ascertained all cargo was fast and the ships ready to sail. Uffa too had joined them in this first night aship, bidding Fare-well to the great city which had been haven and livelihood for the past many years. He would sail on Dauðadagr, for after all, she was a ship of Gotland, and Gotland, his goal.

The crews knew to arrive in good order next morning, sea chests on their shoulders, and with any goods they had yet to stow aboard. They drifted in early, in groups of four and five, and filed over the gangplanks to their respective ships. They returned their sea chests to their customary rowing position, and each captain made a quick count of heads. Death-day was lacking a man, one of the youngest of the crew, a good sort who had never been the cause of the slightest strife. Runulv asked about him.

"Rodvist," he called. "Where is he?"

He did not have time to react to the blank and questioning looks of his men, for of a sudden the young man was upon the pier. Rodvist had neither sea-chest nor any pack with him. His hands were empty, but his face wore a smile.

"Rodvist," Runulv called down. "Where is your chest? Come aboard. We are casting off soon."

"I am staying here, Runulv," came the answer.

"Staying?"

Both crews had stopped at whatever they were doing, to stare at the young Rodvist where he stood.

"Já. Miklagårdr suits me, and I would stay."

A moment passed, in which some colour rose to Rodvist's youthful cheek. "And – I have met a woman, and have been keeping company with her, most of the month." His eyes went to Uffa now. "She is one who lives not far from your lodging."

Uffa had in fact seen Rodvist much with a young woman who plied her trade in a neighbouring house, and as he remembered this, Rodvist went on speaking. "She is tired of that life. She has asked if we might take over your room there, and so we are. I will find work, and she is skilled with needle and thread. Many men live alone in the quarter with no wife to sew and mend for them. She will do so."

Uffa had to laugh, not so much in wonder but in real pleasure. "I grant you my room, and my blessing," he answered. He paused a moment, beaming down at the fresh face of the young man, beginning a new life here in the great and strange city. Perhaps he saw some shadow of himself in Rodvist. At any rate, Uffa held up his hand to stay the young adventurer. He hastened to his own chest of goods, and came back with something familiar to all the men: his pale turban, and his fortune-telling cloak.

"Take these," he said, dropping them into Rodvist's arms. "You are young to know what you want, and wise to follow it."

"What will I tell your parents?" Runulv asked. He did not relish the idea of facing them without their youngest son. Though they had not lost their boy to misadventure, who knew when, if ever, he might return.

"Tell them – tell them I am happy," answered Rodvist, with a grin. He placed the turban askew on his head, and finished with a salute to his brethren. Rodvist's arms were full of the billowing cloak, and he grinned the greater at their cheers and whistles. There were a few amongst them who had thought the same thoughts, dreamt the same dream, but Rodvist would live it for them.

The dock-men of the pier were ready to cast off the bow line of Dauðadagr, caught by Berse, while that at the stern was thrown to Uffa. At a whistle from Runulv the men took up their oars and pushed off. On Eskil's knorr the same scene was enacted. The dock-men raised their own arms in salute, and stepped back, awaiting the next ship of traders.

As the oars of the ships dropped for their first slice of sea water, the breeze picked up at their backs. Once clear of the breakwater they would hoist sail. There was a fitting chill in the air, reminding both crews of their northern route home. Much cold was to come.

Before he must turn his attention solely to his steering oar, Eskil looked back at the great wall surrounding the imperial city. The dome of mighty Hagia Sophia, and many smaller domes, rose above it.

"A place like this – it makes you small," he considered.

THE ICE SHIPS

WINTER enveloped them. Though they had spent but a month within the protective confines of the walls of Miklagårdr, once on the Black Sea they passed into a different realm.

The flakes of snow which had but once drifted within the great city, only to dissolve upon striking stone walls or streets, now fell in clotted clumps, dropping into the dark water around them, and dusting the edges of the coast they sailed past. The mountains ahead, whitened by snow only upon the distant peaks on their approach to Miklagårdr, were now wholly snow-covered. True Winter lay ahead of them, and began now as they sailed north.

They faced stiff cross-winds, not always favourable for their progress. They raised their sails as they could, and relied on rowing when they could not. They reached the mouth of the Dnieper and the ship-wrights there in a day more than it had taken on the trip down, due to this. The boat-yard of the man they had rented the knorr from was utterly quiet, the karv and the dugouts amongst those hauled up upon the banks. The ship-wright hailed them though from his open-ended workshop, where he and another man stood shaping a keel.

As Uffa had suggested, the ship-wright was willing to accept silver, and the small craft he had stored for them, in exchange for the knorr. At last Eskil and Runulv could do the bargaining they had missed in the imperial city, for here there was no agent of the Eparch running his eye over the object they wished to buy, appraising its value, and then approving or disallowing what the seller had asked. Uffa was active in this as well. His years of working at the ship-wright's in Miklagårdr served them here, and the discourse was spirited, with the ship-wright feeling beset at facing three against one, and finally throwing his hands up to accept their offer. They were not unduly sharp with him, though. Eskil, who had sailed the knorr all the way down, and now back, knew she was a worthy vessel. Their bargaining was more for the sport of it, and a welcome return to the trader's art they knew, and had been deprived of.

They replenished their fresh water, enjoyed the ale brewed by the ship-wright's wife, and spent the night at the pier before they set off. The morning found them leaving the vastness of the Black Sea, and sailing up the Dnieper, against the current, its banks white with fresh snow.

Despite snow on the ground the river flowed freely, and it was not cold enough for the men to don their wolfskin suits. These they would save for the hard cold to come. Their heavy woollens and sheepskins would serve until then, and leather mantles shed the wet and snow.

They sailed by day, landing at dusk to clamber down to the snowy bank, flatten the snow, bring stones from the ships, and light their cook-fire. On the third day they reached the rapids. They again landed, though it was still morning, and looked up the river as it dashed its way over a tumble of rocks spanning its width. After they had lowered the masts Uffa considered it, and turned to Runulv.

"In Spring there is water enough, from snow-broth, and the streams running into it, to float a small ship. Or so I have heard."

Now in Winter they must pass this rocky stretch on land. Cradles and skis were let down from the ships, and a great deal of line, for they must not only haul both the knorr and Death-day up out of the water and into their cradles, but lash themselves to the lines and pull. The push-bar they had made for Dauðadagr was again pounded into place, and a second, fashioned by the Miklagårdr ship-wright, added to the knorr's broad stern. A light snow was falling as they did all this, but the banks were far from frozen, aiding them in their efforts, as they could dig a shallow trench in the mud at the bow of each ship to ease their way from water to land.

By the end of the day both ships were on land, and the men spent from the effort. Fate favoured them in that the banks were clear of trees, and hindering underbrush. They stoked up their cook-fire, filled their bellies with hot barley browis, and after brushing the snow off the decks and rigging up their sheltering tarpaulins, bedded down on the planking.

The next day was a swift lesson in hauling over snow, while getting what they could from the tamped oars to help push. The ski cradles were far more stable than those with wheels they had used over the plains of the steppes. But the hauling through snow, though not much more above their ankles, was tiring. They determined how many men they needed to haul, and the rest stood aboard the ships, pushing in rhythm against the snow-covered ground to help propel them along. They switched over twice, to spell both groups. As he had on their way down, Berse acted as time keeper, chanting out a steady beat so no forward effort was wasted, and all pulled or pushed to greatest effect.

"One month and we are soft," Eskil chaffed as they gathered that night to sup. In truth they had needed the rest Miklagårdr had provided, and had all regained the flesh lost from the arduous trip there. But shoulders and legs were now making them aware of the new demands placed on them.

They were past the rough water next morning, and began the work of digging a channel to ease the ships in. Dauðadagr was first, as she was lighter, and they would learn from launching her. They used heavy chocks to stop her ski tips at the bank's edge, and roped the rear cradle to keep it from moving. Then they pushed with all their might and main to propel her in. This was not accomplished without a certain sounding of oaths from most of the men, whether they strained to hold her back, push her forward, or stood upon the deck, oar in hand, to propel her to her natural element. They succeeded, took a needed breather, and then must turn to the broad-beamed knorr and do the same.

Both now afloat, they raised the masts and hoisted sail. Firs and pines ranged along both shores sheltered them from overmuch wind, but there was enough to make use of both sail and water. If Uffa was right and all went well, it might be the last time they did so. Another overnight found them with a cold and clear dawn. There was the broad landing place they had stopped at, where Dauðadagr had been rebuilt into a ship from the loads of ribs and planking they carried. It was heartening, seeing this, and more so now that they would

have no need to break her down again. They sailed on, knowing they would reach the farm ahead later in the day.

The Sun was just past its mid-day height when the small
settlement came into view. The greeting began as soon as
they approached the croft, for the farm dog ran out, barking at their appearance, and then began frisking in the snow
in a way that offered little threat. They drew up along the
banks. Out of the stout and low-beamed barn came a man
and several boys, all with spears in hands, but held upright
and not offensively. Uffa, at the stern of Dauðadagr with
Runulv, placed his cupped hands to his mouth and yelled out
a greeting.

"Sava!"

The man stopped, staring, as Uffa lifted his arms in the
air. The dog had begun barking again, and one of the boys
now whistled it to heel, and the animal trotted back. The
door of the house opened, and two women peered out, and
peeping around their skirts, a few smaller faces, like curious
nestlings in a tree-hole.

The farmer Sava recalled Uffa; he had bought horses
from them twice before. Sava grinned broadly under his
furred cap, and gestured they come ashore. A look at his wife
and daughter in the doorway made clear all was well.

In short order gangplanks were lowered, and the men
off the ships. Uffa approached Sava, speaking in a broken
Slavic tongue, for it was akin to what the adventurers had
oftentimes heard at the trading posts they had rested at
upriver. As they spoke, those from the house came forward,
wrapped in heavy shawls, eager to see the arrivals. Like Sava,
the women were as blue-eyed and yellow-haired as the visitors remembered, with the high cheekbones which helped

also mark them a Slavic folk. The captains had made certain to lay in some gifts to offer, and had them at hand. Runulv held up a good length of patterned fabric, fine-weave wool, in red and blue, with a stripe of yellow at the selvedges to set it off. The elder woman hastened forward, a smile on her face. She recalled the men and dropped a curtsey. None had come down the Dnieper since their appearance more than a month ago.

Runulv, while checking the face of Sava to see if the gesture would be approved, handed the fabric to her, with a bow. Her grown daughter came up now, as did a number of the smaller children, all eager to see the strangers. Eskil, ever ready to flatter a young woman, dug in one of his belt pouches and pulled out a handful of glass beads. He distributed these amongst all the offspring, boy and girl alike, saving three silver beads for the eldest maiden, who blushed but snatched them from his open palm.

Berse stepped forward next. While still in Miklagårdr he had been sent to procure some iron tools which might be difficult to forge upland. He had already traded the remaining shears he had forged in his own workshop, and if truth be told, had given a pair each to two obliging women Uffa had introduced him to. But in the great city he had no trouble obtaining a good pair of pinchers, a large and smaller pair of shears, and a short and finely toothed saw. This was the kind useful for sawn ornament, which the farmer or his sons might like to while away empty hours. Eskil gestured Berse forward and these were presented to the man.

This formality accomplished, and the gifts consigned to the sons, Uffa canted his head towards the paddock between house and barn. Perhaps a score of dark chestnut horses stood there, watching, a few tossing their heads and snorting as they did. The paddock ground was nearly snowless, for the churning action of the horses' hooves. The animals seemed to have grown in size since the crews had last seen them, from the added thickness of their shaggy coats, but their lighter underbellies gave contrast to the wealth of Winter coat they had sprouted. Sava led Uffa, Runulv and Eskil nearer the rail, then chirruped to the beasts. Their ears moved forward and back, and they raised their heads to the newcomers, dark eyes bright with interest.

The men looked over the horses. There were ten and six of them in the main paddock, and a few mares in foal penned in a second smaller one. Another held what must be a fractious stallion, for he whinnied shrilly, as if to attract the attention of the visitors. This was a large herd of horses, and certainly represented the bulk of the material wealth of the family.

Then followed a lengthy period when Uffa spoke to the farmer, haltingly, and with many gestures, in what seemed a range of tongues to those listening, for when the Slavic tongue failed him, he fell back on Greek and even Norse. When he was at last done, he told them what he had learnt.

"The question is how many horses can he spare. Though there are kin of his, living in a forest clearing, who have more. When I bought from him in the past it was for one ship, only. I think we can convince him with our silver to part with what we need."

Uffa led the farmer, followed by much of the family, to the ships. He chose the knorr to board as it was easier of access, and most of the family trooped over the gangplank behind their father. There under the cover of tarpaulins lay the horse collars and harnesses, bridles, reins, and all. They need deprive the farmer of none of this from his own store. There were the two huge cradles, like yokes, awaiting the bearing of the ship. And here, most importantly, running along the keel, the long and broad skis. The knorr and drekar would become giant sledges. Folk were used to sledging in these parts; their snowy Winters forced them to it.

Uffa took care to point out that the crew would be pushing as the horses were pulling; and showed off the grooved blocks pounded over the blades of the oars to serve as tamps, to help them on their way.

They returned to the paddock rail. It was a queer kind of trading, for Sava was so attached to the horses that after the first three, each animal grew more costly in turn. Runulv and Eskil, accustomed to a discount for a bulk purchase, had not seen the likes of this, but then these were animals Sava and his family had bred and raised, and no common transfer to another such as a sack of cabbages would be. At last, and now seated in the farmhouse by the light of the fire, they came to agreement, Sava and Uffa passing silver coins and hack jewellery back and forth. They could take their nine horses, for Sava agreed each ship required three in harness, while three rested. This way each team would always have one fresh animal, each day. To keep the spare horses at their best, the three kept in reserve each day would ride in the ships, two on the knorr, and one on Dauðadagr.

Meanwhile the making of supper was underway in the cauldron hung over the croft fire pit, and in a second large cauldron carried from the knorr. The contents were augmented with wheat berries from the ships, and a sampling of dried fruits was passed around, which pleased the youngsters in no small measure. There was ale to drink as well, a special pleasure for the crews, as they had last tasted it within the imperial city walls. After this the men retired to their ships, confident that now they had the horses, Uffa's scheme was well underway.

In the morning Sava and Runulv made inspection of the beasts selected to draw them onward. They were docile enough under the handling of a stranger, and let Runulv run his hands down their furred legs, and open their mouths. He had seen the simple horse collars Sava used for logging, hanging there in his barn, and was glad those they had bought in Miklagårdr were so padded, for the animals would be in harness every day, save those they rested to keep them fresh.

Uffa spent time with Sava, and turned to the captains as they looked over the horses. "They are never blanketed, even in the harshest of Winters. It flattens their coat, and then they grow cold."

"They are shaggy enough to resemble bears," Eskil answered, and indeed with their Winter coats at the thickest, they could almost pass as small hay stacks.

Sava had snow shoes aplenty for the beasts, flat discs of wood which strapped over the hooves with leather straps and brass buckles, spreading their weight over an area three times the size of its unshod hooves. These were much used on Gotland in Winters of heavy snow, and they gratefully accepted the shoes, to save the fashioning of them.

Though the Dnieper lay as free flowing water about them, further north it would freeze to ice, and here they had the advantage of the horses to haul the ships out. There was snow enough along the bank to glide, once the animals were harnessed and the ships in their ski cradles.

First they rolled away a few of the stones Sava had fronted his croft with at the riverside, and dug another trench to ease the movement of the keels up onto land. Three of the nine horses they had purchased were harnessed, and with the help of Sava and his sons they fastened the traces to the bows. With the cradles in position they eased Death-day's prow towards the bank.

Runulv, farmer that he was, took the reins in the bow of Dauðadagr. Sava stood on the ground at the head of the animals, calling out words of encouragement to them in his Slavic tongue. The sturdy beasts strained forward and pulled the drekar out and onto the cradles. This took control, stopping them at the right moment so they did not overrun the cradles, but Sava had long practice working with the animals, and it was accomplished.

They repeated this with the knorr and a second team of three.

Next they must ascertain who would drive the team from the knorr.

"Have you driven?" Uffa asked the Svear.

Though he had wished to race at the Hippodrome, Eskil shook his head. As a youth he had handled the reins of a small cart, pulled by a single horse, only.

"There will be those of your men who can," Uffa guessed. "You have many Gotlanders, used to handling a team." Uffa looked along the hull to where the Svear would customarily stand, and said the next with a light laugh. "You will not need your steering oar, not now. Whoever you choose, stay at his shoulder and watch until you take the reins yourself. You will pick up enough driving three horses over snow, that one day you might drive a chariot of four, at a run."

Uffa gave a laugh, but for a moment Eskil felt a pang to think that young Rodvist was back at Miklagårdr and its excitements, and he, heading north. Still, after the warring and gaming he had done, and the hazards of this journey, the Svear knew he had rare luck to still live. And Uffa said it took years of training to race a chariot well. Eskil wanted those years to begin to enjoy the life he planned to build for himself on Gotland.

Now all that remained was the final provisioning.

Free of their bulky trade goods, they could lay in plenty of wood for fire-building, as well as ample fodder for the horses. These were thrifty keepers, and required only hay, of which Sava grew in happy abundance. With his sons' help they carried roll after roll of sweet grass hay aboard each ship, and covered them with oiled tarpaulins to keep out the wet.

"Better we hungry than they," Uffa cautioned, "as they must bear us, ships and all." The ships would lighten as they pressed onward, and burnt their firewood. They would take care to collect more where they could, and dry it for use.

One final act awaited, and that was an Offering to the Gods. They had sacrificed one of the farm's ducks, wrapped in Gotland sheepskin, on the way down. It felt fitting to forfeit something of their gains from Miklagårdr this time. Runulv gave thought, then went to the chest in which was wrapped the covered enameled jars he had purchased. One would serve as a rich Offering, for anywhere he sold them they would return much silver. Yet if they reached home, and with all they had traded for intact, their gain would exceed the greatest sum Runulv had imagined. This Offering must be significant. He dug through the chest, looking at one jar after another. Here was one featuring flying birds, picked out in bright enameled colours on the near-black copper base. As symbol of how they hoped to return home alive there could be no more meaningful gift to the Gods.

He pulled it out and showed it to Eskil. The Svear could not repress a wince at the value of it, but nodded. They would not bury it, but instead make direct Offering to the river which had carried them down to Miklagårdr, the source of all their new-found treasure.

"You Offer it," Eskil said. He never knew how to speak to the Gods, and in secret admired those who did.

Runulv took breath, and as he let it out saw how it smoked in the cold air.

"Gods of Asgard, and those who roam here on Midgard, hear our prayer. You have blest our efforts with rich trading. Now we must make good on this. Speed our way to Gotland, and our kin and friends, that we might the more honour your names and acts. Here is a rich token of our success, for the River Gods who enabled our passing."

Runulv pulled back his arm and flung the pot into the dark water. It splashed a perfect circle of up-spray before vanishing into the depths. The ripples were soon lost in the current, and after watching the river swallow it in seeming acceptance, the two captains turned back to their grounded ships.

They led the three reserve horses up the gangplanks, tethered them with feed, and took their leave of Sava and his family.

The stance of both ships upon their skis was nearly the same, and Dauðadagr took the lead, as she was the lighter. The knorr could follow in her ski tracks to good advantage. Runulv took the reins of the team, and on the knorr Eskil took up position next to the Gotlander who drove their three. Never one to stand by in any action, Eskil was determined to soon drive as skillfully as Runulv, ahead.

Runulv gave a cry and a snap of the reins, and they were off, the horses straining forward to move the ship, and then settling in to a steady working pace.

No sooner had the shouts and Fare-well wishes of the crofters died on the air than the stillness of Winter blanketed them. The noise they heard was the snorting of the horses, the jingling of random bits of harness hardware, and the cracking and crunching of snow beneath the shod feet of the beasts, and under their huge skis.

The crew worked with their tamps, practicing their stroke. This was akin to poling in shallow water, something all had done as youths in meres and marshlands. The snow here was not much above the upper ankle of a man standing in it, and fairly soft. As they progressed north they would meet with far more, and harder snow, which Uffa counted upon.

They made camp early. The act of loading the ships into their cradles and hauling hay and firewood had exacted its price, as had the knowledge that now they were alone in a vast and frozen landscape. Once the Sun, which had shown but weakly over them, dimmed behind the trees on the opposite bank, Runulv called a halt.

Then began the first of a nightly ritual with the horses. Those harnessed were freed, and those aboard the ships led down the gangplanks to join them. They were not likely to run off; their herding instinct was strong, and amongst them was both a stallion and a dominant mare, both of which the others would follow. But there was risk of the horses being run off, and that by wolves. To guard against this the stallion and lead mare would be hobbled at night, with the leathern hobbles Sava gave them. Once all nine were together, they formed a circle around the armfuls of hay dropped for them, heads in, strong hindquarters out.

The crews tamped down an area of snow, carried stones from the ships, and used this as the base to light their cook-fire. Kindling fire in such wind was no easy task, and it was done on board under whatever shelter could be managed, and carried out in a pottery bowl. The fire, once laid, would need to burn all night to guard against the appearance of wolves. Two men would take turns feeding it. They would be short on sleep that night, but kept warm by the fire, no small recompense. As it was for most men on land, their horses became their greatest treasure, for they were the means to their safe return, and must be protected at all cost.

As the horses were being cared for and the cooking begun, others worked at rigging up the tarpaulins to shelter them aboard ship as they slept. These ran from mast-lock to stern, and with a side-curtain of cow hide sealed out the worst of the winds and much of the wet and snow. Uffa's demand that they buy so many pottery flasks proved a wisdom, as after they had supped they must melt snow in their cauldrons and fill the flasks with boiling water to warm them as they bedded down on deck. Provision for drinking water was also vital; they had barrels aboard, but they must melt snow so their horses could also drink their fill.

The first night passed without incident, and the hooting of an owl served as reassurance that some living thing was above and looking down over them. They were up at dawn, and readied for the day ahead.

The landscape changed but slowly. For two days the ships were still in sight of the Dnieper, flowing darkly against the snowy banks; they could see it from the decks. Then it was lost in the snow behind them, and along with it, the trials of the falls and rapids they had endured.

As Uffa had promised, they veered from that life-taking passage, heading northwest. To do so they climbed fairly long and steep inclines, which their sturdy horses, aided by the men pushing with tamps, took in their stride.

The aroma of pine drifted to their noses, as they passed stands of these rugged trees, heavy-boughed with snow. And there was the smell of the snow itself, a crisp scent not only of cold, but a slight sweetness like unto sap. It rose as the horses and skis broke the crystalline crust they moved over, and as the men themselves walked about when they were on the ground. The snow hid much of what it fell upon and revealed what it wished. Birch trees grew along their route, bare of leaves and slender branches swaying in the wind. The white of the birches vanished into the snow surrounding them, leaving the dark eyes and slashes of the bark to mark them.

Each day Uffa sought ice or heavily crusted snow, allowing the horses in their snow-shoes to stay on top of the frozen surface. Such gave their long skis their greatest glide. When any wet snow fell in the growing cold it would quickly harden to a crust. As they travelled away from the course of the Dnieper, Uffa must determine their path through memory of his past trips, the Sun above if it shone, and the stars at night. If the day had been cast-over with clouds, it might clear by the time they bedded down. If it did not, the men keeping watch through the night at the fire knew to awaken him if the stars could be seen.

The crews had but one hot meal a day, late in the day, and ate heartily of that. Dried strips of meat were dropped into the boiling grain, as well as shredded cabbage, leeks, and all other enhancements they had laid in. During the day they took breaks as needed, and could scoop out cold spoonfuls of their grain porridge, and partake of their dried fruit. The fresh apples were doled out one to each man a day, and relished. There were enough to take them to Kyiv, or near enough, Runulv reckoned.

Their nightly cook-fire was also used to dry clothing which had become wet, or been washed, especially their woollen stockings, for all knew they must keep their feet clean and dry. Snow was melted every other day that the men might wash their feet, and rub them with the salve of beeswax and linseed oil they used to protect the skin. The rest of them remained rankly unwashed, it was true, but the dictum no foot, no horse pertained to men as well.

At dusk when they stopped to make camp, the rested horses were walked down the gangplank to join the herd. Several of the beasts looked so alike it was hard at first to tell them apart. To the manes of the three who had rested that day was tied a narrow strip of linen, so that those taken aboard the next morning were truly in need of the break. But soon the men grew familiar with all the horses, and even bestowed Norse names on them, while keeping the same commands Sava had used to signal stop and start, or a turn right or left.

The frozen landscape they glided through was not totally devoid of life. They saw at times hares and foxes, both dressed in their Winter white fur, flocks of chattering birds alighting on the snow, and once, even a herd of wild horses, their coats as long as that of sheep in full fleece, pawing at the snow to free the dried grasses beneath. Their own whinnied out to them, and the stallion, who was that day being rested upon Death-day, lifted his head in the air and shrilly called out challenge to the wild herd's own leader. The wild stallion countered by nipping at the mares nearest him, moving them off to safety.

As far south as they still were, the days were longer than on Gotland. And even as they drove towards Kyiv, Winter's back had been broken; it was well past the shortest day and longest night. Some days brilliant Sun lit their travels, making all squint against it. Other days they drove under dull skies, or those marked with snow-squalls, which would clear of a sudden, allowing Uffa to use the Sun to sight their way forward. But deeper cold awaited them the further north they went, with brutal winds. It forced many of the men into their wolfskin suits. These were worn fur-side in, over their regular heavy woollen tunics and leggings, and though bulky, warmed them more than they had thought, for the air trapped in the long fur.

At night the horses gathered together in a tight herd, heads lowered as they drowsed. Their body heat and steaming breath served to warm them. But they kept rumps and strong hind legs outward, ready to strike at approaching predators.

The crews did hear wolves, and more than once, howling and whining at dusk as the men cooked their supper. The horses reacted on the instant, stamping their feet as they crowded closer to the other. Those men still aboard the ships tossed down spears, and all were soon armed, while others fed the fire. They scanned the shadows, but the cries of the pack grew faint. Some of the crew wondered aloud if the wolves knew they wore the pelts of their brethren, and bore a grudge against them for this. But though they heard their howls, the wolves never neared enough to be seen.

They lost track of days; only Brani took note, scoring on the other side of his travel-stick how many dawns they had greeted since they left the gates of Miklagårdr.

A steady rising climb told them Kyiv must be near; the fortress was set upon low hills. They had two days of arduous sledging, relieved only by the hope that they neared Oleg's gates. Then, late the third morning, Brani, standing on the deck of the knorr and stroking with his tamped oar, muttered to himself. "Smoke."

The smell had been but a whiff, but unmistakable. Few were the scents more welcome to those in the wilds than the smell of cook-fires. He scanned the horizon, white in the foreground, forest to the left in the background. Low clouds obscured the view. He caught a second whiff and called out.

"I smell smoke!"

On they pressed, until the source of what Brani's sharp nose had detected resolved before their eyes. The palisade walls of Kyiv were ahead.

A joyous hooting ensued, and Uffa, who was himself pushing at one of the tamped oars, found himself being pounded on the back by one of the men not on active duty. They had made it. It was all Runulv, whose eyes had been on his team, could do to keep the horses moving forward, as nearly every man armed with an oar stopped in his action to whistle or shout out praise for their guide.

Runulv turned his head and grinned at Uffa, then ordered all back to their work, pushing. They did so, and with renewed eagerness, for the nearness of this first over-land goal.

The palisade featured towers built of timber, from which they had been readily spotted, for a horn sounded, joined by a second. The timber paling had been impressive when they had first seen Kyiv, but now, having stood in the shadow of the massive stone walls of Miklagårdr, looked no more than what it was, that of a fortress in the wilderness. This did not diminish their pleasure at seeing it. As they neared, the gate nearest their approach opened.

A group of folk came out, awaiting them, followed by a doubled line of archers, some two score strong. With them were three of King Oleg's great grey wolf-hounds, their plumed tails beating against the legs of the men who held their leads. Yet Dauðadagr was seen and recognised; they knew this from a dark clad figure with a furred, peaked hat who stepped forward. As the ships grew closer the crews knew him as Prince Karlen, nephew of King Oleg, who had accompanied them from his own fortress further up river to Kyiv.

Both ships pulled up, and Eskil made sure he was at the reins of the knorr. The two captains, along with Uffa, Berse, and Brani, were soon off their ships and walking through the snow to greet the young Prince. At his side was King Oleg himself, but Karlen stepped forward, a wide smile on his face, and spoke first.

"You are both alive," Karlen noted. His eyes of turquoise blue-green shone brightly as they moved from Runulv to Eskil. The Prince gave a laugh of astonishment.

The five, given such merry welcome, were quick to admit of their good fortune, and then bowed to King Oleg, who wore his own smile of amusement on his face. It could not be helped, as they had just descended from two good sized ships, hauled by shaggy ponies and pushed by the oars of the crew on the decks above. The men before him, in their bulky wolfskin suits, woollen and fur caps, and heavy mittens looked as outlandish as did their sledges. Still, Oleg's pleasure at seeing them seemed sincere. The King of Kyiv wore his handsome cap of white fox fur on his head, and with his tunic of quilted leather cut the same fine figure he had when they had earlier made his acquaintance.

He lifted his arm in welcome. The second door to the gate was opened, and with much jingling of harness brass the two teams were led through and into the forecourt of his hall. A hot drink of some potency was offered to all as they stood there, warming to both body and soul. It was a spiced and mulled wine, and Oleg and Karlen hoisted cups with the crews as they stood there in the trampled snow. The pottery cups holding it were warm, enough to feel this through mittened hands, and added to the cheer. Despite the cold and the lowering clouds, a number of Kyiivan folk came out to watch, including some of the brightly-garbed women they had earlier seen, laden with their heavy neck-rings of silver, carefully placed over their cloaks and shawls to show to advantage. The crews downed their welcome cup, the strength of which filled their heads with a sense of needed ease. The horses were unhitched by the King's stablemen, those aboard led down, and all animals taken to a barn where they might be looked over, and fed their fill. The crews meanwhile recovered their sea chests, and went straight to the bath house, in as much need of a wash and trim as they had ever been on the journey up, or down.

Later the five sat with Prince and King at the high table in Oleg's hall of carved wood. It was dim within, with only a few oil cressets set upon the table, adding to the sense of enjoying the royal favour of their host. Oleg recalled Uffa, and vowed to ask of him many questions about Miklagårdr, for it had been years since he had ventured there himself. But their first act was to present the gift they had purchased for the Kyiivan King. Oleg had asked for a crystal ball as large as his fist, and clear as rippled water. This was what Runulv and Eskil placed before him, wrapped in a square of blue silk.

The King's surprise when he drew off the cloth was so great that the captains felt this challenge had been nought but a jest.

Oleg folded his fingers into a fist and held it to the globe before him. His utterance was one of wonderment. "You did find one as big as my fist."

"From Basra," Eskil told him. "Mined and shaped there."

More of the strong drink was called for, and all at the table took pleasure in seeing the King's delight over his crystal ball. Uffa, who knew of such things, made bold to speak to Oleg about this.

"If you would use it to good account, King Oleg, dip the crystal first into living water. Or," he went on, in consideration of the abundance of virgin snow they had crossed, "you may wash it in snow. Allow it to dry in nothing more than air; let no cloth touch it. Place it in a pronged stand of gold, silver, or lead; none other than these three metals. It is of Earth, and water, air, and metal complete it.

"When you are ready, rest your palms over your eyes, to help open your own inner sight. Then gaze into the heart of the ball, picturing a small Sun dwelling there, or the flickering flame of an oil lamp. When you see this, lower your eyelids somewhat, and scan with slow movements under your lowered lids, looking above and below the fire at the heart of the ball. You may be granted images there, of animals and folk and even Gods."

The men with him had seen Uffa in his fortune-telling guise, but this was a deeper telling. He spoke with a calm assurance, in a voice so resonant and low that all had their eyes upon the crystal he told of. The King reached out, and with respectful touch, Oleg took up the ball and held it to his eye.

"There is a rain-bow within," he murmured. The light from the oil lamps made this so, but Uffa had a caution to add.

"Such crystals hold power. If the Sun strikes it, it will light a fire on whatever its reflected light hits. That is the fifth part of the crystal's being."

Oleg made a grunt of understanding, and pulled the cloth over the sphere, as if it might ignite the worn wood of the table before their eyes. He looked to his guests and with a nod said, "This pleases me."

Young Karlen then looked at the two captains and asked that he most wished to know. "How many men did you lose?"

Runulv heaved a sigh, but answered. "Coming down, three. Two at the Aeifur falls, one at some lower rapids."

Karlen looked surprised, and a little impressed. "Only three. You did well. If you had taken slaves, you would have lost at least five, perhaps ten."

It was a sobering figure. Men were reckless with the lives of thralls, subjecting them to undue danger. Their lives would be placed at greatest risk, and thus be most likely to die in any mishap.

Oleg nodded in agreement. "Three only, to have gone down the whole of the Dnieper as you did? Odin did indeed keep his single eye upon you."

They told how they had lost a karv, as well as men, but arrived Miklagårdr with all their trade goods intact, for it had been mostly food stores lost in the dug-out upsets. Their royal hosts heard too of how they had re-built Dauðadagr from her pieces, and exchanged their remaining flat-bottomed karv and the dug-outs for the knorr. In this way they were able to sail up to the walls of the imperial city in the style befitting their efforts reaching there.

Karlen asked another question. "That bag the Pecheneg chief gave you – do you have it still?"

"Já," Eskil answered. "It is on the knorr right now, but I know where it is."

Karlen gave a nod of satisfaction. "You are not likely to see more Pechenegs from this point on," he assured them. "Did you open it?"

"Nej." Eskil shot a look at Uffa here. He had had his own dire dealings with that savage tribe. The Svear went on. "I would not open it, because I am a wise man." It made Uffa smile, but Eskil continued, and in earnest. "We did not like even to touch it."

The Prince looked thoughtful for a moment. "Keep it with you," he advised. "When you reach the River Neva I would cast it overboard."

"We will do that," Eskil promised, and all there nodded in approval.

It was now time for all to sup, and the hall began to fill. Torches were lit along the posts supporting the timber frame, and more oil lamps carried out. The fire burning in the long and narrow fire-pit was raked out to coals, length-ening it, and more wood laid on, which soon was blazing out its warmth. The ships' crews came in, along with the men and women who supped with Oleg every night, his warriors, his kin both men and women, a raft of children, and a rus-set-haired woman of real beauty who came to sit at his side. The visitors had not spied her on their trip down; perhaps now that they had made the hard trek to Miklagårdr and returned, Oleg deemed them worthy of seeing his wife.

It prompted a question from Eskil to young Prince Karlen, who sat at his side.

"Have you met your bride," the Svear wished to know.

The colour came into the cheeks of the young Prince. "I have," he admitted, with a downward sweep of his dark lashes. "My uncle chose wisely for me. But I cannot wed her until her father returns from his journeying; he is at Samarkand, but should have left months ago. He might be here by the end of Summer."

"May we see her?" Eskil further prodded.

Karlen grinned. "You? Nej. No one may see her, until we are wed. Even after that I am not sure I would let you see her." And the Prince smiled.

RICH AS LADJA

THE few days' rest at Kyiv proved a needed tonic. In the shelter of the barn the horses could be checked over thoroughly, to make certain none had developed any sores from the harness fittings, or collars. Their coats were in truth so dense as to serve as real protection for their skin. Their wooden snow shoes were unstrapped, so they might trot about freely in the paddocks, and their unshod hooves showed no sign of distress. Now near to other horses, they proved private little creatures unto themselves, unwilling to mingle with any of Oleg's beasts, akin to country folk who disdain those of larger settlements. But they were sound and fit to continue their journey. The men were able to wash all clothes that need washing, and these, hung in the sheltered warmth of the wash house, were rolled and packed away in sea chests when dry.

The cradles and skis bearing the ships were inspected, to make certain no cracking or splintering had arisen over the long and rough distances to which they had been subjected. One day when Runulv and Eskil were standing by their vessels, Prince Karlen came over to join them. He had already driven the drekar a short distance, around the palisade of his

uncle Oleg, that he might know the pleasure and challenge of
handling a team of so great a sledge. But now Eskil thought
of something which had not yet been mentioned.

"Your brother will need to accept the knorr in exchange
of the karvs and dug-outs," he pointed out.

None had spoken of Karlen's elder brother, Prince
Demyan, whose only trait held in common with Karlen was
his brilliant blue-green eyes.

Karlen only grinned. "Even Demyan will not complain of
that," he answered. "And when you tell him how the karv got
away from you, and bounced down the edge of the falls and
nearly killed you, he will laugh."

This felt all too true, but if that misfortune was the price
of amusing the elder Prince, they would pay it.

On their last night with Oleg and Karlen, a special feast
was held in honour of his departing guests. Fish, fresh-caught
from the frozen Dnieper, was offered, roasted whole. They
were sturgeon, as long as a man's arm, and as fat as one could
hope from a fish-pond. These seemed a fitting dish, one from
the river itself.

It was at this meal that Runulv spotted a woman he had
seen before, or perhaps it was the adornment on her shawl
which caught his eyes, for again he saw one of the large
round box-brooches from Gotland. Hers was silver-gilt; he
had seen it on their way down, and a finely wrought piece it
was. When he returned he would have the silver-smith cast
one in pure gold for Gyda.

As a parting gift the next morning the King presented
them with an ice-saw and tackle, that they might try their
hand at fishing for their own sturgeon when they camped for
the night.

This next run, up to the fortress of Prince Demyan, was the shortest of the three legs of their journeying. Prince Karlen had accompanied them down to Kyiv from there, and had predicted the passage, as arduous it was, would take them forty days. The Prince had not been far wrong. Now though, over snow and ice, that number could be halved.

Perhaps no one looked forward to this leg as much as Eskil, for his drekar Sharp Tooth awaited him there. Other than his weapons this ship had been nearly his sole possession. Sharp Tooth, and his own boldness, were the only things which had enabled him to entice the Dane to back the venture. Now if they made it back to Gotland he would have a one-third share of all the profits.

Uffa's task as way-finder was eased, as he could follow frozen water-ways up to Demyan's riverside fortress. They had avoided the dangerous falls from the first leg by striking out overland. Uffa's greatest test in this bold move had been not to over-shoot Kyiv, and end up stranded in the barren steppes. His memory and sense of bearing had again served him, and brought his crew mates through to their first goal. Now their path ran almost due north, with but a slight western cant.

The rest had served horses and crew well. It had been timely, as they met heavy snow as they drove up the water-way. It fell from the skies so thickly that it seemed a sack of flour had been shaken out from the clouds, to blanket them. The warmth of the horses as they worked kept it from collecting on their backs and rumps, but their manes and tails were frosted with ice. Those animals kept in reserve on the ships merely turned their rumps to the wind, and lowered their heads. The crew though must in turn surrender their tamped oars to clear the snow from the decks. Even Runulv, being spelled at the reins by one of his men, did this, using one of their spades to push the snow to the hull wall and shovel it over the gunwale. They must sleep on this decking later, and were grateful for the cow hides which served as ground cloths for them, as everything upon the ships was as wet as if they sailed at sea in a gale.

On the leg from Sava's farm to Kyiv there had been hours when the men would pull off their wolfskin suits, and work the oars in their woollen tunics and leggings. Now the cold was such that none wished to strip down. The winds too were fierce at times, rocking the ships as the horses pulled and the men pushed. At night they made certain to position the prows into the prevailing wind, and led the horses into the lee of both hulls for their own shelter. As soon as they dropped the hay the animals formed their tight circle about it. They had a wooden trough, kept aboard the knorr, and this was carried down and filled with water melted from snow, that the animals might drink. Cooking could only be accomplished by rigging up a fly from the gunwale of the knorr, then hanging hides to two sides as wind-screens. They became so adept at doing this that their fire, kindled aboard ship and carried down in a pottery bowl, never failed them. They took great care to keep their firewood dry, even selecting that lot which would serve as kindling for the next night, and setting it up before the fire to further free it from damp.

So they went on, day after day, with greater or lesser fresh snow to contend with, but extreme cold. The men were frost-bearded, as rimed with snow as were the bent and blasted blades of tall grasses which the winds exposed. Gotland was mild compared to this; snow fell in Winter, but never was the wind so biting. Eskil and the other Svear were more used to severe cold, but the bitterness of the blasts was only mitigated by the labour of the men themselves.

Yet they progressed. There were stretches where the winds had blown the ice nearly bare of snow, and the horses fairly cantered as the skis glided under the hulls. Then they were there, at the home of Demyan and Karlen. The grassy burial mounds outside their walls were now snow covered, but all recalled how they had been nearly linked, mound to mound, and were still. The palisade wall of the Princes' fortress stood just past these, and set above on a slight rise. Somewhere near them Eskil had left Sharp Tooth; she must be covered with snow, as were these mounds holding the dead.

As they expected, a horn sounded. Runulv could only hope Dauðadagr would be recalled by Prince Demyan, and so be deemed friendly. Still, he would not hazard nearing the wooden towers, from which archers might be nocking their bows. They pulled their teams up, and waited. As they stood there, their horses mouthing their bits, snorting, and jingling their harness brass, the men motionless as they studied the timber walls, a gate opened. Out came a single horse, pulling a small sledge, and at furious speed. The horse was festooned with bells which rang out merrily, drowning the slight noise of their own horses' breathing, and hardware.

The driver of the sledge drove for them so recklessly as if to collide with the hull of Dauðadagr. At the last moment he turned his horse's head, with a cry and crack of his whip. He pulled the animal to a halt, and then, spattered with snow, stood up from the low seat he had been perched on. It was dark-haired and swarthy Prince Demyan. He was all grins, and shouting greeting in some unknown tongue.

As welcome it was unexpected, but they had seen no predictable behaviour from the elder brother on their way down, and the men must accept it. Gangplanks were lowered, and the two captains went to meet Demyan.

He was drunk. So much so that as he moved to quit the sledge, he stumbled into Eskil's arms. The Svear set him back on his feet with as much dignity as he could, but the Prince only laughed.

"Karlen. Where is Karlen. What have you done with my brother," he demanded. His words were slurred, and his eyes as glassy as beads.

"He is well, and safe with your uncle, King Oleg," Runulv answered. "And both send you greeting," he added, though in truth neither had done so.

Demyan struck a pose with his finger to his chin, as if he was just recalling why his brother was absent; Karlen had gone with these traders to escort them to Kyiv. His hands were bare, as if immune to cold, and already blanching in the frosty air.

"You are not dead," he decided, and reached out a finger to poke first Runulv's shoulder and then that of Eskil.

"We are not," Eskil agreed. He must keep his message as simple as possible, and broach the topic of his ship later. "And we ask that we might stay a night or two with you, and rest."

In truth, two days would hardly be enough to refresh themselves, but neither captain wished to spend more than a night locked up with Berse and Brani in a small store house, as they had on the way down. Karlen had the better time of it, spending the night on deck with their crews, talking and drinking.

Demyan flung his arms wide. "My hall is yours!" he roared, and then turned, arms outstretched in welcome. He threw his head back and nearly fell over with it.

Eskil could not help his grin, but Runulv was far more cautious. "We thank you, Prince," he answered respectfully. Though the crews of both ships were overlooking all of this, he was eager to warn them that despite the welcome afforded by their host, no liberties must be taken. Such men had quick-silver natures, and all must act with the same decorum as they had at Oleg's hall. Their lives could well depend on it.

A train of warriors had followed Demyan out, all on foot, trudging through the deep snow. Demyan was not glad to see them, and two of them who had sat at the Princes' high table now came forward as if to take charge of their stagger-ing war-lord. They did so, with a practised air of solemnity, and Demyan was led to his sledge and guided to sit down. The reins were taken by one of the men, who walked at the horse's head, while the second paced alongside Demyan, making sure he did not fall upon the snow, as he pitched forward as soon as he was seated.

A third warrior gestured that the ships drive their teams in, and after the captains gave stern warning to their crews, they did so. Runulv had reason to fear what excesses Demyan might sport with, and having brought most of his men alive to this point of their return, was not about to surrender any to riotous drink, the temptations of women, or a slight over a dice game.

He need not fear. The besotted Prince was led to the high table, but not before several young women, who had been lounging, cups in hand, around it, stood and scattered at the sight of the visitors. Demyan whimpered out complaint, holding his hands out as if to stay their fleeing, but his body-guard were firm. He was made to sit in his carved chair. No sooner had he done so that he slumped forward, his forehead hitting the broad boards of the table.

A silver cup was within reach of the Prince's still hand, and a serving man neared to fill it, but was stayed by a gesture of one of the guard. Demyan had drunk enough.

What followed was one of the more unusual nights of the traders' journeying, for Runulv had never sat at table with a host who was entirely unable to perform the duties required of him. Yet he could not regret this. The ale they recalled, remarkable for its bitterness, was poured out for them, and then they were offered the use of the bathing-house. Their animals had been unharnessed and released into a paddock, fed from the Prince's own store, and watered. When the crews returned from their bathing, in fresh clothes and eager for supper, Demyan was gone. One of his men made the gesture for sleep, and all must agree this was the only recourse for the Prince, overcome with drink as he was.

The meal that followed was more than sufficient, though akin to supping in a barracks, for the women who had joined them in the hall on the trip down were entirely absent. It was true they had sat off to one side, and not intermingled with the men of the hall, but they had been an uncommonly fine assortment of females, of which those who had fled upon their entry were examples. Eskil regretted their absence, but Runulv inwardly praised the action of those men of Demyan's who deemed this best.

At the meal's end the crews were led to a secondary hall, one chill enough, for the fire-pit was just being laid and fired, but far more welcome than being locked in a store-room, or spending the night in the snow on the decks of their ships. Still, they were locked in for the night, but from the inside, as a pair of guards sat watch at the two doors. None cared; they were soon warm, had been fed, and though the ale was bitter, had swallowed enough to bring on welcome sleep.

At dawn the men were up, and after washing, were led to Demyan's hall. He was there, sitting beetled-browed at his table, as if trying to recall some fact lost in memory. He started slightly when Runulv and Eskil approached, Brani and Berse with them, and then gave a laugh. The action of this seemed to hurt his head, for his hand went to his brow.

"It was you," he said, as if to himself.

Runulv gave a nod. It was Eskil spoke next.

"And we have a gift for you, oh Prince." This sounded more respectful to the Svear, and considering he was addressing a man for whom he had little respect, was an effort. Still, he went on.

"When we arrived yester-eve you made great remark over the knorr I captain. She is a fine vessel, made by the ship-wrights of the Black Sea, famed for their craft in building ships to withstand the rigours of their treacherous winds and waves. And she is yours."

Demyan blinked his blurred eyes at the Svear. "Knorr? Mine?"

"We paid much silver for her, and she is meant as a thank-offering to you for the karvs and dug-outs. I will right my drekar, and we will leave as soon as we have her on skis."

The Prince at once wished to see his new ship, one he had no memory of acquiring, and after all were swathed in furs out he went, with both captains and crews. Demyan spent much time circling the knorr as she sat on the ice in her cradles, long skis splayed.

The crews went straight to work to find Sharp Tooth. They were armed with spears and shovels, the first to prod through the drifting snow to find her hull, the second to dig the paths needed to right her. She had been keeled over on the sandy bank, and luckily not frozen to any ledge of rock.

Once she had been freed of snow they harnessed three horses, brought the team over, and hitched the traces to her bow. This was no easy task on her port side where she lay, but finally accomplished. Then with the team pulling forward, and the men pushing, they relieved her of her extreme cant.

Prince Demyan had been observer of much of this. As soon as the knorr was quit of her goods Demyan was up the gangplank and aboard. He stood with Eskil at the bow, as the Svear was absorbed in angling the knorr into what would be her resting place until the river thawed. Then the Prince went over every ell of his new ship, inspecting her while she still stood upright. He lifted up the hold decking to check the store of ballast below the deck, and the rounded river rock held fast in netting met his approval. He found a few hidden compartments in the stern, which gave satisfaction; checked the mast-lock for soundness; squinted at the interior rivets in the hull to make sure none had popped under the stresses the ship had known; and spent some time studying the grommets and edges of the furled sail, as if these might reveal clues about the wind she could handle. Finally they must call him off the deck. Demyan joined them on the packed snow as the knorr was slid out of her cradle and unto the banked snow of one of the burial mounds.

This was a day of hard labour, but at the end of it Sharp Tooth was on her skis, her decks swept of snow, and all goods had made the transfer from knorr to snow to drekar.

Possession of such a large cargo ship as was the knorr seemed to place Prince Demyan in mind of new possibilities, and as they walked back to his hall the Prince spent time in converse with several of his men. Eskil guessed what they might be speaking of, and offered his own opinion. "She would serve well as a pleasure barge," he said, for at Uppsala he had heard tales of certain war-chiefs who kept broad-beamed ships in rivers or lakes, merely as respite from their daily cares. This idea struck Demyan, for though he seemed given over to pleasure to the point of danger, a dedicated vessel to which to retire from the demands of the hall appeared utterly novel.

At any rate the crews passed another two nights as guests of the Prince, sleeping in the second hall, though not without the safeguard of his men at the doors, protecting his larger interests.

They filled their water casks from Demyan's wells, and topped up their supply of grain. His steward offered cabbages and onions from their store, and they readily bought all they could. The Prince sent them off in fine fashion, with a cask of the bitter beer for each ship. He stood in the snow and waved after them, and then he vanished. The teams started forward at the cries of the two drivers, Eskil at last upon his own Sharp Tooth. She took the lead now, and Death-day fell in behind her. No sooner had they done so than they heard the sharp cracking of a whip, and lusty cries. Heads turned, to see Demyan in his one-horse sledge, racing after them at furious speed. He came alongside, laughing like a madman, which few of the crew at this point doubted was a strand of his true nature. He overcame Sharp Tooth, and with utter recklessness veered sharply in front of her, nearly spilling himself and the sledge in their path. Then, whip cracking over his horse's head, the sledge sped off back toward the palisade gate. His wild laughter was heard longer than he could be seen, and all were glad to hear the last of it.

This final leg overland would be the longest, a run straight to the hall of Lady Ladja at Staraya Ladoga. Travelling as quickly as they were, they could bypass the fortresses of Prince Efim, and that of Vermund at Novgorod. Berse and Brani knew this, and only regretted the hospitality of Efim, who after all, had given them a fine dinner, and entertained them with skilled musicians and dancers, the latter of which proved most accommodating. Even Eskil was more than willing to forgo their delights, for as well provisioned as they were, and with sound horses and their own willing arms and shoulders, they were making good time.

Their horses had proven as tough as they could have hoped. The resting of a third of them each day aboard the ships was well worth the inconvenience of having large beasts tethered amidships. Most of all the men had provender enough, and of the right kind, to continue on their way, boiling up daily cauldrons of enriched browis. For much of this they had Uffa to thank, for he had been in charge of their provisioning from Miklagårdr. Their fortune-telling friend had not only taken others as far as Kyiv before, but spent years talking with traders who had come long distances over land and water. He knew there must be no shortage of food for them to travel fast enough in Winter cold to reach their goal.

Setting out from Demyan's, they met fair weather almost from the start, with a searing radiance of Sun over their heads equalling the sharpness of the cold. The purity of the air, matched by the whiteness of the endless snow, caused the eyes to dazzle. Soon some of the crew began to complain of dark spots before their eyes. This was snow-blindness, and could cripple a man, rendering him groping and helpless. All knew of the condition, caused from too much glaring light, but only Eskil and the other Svear, who were from further north than Gotland, and thus a snowier clime, had seen it themselves. There was one cure, resting the eyes, but every man was needed to push at the oars and perform the ordinary working action of the ships. But there was a simple aid which they fashioned. As soon as they spotted birch trees they stopped. Strips of the white bark, thin, flexible, and strong, were cut from the trunks. These were further cut down to be large enough to cover the eyes, with an indentation for the nose bridge. Two narrow slits were made where the eyes would sit beneath this mask. Holes were punched at either end that it might be tied over the eyes with a leathern thong or strand of woollen yarn. In this way the light admitted was greatly reduced, and those men who had been suffering snow-blindness gradually recovered their sight. Those vulnerable continued to wear them each day the Sun glared upon the snow, and for this, dull days were welcomed.

Looking back on this final run, Runulv and Berse remembered only the speed at which they moved through the barren snow fields. The fact that Uffa could set their course due north by Sun and stars, with little or no deviation, gave a simple directness to every day's journeying, and robbed it of any telling incident to fix in memory. Most days were as featureless as was the landscape. Even Brani lost count, notching his stick for the days which had come and gone, at times wondering if he had skipped a dawn, or mistakenly notched twice for a single day. They would not recount this time in a haze of memory; the brilliance of Sun and sky and the demands of the cold were too definite for that. But any one day could be exchanged for the next, or the one preceding, in gem-like clarity.

Ice fishing afforded some relief. If they stopped early enough, and if the men who had done so at home cared to try, they would take up the ice saw King Oleg had given them. They worked its sharp tip into the crystalline surface, creating first a hole, and when the teeth had traction enough, they could begin sawing through the hand-span of river ice over which they travelled. The hole cut and then enlarged, hook and line were lowered, baited with a strip of dried meat, which once in water might wriggle persuasively as a worm. They had success at this, hauling up fat bream or perch, at times several in succession. Once gutted and run through with a poker these were roasted over the fire, sprinkled liberally with salt, and shared out, a small flaky piece to each.

One near-dusk Eskil, who was in the lead, whistled out that he would slow his horses. This was as good a place as any to make their night's camp. The animals had just come to a halt when a flare of light appeared on the horizon: fire. Another followed, and another; torches being lit for the night on watch towers, meant to cast light on the near ground if any approached by stealth. His eyes fixed on the pinpricks of flame. It must be Ladja's hall. In a moment of wonderment, Eskil shouted this out.

The whistles and hoots from the men were loud and jubilant. They did not stop, but made instead for the Lady's fortress. There was still light enough in the sky that the ships could be plainly seen from the watch towers by the time they reached her walls, and men upon them blew out warning or welcome from their brazen horns. The crews stayed upon their ships, as respectful visitors should do until they were formally acknowledged, and let themselves be surveyed by those who looked down upon them. Then the gate was opened, with a crowd of men and women spilling out. Down came the gang planks of the two drekars, and the captains and their close companions set foot on the ice before Lady Ladja's fortress.

Ladja herself was in the vanguard, a small but colourful figure dressed in red fox-furs. She was supported by a number of younger women, similarly attired. A man was at her side; surely her son. He must be near his fiftieth year, and bore a sense of command. She lifted her hand in welcome to the men now striding toward her, and turned to the man at her side.

The Lady spoke to him, likely explaining who they were, and had a smile for the arrivals. She laughed in seeming delight at the two large ships, and the beasts hauling them. The same ships and men who had sailed nearly to her door were back, skiing on ice.

The two captains let Berse do the talking for them; she had taken strong liking to the blade-smith on the trip down, and it should be he who took the lead now.

"How glad we are to see your walls again," Berse told her. He made a deep bow, which the captains, Brani, and Uffa joined in. The blade-smith went on in his greeting.

"Your hall was the first we visited, and your hospitality gave us favour with the river Gods. Our trading at Miklagårdr was good, and we have lost few men." Berse turned half way to lift his hand to the horses behind him, jiggling their bridle bits and snorting out steam. "As soon as we can place our ships in open water, we hope you will accept these horses as our gift to you. They hail from a farm near the mouth of the Dnieper, where it spills into the Black Sea. They are stout beasts, despite their size. They have pulled us all this way, and are still sound of hoof and wind."

"As you are," Ladja returned, with a smile.

Her voice took on a much more formal air, and she spoke the next with pride. "This is my son, Truvor. He is chief of Staraya Ladoga, loved by our people, and feared by our enemies."

Truvor was certainly impressively dressed, in a quilted tunic of tawed leather, nearly white in hue; a massive cap of black fur, mayhap bear skin, and knee-high boots of brilliant red. He bore not one but seemingly two swords, for the gold-hilted knife at his right hip was only slightly shorter than the sword on his left. His beard was reddish-gold, with a streak of grey from the chin, and the strands of long hair falling from under the black fur cap similarly paling to silver.

He was greeted with another bow by the arrivals, and responded by an inclination of his great furred head.

"You are welcome," he said next. "The horses we gladly accept. The true price for our hospitality will be the tales of what you have seen and done."

This slight toll was greeted with grins, and much nodding of heads. All had seen how devoid of interest the Winters were to those who must abide along these frozen river routes and steppe snow fields. Visitors were greatly prized because of this.

As Truvor's folk were soon to gather for the evening meal, it took only as long as freeing and feeding the horses for the crews themselves to be seated on benches in the warm and snug hall. The display of weaponry behind the high table did not fail to again amaze, lit as it was now by the dancing flames cast by torches and the oil cressets upon the tables.

Ladja, having divested herself of many of her furs, now appeared in her gold-adorned glory. She gestured that of all the visitors, it should be Berse who sat next her. Eskil sat next Truvor, Runulv at Berse's other side, and Brani and Uffa together, further down the high table. The rest of the crew distributed themselves about the hall, and soon steaming bowls of fish soup were placed on the narrow trestles, along with black bread for dipping. It was a warming welcome, especially after the strong brew they were offered, poured into deep pottery cups. To follow there was a kind of barley browis, which had been baked firm and cut into slabs and fried in the fat of cured pig's meat. It was all hot, of rich savour, and filling, and the men thought themselves blest to be there, and not kindling a fire on the ice to melt snow and boil up their own grain.

After they had dined, and the strong ale had gone round many times, Berse brought out a gift for Ladja. He had given her one of his crafted bronze bells on the way down, as a sign of esteem, and when in the great city of the Byzantines had looked for some fitting token for her.

He placed it before the Lady now. It was a figure of a fish, the length of her outstretched hand, with a jointed tail that swung from side to side. It was wrought in copper and enameled in bright colours, with its scales picked out in careful detail. Ladja picked it up, and the tail flapped, making her cry out in delight. Berse need not say more. She looked upon it with real pleasure, as a remembrance of a young fisherman from Gotland she had once known. Ladja was rendered wordless, and a mist came into her eyes.

"As you still keep his memory," Berse muttered to her.

She nodded her head, the gold on her breast glittering in the thrown light.

Dagr, thought the blade-smith. I hope you are looking down on this, that a woman of Ladja's wealth and bearing recalls you.

Meanwhile Truvor was speaking to Eskil.

"Ladoga is still iced over, but it is beginning to break. I have been down the Neva a stretch, and there you will find open water."

This was what Brani had told them they should find, and Eskil was glad to hear it. Heading west on the River Neva they would find rotting ice enough to enter. Where it narrowed the current flowed strongly, keeping the water open.

The next morning, one as bright as those previous had been, they went out with Truvor to survey the lake. The melt was visible to the eye, dark patches, some large, showing the softness of the layer of ice. After another day or two of rest they hoped to hitch the horses for the final stretch, this time alongside the banks, until they reached the Neva. If Truvor would send a few men with them, they would return with the nine horses as soon as their ships could be launched.

Their Fare-well from Ladja was the most memorable for Runulv and Berse. She had not known Gotland, but had loved a young man from there, one both warmly recalled.

When they turned from her to face Dauðadagr, Berse asked a quiet question. "Will we be rich as Ladja?" He gave his great head a shake; the answer was unknowable. But beyond the treasure they had won, Ladja reminded them of something else to esteem, the value of being a man a woman would long remember.

As they headed out, Truvor's four men with them, Runulv turned and looked back at the timber walls of Staraya Ladoga. Odin was there in his stern, his single quartz eye glinting. Runulv spoke, under his breath.

"I will not pass this way again, but I give thanks to All-Father for having done so now."

OPEN WATER

Gotland

The Year 899, Spring

CERIDWEN paused by her grape vine, that which grew twining about the bench by the front door to Tyrsborg. Each day grew in sunlight, and the vine was leafing out, the palms of every leaf spreading further as they unfurled. Soon clusters of tiny dark beads would appear on the vine, swelling to plump purple grapes. Ceridwen still had her fingers on the tender new growth when she lifted her eyes. Down the hill lay the wooden pier, empty this morning. Her eyes rose to scan the horizon, clear enough that the line between sea and sky could scarcely be discerned. It too was empty.

Gyda, she thought. Runulv's wife could not see the Baltic from their farm, and perhaps this helped her as she awaited him. Runulv had been gone for many months, and though Gyda had her nephews there to help, their presence could not allay her concern. At the Winter's Nights festival,

Ceridwen invited the entire family to the main feast. Gyda's farm animals were bedded down, and her sons, kin, and help climbed into waggons or atop horses to spend the night at Tyrsborg. As the doors and windows were ritually closed, Ceridwen and Rannveig began to intone the natures of those female spirits, the *dísir*, revered at this time of darkness, rest, and new creation. Ceridwen asked aloud for blessing upon those absent from that circle of loved ones, that they might soon return to board and bed.

Today, a fair if chill spring morning, Ceridwen resolved to set out to visit Gyda. And she would not be alone. Eirian was always keen to visit any folk, and would join her. Ceridwen was made glad of this; Gyda's sons were fine looking boys; that might matter to the girl, as it gave some hope to her mother that Eirian might be content to remain here on her island home. Tindr would ride with them, with a gift of honey and beeswax for Gyda. The middle of her boys tended to a hive Tindr had woven with him, and the hunter could check his progress with the bees, and see how the tiny creatures had come through the Winter. And because his father was going, young Juoksa could not be left behind, and he sat in front of his father on the saddle. They rode Yrling's gelding, an animal who wanted work, in the absence of Yrling himself.

They were not empty-handed; by the time they left, Tyrsborg's cook, Gunnvor, had baked and cooled a score of round honey cakes, and Tindr added these to his saddle bags.

Sidroc saw them off, holding back the hound Flekkr, and Helga, Tyrsborg's serving woman, holding Rodiaud. The girl was still uncertain of horses, and so willing to wave her mother and sister off on their respective animals. As they rode down the hill toward the wooden pier,

Ceridwen saw her father-in-law, the elder Hrald, sitting there on the bench, another old man at his side. A third was standing before them, speaking with energetic gestures to them about something, as their laughter could be heard. Ceridwen smiled to herself.

The ride was as pleasant as it could be, trekking first half-way down the trading road, to be greeted by those already at work at their craft, whether the making of shoes or cutting of amber, and then a turn north up the waggon-track taking them to Runulv's inland farm. They rode amongst the abundance of tiny wild-flowers dotting all the island in Spring, and the eager calling of nesting birds lent its own hopefulness to Ceridwen's thoughts.

Once at the farm, the welcome they received was warm and heartfelt. The boys were always eager to see Tindr, and after the honey cakes were sampled, the young clustered about him. Gyda and Ceridwen sat opposite on benches near the outdoor cooking ring. The mistress of the farm and her serving woman had undertaken the laundry just the day before, and some of it was still drying on lines run underneath the house eaves. The washing occasioned the making of a large fire, and the embers Gyda poked up now burst back into life when she added fresh wood.

The two friends spoke of another sea journey, recounting all too well the days when Sidroc and Runulv had sailed together for Angle-land, and the weeks the two women had spent waiting for their return. On that journey, Ceridwen feared they could have been lost at sea, caught in some mis-adventure, or killed outright upon landing. Both men had been restored to them, hale and hearty. For Sidroc awaited a greater joy, to find his wife with child, the babe who would become Rodiaud. The fearful waiting had been rewarded by his safe return, and the shared gift of a coming child.

"Sidroc told me once he knew he was watched by the Gods," Ceridwen said, as they talked over this. "I think the same is true for Runulv."

She gave thought to the sea-captain and went on, hoping to hearten his waiting wife.

"Runulv has weathered storms, and never lost a ship, though once his mast was sheared. Sea-God Njord looks upon him with favour, that is clear, and Freyr draws him back, as if Runulv's ship was one of his own."

Gyda must smile at this kind reassurance, and laid her hand over Ceridwen's. "I thank you. This is true, Runulv has seen fearsome waves, and eluded sea raiders. And I feel there are many other things, which he has not told me, which he was forced to overcome."

Ceridwen smiled back. "Our men rarely tell us the worst," she admitted. "But Runulv has survived all this."

Gyda nodded, and bit her lip a moment. She breathed out a sigh, remembering the day Sidroc had come to the farm with the offer to make this voyage. "The parting was hard; I encouraged his going, and yet was fearful, at the same time."

This was ever the same conflict wives and mothers faced, for all those adventure-bound, whether men or young, and both women sat silent a long moment, considering this.

Ceridwen spoke, again remembering her own parting from Sidroc. "I think the Gods watch Runulv, and this venture. Your risk will be rewarded. This I believe."

Tears were now showing in Gyda's blue eyes; she blinked them away.

"This I believe as well," she answered, with as much firmness as she could summon.

The two friends talked their fill, while turning their eyes and attention to the young around them. They enjoyed the honey cakes as much as did the younger folk, and drank of the birch-leaf tonic Gyda had made, always a welcome refreshment to Ceridwen. Gyda had brewed the freshly-picked leaves with dried blueberries, lending it sweetness and colour. It gave the finished tonic, served cellar-cool, a bright blue hue as Gyda poured it from the mouth of the jug.

Tindr was now sitting at a work table with the middle and youngest of Gyda's sons. They had begged him to teach them the start of the weaving of a second bee skep, and his swift hands were now doing so with the straw they brought from the barn. The eldest son was off with Eirian near the goat pen; he was showing off the twinned kids which had been born a few days ago. They were as small as young cats, and Eirian held one in her arms, while Juoksa held the second. The holding of the tiny thing seemed to bring Eirian such happiness that Tindr's son regretted that his family kept neither goats nor sheep.

Ceridwen, looking out on this, spoke to Gyda. She felt a strong urge to return to Tyrsborg, yet was loath to take Eirian away, when she was enjoying herself so well. "I should go, but will leave them here if I may. Tindr will shepherd them safely back."

Gyda laughed at this truth. The women embraced, and after she exchanged a word or two with Eirian, Ceridwen led her mare to the mounting block, and was off.

At Tyrsborg, Sidroc was at work in the stable with a new leathern strop. He had fixed it to the end of the work bench, so that after he or Tindr sharpened any steel they might further refine the edge. He tried it out on his own seax, stroking the shining blade from heel to tip. A shaft of sunlight pierced the dimness of the stable, warming his back as he stood there. Motes of dust arose about him, but he kept his eyes lowered and upon his blade. It was a quiet task, and the hall and yards quiet too.

As he worked his mind wandered. His shield-maiden had ridden off to visit Gyda, and offer what comfort she could as the months stretched on. He thought of Runulv and Eskil, and the good Gotlanders who went with them, and of Dauðadagr, that war-ship so prized by his dead uncle. His mind slipped to his name-sake son, that younger Yrling, and how sorry he would have been to have missed this adventure, and how glad he himself was that he did not have to forbid the boy from joining it. He thought now of Yrling's twin, his daughter Eirian. He had told Eskil she was destined to go to Wales, and wed a Prince. If so, she had better travel with plenty of treasure as her dowry. He must wait and see on Runulv's return what the yield was. Some men never came back from such journeys, or came back in tatters.

His thoughts were stopped at this point, as he heard a horse approach. He moved to the open doors. It was his shield-maiden, and with a look on her face which was hard to read. She slid off her mare and came to him. There in the doorway she pressed herself into his arms, and kissed him. It was a kiss of unexpected passion, long and lingering.

At its end, and while she was still in Sidroc's arms, his look asked his question, and she answered him.

"Because you are here. And not gone away."

At this she again kissed him, clinging to him as if his weight and strength could truly anchor him to her.

After her lips let him go, Sidroc glanced outside the stable door. Her mare was there, but there was no sign of Eirian, Tindr, and Juoksa. "Are you alone?"

"The others are still at Gyda's, and will follow later."

Hanging on a rod on the wall was one of the airing horse blankets. He pulled it down.

"Come," he said. He closed his hand over the silver disc bracelet on her wrist, and led her to the ladder leading to the hayloft.

She went up before him. When he was next her he used his foot to smooth some near hay, and spread the blanket on top of it.

"Pretend I have just returned, and your tears of happiness are dried," he told her. His face was nearly as serious as her own had been, yet now she saw he was fighting a smile.

"And now show me what you have missed."

A fortnight later Sidroc sat with his father on the bench at the pier's end. It was late in the day, and the men who often times clustered there were gone home, many to sup and return later to Rannveig's brew-house. Father and son had the bench and its view of the Baltic to themselves. Hrald stared at the water, coming at the pebbled beach in countless ripples. The old man's veined hands dangled between his knees; there was a slackness about him, and Sidroc knew, a frailty as well.

The hound Flekkr, having followed them down from Tyrsborg, now came up underneath the hands of the elder Hrald. "Hlaupari," the old man muttered.

Sidroc looked at his father. That name, "Runner" was the name of his father's dog back in Jutland, a dog who would become Sidroc's sole friend in his young boyhood.

"Já, Hlaupari," Sidroc answered. "He lived a long time. Toki and I buried him, together. This one is Flekkr. He was the runt of a litter of scent hounds used for flushing birds, at our upland farm. Yrling and Eirian begged for him, and saved his life. He has been good for them, little Rodiaud too."

His father nodded at all this, and kept his eyes on the incoming tide.

"I – I would like to go fishing," Hrald said. "The herring will be running now, fat shoals of them."

It surprised Sidroc, and the old man half-turned his face to his son, as if expecting refusal. Hrald did not wait, and went on.

"There will not be many days ahead on which I can do so," he judged.

Sidroc's mouth opened to refute this, but then gave thought. His father, worn from a lifetime of hard work, was right. The Spring air and sunshine acted like a tonic to the old man, for a spate of bright and warm days was paired with little or no wind. It warmed the surface of the water, and seemed to give his father some added vigour. Perhaps they should go fishing. It was true, herring and other fish would begin to move now, and aroused by newly emerged insects hovering above the water, rise near to where Sidroc and Hrald could cast a small net from a boat. The lengthening days were spurring Hrald to seek the water with his son.

Hrald voiced his desire a second time, and more poignantly.

"I would like to go fishing with you, again." It had been decades since the two had been out together.

Hrald went on. "That time you went down with the net, and I caught your reaching arm and hauled you out . . . "

His father stopped here, to go on with what must be said.

"If I had lost you . . . "

He was silent a moment, and shook his head before he spoke again. "You were precious to me, boy."

A sigh passed between his father's lips, before he said the next.

"Then another boat took me away from you, for good."

"Not for good," Sidroc corrected. "I found you. Me and my own boy."

The old man moved to wipe his eyes over his long-ago abandonment of his young children. Sidroc shook his own head, and spoke.

"And I did the same as you, to my own boy – I left him, and his sisters. Like you, I was taken away. I could not go back for fear of bloodshed, even war, upon my return. Even without that threat, I would not have gone back. I had finally won my wife, and was done with raiding.

"You chose a more peaceful life here on Gotland, with a good woman. And I did the same. The Gods looking down on us brought us together again, so that you might meet your namesake, now a Jarl in Angle-land."

It was the long and short of it; son had followed father in many ways. Sidroc had no way of knowing how his own Jarl son fared, but hoped young Hrald would be spared from making the same costly sacrifices.

Both looked away, then back to the sea. Sidroc studied the incoming tide, letting go his concern for his son, sensing his father's need. Then he made decision.

"The boat my wife and I arrived in − I still have it." He gave a low laugh at that remembrance, hauling the heavy prow up on this very beach to safety, and lifting his exhausted shield-maiden from it. "I paid dear for that boat, in a sea-battle. It was part of the booty I was awarded.

"It is in a shed at Rannveig's," he went on, tilting his head at the brew-house and its outbuildings. "Tindr and I will look it over, see what needs mending. Then we will put it in the water, and plug any leaks. I think Rannveig still has Dagr's fishing gear; if so, she will let us use it, or the other fisher-folk here will lend us some for our outing."

This said, the old man reached out and laid his hand on his son's arm in thanks.

A week later boat and men were ready. The mast was still sound, though the linen of the sail had rotted to little better than a rag. It mattered not; their intent was merely to row out, drop anchor, and cast their net. Without the sail they had no need for the steering oar, for they would steer directly as they rowed. The vessel had been in the water of the cove for three days, and the final leaks caulked with pine tar and fleece. They would set out just after dawn, when the wind was calmest, and be back well before dusk, earlier if they were favoured with a good catch. They had water, bread and cheese and boiled eggs, and a good net which Tindr and Hrald had together gone over, re-knotting and adding to it as needed.

The wooden pier gave them an advantage, for they would not need to heave the boat across the beach and into water. It made it easy for the old man to step into her, with Tindr steadying him from the pier, and Sidroc taking his hand from inside the boat. Tindr handed Sidroc a long boat-hook, always needful, which Sidroc laid along the keel. They had two oars, both sound. Sidroc also took a spear. It might be useful if they found a larger fish, or to use the butt end to fend off rocks or a floating tree-trunk which might strike the hull. Sidroc had his seax strapped over his belly, and his father had his own knife at his hip. They had warm woollen cloaks against the wind, and Hrald was wrapped in his. Sidroc laid his upon the rowing bench, amidships. He was warm enough, active with lading. Tindr cast off the bow line, and tossed it to Sidroc, then gave them a honking Fare-well, grinning as he waved them off.

Father and son each took an oar, and rowed out beyond the shelter of the cove. It took a few strokes to get into rhythm, and Hrald seemed winded, almost at once. Sidroc slowed his own stroke to match his father's. But fish to be netted would not near the shallows of the coast; they needed deeper water, and the current the fish would ride. Their goal was north, up the coast, and into deeper water, for there they would find no limestone ledge beneath them. Rannveig had told Sidroc that this was a favoured spot of Dagr's, and that early in the season he would meet shoals of fish swimming north, and into his waiting net.

There was something bracing about being out on open water, and the exertion of rowing forced both men to breathe deeply. They sat side by side, a narrow span of the bench between them, and plied their oar with both hands. The water was so clear that even seen obliquely, while seated, it felt their gaze dropped nearly to the bottom of the Baltic.

Sea stacks were there, limestone rauks which were still sub-merged, and far below their shallow draught. But seeing them put both in mind of living creatures, wading out of the water and up onto dry land. If it be true the rauks were night trolls caught by the rising of the Sun and so turned evermore to stone, these must have been frozen in stone before Tjelvar, the first man on Gotland, came with his gift of fire and so kept the island from sinking back into the sea each night.

The breeze picked up, but not unduly, ruffling the water their oar strokes bit into. As thick and white clouds scudded across the blue expanse of sky, the Sun warmed them, only to be withdrawn a moment later as the same clouds hid its face. On their port side they passed beaches of white lime-stone shingle, those of golden sand, and the faces of low but jagged cliffs. Trees were leafing out, glowing gold and green against the darker red and black pines which rose above the lesser growth. The two men spoke but little, and Sidroc could not know his father's thoughts, but when the old man scanned the surface of the water he was sure he looked for signs of fish.

A dark head bobbed up from the surface of the sea, only to vanish again. A seal. It too was fishing, and seals were known for chasing shoals of fish.

"There," Hrald said, pausing in his rowing to point with one hand at the spot where the seal had surfaced. He had been silent long enough that his voice was almost a croak.

They redoubled their efforts, and were rewarded by seeing the sleek creature rise again, thrash in the water, and sink beneath it, a fat-bodied fish in its whiskered mouth. A moment later the surface of the sea was roiled with action, as numberless fish rose and then fell as they swarmed and coiled to avoid the seal's sharp teeth.

"Now," Hrald said. They shipped their oars, and each took up a corner of the net. They would stand and cast it from the starboard side, hoping to snag some of the bounty the seal had stirred up.

Hrald, unsteady on his feet, used his oar to brace himself to stand. As he turned, one hand on his oar, the other reaching for the net edge, he tripped, catching his foot on the bottom of the bench they had been sitting on. He staggered, and then fell in, the oar after, hitting him across shoulder and back as it did so.

Sidroc was also standing, having shipped his own oar. His father's twisting fall overboard happened almost in dream-like motion, so slow did it look. Yet the splash of cold water, the blade of the oar tipping over to strike the old man, was more definite than anything Sidroc had witnessed in many a year.

The oar pulled part of the net in with it, and when Hrald surfaced, sputtering and gasping, he clutched at it, only to draw more of the netting in. It drifted away from his hand, though still fastened to the hull, as he thrashed himself toward the gunwale. The oar was now behind Hrald, and floating away.

Sidroc threw himself, belly first, down across the rowing bench to spread his weight abeam. As soon as his father reached the hull, he might capsize the boat in attempt to pull himself up. Hrald was now pulling at his mantle, heavy with wet, and was able to slip out of it. It floated on the surface, a dark and billowing mass of green wool, before folding over on itself and half submerging. It too was lost.

"Father, come closer," Sidroc commanded. "Try to stretch your legs along the hull, to balance your weight." He doubted his father had the strength to hook his leg over the gunwale, unaided. A strong-shouldered young man might be able to, but not a man as frail as was Hrald. If he could shift his father's weight to run alongside the hull, there would be less chance of capsizing.

Hrald did this, as best he could. Sidroc fixed his own oar in the empty starboard oarlock, and lowered it into the water.

"Take hold," he told his father. Hrald did, and clung to the shaft of the oar with both hands, pulling his own shoulders out of the sea. This freeing of his head from the water lent some calm to his troubled face. But neither man knew how long he could hold on.

Secure as the oar was in the oarlock, and with his father anchoring the blade end, Sidroc angled it toward the stern, then braced himself on the bench, hooking the shaft under his knees.

"Reach your arms towards my shoulders, and clasp my neck if you can," he told Hrald.

It was much for Hrald to release the grip he had on the shaft, but he did so, just catching first one arm and then the other around his son's neck. Holding himself back with his left arm, Sidroc reached out with his right, to wrap his arm around his father's back, just under his arms.

"Tyr," Sidroc muttered.

Many times had Sidroc called upon his patron to give surety to his arm. Now he did so again. But today it was not his own life he needed to save, but that of his father. It was echo of Hrald's pulling him free from the fishing net he was tangled in, when he was a boy.

It was not easy, and the craft rocked perilously, but Sidroc pulled his father out, and onto the bottom of the boat.

Hrald had been struck by the oar, and scraped and bruised by the transit over the gunwale. The water he had been plucked from was cruelly cold, and the old man sat blue-lipped, and shivering.

Sidroc disentangled himself. His first act was to get his father out of his soaking tunic. Hrald barely had strength to lift his arms to help in this. The reddening of his back and sunken chest showed exposure to the chill air was but further assault to the old man's vigour. Sidroc stripped off his own tunic, warm and still mostly dry, and pulled it over his father's head. He guided his father to the bench, where he sat with fists clenched, trembling with cold. Sidroc took his cloak from where it had fallen on the deck and wrapped it about Hrald.

"You have nothing," Hrald murmured. His son was bare-chested, having given his father both tunic and mantle. Sidroc gave a shake of his head; he had as yet no time to feel the cold. He took up his father's sopping tunic, wrung it out, and pulled it over his head. It was tight at the shoulders, and its clammy coldness gave Sidroc a chill. But it would warm up; wet wool did.

The fishing net was still there, held firm by the bow. Sidroc pulled it up, hand over hand. A few fish flopped in it, wry gift from the sea. "Here are fish," Sidroc said aloud, in attempt to engage his father.

"Já," Hrald answered. A smile cracked his thin lips. "I caught them. And you caught me."

As an attempt at a jest, it was a sign of spirit, and welcome. Something silvery flashed along with the fins. It was Hrald's knife, fallen out of the sheath at his hip. Neither had even known it had done so. Sidroc freed it and passed it to his father, who nodded in gratitude for this good fortune.

Sidroc looked about the vessel, and took stock. He had a single oar, a boat-hook, and a spear. There was nothing for it but to treat the heavy boat as if it were a slight and slender dug-out, using the oar as if it were a paddle. He went to the bow, where he could more easily lift the oar up and change sides as he made for shore.

It was slow work, and impossible to make strong progress. The oar was heavy and not made to be lifted and carried over after each stroke, yet this was what Sidroc must do. The current was moving them north, and now the turning tide was fighting Sidroc's efforts, and carrying them further out. Yet there before them was Gotland, tantalizingly close. Sidroc could see how they were drifting, despite his best efforts.

If they could reach shore, Sidroc could kindle a fire; he had always his fire-strike and flint in the pouch at his belt. A fire would both warm his father and dry his clothes; then they could see about the walk home along the beach, or to any near farm.

The pines on the coastline grew only slightly nearer, and they were still drifting north with the current. Sidroc turned to look back and check on his father. Hrald was clutching the cloak across his chest, head lowered, eyes closed. His son lifted his eyes past the stern. There on the water, seemingly half way to the horizon, was the outline of a ship. Sidroc pulled in the oar and stood, bracing himself with his stance, to get a better look. Two ships, he now saw.

It was a risk, one he must take. The current might sweep them to some Gotland beach, but also carry them far up the coast, to land on some deserted headland, away from ready help. Or they might meet strong winds, and be carried out to sea. He needed to get his father warm, and to safety. His father, Sidroc reminded himself.

"Odin," he prayed. "Show now you are Father of us all."

Sidroc had no horn, but a whistle with strong lungs behind it can be heard a long distance. Facing the two ships, he began a shrill and extended whistle, paused, drew breath, and whistled again.

He pulled off his father's tunic. It was light in hue, almost cream-coloured. He took a sleeve and threaded it over the butt end of his oar, then hoisted it over his head and began to wave it in the air. He did this, then stopped to whistle, resting the oar upright against his arm and chest, only to again take up the tunic-adorned oar as flag. The ships might see this. As they neared the island the crews aboard would be scanning the coast, looking for the harbourage they sought. They might spot the tunic aloft, or hear his whistle.

After an anxious wait the ships appeared to make for them, changing course. Sidroc could see both vessels more clearly, and must prepare to meet the result of flagging them down.

"Drekar," he muttered. They were two war-ships, no doubt. Yet they could be Svear, or friendly Danes, come to trade and replenish their stores. If they proved unfriendly, he had but a boat hook and a spear for defence. They must risk it; his aged father was shivering with cold and dangerously close to shock from exposure. If these were raiders they had nothing to steal but this small boat itself, and his seax, and if they were taken aboard Sidroc could ransom their lives with the promise of ready silver once on land.

"Odin," Sidroc breathed again. It was hope of protection, and acknowledgment that much was now out of his own hands, and into those of another.

The ships were driving for them. Sidroc lowered his oar, and narrowed his eyes at that in the forefront. The sail was interwoven white and yellow stripes. He stood a long time, eyes almost burning, at what he saw.

Dauðadagr.

It was Death-day. He again placed his fingers to his mouth and blew out a shrill whistle. After the second, the answering whistle was a distinctive one. Runulv was aboard.

Odin, with his single eye, yet one all-seeing, had guided Dauðadagr back. There was Sharp Tooth behind her, whole as well, blue and white striped sail full, and Eskil the Svear, Sidroc trusted, upon her deck.

Hrald turned on his bench, and lifted his head to take this in. The old man began laughing at their good fortune.

"Runulv! Runulv!" Sidroc's cupped hands framed his bellow. His own was answered from the drekar now, the ship master, Runulv himself, shouting out, "Sidroc!"

HERE ENDS BOOK TWELVE OF
THE CIRCLE OF CERIDWEN SAGA.
THIS IS A NEVER-ENDING STORY.
MORE BOOKS WILL FOLLOW.

You've read the books – now enjoy the food. Your free *Circle of Ceridwen Cookery Book(let)* is waiting for you at www.octavia.net.

Ten easy, delicious, and authentic recipes from the Saga, including Barley Browis, Roast Fowl, Baked Apples, Oat Griddle Cakes, Lavender-scented Pudding, and of course – Honey Cakes. Charmingly illustrated with medieval woodcuts and packed with fascinating facts about Anglo-Saxon and Viking cookery. Free when you join the Circle, my mailing list. Be the first to know of new novels, have the opportunity to become a First Reader, and more. Get your Cookery Book(let) now and get cooking! *The Glossary of Terms* and other background information follow.

THE WHEEL
OF THE YEAR

St Dwynwen's Day – 25 January

Candlemas – 2 February

St Gregory's Day – 12 March

St Cuthbert's Day – The Spring Equinox, about 21 March

St Walpurga's (Walpurgisnacht) – 30 April

St Elgiva's Day – 18 May

St Helen's Day – 21 May

High Summer or Mid-Summer Day – 24 June

Saints Peter and Paul – 29 June

Feast of the Visitation – 2 July

St Lewina's Day – 24 July

Hlafmesse (Lammas) – 1 August

St Mary's Day – 15 August

St Matthews' Day – The Fall Equinox, about 21 September

All Saints – 1 November

The month of Blót – November; the time of Offering for
followers of the Old Religions; also time of slaughter of
animals which could not be kept over the coming Winter

Martinmas (St Martin's) – 11 November

Yuletide – 25 December to Twelfthnight – 6 January

Winter's Nights – the Norse end of year rituals, ruled
by women, marked by feasting and ceremony

LITURGICAL HOURS
OF THE DAY

The Canonical Hours – special daily prayers, as practised by Oundle and other religious foundations, are as follows:

Matins, or night-watch, about 2 A.M.

Lauds, at dawn

Prime (the "first hour") about 6 A.M.

Terce (the "third hour") about 9 A.M.

Sext (the "sixth hour") about noon

None (the "ninth hour") about 3 P.M.

Vespers, the lighting of the lamps, at sunset

Compline, on retiring to sleep

ANGLO-SAXON PLACE NAMES,
WITH MODERN EQUIVALENTS

Æscesdun = Ashdown

Æthelinga = Athelney

Apulder = Appledore

Arx Cynwit = site on the northern coast of Defenas (Devon)

Basingas = Basing

Beamfleot = Benfleet

Beardan = Bardney

Bearruescir = Berkshire

Bryeg = Bridgenorth

Buttingtun = Buttington

Caeginesham = Keynsham

Cantwaraburh = Canterbury

Cippenham = Chippenham

Cirenceaster = Cirencester

Colneceastre = Colchester

Cruland = Croyland

Defenas = Devon

Englafeld = Englefield

Ethandun = Edington

Exanceaster = Exeter

Fearnhamme = Farnham

Fullanham = Fulham

Geornaham = Irnham

Glastunburh = Glastonbury

Gleaweceaster = Gloucester

Hamtunscir = Hampshire

Headleage = Hadleigh

Hreopedun = Repton

Iglea = Leigh upon Mendip

Jorvik (Danish name for Eoforwic) = York

Legaceaster = Chester

Limenemutha = Lymington in Hampshire

Lindisse = Lindsey

Lundenwic = London

Meredune = Marton

Meresig = Mersea

Middeltun = Milton

Readingas = Reading

River Lyge = River Lea

Sceaftesburh = Shaftesbury

Scireburne = Sherborne

Snotingaham = Nottingham

Streaneshalch = Whitby

Sumorsaet = Somerset

Swanawic = Swanage

Turcesig = Torksey

Wedmor = Wedmore

Welingaford = Wallingford

Weogornaceastre = Worcester

Isle of Wiht = Isle of Wight

Witanceaster (where the Witan, the King's advisors, met) = Winchester

ADDITIONAL PLACE NAMES

Aros = Aarhus, Denmark

Basra = in modern day Iraq, once known as the "Treasury of Arabs"

Byzantium = The Eastern Roman Empire, with Constantinople as its capitol

Cathay = China

Cymru = Wales

Dorestad = former trading town on the
Rhine in modern Netherlands

Dubh Linn = Dublin

Éireann = Ireland

Frankland = Much of modern-day France and Germany

Frisia = modern Netherlands

Haithabu = Hedeby (formerly Denmark,
now in modern-day Germany)

Hunefleth = Honfleur, France

Laaland = the island of Lolland, Denmark

Land of the Svear = Sweden

Miklagårdr = Constantinople (Istanbul)

Port Láirge = Waterford, Ireland

Sassanian = Dynasty of Ancient Persia

Serkland = General Norse name for Islamic lands

GLOSSARY
OF TERMS

Althing, and Thing: a regular gathering of citizens to settle disputes, engage in trade, and socialize. Gotland was divided into three administrative districts, each with their own "thing" or meeting, but the great thing, the Althing, was held at Roma, in the geographical centre of the island.

alvar: nearly barren stretches of limestone rock, typically supporting only tiny lichens and moss.

Asgard: Heavenly realm of the Gods.

aumbry: a recess built into the wall of a church, to receive and store sacred objects.

Boethius: Roman senator and consul, executed 524 CE. Author while imprisoned of the influential work *The Consolations of Philosophy*, translated from the Latin into Old English by Ælfred himself. It is this book in which Ceric seeks comfort and guidance.

brewster: the female form of brewer (and, interestingly enough, the female form of baker is baxter . . . so many common names are rooted in professions and trades . . .).

browis: a cereal-based stew, often made with fowl or pork.

chaff: the husks of grain after being separated from the usable kernel.

ceorl: ("churl") a free man ranking directly below a thegn, able to bear arms, own property, and improve his rank.

cottar: free agricultural worker; in later eras, a peasant.

cresset: stone, bronze, or iron lamp fitted with a wick that burnt oil.

drekar: "dragon-ship," a war-ship of the Danes.

ealdorman: a nobleman with jurisdiction over given lands; the rank was generally appointed by the King and not necessarily inherited from generation to generation. The modern derivative *alderman* in no way conveys the esteem and power of the Anglo-Saxon term.

ell: a measure of length corresponding to a man's forearm and outstretched fingers.

fey: possessing magical or supernatural powers; one belonging to the Land of Faery.

fulltrúi: the Norse deity patron that one felt called to dedicate oneself to.

fylgja: a Norse guardian spirit, always female, unique to each family.

fyrd: the massed forces of Wessex, comprising thegns – professional soldiers – and ceorls, trained freeman.

hack silver: broken silver jewellery, coils of unworked silver bars, fragments of cast ingots and other silver parcelled out by weight alone during trade.

hamingja: the Norse "luck-spirit" which each person is born with.

lamm: Gotlandic name for a sheep.

leech-book: compilation of healing recipes and practices for the treatment of human and animal illness and injury. Such books were a compendium of healing herbs and spiritual and magical practices. The *Leech Book of Bald*, recorded during Ælfred's reign, is a famed, and extant, example.

lur: a vertical (or curved) sounding horn fashioned of wood or brass, dating from the Bronze Age, and used in Nordic countries to rally folk from afar.

morgen-gyfu: literally, "morning-gift"; a gift given by a husband to his new wife the first morning they awake together.

nard: (also, spikenard) a rare and precious oil, highly aromatic, derived from the crushed rhizomes of a honeysuckle-like plant grown in the Himalayas, India, and China. Mary Magdalen was said to have anointed the feet of Christ with nard.

philtre: a potion to excite love or lust in another.

quern: a small hand-driven mill consisting of two grind stones, the top stone usually being domed and having a hole to insert a wooden handle for turning. The oats, wheat, or other grain is placed between the stones, and the handle turned until the desired fineness is attained.

rauk: the striking sea- and wind-formed limestone towers on the coast of Gotland.

seax: the angle-bladed dagger which gave its name to the Saxons; all freemen carried one.

scop: ("shope") a poet, saga-teller, or bard, responsible not only for entertainment but seen as a collective cultural historian. A talented scop would be greatly valued by his lord and receive land, gold and silver jewellery, costly clothing and other riches as his reward.

scrying: to divine the future by gazing into a looking glass, a crystal, or water.

shingle beach: a pebbly, rather than sandy, beach.

skeggox: steel battle-axe favoured by the Danes.

skirrets: a sweet root vegetable similar to carrots, but cream-coloured, and having several fingers on each plant.

skogkatt: "forest cat"; the ancestor of the modern Norwegian Forest Cat, known for its large size, climbing ability, and thick and water-shedding coat.

Skuld: the eldest of the three Norse Norns, determiners of men's destinies. Skuld cuts with shears the thread of life. See also Urd and Verdandi.

strakes: overlapping wooden planks, running horizontally, making up a ship's hull.

symbel: a ceremonial high occasion for the Angle-Saxons, marked by the giving of gifts, making of oaths, swearing of fidelity, and (of course) drinking ale.

tæfl or Cyningtæfl ("King's table"): a "capture the King" strategy board game.

thegn: ("thane") a freeborn warrior-retainer of a lord; thegns were housed, fed and armed in exchange for complete fidelity to their sworn lord. Booty won in battle by a thegn was generally offered to their lord, and in return the lord was expected to bestow handsome gifts of arms, horses, arm-rings, and so on to his best champions.

treen: domestic objects fashioned of wood, especially tableware.

Tyr: the God of war, law, and justice. He voluntarily forfeited his sword-hand to allow the Gods to deceive, and bind, the gigantic wolf Fenrir.

Tyr-hand: in this Saga, any left-handed person, named so in honour of Tyr's sacrifice.

Urd: the youngest of the three Norse Norns, determiners of men's destinies. Urd makes decision as to one's calling and station in life. See also Skuld and Verdandi.

Verdandi: the middle of the three Norse Norns, determiners of men's destinies. Verdandi draws out the thread of life to appropriate length. See also Skuld and Urd.

wadmal: the Norse name for the coarse and durable woven woollen fabric that was a chief export in the Viking age.

wergild: Literally, man-gold; the amount of money each man's life was valued at. The Laws of *Æthelbert*, a 7th century King of Kent, for example, valued the life of a nobleman at 300 shillings (equivalent to 300 oxen), and a ceorl was valued at 100 shillings. By Ælfred's time (reigned 871–899) a nobleman was held at 1200 shillings and a ceorl at 200.

yealing: one the same age.

NOTES

Chapter the Seventh

Plegmund. Mercian priest who became Archbishop of Canterbury in 890. He may have been a hermit in Cheshire, before being called to greater responsibilities. He was active in converting the Heathen, and exhorting other Bishops to do so. Plegmund visited Rome at least once, was trusted by Ælfred, and much involved in matters of State with his son King Eadward. Plegmund died either 914 or 923; the record is inconclusive. Canonized as a Saint, his Feast Day is 2nd August.

Chapter the Sixteenth

Constantinople, or Miklagårdr ("The Great City") as the Norse called it; capitol of the Eastern Roman Empire. In 330 CE Constantine the Great designated the old city known as Byzantium as the "New Rome." Eventually the city took his name.

It likely had 600,000 to 800,000 residents when our adventurers visited, of which some 60,000 at any one time were foreign traders. With such numbers we can well understand why Runulv and Eskil would find this city astounding. A combination of strict Roman law and Greek opulence and taste combined to nurture Byzantine civilization, and the great city was its heart.

Constantinople was a vast repository of treasure, much now scattered around the world. One example is the life-size horses seen by Runulv and Eskil at the Hippodrome, which I have placed above the Emperor's viewing stand. The four horses, commonly thought of as cast bronze, are nearly pure copper, which received a mercury gilding for brilliance. Scholars are divided as to their age; they may have been created in Rome in the 3rd or 4th century CE, or even in Greece in the 5th or 4th centuries BCE. During the Fourth Crusade they were carried off by Venetian forces in 1204 as part of the immense spoils of war, to end up adorning San Marco. These "Four Horses of Saint Mark" now reside inside for their own protection, where they may be viewed, but the copies outside are impressive indeed. (They wear horse collars now, as the heads were sawn off for ease of transport to Venice, and then reattached.) The Hippodrome itself was a wonder, holding 100,000 spectators, and adorned with obelisks and all manner of equestrian statues memorializing great horses and drivers.

The Eparch. The Prefect of Constantinople, he was second in power only to the Emperor, and held vast power in a city built on trade. His role was recorded in the 10th century *Book of The Eparch*, detailing some of this official's responsibilities, including determining customs duties; verifying scales and weights; regulating exchange rates between a myriad of currencies and metals; setting interest rates; describing the rights and regulations to be adhered to by scores of guilds (from silk dyers to pork sellers); and establishing trading periods for foreign merchants, amongst many other duties. Stringent laws kept artisans and merchants to a narrowly defined production or trading sphere.

All this worked in ensuring high quality trade, a sense of protection to both sellers and buyers, and maximum profit to the Emperor.

An excellent overview of life in Constantinople and much of the Byzantine Empire is presented in *What Life Was Like Amid Splendor and Intrigue: Byzantine Empire AD 330–1453*. Time Life Books 1998.

CHAPTER THE SEVENTEENTH

Hagia Sophia, The Church of Holy Wisdom. The greatest of all Byzantine churches, Hagia Sophia was built under the reign of Emperor Justinian, in a mere five years (532–537 CE). It rose on the site of two earlier churches, both consumed by fire. Justinian lavished riches and attention on its creation, importing rare marbles from around the entire Western world for its construction. It was the largest Christian building on Earth until superseded by St Peter's in Rome (completed in 1626). Gloriously decorated with mosaics and featuring a massive dome which appears to float above a band of windows, Hagia Sophia remained the centre of the Byzantine Eastern Orthodox Church until its sack and desecration by Venetian forces during the Fourth Crusade in 1204, eventually becoming a Roman Catholic Church. It was desecrated again during the Ottoman conquest of Constantinople in 1453, and saw the slaughter of thousands who had taken refuge within its walls. This marked the end of the Byzantine Empire, and Hagia Sophia was converted to a mosque. Architectural elements appropriate to Islamic religious buildings were added, including four towering minarets outside the main structure.

In 1934, under the secular Turkish government of President Mustafa Kemal Ataturk, it became a public museum. In 2020 Hagia Sophia was again re-designated a mosque by the Turkish government. Dumbarton Oaks, a Harvard University research institute in Washington, DC maintains – amongst all their other treasures – a huge repository of information, photos, drawings, archives, and records about the history of this remarkable building, freely available online. https://www.doaks.org/research/byzantine/resources/hagia-sophia.

Halfdan. This runic inscription, worn now, but likely reading in full "Halfdan was here" was documented first in 1964 by Elisabeth Svärdström in "Runorna i Hagia Sofia" (The Runes of Hagia Sophia). Halfdan immortalised his visit to Miklagårdr in stone on the top floor of the southern gallery. I have placed our adventurers there on the scene to see him finish the deed.

The Spillings Hoard – Gotland's Role in Viking Age World Trade, Gotlands Museum, 2009 is a detailed examination of the conditions and results of early Silk Road trading and Gotland, and as the vast silver and bronze Spillings Hoard was buried on the island in the late 9th century is particularly germane to the world of these novels.

Chapter the Eighteenth

Silk. Foreign traders were never allowed to buy the finest quality of silk; this was reserved by the Eparch for the Imperial family, honoured merchants, and given as special gifts. Still, the lustre and sheen of silk, its ability to take and hold dyes of the most vibrant hues, and its almost magical origins as the product of a humble worm, made it prized indeed. On Gotland, Viking Era silk has been found in only one grave, that of a female in the 600-grave site at Ihre (or Ire), on the island's west coast, but lucky we are to have it. This was a fragment of samite (a heavy twill-woven silk, which often included either silver or golden thread), and a fragment of silk tablet-woven work. For a detailed examination of the silk trade and the Viking thirst for it, see *Silk for the Vikings*, Marianne Vedeler, 2014.

CHAPTER THE NINETEENTH

Arsenikon and sandaraca. The toxicity of many dyes and pigments was well known even in ancient times, but the desire for the vivid hues produced by working with them did not prove much of a deterrent. Lead, mercury, cadmium and other hazardous heavy metals were commonly used by many artists and artisans up to modern times, and the deleterious health effects to painters, gilders, and the grinders and preparers of paints and dyes can only be imagined. (The expression "Mad as a Hatter" is rooted in the use of mercury by those fashioning hats, for example; and some scholars have suggested Vincent van Gogh's mental illness to be at least partly derived from his extensive use of the oil paint Naples Yellow, made from lead antimonate.)

Arsenikon and sandaraca were particularly notorious. Arsenikon, or yellow arsenic sulfide, later known as orpiment, was used as a cosmetic by the Egyptians, employed by the Assyrians as a medicine, and described by Pliny in the first century. It was Strabo who described the toxicity of arsenikon as being so great that only criminals in northern

Anatolia were sent to mine it. It was one of many pigments used in the illuminations of the 9th century *Book of Kells*, and continued in use right up to the Impressionists in the late 19th century. Similarly, sandaraca is red arsenic sulfide, and would yield a range of red and orange-red shades.

CHAPTER THE TWENTIETH

Wilfrid Blunt's *The Golden Road to Samarkand*, 1973, follows the footsteps of two thousand years of journeying to the sources of the fabled riches carried upon various routes of the Silk Road. Winter hardship was extreme, and Blunt writes engagingly of hardy traders attired in bearskin stockings worn fur-side in, tough horse-hide boots, and wolfskin suits to trap body warmth.

ACKNOWLEDGEMENTS

Sincerest thanks to all my readers for their devotion to the Saga series. Whether you have just discovered the series or been with me for years, know I cherish your interest and affection for the Saga Folk – the characters. I strive to be constantly worthy of your time and attention, and thank you for helping me "grow the Circle", through reading or listening to the books, requesting them at the library, and most of all telling friends about the Saga adventure.

My thanks, always and ever, to Beth Altchek and Libby Williams for their discerning ear and dedication to these stories (and their author). Your interest in the Saga Folk and their development over many volumes speaks more than the reams these books have been printed on. I am in your debt, happily and gratefully so.

My First Readers are an enthusiastic group of discerning and articulate fans, whose input I greatly value. My warmest thanks to the following for reading and commenting on *Treasure*: Wendy Adams, Tony Allen, Judy Boxer, Liz Faulkner, Elaine MacDonald, Kristen McEnaney, Debbie Newsholme, Melinda Osman, Amanda Porath, Linda Schultz, Kristin Sponsler, Lorie Witt, and Veronica Zysk. I am fortunate indeed to have you with me, and to share the excitement of a new title.

To Uffa Nysell, builder extraordinaire here on Gotland, my thanks for allowing me to use your name and likeness for the redoubtable Uffa of this novel.

If you'd like closer engagement with the world of the Saga, the Octavia Randolph Official Circle of Ceridwen Saga Forum on Facebook awaits you, where you shall find fellowship in discussing the Saga novels and the Anglo-Saxon and Viking Era settings in which they take place. The Saga Forum is a veritable "treasure room" of information and celebration, from medieval foodways to smithing, fashion to fortress building, parchment making to rune carving, early Christianity to the Gods of the Norse, and much more. Such a welcoming home for my books and their readers would not be possible without the tireless activity, creativity, and oversight of Misi, Jessica Charboneau, and Wolf CrescentWalker. My debt to you is boundless, as is my gratitude.

ABOUT
THE AUTHOR

Octavia Randolph has long been fascinated with the development, dominance, and decline of the Anglo-Saxon peoples. The path of her research has included disciplines as varied as the study of Anglo-Saxon and Norse runes, and learning to spin with a drop spindle. Her interests have led to extensive on-site research in England, Denmark, Sweden, and Gotland. In addition to the Circle Saga, she is the author of the novella *The Tale of Melkorka*, taken from the Icelandic Sagas; the novella *Ride*, a retelling of the story of Lady Godiva, first published in Narrative Magazine; and *Light, Descending*, a biographical novel about the great John Ruskin. She has been awarded Artistic Fellowships at the Ingmar Bergman Estate on Fårö, Sweden; MacDowell; Ledig House International; and Byrdcliffe.

She answers all fan mail and loves to stay in touch with her readers. Join her mailing list and read more on Anglo-Saxon and Viking life at www.octavia.net. Follow her on Facebook at Octavia Randolph Author, on Instagram and for exclusive access and content join the spirited members of The Official Circle of Ceridwen Saga Forum on Facebook.